A GIRL
LIKE
CHE
GUEVARA

A GIRL LIKE CHE GUEVARA

 A NOVEL

TERESA DE LA **CARIDAD DOVAL**

SOHO

Published by
Soho Press, Inc.
853 Broadway
New York, NY 10003

Library of Congress Cataloging-in-Publication Data

TK

ISBN 1-56947-358-7

Designed by Kathleen Lake, Neuwirth & Associates, Inc.

10   9   8   7   6   5   4   3   2   1

To Hugh, my husband, editor
and always supportive Panda Bear. ¡Gracias!

⊰ ACKNOWLEDGMENTS ⊱

I wish to thank Laura Hruska, for believing in this book and for her wonderful editing and valuable suggestions; Dr. Kimberle López for her detailed revision of the manuscript and encouraging words; my mother, who taught me to love books; and I also wish to acknowledge the memory of Liza Nelligan, for her friendship and support.

⊰ CHAPTER I ⊱

"DIVINATION IS LIKE reading your Life Book," said Sabina soberly, looking me in the eye. "Sometimes we can change a few words here and there, but at others we can't even add a comma. That is what I call fate. Do you understand, Lourdes?"

I nodded. Four pieces of coconut shell fell from the *santera*'s fingers and scattered across the tabletop. A few motes of dust rose from the dark cedar surface and floated in the air as the shells clattered and stopped in front of me.

The *santera*'s head was crowned with a neatly tied red kerchief. Her gleaming dark skin and immaculate white dress did not match my idea of a witch. She seemed to embrace me with her eyes, but still my hands trembled, so I pressed them beneath my legs. I was sixteen, a short, copper-skinned *mulatica*. I seldom wore skirts because of my thin calves. That day, however, my grandmother had made me wear a turquoise dress and a string of blue plastic beads in honor of Yemayá, the goddess of the sea.

As salty drops of water moistened my forehead, Grandma Inés, my maternal grandmother, did her best to comfort me. The grip of her hand on my shoulder lent me courage and confidence. I began breathing more easily despite the thickness of the air in the room which smelled like Florida water, cocoa butter, and aromatic herbs. The warm atmosphere of Sabina's house began to wrap around me like a silky, fragrant veil.

Two days before the consultation, Grandma Inés had had an inauspicious dream in which I appeared, crying and surrounded by fire and blood. She regarded it as a serious warning. In her opinion, my upcoming stay at the School-in-the-Fields—four months spent far from Havana, working in the tobacco fields and away from the family—was an event that required the special protection that only her saints, the *orishas,* were able to confer. Despite my protests (I considered myself an atheist), she had taken me to the *santera*'s house to have a spiritual consultation before I left for the Pinar del Río camp.

Sabina took a sip of rum but didn't drink it. She kept it in her mouth for a few moments and then spat it on the floor in front of the altar, a small, round table where two black dolls adorned with blue necklaces were displayed among corn ears, bananas, and oranges.

"Light be with you!" Sabina said in a hoarse, strange voice. "May Elegguá, lord of the roads, and your *orisha*, Yemayá, accompany you all your life and particularly during the next four months! Light be with you! *Siacará!*"

"*Siacará!*" repeated Grandma Inés. I also muttered *Siacará* to myself, a protective phrase used to exorcise any bad spirits.

An invisible presence softly caressed my neck. I shivered. As on the gusty morning when I had seen the ocean for the first time, I stood trembling, this time at the threshold of a supernatural world, afraid of being engulfed by it.

When Sabina spoke again, she had recovered her soft Guantanamero accent. "Now, Lourdes, take two shells and drop them while you think of a question."

"Remember what you have to ask, girl!" Grandma Inés interjected. "Do not waste our time thinking of nonsense!"

I chose two shells. The rough pieces of coconut felt wet and slippery as if they had been soaked in water for a long time. *Will I be okay at the School-in-the-Fields camp?* I asked.

Every year in January, all Cuban secondary and high school students were sent to the countryside. This was part of a nationwide project designed to combine study and work at a place known as the School-in-the-Fields in Pinar del Río. In 1982, however, the minister of education decided to extend our stay from six weeks to four months, until April. That would be our modest contribution to the tobacco harvest, he said.

Mami and my two grandmothers didn't like the idea at all. *Papi* and I did. Though I knew I would miss my family, I felt proud that our high school had been selected to stay in Pinar del Río longer than the others. It was a revolutionary distinction, my father explained to me. If I went and worked hard enough, that would be taken into account when I applied for membership in the Young Communist League. If the Party ever sent me on a mission to other countries, which had been my dream for years, I would be more prepared to meet the challenge. So I was happy to go. I wanted to prove to *Papi* and to myself that I could really be like Che Guevara.

I threw the shells on the table, where they stood aligned, their whitish pulp sides facing up.

"Perfect!" Sabina smiled, beaming at me. "Do it again."

I selected another pair of shells and dropped them. This time they showed me their dark surfaces. Both Sabina and my grandma said, "*Uff.*" The *santera* ordered me to stop. Grandma Inés lit a candle and placed it on the altar.

Sabina burned incense and then began to throw the shells herself. Finally, she addressed Grandma Inés and declared, "It was good that you brought Lourdes to me before her trip to Pinar del Río. She does need protection because life is going to put a few obstacles in her way. Your granddaughter is strong and brave," she continued, speaking as if I weren't present. "She will come out unharmed despite the difficulties she'll have to face. Many difficulties! But that is life. Suffering and growing."

"What—what will happen to me?" I stammered. The atmosphere of the room, illuminated only by the candle, seemed viscous and suffocating. The silky veil had turned into a noose. The *santería* paraphernalia that Sabina kept in the corners didn't help—an aged crucifix with a mulatto Jesus hanging from it, the serious-looking black dolls, three dried coconuts, several life-size images of saints, and countless plaster statuettes. Inanimate objects became ominous messengers of the future. "Shouldn't I go to the School-in-the-Fields?"

"You will go, indeed," Sabina answered. "You have to go. Fate, as I said before, is unavoidable. If it doesn't catch you there, it will catch you somewhere else. What I see," and she looked again at the table where the shells of divination lay in disarray, "is that Evil will surround you, so be very attentive. There will be a lot of malice, my daughter, but you'll conquer it by the power of your mouth."

"What do you mean?" Grandma Inés asked.

Sabina shrugged. "I really don't know, but this is what the shells tell me. Lourdes will desire something very ardently, suffer for it, and achieve it in the end, but it won't bring her as much satisfaction as she expected."

"Something." Grandma Inés repeated, intrigued. "What?"

"Or someone. The shells aren't very precise. They just say she'll get it, whatever she wants." Sabina paused. She turned to me and added gravely, "But this is not the most important matter, *niña*. I can see that many of the people you will have to deal with are wicked, dangerous, or in danger themselves. You have to be extremely careful!"

Grandma Inés crossed herself. The mulatto Jesus on his cracked crucifix appeared somber. I didn't dare move a finger.

The *santera* went on, addressing Grandma Inés again. "Lourdes's life has been too sheltered up to now, but this is going to change soon. The saints aren't entirely happy with her. Saints can be very irritable, almost capricious, as you know. Did she offend them somehow?"

"Lourdes hasn't shown any interest in learning how to be agreeable to Yemayá, though Yemayá healed her when she was so sick a year ago." Grandma Inés sighed. "The ingratitude! I am always telling her, the *orishas* help when you honor them, but if you ignore them, they ignore you."

Yemayá, the dusky Virgin of Regla, was my *orisha* according to Grandma Inés. She was my black guardian angel, my mother in the spirit world. Grandma swore that Yemayá had been responsible for the disappearance of a terrible rash that afflicted me after my fifteenth birthday. She had saved my life with a quick, miraculous cure that astonished the doctors who had for months tried unsuccessfully to heal me.

"Your granddaughter isn't very careful, is she?" Sabina sighed. "These youngsters of today are way too loose!"

I immediately remembered Grandma Gloria's last scolding. "You are too loose! *Cochina!*" my paternal grandmother had shouted. She had just caught me touching myself "down there," playing with my *papaya,* and I was grounded for two days. But how did Sabina know this? I blushed.

"Well, it is not her fault," conceded Grandma Inés, "but her father's and her other grandmother's. My son-in-law, Rafael, thinks that he has God by His beard because he is a university professor. And stuck-up old Gloria—*Uff!* They all fart higher than their asses and don't care for the saints. I try to help, though. This morning I went to the Regla Catholic church, attended Mass, and said a prayer just in case. I also offered a good, fat pigeon to Yemayá in Lourdes's name."

"Thank God!" exclaimed Sabina, slapping the table after a last scrutiny of the shells. "Thank God you don't forget the offerings. They are most important. Anyway, I'd better give Lourdes a strong protector. She is lucky after all, because Yemayá, no matter how irritated, is still behind her."

"You mean she has to wear a charm?" Grandma Inés asked, concerned.

I cringed. My Marxism teachers said that those who wore crucifixes, medals with images of Catholic saints, or *santería* charms suffered from "ideological deviation." I had been a Pioneer. I wanted to become a Young Communist, to be like Che Guevara. Would a Che follower wear an amulet? No way!

After a moment's pause, the *santera* replied, "I know it *may* cause trouble. But it won't harm her to wear a little jet stone, an *azabache*, hidden inside her clothes. No one will notice it if she is careful." Sabina opened a sweet-smelling sandalwood box. She took a bright black stone out and handed it to me. "*Azabaches* are the safest charms against the evil eye. I have blessed this one. It will certainly protect you."

"Thanks," I said firmly, "but no thanks."

"Do not worry, Sabina." Grandma Inés glared at me, then she took the black stone and put it inside her purse. "I'll make sure Lourdes takes the *azabache* to Pinar del Río."

In your dreams, I thought.

"Now we'll consecrate her head to Yemayá," concluded Sabina.

"Let's hope our work will be enough to guard her against the dark forces this girl will encounter in the School-in-the-Fields. Let's just hope so."

And the ceremony took place, with honey and flowers and perfume and more candles, while a tiny turtle, also consecrated to Yemayá, observed the scene from the bottom of a big wooden pan painted blue.

⊣ CHAPTER II ⊢

SMELLS OF SWEATY flesh. Noisy complaints that filled the bright Havana morning with red anger. "Where is that *cabrón* bread van?" Purses and newspapers, paper and sackcloth bags brandished like weapons. Smoke from cigars. "I shit on the baker's mother." Whistles. "Who is the last one? If there is no last one in this line, I am the first one!" Laughs. A silent prayer. A loud curse. A coffee-tinged smile.

The bread line curled around itself like a nervous snake. There were at least fifty people in front of me. I stood, resigned, at the tail of the queue, behind a thin, toothless old lady who kept mumbling obscenities. On Saturdays, the van that brought bread from the city bakery, *La Gran Vía*, to our neighborhood bread store—the *panadería*—would often arrive an hour or more late. We were used to it and accepted the fact that Manolito, the chunky van driver, liked to sleep later on the weekends. After all, he was quite punctual the rest of the week.

Twenty long minutes crawled by. Manolito must be "either dead, drunk, or completely lacking in shame," the enraged toothless lady said. It was 10:15 in the morning and he hadn't showed up yet.

"Maybe his van broke down on the way," a skinny old man whispered.

The toothless lady shushed him, "*Siacará*, Pedro Luis! Shut up! Don't even mention it!"

We all lingered outside the *panadería*. The sales clerk wouldn't allow anyone to enter until the van arrived. I guessed that he hated selling bread. He probably hated waking up early on Saturdays. Hated having people around. In fact, as many of us suspected, he hated people, and enjoyed making life difficult for us. One of his more annoying habits was to refuse to serve a client if he didn't have the exact change, fifteen *centavos*. It was useless to try to bribe him by politely saying, "Keep the change." He wouldn't do it. He took great pleasure in thwarting his customers. And his favorite words were, "I'm out of bread! *Fuera!* Scram!"

Had there been any possibility of buying our daily pound of bread in a different *panadería*, I'd have gladly done it, even if it meant walking a few extra blocks every morning. I wondered if someday, when we had already built a communist society, people would be able to choose their own *panaderías*. Or perhaps all the communist employees would be kindhearted and smiling, and would treat their clients more decently than our grouchy clerk.

Two disheveled, hungry-looking women sat on the greasy sidewalk. They had probably been waiting since 6 A.M. I entertained myself by browsing through our tattered ration card, where the sold items were marked with a red check in the third column. I had seen its first page so many times that I could recite its contents by heart.

PRODUCT	MONTHLY AMOUNT	JANUARY 1982
Rice	6 pounds	✓
Sugar	6 pounds	✓
Beans	20 ounces	✓
Coffee	4 ounces	✓
Meat	1 pound	
Bread	30 units	✓✓✓✓✓✓✓✓✓✓

We had already used our monthly coffee ration, but Grandma Gloria always managed to obtain three or four additional pounds on the black market. *Papi* couldn't go to work without drinking a cup of strong coffee in the morning. I knew it wasn't proper for a revolutionary to buy things from individuals who sold them for a profit, but when I told *Papi* about my concern, he explained to me that he *needed* the coffee in order to do a good job teaching. Besides, Grandma Gloria liked coffee, too. She was a great old lady, a hardworking *viejita*, and shouldn't be deprived of anything. "I am not a fanatic," he would say. "I won't allow my mother to go without it when there is so much coffee in Cuba." Buying more coffee than the few ounces allowed by our ration card wasn't such a big deal, he noted. Not like buying, let's say, an American tape recorder or a cassette with Julio Iglesias or—horror!—The Beatles' forbidden songs.

Meat, however, was much more difficult to find, even in the black market where Grandma Gloria had so many friends. I had not had a steak since the beginning of December. When would our January rations come? I hoped it might be that very week. Then Grandma Gloria would make steaks for dinner. A well-done, round, onion-covered steak danced before my eyes, escorted by crispy french fries. My stomach, unsatisfied by a breakfast of watery milk sweetened by two spoonfuls of sugar, supplied a musical accompaniment to my longing.

At eleven o'clock the *panadería* clerk faced the expectant crowd. After a long pause, he barked, "*Carajo*, I am going home."

Insults and pleas greeted his announcement.

"Lazy bum!" the toothless lady shouted. "*Cabrón!*"

"Yeah, he doesn't need to wait for the bread," the skinny man squealed. "He steals ten pounds every day and already has a reserve!"

"Can't you wait ten more minutes?" I dared to ask.

"Please! Stay until twelve!" another pleaded.

"What if the bread van arrives after you leave?"

He ignored us, closed the door of the *panadería,* and left. The toothless lady spat behind his back. The line began to dissolve.

When I reached my house, the bread van appeared at the corner of Vista Alegre Street. Seeing that the *panadería* was already closed, Manolito didn't bother to stop. The aged, yellowish truck vanished down Porvenir Avenue, taking with it our weekend breakfast.

A CRY came from the left side of the street. "The meat! Hey, the meat van is here! The butcher's starting to unload it!"

Immediately, all heads turned. Like an army of orderly ants, they changed position and went straight from the grocery store—where they had been waiting for the arrival of the potato truck—directly to the butcher's. According to ration regulations, red meat would be available every two weeks, half a pound per person.

At home no one answered. Where were my mother and grandma? This was an important matter, indeed.

"Grandma, *Mami,*" I shouted from the garden, "the meat—"

"*Bueno,* Lourdes, I heard you," Grandma Gloria replied. Her still slightly Galician-accented voice came from the kitchen. "Stop squeaking!" Then she called to my mother, "Barbarita, go for the meat! Hurry up or you will only get bones!"

The butcher's door opened. A red-haired girl was the first to enter, proudly swaying her massive bottom.

"Barbarita!" Grandma Gloria screeched. "Good God, where does this mulatta go when one needs her?"

"Just a second, Gloria," I heard *Mami's* response coming from the bathroom. "I am getting ready to take a shower and—"

"Take your shower later," Grandma ordered brusquely. "We'll have water all day, but you know that the meat delivery is never enough for everybody. If we don't collect ours now, we'll have to wait until next month. Move!"

Mami darted out of the house with a vinyl bag in her hand and I watched her take a place at the end of the meat line. Her black, wiry hair shone in the sunlight. She kept her head bent. The tone of voice Grandma had used was so rude.

A suffocating weight of sorrow and guilt fell on me. When I passed the kitchen, Grandma Gloria was sprinkling powdered cinnamon over a recently made, still steaming, rice pudding dish. Her long-fingered, aristocratic hands, where bluish veins ran like tiny streams in a porcelain valley, held a silver teaspoon. Pretty hands, which were so often cold. I remembered Grandma Inés's black fingers, short but protectively warm.

"This is Waiting-in-Line Land," Grandma Gloria sighed. "Let's hope your mother is luckier than you were yesterday in the bread line." She approached me and put a teaspoonful of rice pudding close to my lips. "Try a little bit, *niña*. I prepared it especially for you, to make up for your poor breakfast."

I grabbed a dish of rice pudding and went to the living room to eat it in front of the TV. We had nice furniture: a black leather sofa and two armchairs, a mahogany coffee table, and a rocking chair, all older than I was, but well preserved thanks to Grandma Gloria's care.

It was time for the Russian cartoons, which I still enjoyed, despite the fact that I considered myself a grown-up. I plopped into my favorite armchair but couldn't concentrate on Tolia's adventures. Instead, I kept looking at my parents' wedding picture, framed in silver, which hung next to a Che Guevara photo. *Mami's* skin reminded me of a warm glass of coffee and milk, while *Papi's* had the creamy hue of vanilla ice cream. Dr. Rafael Torres, *Papi* to me, taught Political Economy of Communism at the University of

Havana. He maintained a dignified countenance at all times; he was *"El Profesor."* *Mami* worked as a clerk at a clothing store in Old Havana, and she was quiet and shy. In that photo, I realized, she looked even more mousy than in person.

Without waiting for the cartoons to end, I turned the TV off and left the empty rice pudding dish on the coffee table. Grandma Gloria would pick it up.

Then I went to my bedroom, which was warm, bright, and still childish. A canopied bed, a pink wooden shelf where my set of *matrioskas* was prominently placed, and an ample, curtained window that opened to the garden. The *matrioskas* were seven wooden dolls that *Papi* had bought for me in Leningrad. I had chosen Russian names for them. They were my babies. I knew I'd miss them all, particularly Aniuska, the tiniest one, during my stay at Pinar del Río. At the same time, I reproached myself for such weakness: I was a future *guerrillera,* though the Latin American guerrilla war wasn't my big concern just then. I had a bigger problem, a home problem, in fact.

Something was wrong, I thought. But what? Grandma Gloria was cooking, *Papi* was lecturing at the university. My parents wouldn't send me to get groceries because the butcher and the grocery store clerk would steal shamelessly from me, an absent-minded teen. So only *Mami* could go for the meat. But why didn't Grandma Gloria address her—differently?

And yet how could I criticize Grandma Gloria? How could I, when everything around me proclaimed how much she loved me and cared for me? My twin-size bed that she made every morning, the sheets she herself would iron in the winter, the pillowcase on which she had embroidered a colorful Pinocchio. The photos on the walls were also evidence of her love: Grandma Gloria by my side during my Pioneer initiation, tying the red kerchief around my neck. Grandma Gloria holding my hand on a visit to the Havana Zoo, while I made faces at the elephant. Grandma Gloria helping me blow out the candles at my tenth birthday party. Grandma Gloria smiling behind a dreamlike meringue cake that she'd made, better and softer than those sold in the stores. Grandma Gloria watching me dance with *Papi* at my *fiesta de quinceaños*. Grandma Gloria—

I plopped down on my bed and tried hard not to think of *Mami*. Instead, I began making a mental list of all the things I'd need to take to the School-in-the-Fields camp. Work clothes: they were ready. Rubber boots: *Mami* had to buy them. A straw hat: I could use last year's, if it was still wearable. A tin cup and a spoon, a big bucket to carry bath water, and a small one to pour it over me. A mosquito net, two thick blankets, some books—food. Oh, Grandma Gloria would take care of that, I didn't need to worry about it.

Now, dress clothes. *Caramba. Nothing looks really good on me*, I groaned. *All my pants make me look thinner and more assless than I already am. Mami* had just bought me a long, ample skirt, but camp rules only allowed us to wear pants. Skirts and dresses were forbidden. Oh, if I could only have a pair of American blue jeans, a *pitusa*! They made even skinny girls look curvaceous. How chic and sexy those Lee blue jeans were! And the Levi's! And the Jordaches, with a pretty horse's head embroidered on the sturdy cloth!

I longed for a good *pitusa*. But I would never dare to ask my parents to buy them for me. First, because they had to be bought on the black market. Getting American blue jeans must be a hundred times harder than procuring a few ounces of Cuban coffee! Secondly, because I felt deeply ashamed of my desire to own a Yankee item.

Why didn't the Soviets make *pitusas*? Why didn't our stores sell Cuban-made blue jeans?

Consumerist, frivolous, vain girl, I scolded myself, and then fell asleep.

★ ★ ★

AT FIVE O'CLOCK *Papi* came in. I heard him close the front door and walk toward my room. When he peeked inside I pretended to be asleep. I didn't feel like talking. He walked to the kitchen.

"How was your day, *hijo?*" Grandma Gloria asked him.

"Fine. But buses are impossible. I waited forty minutes for the thirty-four! *Uff!*"

"Maybe you'll get a car soon. One of those new Ladas. You deserve it."

"Hope so. I've been expecting to get one since 1980."

"Here, *mi rey*, have some rice pudding."

Grandma Gloria had a thing for titles of nobility. *Papi* was her king, I was her princess. But *Mami*—what was she? I imagined *Papi* seated at the kitchen table, tasting the rice pudding, savoring it.

"Where is Barbarita?" he asked.

"At the butcher's. The meat came today. Do you want to take a bath? I can heat the water right now."

Papi didn't like to take showers. Grandma Gloria would warm water for him in a huge aluminum pot and pour it in the bathroom bucket, even during sultry summer afternoons. She did the same for me and for herself. "Cold water is harmful to the body," she said. When *Mami* took a shower, Grandma Gloria wrinkled her nose. And I was only allowed to take cold showers when I visited my black grandmother.

"No, thanks, *Mamá*," *Papi* answered. "I'll be you-know-where. If Barbarita asks, tell her I called from the university. That I have a department meeting and won't be home until eight or nine."

"No problem, dear. Have fun."

Papi left again, silently. I spent a long time wondering where you-know-where was.

When I woke up and looked through the window, a waxing moon cut the sky like a golden, curved needle. Grandma Gloria watched a Brazilian soap opera in the living room. *Mami* had not returned yet. Meat lines lasted three or four hours, sometimes longer.

The silence of the house blanketed me as I entered my parents' room. Aimlessly I sat on the stool in front of *Mami's* vanity table, which had previously belonged to Grandma Gloria. The vanity table was elegant, with carved legs covered by a white taffeta skirt. A fine piece of furniture chock full of perfumes, eye shadow, facial powder, and mascara, it exhaled the indefinable scent of womanhood. I turned on a table lamp and studied my face in the mirror.

My brown skin didn't look too bad in the soft, intimate shadow created by the alabaster table lamp. But if only my eyelashes were a little longer, my eyes green like *Papi's,* my hair silky and straight like Grandma Gloria's . . . I pensively rubbed my nose—the only one of my facial features that I was rather fond of—and opened the top drawer. Though *Mami* seldom wore makeup, she owned an impressive collection of lipsticks and rouges. She didn't mind my using her cosmetics, but I preferred to do it when no one else was around. I knew I was not yet an expert in the difficult art of applying them.

While I searched inside the drawer, my fingers met something soft and gooey. Curious, I took the thing out and examined it. A five-inch black doll, similar to those I had seen in Sabina's house during the consultation, looked back at me with glassy eyes made of green plastic beads. The doll was wrapped in a piece of cloth that I immediately identified as belonging to one of *Papi's* old *guayaberas.*

I sniffed the sticky substance that covered the doll, which smelled sweet, and then carefully licked it. It was honey! On the back of the doll there were two names handwritten, Rafael and Barbarita, with *Mami's* name on top of *Papi's*.

I put the doll back in its place and found another, dressed in a blue-and-white gingham gown. Like Grandma Gloria's muumuu, I realized. A gray rag imitated hair. Its eyes were also green. It wasn't coated with honey but sprinkled with salt. A long, rusty pin had been stuck into the doll's chest, where its heart was supposed to be.

For a few minutes I kept looking at the doll and shaking my head. What was going on? *Papi* asked Grandma Gloria to lie, to say he was at the university, while he actually went to "you-know-where." *Mami* dressed black dolls in gowns made from *Papi's* and Grandma Gloria's cast-off clothing. *Grandma Inés must have taken Mami to visit old Sabina, too. This is santería stuff!* I remembered that the previous month, *Mami* had spent a weekend at Grandma Inés's house. She explained to us that her mother was sick and she had to help her. The very day she left, I overheard Grandma Gloria saying to *Papi*, "I am afraid that this mulatta and the old witch are having some special 'work' done to hook you again. Black mischief! When you least expect it, they'll cast a spell on you!"

With a cocky smile, *Papi* had answered, "More than a spell is going to be necessary now, *Mamá*. Things have changed."

Things were definitely not OK. A quiet bitterness hovered over the Vista Alegre Street house. When the family ate together, eyes avoided meeting other eyes. Grandma Gloria would do all the talking without getting, and perhaps without expecting, any response, generally praising her own food and detailing the efforts she had made to get the right ingredients, before she fell silent, too.

Mami entered the bedroom. Her unexpected appearance made me jump.

"What are you doing here?" she asked.

"Trying your red lipstick," I answered, blushing.

"Take it with you if you want, but don't stay here all night bothering me! I am exhausted!"

"*Bueno*, okay," I said. "Don't get mad. I was just going."

I walked fast toward the door, eager to leave the room before she noticed I wasn't wearing any makeup. But *Mami* followed me. Suddenly she put her arm around my shoulder and muttered, "I'm sorry, Lourdes. I am not angry at you, just so, so tired. I had to clean the house in the morning, iron the clothes that you are taking to the camp, and then wait on that damned meat line . . . But I didn't mean to shout at you. My dear *niña*, my baby, you are the only thing I have."

I knew I should have said something nice in response, but I couldn't. Silently, I left the room and joined Grandma Gloria in the kitchen, where she was busy preparing an onion-covered steak for me.

My mind sought an explanation. Did *Mami* intend to harm *Papi* and Grandma Gloria with Sabina's or—I shivered—Grandma Inés's help? Would there also be a black doll clothed in a gown made with one of my dresses? And where was *Papi*? Why hadn't he returned from "you-know-where"?

⊰ CHAPTER III ⊱

THE THREE BIG houses towered loftily over the smaller buildings that neighbored them. The *panadería*, the grocery store, the meatless *carnicería*, even the only two-story apartment building on our block appeared diminished and humbled when compared to the houses. Like elegant, tall, long-legged belles accompanied by a cohort of dwarfish, poorly dressed maids, they "set the tone" of the barrio. They were called *las casonas*, and they were the great houses of Vista Alegre Street.

Grandma Gloria had told me that all the *casonas* were built at the beginning of the century, in the twenties, a time of such economic prosperity that it was called the Dance of the Millions and the Years of the Fat Cows. Money had been so abundant, she remembered, that the marble used for our dining room table and for the staircase was brought directly from Italy, bought especially for our house. Her huge marble bathtub with curved bronze legs had come from Venice.

The three *casonas,* designed by the same architect, Eugenio Rayneri, complemented one another, but each had a distinguishing feature that set it apart from its sisters. Ours had two small turrets on the roof. Below the house next door, two vigilant bronze lions guarded the main entrance—though, unfortunately, one of them had lost its tail. The third *casona* proudly exhibited the only gazebo in the entire Lawton community.

Our neighborhood, thanks to *las casonas*, was considered "bourgeois." Even though the three houses lacked paint, even though their picket fences were partially broken and their gardens had grown unkempt and wild, they preserved an indelible air of grandeur that placed them miles apart from the rest of the more modern and modest buildings of the barrio. The former belles had aged, if not gracefully, at least with aristocratic dignity. They had turned into gray-haired ladies who displayed, around their wrinkled necks, half covered by their worn-out dresses, a priceless string of cultivated pearls.

The first *casona*, located on the left corner of our street across from the grocery store, belonged to Dulce, whose notorious existence offered me an early glimpse of what a woman-woman relationship was. Then came the apartment house. Grandma Gloria said that the people who lived there were vulgar, penniless, and dirty, and fought noisily at night. (Later I'd learn that Aurora, my best friend at the School-in-the-Fields camp, lived in one of the apartments.)

Ours was the second "great house" of the block. My parents' room, my bedroom, a bathroom, and a storage room occupied the first floor, as well as a big living room, the formal dining room with the marble-top table that we seldom used, and a tiled kitchen. Grandma Gloria had the second floor—two bedrooms, the huge bathroom with the Venetian bathtub, a terrace, and a den—all for herself.

Separated from us by our front gardens, in the lion-guarded *casona*, lived Marietta and her son, the monster, Crazy Jorge. The fact that Crazy Jorge was the "boy next door" enabled him to break the windowpanes of our house at a higher rate than he destroyed others. "Jorge is a monster in all senses of the word," Grandma Gloria would say. Despite his teachers' efforts, he was incapable of finishing twelfth grade, and was kicked out after starting a fire in the boys' bathroom of our high school.

"This guy will end up in jail" was everybody's prediction. A few months after being expelled from school, Jorge acquired even more notoriety by leading a street fight which involved throwing bottles, daggers, and knives. The monster was eighteen, two years older than I was. He didn't go back to school. He didn't work. He did nothing, or, at least, nothing good.

Crazy Jorge's mother was an attractive blonde, a divorcée as soft-spoken as her son was foulmouthed. "I don't really know what to do with him," she'd say when confronted by an angry neighbor or a frantic schoolteacher. "I understand how you feel, but as God is my witness I just don't know what to do with my boy." Consequently, she did nothing. Except, perhaps, screaming at Jorge when she felt like it, which didn't affect his behavior in the least.

Marietta seldom worked. Indolence, as *Mami* said, ran rampant in that family. She was "between jobs," on vacation, or on medical leave. But when barrio gossipers labeled her a slothful floozy, Grandma Gloria immediately came to her defense. She described our neighbor as "a very refined lady who once made a mistake." The mistake was Crazy Jorge.

Despite the boy's behavior, Grandma Gloria and *Papi* got along very well with his mother. *Papi* admonished Jorge, counseled Marietta, and fixed broken faucets and old appliances in their house. "Let that good-for-nothing kid and the slothful floozy solve their own problems," *Mami* protested. "You don't even change a lightbulb here, Rafael! Why do you have to run there every time she gets a fart stuck in her ass?"

Marietta cooked caramel puddings for Grandma Gloria. She also flattered her by attentively listening to her stories. "When my husband and I went to a cocktail party hosted by Senator Palma—" Grandma Gloria would begin.

And Marietta would coo, "Oh, you knew important people, didn't you?"

Grandma Gloria and the blonde sat together in the inner courtyard to chat. They feasted on flans, cookies, and mango juice. Sometimes *Papi* and I joined them. But not *Mami*! *Mami* was not fond of Marietta and she let it be known.

"Well, it is *my* house," Grandma Gloria stated emphatically after *Mami* once made a scornful comment about the guest. "And *my* friends are always welcome here. Those who don't like it may go someplace else."

Though it was no secret that *Mami* hated Marietta, I couldn't say that I disliked our neighbor. She treated me decently, often smoothing my rebellious tresses and patting my back. I never failed to notice her fragrance, a Bulgarian perfume called *Gato Negro*. Marietta was thirty-five or thirty-six years old, and her golden hair was waist-long. She wore modern, flowery dresses, tiny shorts, and sometimes bold red miniskirts. *She may be a slothful floozy but she is also so chic,* I thought with a tinge of remorse. Was I betraying *Mami* by not sharing her antipathy?

How different Marietta and *Mami* looked, though they were the same age! And it was not just their skin color. *Mami* only wore perfume when she went out with *Papi*—which was almost never—and her clothes were—well, we had a word that described them to perfection in our high school lingo. They were *cheas*, old-fashioned, utterly unstylish, absolutely uncool. Secretly, I wished *Mami* looked more like our neighbor, or at least dressed like her.

"Marietta looks so European," Grandma Gloria loved to repeat. "Few people like her are left in this country." "European" was one of Grandma Gloria's favorite words. I tried to understand, thinking that, as she was "European" herself, it was only natural that she preferred her own kind. But it always hurt me a little to acknowledge the fact that I would never be "European" enough for her taste.

TWO DAYS before my departure for the camp, *Mami* and Grandma Gloria had already collected everything that I would be taking with me. Clean clothes, canned food, a can opener, laxative tablets, vitamin C, aspirins, work gloves, a wool beret and a scarf for the cool mornings, toilet paper . . . This was an important item. Due to the difficulty in finding toilet paper, all the family members had stopped using it during the last month. We had saved the rolls— which were purchased at the grocery store with a ration card, one per person every four weeks—so I could take them to Pinar del Río. We had temporarily resorted to the little ass rags, *los trapitos de culo*, small pieces of cloth that were used, then washed and let dry until they were needed again.

Finally, I was ready! Nothing was missing except a *linterna,* a flashlight. We didn't have flashlights at home and they weren't sold in the stores very often. But *Mami* insisted that I take one with me, in case I had to go to the outhouse at night or for any other emergency. She had asked all her friends and acquaintances, but the few people who owned *linternas* were not interested in selling or lending them.

Mami had given up all hope when *Papi* surprised us by bringing home a shiny, brand-new Russian flashlight. He'd bought it from a colleague, who had just returned from Moscow, for two hundred pesos. *Mami* was elated. "This is gold, *niña,*" she said, caressing *Papi's* purchase with delight. "Pure gold!"

I'd have preferred not to take something so valuable with me. It might be broken, or stolen, and I knew my parents would ask me about its fate every single Sunday. But *Mami* was inflexible.

"You will take the flashlight," she said flatly. "Darkness is dangerous," she added, a little miffed because of my evident lack of enthusiasm. "It makes me feel better to know that you won't be stumbling around if you have to go outside at midnight. And what would you do in case there is a blackout at camp?"

Likely, the same as we all did when there were blackouts in the city; sit, talk, and kill mosquitoes until we felt sleepy enough to go to bed. Grandma Gloria had two old hurricane lamps and we used them often, as there were "scheduled" blackouts at least once a week. At camp it would be more interesting, as we might be allowed to make a fire. While *Mami* and I were discussing the issue, darkness fell, ending our talk.

"*Cojones!*" *Mami* exclaimed. "Just what we needed now, a damned blackout!" And then, more calmly, "*Bueno,* we'll get to try the new flashlight before you leave."

I couldn't help smiling, because *Mami* didn't usually curse. Well, she would say shit and *coño.* She might even send somebody to the house of *el carajo,* that is, to hell, if she felt *really* upset. But this was her limit. *Cojones*—balls—was, in her opinion, a highly improper term.

"Sorry. I've been a little fidgety all day," she said in excuse. "It's because you are leaving." She sighed, but didn't sound convincing. I suspected there was something else going on.

Mami sat on the sofa and held my hand. "I've always been afraid of the dark. I am glad you are not."

Papi turned on the flashlight. Then we found out that it possessed an interesting peculiarity. Besides the regular yellow light, when a button on the side was pressed it would emit a blue or a red beam. "It makes the house look like a disco club!" *Papi* commented. "Curious, no?"

"When have you been in a disco club, Rafael?" *Mami* jumped up, furious. "And with whom? Because I've never set foot in one!"

"Neither have I," *Papi* replied quickly. "But I have seen them on TV—color TV, when I was in Prague."

Mami didn't seem pleased with his response but she only said, "Hmmm!"

I smelled tension in the air. Right at that moment, as if to make things worse, Marietta's pleading voice came from the garden of her house, "Rafael! Gloria! Could anyone come here, please? I've lost one of my contacts. And I don't even have a match!"

Papi immediately shouted back, " I am coming! Is Jorge there?"

"Yes! But he can't find it either."

As *Papi* walked out—with the flashlight, of course—*Mami* followed him. "So you're leaving us in the dark?" she asked angrily. "You'd rather help that floozy instead of staying here with your wife and your daughter? What kind of father are you?"

"Barbarita, please!" He stopped and faced her. "Don't be ridiculous! I'll be back in a couple of minutes. That poor woman needs help!"

"Poor woman, my ass," said *Mami* under her breath.

Papi dashed over to Marietta's house.

For the next half hour *Mami*, Grandma Gloria, and I could see the changing beams of light move around inside our neighbor's *casona*. Blue in the living room. Yellow in the kitchen. Red in the dining room. Then they moved out. Red in the garden. Blue around the lions. Yellow next to the picket fence. Colors kept mutating. They were stupidly wasting the batteries, *Mami* grumbled.

It occurred to me that *Papi* and Marietta couldn't be looking for the lost contact in such a random way. It had to be Crazy Jorge who was playing with my flashlight while *Papi*—

"Rafael probably found a hurricane lamp or a box of matches," Grandma Gloria said. "And he is searching inside the house, while Jorge and Marietta look outside."

Mami replied with her usual, disapproving "Hmmm!"

After the electricity returned, it was always necessary to dry the refrigerator with a kitchen towel, as the ice in the freezer melted during the blackout. I hated this chore, particularly on cool January nights, when my fingers were numbed by the chilly water that flooded our twenty-year-old Kelvinator. I quietly crept toward my bed before this happened, thinking it'd be better not to risk catching cold just two days before my departure.

The following morning I couldn't find the flashlight. Grandma Gloria didn't know where *Papi* had put it. As soon as he returned from the university, I asked him to give me back the *linterna* so I could pack it.

"Lourdes, *niña*, I am so sorry," he mumbled. "I was going to tell you yesterday but you'd gone to sleep."

I had a bad feeling I wouldn't see my new *linterna* again.

"The flashlight—uh—Jorge broke it," he went on. "Without bad intentions, naturally. He didn't mean to, but he shattered the glass. Jorge is such an awkward, clumsy guy—"

"What?" I cried out. "The monster broke *my* flashlight? Why did you let him?"

"Hush, Lourdes! It was an accident. And I do not want *Mami* to know. She can't stand poor Marietta. You know that, don't you?" I nodded. "Now, if she finds out what Jorge did, it won't contribute to neighborhood peace. But if *Mami* thinks you have taken the flashlight with you and lost it at camp, she won't be as angry."

Accustomed to obeying *Papi* without questioning since my childhood, I lowered my head and said nothing. It didn't seem fair, though. But I finally whispered, "*Bueno, Papi.* Alright."

That very day, the last one I'd spend at home, *Papi* went out in the evening and returned at nine o'clock with a carefully wrapped package. I was watching the Brazilian soap opera with Grandma Gloria, and didn't pay much attention to the mischievous smile he flashed at me as soon as he came in. Five minutes later I heard *Mami's* delighted squeals, and her urgent calls, "Lourdes, come here! *Dios mío,* it is so pretty! Hurry up!"

I ran to my parents' bedroom. Lying on their big bed, desirable and blue, was a brand-new *pitusa*. A pair of authentic, American, stylish Lee blue jeans, the kind I had silently and hopelessly coveted for months.

"Thanks, *Papi,*" I murmured. And I didn't know what else to say. I felt as if I were an accomplice to some secret, shameful crime. But this unpleasant feeling was quickly erased when I tried my *pitusa* on. It fit better than any of my other pants. It enveloped, cuddled, and seemed to enlarge my rear end.

Papi whistled.

"You look great, Lulu!" *Mami* exclaimed. "But you aren't taking that *pitusa* to the camp. It'll get all dirty and frayed in two days, and it cost way too much."

"Come on, Barbarita. Let the girl take the blue jeans to Pinar if she wants to," said *Papi,* grinning at me behind *Mami's* back. "After all, I got them for her. Lourdes is not a baby anymore. We can trust our daughter to take care of her things."

"If you say so—" *Mami* shrugged.

I avoided her eyes but couldn't resist the temptation to exchange a knowing glance with my father.

"I think *Mami* is right, though," I replied. "The School-in-the-Field camps are rather iffy places, where things easily get lost."

That night the blackout surprised us at ten o'clock. When the lights went off, I was already in bed curled with my *matrioskas*, pressing my cheek against the Pinocchio embroidered on the pillowcase.

At eleven I noticed that the moonlight was falling directly on my bed. I got up to shut the window. Grandma Gloria had told me that the chilly touch of moonlight caused fevers, epilepsy, madness, and strange maladies. I looked over at Marietta's house. For the first time I asked myself why she and her son had five bedrooms, why they needed such a big *casona*. In a really egalitarian society, I thought, houses like hers—and ours, too—shouldn't belong to small families, but to large ones, to museums or to public schools.

In the middle of my reflections, I saw a red light shining in Marietta's den. It immediately turned blue. And then I heard her voice, as clear as the bright January moon, saying in mortified tones, "For God's sake, Jorge, stop playing with that stupid gadget! Don't you have anything more constructive to do?"

I closed the window and went back to my bed. I found it difficult to sleep that night. I spent the next two hours wishing, despite my sincere desire to emulate Che Guevara, that I could stay home with *Papi, Mami,* and Grandma Gloria, that I didn't have to leave my home and face the dangers that Sabina had prophesied I'd encounter at camp, that I could preserve for a little longer the rosy illusions of childhood.

◄ CHAPTER IV ►

THE WAITING ROOM was full of nervous kids, anxious relatives, tin buckets, boxes, wooden suitcases, and bundles of blankets. There were plastic bags bursting with oranges, grapefruits, and bananas, and heavy jute bags containing Russian canned meat, canned soups, and condensed milk. The air was filled with advice, pledges, loud music from a portable radio, laughter, and muffled sobs.

I couldn't wait to leave, tormented by my parents' gloomy looks and endless nagging. They stayed in the waiting room until the last minute, patting me sadly and stuffing my handbag with sweet bread bought at the train station store and peanut brittle sold by a furtive street vendor.

"Are you warm enough, Lourdes?" *Mami* asked. "Let me see, *niña*, do you have a jersey under the shirt?" She felt under my denim work shirt. How embarrassing!

The *azabache* and an "Outstanding Communist" medal hung from a silver chain that Grandma Inés had slipped around my neck. First I had told her I would never wear the amulet, but she reminded me that Fidel and the *barbudos* had worn charm necklaces and crucifixes in the Sierra Maestra Mountains and then I relented.

But I insisted on wearing my medal, too. I had been honored as an Outstanding Communist a year before. *Papi* and I felt very proud of my award.

"Remember to put your socks on at night," *Papi* said. "It's always cooler in the countryside."

"If you haven't had a bowel movement by the second day, take a laxative," *Mami* added. "Be careful and don't confuse them with the vitamin C pills!"

I wanted to yell, "*Coño*, shut up!" Instead, I smiled and nodded obediently. I looked at my parents. *Mami* was wearing her blue-and-red polka-dotted dress which needed to be ironed. *Papi* had donned his spotless white *guayabera*, ironed, no doubt, by *Mami's* hands.

"Don't bathe in cool water," she went on. "It's better to have earth on your body than your body under the earth!"

Mami's short, curly hair stuck out of her head like an alert cat's ears. *Papi's* golden mustache quivered slightly as he whispered to her, "Keep your voice down, Barbarita, please."

Mami often deferred to *Papi*. But that day she ignored his request and said even louder, almost defiantly, "Stuff yourself, Lulu, we'll bring more food next Sunday! Don't work too hard! Be careful with the machetes!"

The whistling of the train put an end to the deluge of advice. I kissed *Papi's* rosy cheeks covered with his soft blond beard and *Mami's* brown, smooth face. Then I ran to meet my classmates who were already lining up forlornly. The silence that had fallen over the train station was broken by *Mami's* shouts as she trotted after me, "*Niña,* don't forget to wear your grandma's cashmere sweater at night! And don't sleep near an open window!"

I pretended not to hear her. How I hated to be called *"niña"* in public! *Mami* knew that, yet it made no difference to her. A few girls simpered but soon other mothers followed *Mami's* example, giving their last admonitions to their mortified offspring, and I felt better.

Finally, our group boarded the train. I chose a seat by the window. With considerable effort, I placed my weighty suitcase under the seat and my two heavy handbags beside me.

Fat Olga and Marisol sat in front of me. The two girls offered a vivid contrast. Even when seated, dark, lanky Marisol was erect, like an arrogant pine, while Olga, freckled and roly-poly, rested in her friend's shadow with the grin of an impish elf.

A tall girl entered the car. She wore black pants and a brown shirt, the same color as her large eyes.

"*Hola*, Aurora!" Fat Olga said.

So here we have the famous Aurora, I thought, examining the newcomer closely. I knew her name because the boys in my class were always talking about her, though we had never been in the same class. Some called her The Beauty, which I now saw with a tinge of envy, was no exaggeration. As Aurora walked, her hips undulated as if they were dancing to their own inner rhythm. Her waist-long braids struck her back in cadence with her steps. Her breasts pushed against her tight shirt and I wondered if she had forgotten to put on a brassiere.

Aurora stopped by my seat and asked, "May I sit by you?" I hurried to move my bags. Aurora plopped down and stretched her long legs. I smelled the strong fragrance of violets.

An old lady knocked on the train window and said something to Fat Olga who jumped up and ran out. A brigade of boys, herded in by our high school principal, began to occupy the rest of the seats. Alberto Díaz, our principal, was short and with his inflated belly he resembled a worm that had swallowed an orange. His posterior—

big, ample, almost feminine—waggled like that of a well-fed pig. The train whistled again.

"Where did Olga go?" Marisol asked. "We're going to leave without her!"

A third whistle heralded the immediate departure of the train.

Marisol ran to the door screaming, "Olga! Come back!"

"Sit down!" the principal scolded her. "Where do you think you are, in an Old Havana tenement? Sit down and shut up!"

"*Viejo cabrón!*" Marisol muttered, returning to her place.

"Hey, Aurora," a blond, muscular boy called to her. "Why don't you come here and sit by the window with me? You can't see the view from there."

Aurora switched her seat but her perfume lingered.

"As if she cared about the landscape," smirked Marisol.

Suddenly Fat Olga made a triumphant entrance carrying two onion pizzas inside a greasy paper bag.

"*Hija*, you almost missed the train!" Marisol cried. "Didn't you hear the whistles?"

"I shit on the whistles three times over," replied Fat Olga. "My grandma went to the Pizzeria Parque Central just to get these pizzas for me."

The train started. Someone began to sing.

Al campamento William Soler
las guaguas llenas van a llegar.
Con patriotismo va nuestra escuela
de cara al campo a trabajar.
(At the William Soler camp
the crowded buses will arrive.
Our school goes patriotically
to work in the fields.)

I felt drowsy, lulled by the song and the rhythmical crac-crac of the train. The fragrance of Olga's onion pizzas and Aurora's perfume floated through the car. I fell asleep when the first Pinar del Río hills appeared, bordering the road like green velvet giants watching over the country towns.

⊰ CHAPTER V ⊱

A WIRE FENCE SURROUNDED the camp in its rusty metal embrace. The whole place smelled of dampened earth. A dark cloud hovered over our heads. A flock of sparrows that had alighted on the roofs fled in panic as we approached.

A strange feeling came over me as I went through the gate. I saw two dilapidated barracks and a brick dining hall. The barracks were big, flat constructions with narrow windows. Among thick trees at a stone's throw away stood a hip-roofed cabin that resembled a witch's house.

I felt an inexplicable impulse to run away. My friends considered me a *pendeja,* a coward, and said I feared my own shadow, but this time the other kids seemed similarly unhappy. Even the two adults who accompanied us—Juanito Lopesanto, a handsome math teacher, and Comrade Katia, our Marxism instructor—were not in very high spirits.

"What an odd place!" Comrade Katia said. She took off the round, gold-rimmed eyeglasses that gave her face a severe air and added, "Doesn't the sky look bloody?"

The sunset had wrapped the camp in a reddish halo, as well as the distant hills and the clouds that crowned them. The earth that covered the road was red, the tin roofs of the barracks, gleaming with the last rays of the sun, were red. The flowers of an enormous tree, a *framboyán* tree, which presided over the camp, were red. A whiff of stale dust greeted us when we entered the girls' barracks. Although large, the building looked crammed full. Two hundred bunk beds, covered with jute mattresses, were jammed up against one another. Three torn, greasy posters—all of Che Guevara—adorned the walls. They, at least, reminded me of home. Fat Olga sneezed. Marisol opened a window and bright motes of dust danced in a weak ray of sun, defying the law of gravity and our efforts to clear the air.

Aurora chose an upper bunk and began unpacking her suitcase. I followed her and took the lower bed. Fat Olga and Marisol occupied the next bunk bed. Aurora sprayed perfume on her sheets and complained about the cool breeze that entered through the window. "My blanket is too thin! There is only one heavy blanket at home and it belongs to my brother Armando so I'll freeze my ass here. *Coño!*"

"You can use mine, if you want," I offered. I overcame my usual shyness in the hope of getting acquainted with such a popular girl. "Let's pile them over us and sleep together."

Aurora agreed. She helped me make the bed. While we arranged sheets and blankets, I observed her hands. Her long nails reminded me of the white and pink shells I had collected on Varadero beach, where my parents and I had spent a week during the summer. In my mind I went back to the *Hotel Internacional*, where we had stayed. With its carpeted rooms, mirror-covered walls, and glittering chandeliers, the hotel had seemed like a fairy-tale palace.

The trip had been a reward from the Party for *Papi*. Our room—spacious, fresh, decorated with pictures of marinas—had air-conditioning and a color TV. Nothing was rationed in the restaurant and the guests could order as many dishes as they wanted. *Mami* and

I had gone for long walks together while *Papi* stayed in the lobby, sipping *mojitos* or talking to a group of sturdy Bulgarian tourists. I'd busied myself picking up shells and small starfish. But *Mami's* expression had been strangely bitter. It was then I began to suspect that something was wrong between my parents, suspicions that had been confirmed by *Papi's* escapes to you-know-where and *Mami's* black *santería* dolls. Even that night, the first one we spent in the camp, I couldn't avoid worrying about them.

THOUGH CAMP rules forbade it, many girls curled up together in pairs, creating a flesh barrier against the cold. After a few unsuccessful attempts to stop the practice, the teachers pretended not to notice. It happened in all School-in-the-Fields camps.

Aurora and I slept quietly but others did not. Long after the lights were turned off, the sound of beds creaking and moving punctuated the nights at regular intervals until daybreak. The very first night, Fat Olga's cries of ecstasy could be heard at 2 A.M., followed by Marisol's agitated breathing, while their bed bounced in a very revealing way.

Aurora's warmth comforted me in the darkness while we huddled together, transmitting a feeling of security and peace. Sleeping with her was almost like sleeping in my own bed at home and made up for the harshness of camp life. The bunk beds were very narrow. Sometimes when Aurora squirmed her thighs rubbed my *papaya*. I enjoyed the contact: I didn't see anything dangerous in our involuntary touching.

FOR MY last birthday *Papi* had given me a copy of *Che's Journal*. I brought the book with me and read it in the evenings. Once, I became so absorbed that I forgot the time. When I noticed that the barracks were empty, I ran to the dining hall and hurriedly grabbed a tray containing burned rice, some sauceless macaroni, and a spoonful of saffron jam. All the tables were occupied. A weak lightbulb illuminated the scene of fifty kids devouring their meals, tin spoons hitting their trays, burping, laughing, and talking loudly despite the presence of the principal who glanced reprovingly at the noisiest from time to time. The place reeked of reused grease and burning wood.

I wandered in, trying to find an empty chair, when the principal spotted me. "You can't find a seat?" he yelled. "Well, then you are going to eat on the floor! It will teach you to get here on time!"

Some kids laughed, others whistled. I trembled at the old man's angry words. Through a veil of tears I saw Aurora seated next to a blond boy. Was she laughing at me, too? I thought of leaving the tray and running away but I was both hungry and paralyzed with fear. Then the blond boy left his place and walked toward the door, swallowing the last of his macaroni on the way.

"I shooed him off," Aurora said as I sat by her. "I couldn't let you eat on the floor like a dog!" She put her arm around my shoulder and smiled. I smiled shyly in return. The threatening shadow of the principal was eclipsed by The Beauty's face.

After the incident in the dining hall Aurora and I became great friends. I felt so grateful that I would have followed her to the moon had she requested it. Unconsciously, I began to imitate some of her mannerisms and tried to talk and walk the way she did. Not an easy task, though. We couldn't have been more different. She was at least six inches taller, with a nice round ass, where mine was small and bony. She was a white beauty. I was a plain *mulatica*. Not even an arrogant, long-legged, big-rumped mulatta, distinguished by the ampleness of my posterior. Mine looked like a sad, deflated cushion under my pants. My skin was the color of a paper bag—*cartucho*, as Grandma Gloria called it—and my hair, wiry as a bunch of aluminum rods, wouldn't move even in the middle of a hurricane.

But Aurora loved to have admirers, to be worshipped by faithful, obedient satellites, and I happened to be good at worship. I kept our place in the food line while she stayed in the barracks, took a bath, or wandered around. I polished her nails, massaged her feet after work, brushed her hair, and scratched her head to scare away the fear of thunder that seized her on rainy nights. In the tobacco house, I gladly helped Aurora sew her *cujes* and supplied her with leaves.

The tobacco house was a large, unpainted hall, almost as big as our barracks, equipped with rustic wooden benches where we sat to work. Light came through three small windows located on the northern wall. A family of bats shared the place with us but they kept tolerably quiet. A sweet-tempered owl dwelled in a roof corner and we named it after Comrade Katia because of the dark circles that surrounded its eyes. Chabela, a kind, motherly girl, adopted Katita and treated the owl to snacks often taken from her own meals.

A mango tree grew outside the tobacco house and we soon found the fruit hidden among its leaves. I, too, learned to climb it to retrieve the golden balls that left a slightly acid taste in the mouth.

Our job was to sew green leaves of tobacco onto dried sticks of wood called *cujes* using special needles. An individual's production goal was fifteen *cujes* in the morning and ten in the afternoon. The *cujes* were then stored in a high, shadowy place so the leaves could dry. A strong aroma penetrated even the kerchiefs we wore to help fight the overpowering stench.

There were "long" workers like Marisol, who could reach the expected goal every day, and "short" workers like Aurora, who never achieved half of it even if I helped her. But then, most of us came up short.

Only girls sewed. Boys, grouped into supply brigades, picked leaves and found *cujes* in the fields, then brought them to the tobacco house. A boy named Papirito was in our supply brigade and he always did his best to get close to Aurora and to hand her the smallest *cujes* he could find. (The smaller a *cuje*, the less leaves were needed to be sewn onto it.) Papirito would stare at The Beauty, laugh every time she made a joke, and listen to her chatter reverentially.

"*CoÑo*, I feel like eating something sweet," Aurora said one afternoon, while we were working in the tobacco house. "I'd do anything for a guava pie!"

Papirito, carrying a *cuje,* came closer to us.

"Uh—I'll find some guava pie for you, Aurora," he whispered. "Just wait."

She didn't answer. She may not have even noticed him.

When we arrived back at camp, Papirito rushed to the boys' barracks and returned, panting.

"Here, I have half of a guava pie left." He offered it to Aurora, lowering his eyes.

The Beauty grabbed the piece of pie and quickly devoured it, not even thanking Papirito. He didn't seem to mind and stood there, looking at her with puppylike adoration.

"I am sure that Papirito wants some kind of payment," joked Fat Olga. "What about a kiss, Aurora?"

Papirito ran away, his ears as red as the *framboyán* flowers.

Aurora confessed, licking her fingers, "I was so hungry, *hija,* that I'd have kissed even him!"

I couldn't understand why Papirito kept circling Aurora like a moth around a candle. Shy, sheepish Papirito looked like an unfinished sketch of a boy. He wasn't just plain ugly, with the normal uncoordinated, pimpled, sweat-stained ugliness of most teenagers.

He had all that plus he smelled of cough syrup, and had bad breath. His skin was a sickly whitish hue, splashed with freckles. He was frequently sick. Life had always kicked Papirito in the rear. Not only was he afflicted with agonizing asthma attacks, but everybody picked on him. His boots vanished from under his bunk bed and reappeared inside garbage cans or in the filthiest part of the latrines. Boys would put dead frogs, dirty papers, and rotten food on his pillow, throw mud balls and orange peels at him during the breaks, and brazenly steal from the well-filled bag of food he had brought from Havana. They called him "The Mouse."

A hostile circle enclosed Papirito everywhere he went. Not even the younger kids respected him. Things hadn't been much different at school back in Havana, but then the teachers' presence made his life less difficult. The School-in-the-Fields proved a perfect arena for the bullying tactics of his classmates.

No one wanted to be seen with Papirito, but once in a while I would chat with him in the tedious early evenings as we sat on a bench near the girls' barracks, under the leafy *framboyán*. Occasionally a flaming red flower dropped on us from the splendid tree, which was about twenty feet high, a mass of foliage and color whose protective shade attracted many a couple after dark.

Indifferent to the romantic setting, Papirito and I talked mostly about books. My favorite was *Che's Journal*. Many times I imagined going to Bolivia and joining the *guerrilleros* near the Ñacahuasí River. Papirito preferred poems, and had brought Lorca's *Romancero Gitano* with him. We read it together. But our conversations never lasted long. Intruders were always ready to interrupt with sarcastic remarks that sometimes included me. When that happened, I quickly cut Papirito off and didn't talk to him for a couple of days.

One afternoon we were quietly reading poetry when a tenth-grade girl shouted, "Papirito, are you looking for a girlfriend?" A group of bored onlookers encircled us, anxious for a few minutes of cheap amusement.

"No, *hija,* he has many. Hundreds of them!" Marisol said. "Even Lourdes is hooked—"

"Oh, how could you do that to me, Papirito? I adore you and you despise my love! You prefer Lourdes, the thin lizard! Traitor!"

The teaser ran away laughing. I hated her—and Papirito. Too timid to chase after her and slap her, as Aurora would have probably done, I fled to the barracks, embarrassed and hurt. Papirito was left alone under the tree, innocent of everything except being a submissive, defenseless little boy.

Only Chabela defended him. Chabela dreamed of studying psychology at the university and had excellent grades. She would scurry from weeping girls to lonely boys to comfort them. She scolded Marisol. Chabela had a pointed nose, bright eyes, a slight overbite, and was determined to rescue the whole world.

DURING THE first cold nights when Aurora stayed outside the barracks necking with a boyfriend, I thought of Papirito and felt really sorry for him. My sympathy was tainted by self-pity: I recognized in myself many of the attributes that made him the butt of the camp jokers. We were both shy, only children; library mice." We were skinny, short, and had few friends. But, at least, I had Aurora. Papirito had no choice but to keep to himself, as lonely as our high school librarian, aged Comrade Ramón. Sometimes Papirito looked almost as frail as old Ramón was.

Maybe because I became Aurora's best friend, or because he knew of my silent sympathy for him, one evening Papirito hesitantly confessed to me what he thought was a deep secret. "I'm in love with Aurora," he said. "Whenever I see her, I am grabbed by her smell of violets. But don't tell her or anybody else, please."

I promised him eternal silence, aware that my discretion would not help him much. Aurora already knew that he liked her, as did everybody else in the camp.

That night I dreamed of Aurora for the first time. Since our arrival in Pinar del Río, I had dreamed only of my beloved *matrioskas*. When I was in Havana, I would put them into their little cradles at ten o'clock and kiss them good night. At camp, I had missed my dolls and shed a few tears thinking of them. But after Papirito's confession, the dreams of the round, stunned-looking faces of the *matrioskas* were replaced by images of Aurora's brown eyes and graceful body. I saw her sewing *cujes* in the tobacco house, eating a yellow-and-red mango and smacking her lips. I saw her changing clothes before she got into bed . . .

⊰ CHAPTER VI ⊱

THE THICK ATMOSPHERE of the tobacco house weighed on us like an invisible sticky net. It smelled like rotten mangoes and bat guano. Bits of leaves floated in the dense air. It was suffocating, humid, and dark, not with the fresh, cool, darkness of the night, but with a stifling, heavy dimness that oppressed the spirits and the lungs.

We all worked hard—it seemed even harder because we never had enough to eat. At 5 A.M. a siren rang in the barracks, breaking into our sleep of exhaustion. We reluctantly abandoned our bunk beds and began to dress, cursing the siren, the *cujes,* and the camp principal. We left the barracks, hastily washed, and rushed to the dining hall.

After an endless wait in line, a glass of sugarless, smokey-smelling powdered milk and a small piece of bread were served at six o'clock. Sometimes the bread was stale, sometimes the milk was scorched. I thought of the hardships suffered by Che Guevara and the *guerrilleros* in Bolivia and tried not to complain.

At 6:45 we performed the "civic act." Each brigade reported on the production goals reached the previous day and we shouted patriotic slogans loudly. *We are all ready to die for the Homeland, the*

Revolution, and Socialism. So as to honor the memory of the Playa Girón martyrs, we will produce more and more every day. At 7:30 we left for the tobacco fields.

You are the New Man dreamed of by Che Guevara. At 12:15 the brigades returned to the camp and had lunch. Burned rice, smelly fish, boiled potatoes for the New Man. Then back to the fields until 5 P.M., when our tired bodies were drawn to the bunk beds in our barracks. After six came the daily routine of filling buckets with icy water from the camp cistern and waiting in line for a turn to take a quick bath. Then we would kill time until seven, when lines were formed again and *the young soldiers of the Cuban Revolution* waited with famished resignation because *the future belongs completely to Socialism.* Dinner was served at 7:30. Potatoes, fish, and rice again and perhaps the bonus of a boiled egg. Sometimes Comrade Katia organized a political workshop afterward. *Study, work, rifle. Viva Fidel!* Usually we had free time until ten o'clock, when the lights were turned off and the camp began to bubble with nocturnal life. Boys and girls slipped out of the barracks to compensate for a dull day of work and meager rations with ample servings of love.

Time obeyed strange laws in the School-in-the-Fields. During the workdays in the tobacco house, hours were elongated. We girls, bent over our *cujes,* could almost hear the seconds repeating themselves, then the interminable minutes dragging by. The boys who mechanically picked tobacco leaves, threw anything green that they found into their baskets, including weeds and thorns. Eternity was no longer an abstract concept for us. The evenings were long carpets of apathy which had to be trod under the lethargic surveillance of wearied teachers. But at night the rhythm changed. Hours flew. Minutes became nanoseconds.

On Saturday evenings, the most energetic and fun-loving

would organize *bailables*, miniparties whose main attraction was the strident music from the radio that the loudspeakers blasted until 11 P.M. The *bailables* were pale copies of parties thrown in Havana, but they at least diluted the monotony of the long and chilly Pinar del Río nights.

Teachers slept in our barracks, female teachers with girls, male teachers with boys. Comrade Katia and a skinny spinster known as *La Flaca* slept in mine. They generally minded their own business. Poor *Flaca* was always so tired that she fell asleep right after dinner without paying any attention to the loud conversations and peculiar noises that came from the bunk beds. Comrade Katia, armed with a flashlight and her eternal eyeglasses, read quietly until 1 A.M. every night, absorbed in her Marxism manual.

The male teachers had more energy but they did not care what the boys did. Sometimes they would slip out of the barracks too. Sexual intercourse between teachers and students was outlawed, but because of this rule the flavor of these relationships became more spicy. A "teacher boyfriend" was a trophy.

As I was not accustomed to hard work, I went to bed exhausted and fell asleep immediately. But sleep was no longer the unruffled lake into which I used to dive peacefully every night in Havana. It had become an agitated, frightening ocean. Aurora appeared in almost all my dreams and this involuntary fixation troubled me deeply.

When I was a child I played only with the neighborhood girls. Grandma Gloria said that boys would touch my little *papaya* and force me to do dirty things. (She didn't know that I had learned a few dirty things just by myself.) Grandma forbade me to talk to boys and, being a timid, docile *niña*, I never disobeyed. Because of my shyness, flat butt, and thin legs, boys showed no interest in me either as a playmate or as a future girlfriend. But for a long time their indifference didn't bother me at all. The boys I knew looked filthy and nasty. (Oh, that horrible Crazy Jorge, the monster next door!) The games they played were noisy and rough. They scared me.

Later on, in high school, I went out with girls or they visited me. Except for Papirito, I had never had a male friend. But when my dreams of Aurora began, I wondered if, despite their roughness and lack of cleanliness, I should be paying more attention to boys, perhaps I should be dreaming of *them*.

Why did I dream of another woman? Grandma Gloria would say that was ten times worse than having a boyfriend! And the tingling "down there" that often woke me up! And the electric feeling in my *papaya* that Aurora's touch caused! I began to distrust myself. Something odd and dangerous was incubating inside my body, I feared, like those whitish, disgusting worms that dwelled hidden within the tobacco plants.

EVERY EVENING, after taking a bath, Aurora began her meticulous grooming routine. Twice a week, wearing only a loose transparent blouse, she would spend an hour sprawled in our bunk bed, shaving her legs and armpits. Later she would brush her hair—or ask me to do it—until it became a cascade of brown rain. Then she would get dressed as carefully as if she were attending a *quinceañera* party in Havana. She would attire herself in her favorite outfit—a black T-shirt, a black-and-white bandana, and black corduroy pants. Unlike most girls, who, during the first days in camp went to the bathhouse or hid behind a bed to change clothes, Aurora undressed in front of us without the slightest shyness.

Her makeup was a serious and complicated business. She used a red pencil to outline her mouth, and filled in her lips with an aged pink lipstick. She would apply the same red pencil to her cheeks, rubbing them with a piece of paper. Swallowing toothpaste guaranteed her sweetened breath. Then The Beauty was ready for her nightly adventures.

"Men are so dumb," she said. "I just went out with Tomás, you know, that blond guy. Vladimir waited for me to finish necking with Tomás and then said he was in love with me too. When I told him that I liked Tomás, he seemed more in love than ever. I really don't care for *either* of them, but they are both crazy about me. And I do like to make them suffer."

The following night Vladimir was favored and Tomás discarded. Aurora changed lovers as easily and shamelessly as she changed clothes.

"Aurora, *hija,* why do you have so many boyfriends?" I asked her. We were in our bunk bed. I brushed her hair while she polished her long, scarlet nails.

"Lourdes, what a question!" She looked both surprised and amused. "Because I like to make love, girl!"

"But you don't have only one guy, you have several—"

"What can I do?" she said proudly. "Men are after me all the time, *chica.* And I really like it when a guy dunks his bread in my *café con leche.*"

"Isn't it bad to have many lovers?" I insisted. "They may think you are too easy."

"Don't be old-fashioned, girl." She laughed out loud. "It isn't bad at all! It's very good! Listen, I had two guys at the same time in Havana, before we left. I saw one after classes and the other one at night. I took it up the ass with the afternoon guy. *Uff!* He is a musician and plays the drum for Los Van Van. He always has money and once took me to the Tropicana. The other one is a carpenter. Great in bed but always penniless. Oh well—I just had to be cautious so neither of them would suspect he wasn't the only one."

I imagined Aurora kissing the drummer, the carpenter, Vladimir, Tomás. I longed to learn about the ways of love, of which I was still ignorant. How would it feel to be a white, desirable, pretty, big-assed girl, at least for a day? How would it feel to be kissed by her?

LOVE, WITH its pains and glamour, was a constant, essential theme of the camp tunes, *las cadencias*. They were very short songs—only four verses—that we would sing on our way to the fields and inside the tobacco house. Many tunes had a moral, while others offered love advice to girls. The most popular among them stressed the traditional evil of males, and their ungrateful response to female devotion.

We had two good singers in our brigade—Chabela and Fat Olga. One of them sang the first two verses and the rest repeated the response, which was a high-pitched *cua-cua-cua*. The next two verses followed, and then the chorus, *Alo, alo cua-cua-cuá María Cocuyé, cua-cua-cua*. As we made our way through the long corridors of sunflowers and plantain trees, Fat Olga admonished us:

> *Los hombres de hoy en día*
> *son como los tranvías,*
> *que cada cinco minutos*
> *están cambiando de vía.*
> *Alo, alo cua-cua-cuá María Cocuyé, cua-cua-cua.*
> (Men of today
> are like the trams,
> every five minutes
> they change their way.)
> *Alo, alo cua-cua-cuá María Cocuyé, cua-cua-cua.*

There were also political *cadencias*, like this one about Che Guevara:

El Che nació en Argentina
con una estrella en la frente
alumbrando el continente
de la América oprimida.
(Che was born in Argentina
with a star on his forehead
illuminating the continent
of oppressed America.)
Alo, alo cua-cua-cuá María Cocuyé, cua-cua-cua.

I copied my favorite *cadencias* into a green grammar notebook. I also wrote down the lyrics of popular songs, Young Communist slogans, reminders of things that needed to be done, and questions I should ask the teachers when we were back in school.

Elena was the best *cadencia* singer we had ever heard, even better than Chabela and Fat Olga. She and her father, Pancho the Widower, lived near our camp in the hip-roofed cabin, the "witch's house."

Pancho was big, tall, wrinkled, and grouchy. He drove an old, dusty orange Ford since he was no ordinary peasant, but *"El Responsable,"* the overseer of the fields where the School-in-the-Fields brigades worked. He never seemed happy with our work. He considered the *Habaneros* careless kids, greenhorns. He'd go to the tobacco house twice a day and shout at us because we were too slow, too sloppy, or because our *cujes* came up half empty. He despised the boys and laughed at the girls when he wasn't mad at us and cursing. We all disliked him.

But his daughter, Elena, was kind and beautiful. A slender mulatta with a prominent rump, her good hair and blue eyes attested to her mixed heritage. On her father's side, she was a descendant of the Canary Island immigrants, who had worked in the tobacco plantations since the beginning of the century. Her mother must have been a black woman, or a very dark mulatta like *Mami*. I asked myself in despair, why had Elena gotten the most desirable traits of both sides, the blue eyes, the big ass, and the wavy hair, while I had been born brown-eyed, assless, and with a bird's nest on my head.

Only two things marred Elena's beauty; a two-inch scar that crossed her left cheek—though she kept it covered with her long curls—and her shabby, faded clothes. She often wore her father's ragged, sweat-stained shirts, and old-fashioned skirts that looked like they had belonged to her grandmother. The most generous girls in camp asked their parents for used pants and blouses and passed them on to her. I'd have done the same but I knew it would be impossible for Elena to squeeze her well-developed body into my childish, size-four garments.

Elena had traveled out of the small town she lived in only once in her whole life. She had gone to Viñales with her father, for a doctor's appointment. She had never been in the capital and she reverently admired us, "the people from *La Habana.*" Every evening she would join a brigade and sing *cadencias* all the way back to the camp, where she stayed until nightfall to escape the loneliness of her home. Elena said that our barracks were "a little Havana," so lively and full of amusing things to do. We secretly laughed at her naïveté.

She helped in the kitchen, cleaned the principal's office, and chatted with the girls, because, like most country women, she was too shy to get close to the boys. "How can you do that? You *chicas* from *La Habana* are really bold," Elena would murmur with her sweet-sounding accent when she discovered a couple necking openly under the *framboyán*.

Students and teachers liked Elena and felt flattered by her

candid admiration. I tried to get her interested in books, but she didn't care for reading. Aurora taught her how to use makeup. She was much more successful. Comrade Katia talked to her about the Socialist Agrarian Reform. "Elena is the symbol of a new generation of *guajiros*," the teacher liked to say. "They are the peasant children of our revolution, the future developers of communist agriculture."

Boys would hang around the *guajirita*, their lust only contained by the machete that old Pancho carried with him everywhere and by his repeated threats to cut off the balls of the *cabrón* city boy who dared to touch his daughter. So our male comrades were limited to admiring Elena's beauty at a respectful distance.

One of these admirers baptized her *la sinsonte*, the mockingbird, because of her melodious voice. But amid the prevailing goodwill that paved Elena's way in the camp there was Chabela, the wannabe psychologist, the only one who didn't trust the *guajirita*. When the others praised Elena in front of her, Chabela would shake her head saying, "This girl pretends to be so pure and shy, but I have seen her swimming naked in the creek. She may have the face of a cherub, but she also has a woman's eyes, sharp and piercing as her father's machete.

"Your face tells lies,
your eyes can't.
You deceive others,
I know who you are.
Alo, alo cua-cua-cuá María Cocuyé, cua-cua-cua."

The *cadencia* singers felt particularly inspired when crossing the fields sprinkled with morning dew. Our boots, heavy with mud, became stuck in the wet ground which smelled gloriously in the early hours of the day. The girls' loud, cheerful voices produced a special exaltation of the mind and the body, a blend of joy in our youth and of pain for the years that passed us by without being noticed. Fragile and tender feelings floated behind the brigades like pink gauze.

⊰ CHAPTER VII ⊱

THE ENEMY HAD spotted our team. I couldn't see the soldiers yet, but I knew they would surround us in a few minutes. Time was running out. Fortunately, I was in charge. Without the slightest fear, I stood up and addressed my subordinates. *Now, prepare your rifles. Don't fear, comrades! Che Guevara is with us! Fire!*

Perched in the branches of a small tree, I lived my *guerrillera* fantasy until Fat Olga brought me back to reality with a loud chuckle and a mango seed skillfully aimed at my head.

That Saturday after lunch, Fat Olga, Marisol, Aurora, and I sneaked out of camp when the principal and teachers were in a meeting. The fact that we were not supposed to leave the grounds made our four-hour adventure incredibly thrilling. We strolled around the tobacco fields, chased an old, bored cow, and ate greenish mangoes that tasted to us like forbidden fruit. Finally we stopped by a creek near Pancho's house. Neighboring *guajiras* would bathe there at dusk, tormenting our boys with the spectacle of their aquatic games.

It was an unusually warm afternoon and we, too, went for a swim in the creek, our brassieres and panties as bathing suits. Fat Olga, being Fat Olga, took everything off and showed off her titties. We looked at each other, comparing bodies. Then I discovered the secret of Aurora's charm. She looked more like a woman than any other girl in the camp. Most of us still carried some of the unwanted traits of childhood, but Aurora had gotten rid of them all. Her face, waist, breasts, and pose were those of a fully mature woman. Her *papaya* was covered by dark, curly hair. Though I tried not to stare, my eyes seemed to be fastened to her body.

The creek water bubbled like milk when it boiled in Grandma Gloria's pot. The nearby bushes were bathed in liquid dust. Slippery blue rocks paved the creek's bottom and frightened little fish caressed my legs. I floated close to Aurora while red-throated hummingbirds and green *periquitos* flew and chirped above us. Marisol and Fat Olga swam so closely together that they looked like a gigantic fish with four tails. But soon I broke the magic of the moment, abandoning my friends to take refuge from the sun under a palm tree, refusing to become burned to a crisp. During the short Caribbean winter, Grandma Gloria was convinced that my skin acquired a paler hue, which she wanted me to preserve as long as I could. I entirely agreed with her. Grandma Gloria bought me parasols and wide-brimmed straw hats, and frowned whenever my parents took me to the beach. "A crackling, that's what you are going to make out of her," she protested. "*Un chicharrón!*"

I was curled up in the grass, protected by a towel, when I heard the sound of soft footsteps. I looked around, scared. If Comrade Katia—or worse, the principal—found us there, what would happen? For the first time since we'd come to camp, I remembered Sabina and kissed my *azabache* in a silent prayer to Grandma Inés's dark gods.

"*Hola*," Elena said. "How are you?"

I sighed, relieved. Elena waved to the girls who were still playing in the creek and yelled, "Come here! What are you doing? The Mother-of-Water will be furious! Get out or she'll drown you all!"

Fat Olga ran out of the water. She grabbed my towel to dry herself. Marisol and Aurora followed her. When we all gathered around Elena, four nervous, wet, and half-naked girls, the *guajirita* launched into a lengthy explanation of the dangers that lurked in the creek. "An old Mother-of-Water is the owner of this place, the one who keeps it running," Elena explained, impressively. "The Mother looks like a big snake with paws and horns. The paws come out of her belly and are as big as tree trunks. She is very astute and can sometimes be dangerous. She may be listening to our conversation right now."

Aurora whistled. Fat Olga farted. Marisol shrugged. We had listened to the *guajirita*, smiling sometimes to pretend we were not afraid. But when Elena finished, Fat Olga peered nervously into the creek and said, "I think we should return to the camp now. The teachers' meeting must have finished an hour ago!"

Back in the barracks, we discussed Elena's words, which seemed less frightening than they had been by the creek. Could there be such a thing as a Mother-of-Water? Marisol said it must be a fable concocted by selfish Elena, who didn't want us to enjoy the fresh waters of the creek. Aurora remarked that it was natural for an uneducated *guajirita* to be superstitious. Fat Olga admitted that there might be a snake living nearby and the peasants' imagination had added horns and paws to it.

The story of the Mother-of-Water had not impressed me. I could only think of Aurora's tight body, with the dark boa of her hair curling around her neck, and her gleaming, dripping white thighs . . .

That night I didn't dream of Aurora. I didn't dream of anything because I didn't sleep at all. I squirmed in our bunk bed, rubbing against her, remembering over and over the scene at the creek. I saw the drops of water quivering on Aurora's throat like a liquid necklace, her breasts as full as ripened mangoes, the hair between her legs. I thought of kissing her softly on her lips. And in my mind, I called her *mi amor.*

Aurora the Beauty, the lady of the night with her long hair, round ass, and ivory legs. Brown eyes. Scarlet nails. Come close to me. Your face in the mirror. Look at me. Aurora, the smell of violets and salt. Ah, I dream to touch you there, Aurora . . .

THE FOLLOWING morning in the tobacco house I helped my friend diligently. I sewed most of Aurora's *cujes* and enjoyed a guilty pleasure when the large, rusted needle hurt my fingers, as if this discomfort would atone for my sins of the night before. For a few days I felt utterly miserable. There was no remedy. I had become a *tortillera,* a dyke like Fat Olga and Marisol, and soon the whole camp would notice. Aurora, the teachers, my classmates, my parents, and the rest of the world would eventually find out and despise me. Worst of all, I wouldn't be able to join the Young Communists. Che Guevara had stated that all gays should be sent to labor camps so as to make men out of them. He hadn't said anything about lesbians, but the rule must be the same for them. The New Man and the New Woman ought to be straight. What had I done? Was it my fault? Perhaps I had started dreaming the wrong dreams after sharing a can of condensed milk with Fat Olga!

We all knew that Fat Olga and Marisol were more than good friends. They worked side by side in the tobacco house, they ate at the same table, and sometimes from the same dish. They strolled together in the campgrounds and they slept together without clothes. But their affair was considered gross and indecent. Boys ridiculed them, calling them *tortilleras*—though not in front of them because Marisol, with her round shoulders and huge hands, was to be feared when she was incensed. Girls also criticized their relationship and had seldom invited Olga or Marisol to their Saturday night parties when we were in Havana. Even in camp they didn't have many friends. They had mostly kept to themselves until Aurora and I began to hang out with them. Now this affinity distressed me almost as much as my odd dreams. Should I stop talking to them, move to another bunk bed, forget about them—and about Aurora?

My mind's pendulum swung in the opposite direction. I considered asking Fat Olga, who was far more approachable than big-mouthed Marisol, what they felt for each other. Later I could compare it with my own feelings for Aurora. But what if Fat Olga took my inquiries as a personal insult? What if she told Aurora?

In the end I did nothing. Although most kids joked about Fat Olga and Marisol, their relationship had never been seriously discussed by anybody in the camp. It was not even acknowledged by the partners themselves.

UNTIL THEN, I had only known one homosexual and that was Dulce who lived in the third *casona* of Vista Alegre Street. Grandma Gloria disliked her because she was "too outspoken" and "didn't look like a lady." Dulce never wore makeup. She drove her own car, an old but defiantly purple Plymouth. She occupied by herself a large, two-story house, with an immense garden into which the neighborhood boys crawled to steal oranges after dark. I had often glanced at the blooming trees that sheltered the garden's entrance, fresh and inviting, like temptation. A woman who the neighbors mockingly called *La Tetona*, Big Boobs, visited Dulce almost every day and stayed at her house during the weekends. Grandma Gloria would greet Dulce briefly if they met in the street, but turned her face away when she passed by Big Boobs. Sometimes I'd spy Dulce and Big Boobs seated inside the gazebo. I could hear muffled giggles. But I never learned anything of substance about them. The leafy trees, like a protective barrier, hid the couple from my intrusive prying.

When I finally understood what a dyke was and the stigma attached to this condition, I couldn't avoid secretly admiring Dulce. The woman lived her life the way she wanted despite the barrio's constant criticism. She was no *pendeja*! Attracted by the aura of mystery and secret vice that surrounded Dulce, I often thought of visiting her house with some excuse. I'd ask her for matches or for a cup of sugar. Would she allow me to enter? What would the house be like inside? But I was too shy to approach her. During the Mariel boatlift in 1980, Dulce and Big Boobs left the country. Then I despised her because she had turned out to be a counterrevolutionary, an abject *gusana*.

AS THE days passed my feelings for Aurora became more intense. My fantasies arose in the mornings among the *cujes* and tobacco leaves. They crept over me during the boredom of the evenings and in the darkness of the camp's hectic nights. When I was by myself the thoughts came, thoughts of what I'd like to tell Aurora, to do with her, how I'd kiss her and stroke her long brown hair. I had never been with a boy before, let alone a girl, and yet in my dreams I never let my inexperience hold me back. I held imaginary dialogues with her in which I was sharp, ebullient, and ingenious, and The Beauty was always captivated by my cleverness. But when we were together, in bed or in the tobacco house, it was Aurora who did most of the talking. I nodded and smiled, just like Papirito. I didn't even dare make a joke. I'd have been so embarrassed if she didn't laugh! Besides, I felt hopeless. Aurora was always bragging about how good and hard her lovers' *pingas* were. Thin, short, assless, and *pinga-less*, what could I reasonably expect from her?

★ ★ ★

THE FIRST days after I recognized I had a crush on Aurora, my biggest fear was that she would discover it. Yet, sometimes, I wanted her to know. I fantasized about confessing, *Aurora, I like you. Would you be my girlfriend?* I imagined her big eyes winking under the shadow of the mosquito net. *Yes, Lourdes. Oh yes.* Then a smell of violets would fill the air and my hands would caress the tempting globes that lifted her see-through blouse. I'd wrap myself in the dark boa of her hair and nibble her soft neck—

But Aurora didn't seem to notice any change in my attitude. Silly girl! How could she be so blind? Why did she think I was always behind her, always helping her?

One afternoon, when I had sewn nearly all of her *cujes*, she hugged me affectionately and called me "little sister." This saddened me because the abyss that separated us was doubled now. I hid my tears but a powerful, angry voice kept resounding inside my head the rest of the day. *I do not want to be your sister! Don't you see you are my* amor?

⊰ CHAPTER VIII ⊱

RELATIVES IN HAVANA sent packages of food brought to us by the teachers who occasionally traveled to the capital. One morning, Comrade Katia, who had gone to Havana to attend a Party meeting, came back and handed me three steaks, four tamales, and a brief note from *Mami*. *Mami's* note read:

Dear Lourdes,

How are you feeling? I miss you a lot, *niña*. Life is so difficult and full of traps. Keep your eyes open because when you least expect it, someone may hurt you. Evil is everywhere and you have to fight for what you want.

Take care. Eat enough fruits if you can find them, go to the bathroom regularly, keep warm. I'll see you on Sunday.

Kisses,
Mami.

When I finished reading, I was shaken. The note gave me a message: *You have to fight for what you want.* I repeated it aloud, enjoying my new assertive tone. I'll fight for Aurora! I'll tell her I like her. That's what people normally do when they are in love. She *may* accept me! But if the others suspect—No, no one will find out. We will be careful, I told myself.

Aurora might be tired of boys. She had had so many! But I wouldn't dare to say, face-to-face, that I loved her. That was too difficult, too scary. I'd write a letter to her.

Since our barracks didn't offer any privacy, I resorted to a lonely spot near the outhouse and sat on the grass, writing the letter for an hour. I worked hard to elude a crew of albino cockroaches that resented my presence in their domain and kept charging against my feet. The grass was as prickly as if a thousand needles had been scattered on it. I felt the chilly stab of the evening wind. My back ached. The emanations from the latrines hardly inspired romance, my hands perspired abundantly despite the cold weather. The pencil and the paper were already sticky.

Dear Aurora, I wrote. *I want you to be my girlfriend. I would like us to have a serious relationship because I am crazy about you. You are my amor. Please let me know if you also like me. With lots of love. Lourdes.*

So the letter was finished. But would I deliver it? Probably not. My courage seemed completely gone. I was a coward, a *pendeja.* I had always been.

Though I didn't really know if I *loved* Aurora, I didn't have any doubt about the fact that I *desired* her. But that was wrong. I had sworn many times to be a loyal follower of Che. And Che despised homosexuals. My thoughts were a chaotic mess of lust and guilt as I remembered the consultation with Sabina and what the *santera* had said. *Lourdes will desire something very ardently, suffer for it, and achieve it in the end, but it won't bring her as much satisfaction as she expected.* Why not? And when would I get it?

As soon as the camp lights were turned off and only the living lanterns of fireflies illuminated the fields, there was constant movement in and out of the barracks. We all breathed sex at night. More than half of the kids had a partner. Couples agreed to meet in odd shelters, carefully selected during daytime. The tall, dewy grass behind the boys' barracks was a favored spot. After curfew, boys and girls hastily crept out of bed and did not return until 2 or 3 A.M. Then they complained about being tired in the morning, and the teachers would smile knowingly. They really didn't mind, since most of them would creep out too. The only difference was that they did not have to work in the fields the next day.

The evening that I wrote the letter, I folded it and put it inside my green notebook at the bottom of my suitcase. She'll see it tomorrow, I told myself. If I am not a complete chicken I'll give it to her before breakfast and we'll talk in the tobacco house during the break.

But my *amor* was later than usual. I waited for her nervously, smelling our pillow that preserved Aurora's scent, a mixture of violets and sweet sweat. When she came back, at about 2 A.M., she sneaked into our bunk bed. I was exceedingly aware of her warm hip rubbing against mine, of the soft hair tickling my shoulder, and I wanted to grab one of her long locks and suck it.

"Juanito Lopesanto took me to the grass behind the boys' barracks," Aurora bragged, shaking my arm. "Juanito Lopesanto, Lourdes! Imagine that!"

A painful lump lodged in my throat. All of us considered Juanito Lopesanto, our math teacher, *un buena gente,* a "cool guy." He assisted us during the tests and covertly suggested the appropriate answers when we asked him for help. Despite the dry subject he taught, he loved to tell jokes. Juanito had a very impressive, black, curly musketeer mustache. With his easy smile and his six feet of muscle and bone, Juanito was the most popular teacher in our high school.

"*Ay, coño!*" screamed Fat Olga excitedly. "How was it? He is very attractive, isn't he?"

"Oh, it was pretty good."

"Did you do it? All the way?"

Fat, greedy Olga!

"No, *chica*, not yet," Aurora answered. "A woman has to give herself some value, you know."

"Was he hard enough?" asked Marisol, with a contemptuous inflection. "He isn't that young, eh?"

"What do you mean?" Aurora replied, offended. "He *isn't* old, no way. It was harder and better than all the boys' *pingas you* have ever known!"

That didn't say much. But Aurora's knowledge of the matter was quite sufficient, and if she declared that Juanito's *pinga* was good and hard, such a statement had to be true. She was the expert.

"Are you going to do it soon?" asked Chabela.

"I can't tell you yet. Maybe in a week," answered Aurora modestly. "Or in three or four days."

"That's too soon!" Chabela said. "Why don't you wait until we get back to Havana?"

Aurora shrugged. "Well, I really like him," she said. "And he likes me, of course. He wanted to do it today! But don't talk about this with anybody. You know, he is a teacher—"

"Don't worry." Chabela reassured her. "I'll be a tomb."

"Oh, we don't gossip!" Fat Olga declared in a very dignified tone. "Speak, *hija,* speak. *No tengas pena,* don't be shy."

"If you just knew! Juanito Lopesanto is really strong and he knows how to tongue kiss. And he has a *pinga* about the length of a milk bottle," Aurora disclosed, writhing. I couldn't see her face, but imagined her conceited smile. Our sheets jumped up and down, tossed by her shameless movements. I listened silently, curled into a rueful ball.

"*Ay, coño!*" cried Fat Olga again. In spite of my pain, I couldn't avoid wondering if her excitement was caused by Aurora's story or because of what was happening under her own blanket.

"The only problem we have is that he doesn't want to use condoms," Aurora complained with a loud sigh. "Men are *so* selfish!"

"So *how* are you going to do it?" asked Fat Olga in a low, tentative voice. "In the ass or—?"

"Olga!"

Strident laughs destroyed the serenity of the night, causing an outbreak of irate complaints from half-asleep girls. Comrade Katia hissed from her bunk bed and ordered, "Everyone shut up! It's three A.M.!"

I stayed awake for a long time, desolate, touching my *papaya*, rubbing my thighs together, desperately swallowing my tears.

The next morning I considered destroying my love letter. I wouldn't give it to Aurora now. She was in love with Juanito. Juanito Lopesanto, of all guys! Not a dumb boy like Tomás or Vladimir, but a teacher, a real, handsome man!

I had lost the battle before even starting it. What would Aurora say about my hopes? She'd sneer, *This foolish* mulatica, *who does she think she is? Doesn't she know that I don't like schoolgirls, only very macho men?* But I kept the letter, hidden inside my green notebook. Despite Juanito Lopesanto and his giant *pinga*, I still dreamed of my *amor* reading it someday.

During the nights that followed, when Aurora went out with Juanito, I wriggled in the solitude of our bunk bed, thinking sadly about the golden rod of men, the stone dream that girls liked good and hard. Why didn't I have one? It was the fiery knife, the stem of life, the burning sword of desire. Oh, if I could just have one!

I revered Che Guevara, the bravest of all men. I had repeated over the years that I wanted to be like him. *We Pioneers want communism. We'll be like Che!* Our Pioneer slogan had acquired a new meaning. If I had a big *pinga*, would that make me like Che?

⊰ CHAPTER IX ⊱

THE STENCH OF kerosene filled the dining hall, blending with the smells of rotten cabbage, boiled rice, and burning wood. Enormous shadows danced on the walls and the pale light made a bowl of watery pea soup look like chicken bouillon. Besides the soup, the meal consisted of a dish of dry yellowish rice with yam. Aurora and I ate fast, trying not to think of the flies and bugs that could have accidentally dropped onto our trays.

Right before dinner Comrade Katia discovered that the light-bulb in our dining hall was missing. As there were no spare bulbs around, the principal resorted to Pancho the Widower, who sent Elena to the dining hall with an old kerosene lamp. The two women who helped in the kitchen every day, from six in the morning to 9:30 at night, and who stole flagrantly from the camp's meager supply of provisions, were blamed for the robbery. Lightbulbs were rationed in the countryside and a family of four would receive only two a year. The *guajiras* were constantly *llorando miserias*, asking us for things—old clothes, broken pans, soap, blankets—so our mistrust was more than justified.

The teachers who walked around the tables had trouble maintaining good discipline in the dining hall even with adequate lighting. The dimness didn't make their task easier. Every five minutes a kid stumbled over a chair, bumped into someone, or spilled water on a table.

"We should have sent them all to bed without food," the principal said grumpily.

"This is chaos," sighed *La Flaca,* shaking her blouse to get rid of the rice leftovers that someone had maliciously thrown at her.

"This is *counterrevolutionary* chaos," Comrade Katia added.

The following morning our principal delivered a long, very serious speech. For more than an hour the old man harangued students and staff about the importance of respecting communal property. "Whoever steals from the camp, steals from the revolution, steals from Fidel. And Fidel is our father and the father of the revolution," he emphasized, pointing an accusing finger as if he were *El Comandante en Jefe* himself. "You have to respect him!"

"Shit, Fidel is not my father," Fat Olga muttered. "I have my own *Papá!*"

"If it were not for Fidel, you wouldn't be here today," continued the principal.

"So he is a great *cabrón!*" Marisol said to Olga. "Because I don't *want* to be here, do you?"

I was horrified at their lack of respect. How could they talk like that?

"He freed our country!" The principal concluded. "He is the star of our flag, the savior of all Cubans. When a Cuban steals from Fidel, he becomes a *gusano,* a miserable worm. We don't want any worms in our camp!"

Next Sunday the secretary of education sent us a new lightbulb on the parents' bus, which seemed to be the end of the unpleasant thievery episode. But it was just the beginning.

The following week, Hilda, our cook, discovered that the camp's only rice cooker had vanished. Hilda was an old Communist Party member, which placed her above suspicion. She and the other *guajiras* swore they had seen the cooker the previous night on the top shelf of the kitchen. It had obviously disappeared before 6 A.M.

"Now, this is a mystery," said Comrade Katia. "If I were not a Marxist, I'd say we have spirits in the camp."

That day, instead of regular rice, our meal consisted only of boiled rotten potatoes. They smelled and tasted like charcoal. We unanimously cursed the thief. Food was scarce. Food was sacred. And a *cabrón* had made its preparation more difficult!

In the evening Aurora entered the barracks, happy and excited, chewing a piece of home-cured ham. *Jamón curado!* Where had she found it? "Eat and don't ask," she grinned, handing me a slice.

I ate it with the same guilty feeling I had in the mornings, when Aurora put on her work clothes and I stared at my friend's breasts.

After that, once in a while Aurora would come up with a pork rib, a chicken leg, or a pint of fresh milk. She finally confessed to me that Juanito Lopesanto had "connections" with Hilda and her husband. The *guajiros* sold him food and cigars. At that point I didn't consider such trade dangerous or even strange. It was certainly wrong, but I knew that everyone bought and sold things on the black market, both in the city and in the countryside.

AN ORANGE and prawns salad served with mayonnaise on a gleaming porcelain dish. Lobster cocktail swimming in a delicately shaped glass that produced a musical sound when touched by the engraved silver spoon. Roast leg of pork, king of the banquet, surrounded by white rice and black beans cooked together, the delicious *congrí*. Fried steak with onions bathed in garlic dressing, served with a perfectly round mound of steamed white rice. Mouthwatering desserts: caramel pudding, grated coconut with cheese, *torrejas*—fried slices of bread soaked in a milk and cinnamon sauce, topped with syrup . . .

I had eaten all this as a golden chandelier swayed above my head and classical music played in the background, when my family and I had stayed at the *Hotel Internacional,* during that unforgettable week in Varadero. It had been a marvelous experience. But what came to mind more often in camp was not the sapphire bordered beach nor the luxurious hotel rooms but—the restaurant. Food.

Ah, food. In our erratic and often broken dreams, food was a recurrent theme. Steaks, chicken, ice cream, fruit juices. *La comida.* In the School-in-the-Fields, we cheated hunger with stale bread, crackers, condensed milk, or the green, insipid bananas that grew in nearby trees—anything that could be used to alleviate our stomachs' noisy complaints. Only Sundays were different, thanks to our parents' visits.

Mami and *Papi* would bring me chicken soup and ham sandwiches, or *ropa vieja,* shredded meat, and macaroni salad. These delicacies couldn't always be found in Havana, but my family managed to procure them while my School-in-the-Fields period lasted.

Of course, not all of my comrades were as lucky as I was. Some kids were visited only once or twice during the whole term. Others didn't get a visit at all, *los pobrecitos.* They would glance with envious eyes at their friends' feasts or stay in the barracks until the parents' bus departed.

For me, the Sunday lunch was invariably a banquet. *Mami* would bring a portable brazier and cook on it while tantalizing smells permeated the camp. Smells of black beans seasoned with pepper, tomatoes, and a spoonful of sugar. Smells of Grandma Gloria's chicken-fried steaks. Smells of Grandma Inés's pork chops. Cans of condensed milk and Russian meat, guava bars, cream cheese, and hard-boiled eggs were left with me as a reserve. My resources ordinarily lasted until Wednesday. On Saturday nights, and despite the *bailables,* thoughts of the good food that was on the way made me want to go to sleep quickly, as if by doing so Sunday would arrive earlier.

Aurora belonged to the unfortunate group that never had a visitor. The second Sunday in camp, after asking *Mami* and *Papi* for permission, I invited her to eat with us. We shared a plate of pork chops accompanied by french fries and tamales. Aurora's jaws moved incessantly and fast, and her full lips were coated with glossy lard.

"Eat, *niña*, eat," *Mami* said to Aurora, stroking her hair. "Stuff yourself. Do you want more pork?"

All this was crowned with the jewel of a flan. *Papi* cut the flan, opening it like a book, and the eggs, sugar, and milk moved rhythmically inside as if in a *rueda de casino*, the elegant dance of our *quinceaños*. Aurora swallowed every last morsel of her portion and impulsively stood up and hugged *Mami*.

"Thanks, *señora*," she said. "That's the best lunch I've had in my whole life." She rushed into the barracks. I thought Aurora was crying as she ran away.

"Strange girl," commented *Mami*. "But why isn't her mother here? Save a tamale for her."

DURING THE empty Sunday afternoons, after the visitors left, sadness would fly from one bunk bed to another like a giant moth with heavy wings. Everything was gloomy, even the blooming *framboyán*. The outhouses looked darker and filthier. The two big garbage barrels behind the kitchen became smellier. Faces seemed wearier, nails dirtier, barracks uglier. The atmosphere turned oppressive as the parents' bus disappeared on the dusty road leading to the highway.

I would take something sweet with me and withdraw to a broken-down bench, half-hidden by the shrubbery surrounding the boys' barracks. There I sadly dreamed of my bedroom shelves full of books, my cherished *matrioskas*, watching TV sprawled out on our living room leather sofa, and having chocolate ice cream in Coppelia. Not even Aurora's presence could console me then. She also seemed to be covered by the thick curtain of dullness that wrapped the camp and its inmates. However, sometimes I would also think of her bulging breasts, not with the usual twinge of guilt, but with the same quiet pleasure evoked by reminiscences of Grandma Gloria's mush and fried eggs.

One Sunday evening, when the entire camp was under the sway of despondency, I pensively nibbled a piece of chocolate cake when a string of obscenities coming from the boys' barracks startled me. *Maricón de mierda*, someone said. *Oh, you fucking fag.* No man calls another one *maricón* unless he is really furious. *Maricón* is an unforgivable insult. But this time the inflections of the speaker's voice lacked the high-pitched tone of affront or the gravity of repressed anger. It sounded like a tender lament, a languid prayer of love.

Amazed, I stood up and got closer to the window. On a lower bunk bed, two boys squirmed under a stripped blanket. One of them was Berto the Duck, a skinny kid who always wore a silver bracelet on his right wrist. The other one was Ernesto, a big, handsome mulatto who lived in a tenement not far from Grandma Gloria's house. I had never talked to him, but knew his name because he had been selected as a *vanguardia*, an exemplary worker.

"You fucking fag," Ernesto repeated in a sweet voice. He fell by his mate's side while a violent drumming reverberated inside my head.

Gong. A tremendous drum plays the rhythm of the boys. Give me your flower. You take my sword. The moon inside the cloud. The cloud around the moon. Duel of arrows. Mine in yours. Yours in mine. The moon enters through the window, dancing, singing, laughing, playing the rhythm of the boys.

The Sunday torpor evaporated. I felt revolted and aroused at the same time. Part of me was nauseated and didn't want to continue looking at the now motionless bodies. *Indecentes!* But another, depraved part had enjoyed the show—and wanted to see more. Then Berto got up and put the blanket over Ernesto. He approached the window where I stood watching them and closed it with a satisfied smile on his flushed face.

I left hurriedly, as quietly as I could. Near the girls' barracks I caught sight of another careless couple. A tall, dark boy lay with his chubby naked girlfriend under the *framboyán*. Her breasts pointed to the sky. The moonlight illuminated the scene with a shameless clarity. The breeze had become sticky and acrid. The red *framboyán* flowers glowed in the sunset. The tree branches curled seductively in the air like Ernesto's arms around his partner's neck.

An electric itch crept all through my body when I finally got in bed. Aurora was out with Juanito, so I turned to sweets for comfort, eating a dozen bonbons that sent me to the latrine every two hours the following day.

⊰ CHAPTER X ⊱

THE FIRST THING I perceived when I entered the outhouse was the strong, pervasive odor. Old and fresh, hard and soft, shit reigned inside the latrine holes, on the slippery earthen floor and on the walls. It was Queen Shit's domain.

Initially, ragged jute curtains had separated the latrines. But soon most of the curtains had been torn up, so we had to defecate in plain view. Then the holes had filled up and overflowed. Fetid streams invaded the outhouse. I learned to walk there as if I were crossing a minefield. The principal had assigned the task of cleaning our outhouses to the self-service brigade, where the sick worked until they were ready to return to the fields or the tobacco house. The self-service crew remained in the camp to help the cook, sweep the barracks floors, and sanitize the latrines.

One morning I woke up with a cold and Comrade Katia sent me to self-service. Papirito was in the same brigade that day because he had suffered an asthma attack. Naturally, he had been assigned to outhouse cleanup. He looked so sad and pitiful carrying big buck-ets of water, coated with shit up to his freckled nose.

The boys' barracks were similar to ours, only messier and dirtier. Most beds weren't even made, displaying gray or yellowish sheets where cigarettes, food, and muddy boots had left their marks. I was sweeping the floor when Vladimir came in and headed for a tidy bunk bed covered by a red bedspread.

Vladimir was coveted by a considerable number of girls. Though he had an official girlfriend, Natasha, he regularly cheated on her, which made him even more interesting in the eyes of the others. Aurora had once let him dunk his bread in her *café con leche*. Vladimir worked as little as possible, made fun of everybody in camp, including the teachers and the *guajiras*, and was a first-class bully. I couldn't stand him.

He began to search through a bag full of food. I inspected him but could not discover any reason for his alleged sex appeal. He exuded defiance. His face was adorned with countless purple pimples and he had already acquired the disgusting Cuban macho habit of touching and scratching his testicles every five minutes. The *cojonudo* sniffed several packages and selected a piece of bread wrapped in nylon. He tasted it, then turned around, noticed my presence and asked, "Want to try it?"

His offer caught me by surprise. Vladimir wasn't the generous type—none of us were when dealing with food. The bread looked stale and its oily spread had become thick and rancid, but when you are hungry, bread is never too hard, as the saying goes. I accepted it.

We were still chewing when Papirito entered the barracks and confronted us with an unusually threatening expression on his pale face. "What are you doing with my stuff?"

Vladimir ignored him. He finished the bread and flipped through the bag again until he discovered a glass jar containing a white dough. He smelled the jar and dropped it. "Yuck, it's rotten! Why do you keep this shit here, Papo-rroto, sweet ass?" The jar split open like a coconut and the white dough scattered over the reddish cement floor.

My first impulse was to defend the poor Mouse, but I realized that siding with him could only lead to conflict with Vladimir, by far the most abusive and crude guy in camp. I continued sweeping and feigned deafness.

"Clean this mess up now," Vladimir said to me and left.

Papirito burst into tears. Men do not cry in Cuba; at least, they are not supposed to cry in front of people. I felt guilty and tried to reassure him. "*Bueno,* it's over," I murmured. "Vladimir plays too rough. But don't worry, it's almost lunchtime and he isn't coming back."

Papirito didn't even look at me. He must have been mad because I ate his stuff, I thought, ashamed. He still smelled slightly of shit but I didn't care. I got closer to him and said, "Listen, I did not know—Vladimir gave me the bread and I honestly thought it was his. I am sorry."

He didn't answer. I knelt on the floor to find out if something could be saved from the white dough that a long time ago had been *arroz con leche. Uff!* It stank. "It's spoiled, Papirito," I whispered, because a noise at the door made me afraid that Vladimir was returning. "It would have caused you a real stomachache."

Big round tears dropped down Papirito's cheeks and wet his lips. I tasted the bitterness of his tears in my own mouth and felt irrevocably touched by his deep anguish. "Are you hungry?" I tried to pat his shoulder. He stepped back and I added, confused, "Let's go to the kitchen and I'll get you something good."

"Leave me alone, please."

The *guajira* Hilda shouted my name. I had to run and help her. Papirito stayed in the barracks, weeping. When I looked back he was lying on the bed, face down, shrunk against the red cover that engulfed his feeble body like a shroud.

Later on, while I took the worms out of the lunch rice, the cruelty of Papirito's tormentors and the senselessness of the whole School-in-the-Fields project hit me. Why did Vladimir and others pick on

Papirito when he didn't bother a soul? Why did he have to work in the fields when he was always so sick? Why were all of us there? It took forever to kill the worms. They struggled to escape from my nails. Some flew. I kept thinking strange, rebellious thoughts. *Papi* had told me that my duty as a revolutionary was to help build Socialism. But were we building Socialism by cleaning outhouses and eating rotten fish? Pancho the Widower complained every day, saying that we wasted more leaves than we sewed and that our work was useless.

In my mind I relived the episode in the barracks a thousand times. Had I been a *pendeja?* I should have confronted Vladimir, shouldn't I? What would Che Guevara have done, had he been in my place? What would Che have done, had he been in Papirito's place?

MY LIFE continued as usual, lulled by routine, quiet and monotonous. My rebellious thoughts soon faded. When my cold disappeared I returned to my regular brigade and forgot about Papirito and Vladimir. But Papirito didn't forget me. Not only did he want to talk about books as we had done before, but he took to following me everywhere. He would wait for all the brigades to finish supper to offer me a cookie or a *pastelito.* In the tobacco house, he divided his attention between Aurora and me, giving both of us good, small *cujes.* He even tried to help me sew them.

Oddly enough, he avoided mentioning Aurora's name in our conversations. If I alluded to her he would blush like a girl, but say nothing. A pariah until then, Papirito was delighted with my companionship. For a while I didn't mind his attentions and felt proud of having a satellite, but soon his visits became boring and even disturbing. He would pester me while I waited in line for lunch, and interrupt my conversations with Aurora. He constantly asked me if I wanted to read a three-day-old newspaper or one of his dated novels. He got so close to me that I could feel his acrid breath. He clung to me like a famished flea on a fat dog.

Then other kids started making mocking comments. "Lourdes has a tail" was considered a knee-slapping joke because of the double entendre. It annoyed me immensely. Monkeys have tails, everybody knows that. And I looked just like a small chimp!

I longed to put an end to our tiresome association, and only pity prevented me from shooing Papirito away. The end came one rainy evening when my "tail" went to the barracks and asked Marisol to tell me that he was outside waiting for me.

This simple message brought the burden of his neediness to an unbearable extreme. My pathetic satellite had become way too bold! He should have known that only boyfriends or very good male friends would go to the girls' barracks and ask one of us to come out. The act implied an intimacy that by no means existed between Papirito and me. Probably delighted with the idea of giving me a hard time, Marisol ran toward my bunk bed. I had been polishing Aurora's nails and was shocked by the loud announcement, "Lourdes, your *suitor* is outside! Should I tell him to wait or to come to your gracious presence?"

"Which suitor? What are you talking about?" I asked, dumbfounded. Aurora took her hand away.

"'Which suitor?' Listen to her, the innocent! As if she didn't know!" Marisol retorted. She began to take off her rain-soaked blouse. "Papirito!"

Aurora broke up laughing, holding her stomach. Elena, who had come to camp because her house was flooded, smiled. Fat Olga laughed so hard she got the hiccups. Were they making fun of me, or of Papirito? Or both of us?

"Imagine what they would look like together in a queen bed!" Marisol cackled, putting on a Betty Boop T-shirt. "Ebony and Ivory!" I didn't argue with her, knowing that my protests would only make the taunts worse. Instead, I stomped out of the barracks, ready to grab Papirito by the neck and strangle him.

He had sought refuge from the rain under the *framboyán*. He looked mousier than ever, wet and weak. But the pity I had once felt for him vanished. A violent desire to kick that feeble face replaced it. Little *cabrón*, getting me in trouble, causing people to laugh at me!

"Hello, Lourdes. I wanted to ask you if—" he began, smiling bashfully.

"Wait, Papirito, wait, you are always asking me things," I cut him off. "I don't mind if we talk sometimes, but don't come here to call me again because I don't like it. It doesn't look right, get it?"

He became red with shame and mumbled, "But I thought we were—"

"I don't care what you thought!" I replied, feeling a wicked delight in his confusion. "I can't see you today. Go to your barracks and I will let you know when I have time to chat. But don't come here again. Ever."

Papirito left, dropping two *framboyán* flowers on the muddy pathway. I watched his bent figure, a headless shadow moving slowly beneath the rain. I felt sorry and relieved at the same time.

I went back to the barracks. My suitcase, which I had forgotten to lock, lay open on the floor. Marisol, Fat Olga, and Elena smirked as they saw me. Then I realized that Aurora had found my grammar notebook and was turning its pages. She looked curious and surprised.

I gasped for air. The letter! I wanted Aurora to read it, but under different circumstances. What if she shared it with crude Marisol and Fat Olga? She wouldn't do that to her "little sister," would she?

I sat on our bunk bed without saying a word. Elena began to sing a *cadencia*.

Si de niña me quisiste
si de niña me adoraste,
no me vengas a decir
que por niña me dejaste.
Alo, alo cua-cua-cuá María Cocuyé, cua-cua-cua.
(If you loved me when I was a young girl,
if you adored me when I was a young girl,
don't say now that you are leaving me
because I am a young girl.)

WHY DID Aurora seem to avoid my eyes?

At that moment, Chabela stepped inside the barracks and yelled, "We have chicken for dinner! Did you hear that? Chicken!" she repeated, overjoyed, her clothes still dripping. "Hurry up!"

A throng of girls rushed to the dining hall, skipping and giggling in the rain. I waited to be alone and leafed through my notebook. The letter had disappeared. Who had taken it, Aurora, Elena, Marisol, Fat Olga? Where was it? Completely demoralized, I considered my chances of reaching Havana in a couple of days if I fled from the camp that night. Then Comrade Katia passed by my bed. "Go to the dining hall, Lourdes," she said. "Don't you want to eat tonight?"

The fifteen minutes we spent in the yard waiting to enter the dining hall had been magically lightened by Chabela's announcement. It was as if a big, flamboyant, multicolored rooster had perched on the roof of the barracks intoning a festive *ki ki ri kí*.

Hilda had prepared a sumptuous supper. The chicken, cooked with potatoes and onions, was served with white rice and orange jam. A feast! But I was too worried to enjoy the meal and take part in the general euphoria. Aurora busied herself with a big chicken thigh and didn't show any interest in starting a conversation. However, sometimes she looked at me with a suspicious flame dancing in her brown eyes. I decided to ask her about the letter before bedtime. The agony of suspense was ten times worse than the most terrible certainty.

Marisol and Fat Olga had gone to another table. Were they gossiping about me? How I regretted having written that letter. I should have destroyed it a long time ago. Why hadn't I? It was all Papirito's fault. If he hadn't come to the barracks, nothing would have happened. He had ruined my life!

I tried to concentrate on the meal but it was useless. Repressing my memory of the letter, I kept remembering a steaming *arroz con pollo* prepared by Grandma Gloria. I felt again the pain of the skin sores that had once afflicted me and the icy touch of death I had felt. I smelled Grandma Inés's cologne. I saw the beheaded chicken that had healed me thanks to the *orishas'* intervention—all of these memories brought back by the aroma of a hot chicken leg.

⌐ CHAPTER XI ⌐

*C*HICKEN. OIL, SPICES, *onions, saffron, red peppers, olives, rice. Yellow, red, and green.* Arroz con pollo. *A whirlwind of white feathers, blue flowers, herbs, tobacco, and blood. Offer a coconut to Yemayá.* Papi's *arms are as white as coconut flesh.* Mami's *face is as dark as coconut shell.*

The last chicken I ate at home had been cooked by my white grandmother, Grandma Gloria. What a scrumptious *arroz con pollo!* The last chicken I saw alive had been used by my black grandmother, Grandma Inés, in a *santería* rite. She had rubbed it, still throbbing, all over my sickly body. *Siacará!*

Grandma Gloria. Grandma Inés. How I missed them in the camp! How different they were! But I loved them both—well, maybe I favored Grandma Gloria, as we had lived together all my life. She enjoyed telling me stories. I already knew all about the *Almirante Cervera*, the transatlantic ship on which she'd come from Galicia, in third class, at eighteen years of age, looking for a brighter future in the New World. The beginning, she admitted, had been difficult. She'd worked at different menial jobs until she settled as a baby-sitter, a *manejadora*, for a rich family in Havana.

But then I managed my affairs so well that I ended up marrying the eldest of the boys I was hired to look after. Your grandfather was twenty at the time—three years younger than I. I charmed him! Your great-grandfather, a Spaniard himself, may his soul be now in heaven, planned the wedding in two months. He knew that hardworking, well-fed women from the Homeland were better suited to be mothers and wives than lazy Cuban girls.

My great-grandmother, the descendant of a Cuban abolitionist, was in complete disagreement with her husband's ideas. She despised the woman who had entered the house as a hired hand. How could she share the same table with her Gallega maid? *She never accepted me. She kept calling me la Galleguita puta—the little whore from Galicia—until her last day.* Cochina!

After the wedding, which took place in 1933, a month before Machado's fall, my grandfather took his wife on the required tour of European capitals, hoping to polish Grandma Gloria's rustic edges. They spent three weeks in Italy, two in Spain, and an entire month in France. In pictures taken during the trip, Grandma Gloria looked majestic with her elegant shawls and French dresses, and her aristocratic pose as an Iberian matron.

We also visited my old village. Look at this photo. These girls are all aldeanas, like I used to be. But they didn't have any ambition, they were happy with the crops, the sheep, a cow, and any man—with their bread-and-butter lives. I was different. I always wanted to climb—Arriba!

When we returned, my husband bought this house, which was new and painted white, not old and run-down as it is now. Lawton was a fashionable neighborhood then, and Vista Alegre its best street. With my own hands I planted the mango tree in our backyard. I took French and piano lessons. I wore two-strand pearl necklaces and diamond rings.

Inside the drawers of her mahogany dressing table Grandma Gloria had stashed many velvet boxes that contained old gold chains and rings, earrings and pendants, platinum bracelets . . . Occasionally she would let me admire her treasures, though she became nervous when I touched the stones. *Cuidado, Lourdes! Jewels are not toys. But be a good girl and someday you'll inherit all this.*

Grandma enjoyed telling me about the second chapter of her Cuban life. *On Sundays I would drive to* Los Pasionistas *Catholic Church for the morning mass in my father-in-law's Studebaker President. Your grandfather and I would go to cocktail parties in the afternoons. Our friends were doctors, architects, a senator—The* El Encanto *salesgirls all knew me. I became a lady, Lourdes. I went from rags to riches, as the saying goes.*

The single trace she kept from her old days as a servant was her ability to do wonders with olive oil, spices, and any kind of meat. Oh, her *arroz con pollo a la Chorrera,* with the lustrous pieces of chicken in an ocean of fluffy yellow rice, decorated with green peppers glowing like dewy tobacco leaves. Even in times of scarcity Grandma Gloria succeeded in giving a masterful flavor to all her culinary creations. *But my heart broke when I had to use ordinary green peas instead of Spanish olives and the asparagus and the apples you didn't get to know vanished from the kitchen.* Ay!

Grandma Gloria adored *Papi,* her only child, but on one occasion she almost disowned him. It happened during the dangerous convulsions in the fall of 1962. *My husband had died the year before and your father should have respected the fact that we were still mourning. But he did not. He brought a dark-skinned, curly haired* mulatta *to our home! And then he announced he was marrying her!*

I could see *Mami* entering the Vista Alegre Street house for the first time, looking in awe at the paintings framed in silver, not daring to touch the big marble-topped table, lowering her voice when she spoke. *Mami* was then a bashful twenty-two-year-old girl who lived in Mantilla, a poor barrio on the outskirts of Havana.

Grandma Gloria spent weeks hurriedly locking her bedroom door when she heard *Mami's* timid steps in the living room. But her opinion received the same consideration that her own mother-in-law's remarks had received thirty years earlier. *They ignored me and went ahead with their plans. They walked all over me. Then you came, my* niña. *Thank God your hair isn't too wiry and your nose is aquiline, like your grandfather's. And I forgave them—*

MAMI'S MOTHER, Grandma Inés, had gleaming skin that looked as if it had just been oiled. Only her chalky teeth put a stroke of white in her round, inky face. She always wore ample cotton gowns, yellow or light blue, and a white turban, as lacy as a meringue pie, wrapped tightly to her head.

My first memory of her is of a dark, affable presence at my fifth birthday party, which Grandma Inés attended, bringing me an unusual present; a necklace made of blue glass beads. *Lourdes is a daughter of Yemayá. She needs to use this* ileke *in order to be safe from evil eyes. One never knows what may happen to Yemayá's daughters. I want her to wear the necklace until she is old enough to have some good protection work done.*

Grandma Gloria showed regal disdain for the gift. She called it a witchcraft amulet, a vestige of barbaric African rites. *Papi* shrugged and smiled the grin of a professor of Scientific Communism. But *Mami* made me wear the *ileke*. She hid the beaded necklace under my uniform blouse and told me to keep silent about it.

Soon Grandma Gloria started urging me to get rid of the *ileke* and bad-mouthing the *santeros. They are child-eating sorcerers. They kidnap and kill children to offer innocent blood to their diabolic Negro gods.* Through the magnifying glass of my childhood terrors, the *santeros* and their *orishas* appeared as large, dark personifications of evil with voracious mouths ready to swallow me. For a long time I was torn between two loyalties until Grandma Gloria prevailed, and I dropped the necklace inside a neighborhood garbage bin.

★ ★ ★

WHEN I was fifteen I was afflicted with painful skin sores on my arms and upper back. They were the result of allergies, according to some doctors, or caused by internal blood poisoning, others argued. The itching became so tormenting that I scratched my back raw. I would wake up wrapped in bloody sheets with pieces of torn skin under my nails. Violent attacks of fever followed, leaving me exhausted in a delirium of bleeding ulcers.

Mami applied zinc oxide and soaked towels over the wounds. Grandma Gloria bathed me in the sedating coolness of chamomile infusions and spread starch on the sores. Doctors recommended a variety of creams, lotions, and pills. Don't scratch the itch, they ordered. Easy to say and hard to do. . . .

The fever kept me floating in a limbo of fire. I knew I was fading away in the midst of pus and blood. One morning at dawn, an old man with reddish eyes sat on my bed and asked me if I was ready to go. A pale otherworldly light emanated from him. When I opened my mouth to call for help, the man disappeared, leaving a huge cockroach in his place. "I'm going to die," I said to *Mami*. "*Adiós.*"

The following day Grandma Inés asked *Mami* to bring me to her house. I needed to have healing work done as soon as possible. My affliction couldn't be alleviated by human means since it was a *daño*, she explained. "It's a spell cast by an evil eye. I'll have to perform a cleansing rite and restore Lourdes's life path."

Not a soul objected, not even Grandma Gloria or *Papi*. Desperation overcame prejudice and on a warm summer morning *Mami* rented a car and took me to Grandma Inés's house. She carried an extra set of clothes for me—a white cotton dress, white socks, and a pair of brand-new white tennis shoes.

Grandma Inés's house smelled of strong coffee, fried plantains, and of the curative herbs she burned in a dish made out of a large, iridescent shell. A palm tree grew in the backyard, among flower beds of forget-me-nots, and a bougainvillea creeper ornamented the porch. The house was just one large room where Grandma Inés, her youngest daughter, and her two little granddaughters slept, cooked, and ate.

Grandma Inés was wearing a light blue gown and a necklace made of blue beads. She carried me inside in her strong arms. I looked around and blinked. Thirteen candles on shelves, tables, and chairs lit the room. Three oranges, five bananas tied with a red ribbon, three ears of corn, and two fresh coconuts lay on the floor surrounding a plaster statuette of the Virgin of Regla, Yemayá. Two small cauldrons and a life-size statue of *San Lázaro* stood in a corner. A cage covered with a blue tablecloth rested at the saint's feet.

While *Mami* waited on the porch, Grandma Inés instructed me to take off all my clothes. Nudity wasn't a problem for me; I had lost my sense of shame after seemingly endless, detailed medical exams. When I was ready, Grandma lit a cigar and puffed for a while around me, said a long prayer in a strange language and then sprinkled me with cologne, accompanied by the continuous recitation of the three-syllable cabalistic cry, *Siacará*.

Siacará, Grandma Inés screamed when she took a live chicken from the cage and beheaded it with one powerful slash of a kitchen knife. *Siacará*, she repeated when the chicken's blood stained her shoes and my legs. *Siacará* as she took the bird with her right hand while keeping the cigar in the left one and carefully rubbed my body with the chicken's throbbing remains.

"Babalú Ayé, lord of all the plagues, listen to me!" Grandma Inés yelled. She removed the chicken heart, big, red, and bloody, and threw it in one of the cauldrons. "Beloved *San* Lázaro, compassionate *orisha,* assist me, heal my granddaughter! Return the evil to its source! *Siacará!*"

She anointed me with a concoction of herbs and applied *cascarilla*—a powder made from eggshells—all over my sores. Then she helped me put on the white cotton dress.

"*San* Lázaro, protector of the sick, will watch over you now!" Grandma proclaimed. "He will scare away your enemies and will turn their malice against them!"

Next, she used the other cauldron to heat up an *ajiaco,* a tantalizing blend of jerked beef, yucca, sweet potatoes, pumpkin, and green plantains. I felt the smooth consistency of the yucca and the jerked beef slipping down my throat while spirals of fragrant smoke sneaked into my nostrils and eyes. It was a dish bursting with life and unquestionably the best meal I'd had in weeks. While I gulped the *ajiaco* down, Grandma went out and buried the chicken under the palm tree. Only then was *Mami* allowed to join us.

"I've taken the spell off her!" Grandma Inés boasted. "Let us thank *San* Lázaro, who lent us his healing hands and Yemayá, who saved our *niña* from this hardship."

In a week my sores were dried. Soon the itching and scratching became a vague memory mixed with the acid smell of chicken blood.

A few days after the cleansing rite, Grandma Inés visited the Vista Alegre Street house to make sure I was doing well. "I am going to offer Yemayá a good goat in your name. Her next fiesta will be in my house," she said. "I hope you can attend. We are having a *bembé* there, as your cousin Cándida is going to be initiated. We'll have drums, food, dancing, and lots of fun. You've never seen anything like it. Your mother has, but she's forgotten about it. And *bembés* are worth seeing."

"What is it, to be 'initiated,' grandma?"

"It's when somebody is consecrated to an *orisha*."

"Who is an *orisha*? A saint?"

"An *orisha* is a god or a goddess. Yemayá is your *orisha*, as *San Lázaro* is mine. Everybody should be protected by one because there is a lot of malice in this world. Look at what happened to you. We all need to be cautious, my child. The Devil is free!"

"So, do I have an *orisha* now?" I asked.

"Sure you have! Yemayá helped me have you cured. She told me what to do. She and *San* Lázaro are very powerful. *San* Lázaro is really the wise Babalú Ayé, the most compassionate *orisha* in the world. Thanks to him the sick heal and a dying person comes back to life. Babalú Ayé can close the gates of death. Yemayá is the great ocean-mother of the world. She dotes on her children. See, you are lucky to have her on your side. Yemayá is an invincible *orisha*, the prettiest of them all."

"What does she look like?"

"She is a beautiful mulatta, tall, with ample hips, and good hair. At the fiesta you may present her with a dove, a seagull, or just a blue flower to make her happy so she will want to continue assisting you."

Papi's appearance put an end to this conversation, and Grandma Inés left.

The *bembé* became my obsession during the following weeks. Unfortunately, neither Grandma Gloria nor *Papi* approved of it. "A nigger party!" Grandma Gloria hissed. "You won't lose anything by missing it, *niña!*"

"You belong to a new generation," *Papi* told me severely. "It's OK for older people to believe in their saints, but such beliefs are inappropriate, even ridiculous, for a young revolutionary like you. The *orishas* didn't heal you," he added. "It was just a coincidence, or your own mind at work. The Soviets are now studying the extraordinary powers of our minds."

Mami said nothing but didn't seem too enthusiastic about the fiesta either. In the end I was not allowed to attend.

The day after the *bembé*, Grandma Inés sent us sweets and a big plate of the delicious roast goat, which is the *orishas'* favorite food. That night I dreamed of Yemayá, arrogant and graceful, with long inky hair, dressed in blue.

WHEN WE left the dining hall I managed to control the shaking of my lips and asked Aurora if she had seen my notebook. She didn't answer immediately. I thought, *Please, Yemayá, help me!*

Finally Aurora smiled in her usual fashion and said, "Oh, that old green notebook! I took a page from it because I needed to write a note to Juanito. Hope you don't mind." And then she added, "What a treat we had for dinner, no? I had almost forgotten the taste of chicken!"

Once in the barracks, I searched my suitcase again and found the letter, that crumpled page with uneven lines, hiding between two work shirts. I put it in a much safer place, under the mattress, silently thanking Yemayá. The chicken that had perched on top of the zinc roof opened its colored wings and left the camp. I thought I could distinguish its silhouette against the night sky, surrounded by a cloud of incense, tobacco smoke, and a splash of cologne. *Siacará!*

⊰ CHAPTER XII ⊱

WE WERE BORED but we never stopped fighting the monotony with *bailables*, games and other survival strategies. Among them was the love-letter contest to be held the night of February 14. Boys and girls wrote real or mock love letters to each other and placed them in a mailbox. On Valentine's Day, all missives were to be collected and read and the best one chosen.

Could I submit my love letter to Aurora? I soon discarded the idea. Aurora had been in a very bad mood for the last two or three days. Although she still went out during the night to meet Juanito, things weren't going well between them. Several times she returned in a few minutes, a clear sign that Juanito had not shown up for their date. Once she even referred to her lover as *"viejo cabrón,"* Old Bastard.

I waited impatiently for Valentine's Day. Juanito and Aurora wouldn't appear together in public. I'd have Aurora to myself. We'd wander around arm in arm. We'd have fun. But right after dinner Aurora announced that she was staying in the barracks. "I'm not feeling well," she said grumpily. In vain I pleaded with her. She insisted on getting into bed at nine, and I ended up going to the love-letter contest by myself.

That day had not been a lucky one for Aurora. Her favorite piece of clothing, a tight black T-shirt, was missing from the fence where she had left it to dry the night before. "I have told you a hundred times not to leave clothes on the fence overnight," I scolded her, sounding like Grandma Gloria.

"If I don't wash my own clothes in the evening, when am I going to do it?" Aurora replied, upset. "I do not have a mama at home to wash them for me on the weekends!"

WE HAD worked hard to decorate our camp for the celebration. Chabela had glued a red cardboard heart to the dining hall's door. Bows made with pink and white kerchiefs were displayed on the windows of the girls' barracks, their tips waving happily in the breeze. The little benches were covered with yellow and purple wildflowers. Garlands made of magazine pages hung from trees, adding a festive touch.

Fat Olga and I met near the principal's platform. "Don't you think that Aurora is acting strange?" she asked. "It's the first Saturday evening she hasn't gone out."

"Juanito Lopesanto will pick her up soon to dunk his bread in her *café con leche*," I answered. "She was probably lying when she told me she didn't feel well, because she wanted to go out with him."

Then I realized that Juanito was just two feet away from us, talking to Comrade Katia. Comrade Katia, the Marxism instructor, had been blessed by nature with a colossal ass. Juanito stood close to her—very close! As they were chatting he ogled her way too often. *La Flaca*, our grammar teacher, was there too, her wrinkles concealed under a thick coat of cosmetic powder.

"I bet Elena will receive some love letters tonight," Fat Olga said, eyeing the *guajirita* who wore an old, patched gingham dress and yet looked graceful in it.

I sighed. Of course she would. But what about me? Would I get at least one note? Ha! In my dreams! I was the ugly duckling. The *brown* ugly duckling! I gazed at the stars that were beginning to glitter in the still bluish sky. The last rays of sun were fading in the west.

"Beautiful evening, huh?" someone said. I recognized Papirito's voice behind me. I pretended not to hear. He walked away.

The radio was turned on, the loudspeakers blasted, and Los Van Van invaded the campgrounds with their recent hit, "The Dance of the Tired Out Ox." Fat Olga moved her chunky hips, following the rhythm. Other kids cheered and whistled. A bottle of *Coronilla* rum, hidden inside a paper bag, circulated furtively among the boys. The teachers pretended not to notice. Sitting like a genie amid a cloud of smoke from a lustrous, large *Cohiba* cigar, even our principal seemed cheerful. Everybody was happy, ready to enjoy the cool Saturday night. Everybody—except me.

The contest began, with Vladimir as the self-appointed reader. After casually touching his crotch, he took a letter from the mailbox and opened it. "Addressed to Aurora," he announced. "From a gentleman caller."

"Why do boys always have to write to her?" complained Fat Olga. "She is not *that* pretty, is she?"

"Boys don't like 'pretty' girls, only easy ones," replied Natasha. She was Vladimir's official girlfriend, a pale, scrawny teenager with an old woman's face and personality. "And Aurora is easier than an open-book test!"

Aurora would enjoy showing off. Should I rush to the barracks and call her? Then I noticed that Juanito Lopesanto was stroking Comrade Katia's tanned arm. She smiled as he patted her, and he smiled back. Hmmm! The principal was also smiling as he spoke to Elena, puffing tiny white clouds of smoke into her face. A current of lust floated in the air.

"Dearest Aurora," Vladimir read. "I have been in love with you since the first time I saw you. I think of you every day and every hour; when I wake up, when I work, and when I eat the fine, good food my *Mamá* brings on Sundays—"

"Papirito wrote it!" someone shouted. Crude remarks followed.

"Papirito, moron, Aurora is too much for you!"

"You don't have gasoline for that car, Mouse!"

"Cut your *pinga* off and give it to the dogs!"

A vicious gang surrounded Papirito, sounding like a pack of wild dogs howling in the darkness. I hated them. The boy was a fool, yes. But why couldn't they leave him alone? Normally Papirito begged for mercy or remained silent, but this time he found courage to break out of the ring and escape, though not before being shoved and hit.

The game continued. The principal, Juanito, and Comrade Katia left. Elena departed without waiting for the love letters addressed to her to be read. Marisol took Fat Olga by the arm and they disappeared behind the boys' barracks. I stayed by myself, lonely, sad, ready to cry. Fortunately, Chabela came to my rescue. We danced together to the Los Van Van's rhythms until the end of the party.

After all the letters had been read, the bottle of rum drunk, and the music finished, the fun ended at 11:30. We headed off to our bunk beds, sweaty and tired, still humming the song of the tired out ox. Only then did the boys discover that Papirito wasn't in their barracks. They called him but he didn't answer. They looked in the latrines, near the sinks, and in the dining hall but he didn't appear. Vladimir and two of his buddies went after him, perhaps hoping to end the night with a beating.

The first explorers did not succeed in finding Papirito, so the teachers joined them. The boys were divided into two teams, one led by Juanito, the other by the principal. Comrade Katia organized a group of girls to help the searchers. Armed with flashlights and candles, they raked the grounds. The night lightened. Loud voices and the aroma of jasmine and forget-me-nots permeated the air while the teachers cursed Papirito. The principal was furious. With a flashlight in his pudgy hand and a red, choleric face, he threatened not to allow the parents' bus to enter the camp the next day if Papirito didn't show up.

"He won't dare!" Fat Olga said. "If my *Papá* can't see me after traveling a hundred miles, he'll kill him!"

Boys amused themselves by imagining what would happen to the fugitive when they laid hands on him. Some couples found time to neck under the very noses of the principal and teachers in the darker areas of the camp. It was the party after the party.

Two hours passed. The search became frantic. The principal, on the edge of a nervous breakdown, asked Pancho for help. The *guajiro* went out with a lantern and explored the creek of the Mother-of-Water. Papirito wasn't there either.

I felt a tightening in my stomach, the first symptom of remorse. I knew I had treated Papirito miserably. I hadn't given him a chance. Just a few hours before, I had been awfully rude to him for no reason at all. I was ashamed.

The teachers were first amazed at Papirito's boldness, then more upset than amazed. "If this dimwit escaped, he's going to be kicked out of the camp the first thing in the morning!" the principal yelled. "He had to do it the *only* night that I could rest for eight hours! What a lack of consideration!"

"The quiet kids, they are the worst!" Juanito remarked.

"That's true. One never knows when they are going to show their little claws," *La Flaca* agreed.

"Papirito!" we called.

But only a weak, distant echo answered back, "Itoito—"

Despite the principal's curses and threats, despite our careful inspection of the campgrounds, Papirito didn't appear. Perhaps for the first time in his life *he* was in control. And he knew it.

By 3 A.M. all students were sent to their barracks, but no one slept. The teachers and a few farmers continued walking around the camp and the nearby fields, with diminished hopes. I lay down in my bunk bed and guilt suffused me.

IT WAS Pancho who discovered him with the first light of dawn as hundreds of sparrows punctured the pale morning air. Clinging to the top of the *framboyán's* leafy branches, showing no sign of leaving, was Papirito. A sleepy crowd gathered around the tree. I joined them. I shouted and made desperate gestures, trying to persuade him to come down. But he didn't seem to recognize me. His eyes, abnormally wide, looked through me, his gaze lost in the distance.

"Come down at once, shit eater!" the principal ordered. "*Carajo*, if I have to go up there and get you—"

Unlikely, because the man weighed about two hundred pounds, a fifty-year accumulation of tired flesh. The *framboyán* branches shuddered.

"Come on! The boys won't bother you again!" Comrade Katia promised.

I wanted to assure Papirito that I would be his friend forever, that Aurora would love him, that we would all respect him from that day on, that no one would call him Mouse again. But I couldn't because I saw in his eyes that he was already beyond my reach.

"Papirito, for the last time, come down!" the principal barked. "Right now!"

So down he came, head first. He jumped from the *framboyán* and bounced against the ground. His head split open like a jar of *arroz con leche*. His blood stained the boots and pants of the horrified onlookers who backed away.

I fled to the barracks, got into bed, and hid under Aurora's blanket.

★ ★ ★

IN THE evening, Papirito's parents arrived. His body, wrapped in a red bedspread, had been sent to the village hospital in Pancho's puffing '56 Ford. Papirito's mother screamed insults at the principal and teachers, cursing God, Fidel, Che Guevara, and all the saints. Papirito's father—a tall, sad, handsome man—went to the boys' barracks and silently began to collect his son's belongings. He picked up even the muddy boots Papirito had worn, but left the bag of food that he and his wife had brought.

"You use it, boys," he said to the kids who loafed timidly around the bunk bed. "I am not taking it back."

No one ate the food. Not even Vladimir, not even the hungry boys who never had visitors. The bag full of delicacies stayed on Papirito's bunk bed until our last day in camp.

AURORA WEPT quietly. I stroked her hair, struggling to restrain my own tears. I hated myself for not confronting Vladimir when he stole Papirito's food. I hated myself for treating Papirito so harshly that rainy afternoon, and for ignoring him before the contest. I hated myself for having hated him. Had I been more compassionate, he might still be around.

I remembered Benjamín's death in Bolivia. Che Guevara had written in his journal that it was an absurd loss, that young *guerillero* drowned in a river. Wasn't Papirito's death absurd too? The wind blew and whistled outside, tossing a rusted can against the *framboyán*. Or was it Papirito's ghost, reminding his tormentors of the many times they had emptied a can full of urine on his mattress at bedtime?

The dreadful events of the day lingered in my mind for hours. When I closed my eyes I saw rivers of blood. Crimson currents. Red stars looking down. A giant heart dripping blood. Trembling flesh painted red. I saw the cherry flowers blossoming where Papirito's face had been.

Sabina's warning sounded in my ears: *Evil will surround you, so be very attentive.* I held my *azabache* tightly. The hooting of an owl resounded through the barracks. Had Evil killed Papirito? Would it harm me, too?

CHAPTER XIII

*C*LAP-CLAP-CLAP. *Click-clap-click. Brumm. Clap-clap-clap,* the drops hitting the zinc roof sounded. Thunder boomed in the distance. The hidden fragrances of the soil surfaced, called forth by the rain. The wind hissed outside and rushed into the barracks, bringing in particles of damp earth, wildflowers, and tobacco leaves. *Clap-clap-clap. Click-clap-click.* We were cradled in our bunk beds by the comforting sounds, breathing in the cool air.

The spell was broken when Fat Olga discovered that water had sneaked under the door, and our bags, shoes, and suitcases were swimming in the muddy lagoon of the cement floor. I managed to catch my boots before they were lost. Aurora rescued the can of cookies brought by *Mami* the previous Sunday.

A flash of lightning illuminated the barracks for a second, followed by an earsplitting thunderbolt. *"Ay!"* Aurora screamed, getting so close to me that I felt the tickling of her hair on my neck. The darkness became more intimate. I wished that the storm would never end and that thunder lasted until the end of time—

Ten minutes later Marisol asked, with unusual politeness, if she could join us. The roof leaked over her bed and she was freezing. I would have preferred to spend the night alone with Aurora but gave Marisol a reluctant welcome. Refusal would have hurt her deeply.

That afternoon she had had a memorable fight with Fat Olga and they weren't on speaking terms yet.

Once the three of us were together, I offered to tell them a story. "No way! Your made-up stories are too boring," answered ungrateful Marisol.

"Let's share real-life stories instead," suggested Aurora. "If you keep quiet, I'll tell you a secret that no one else knows yet."

Marisol and I quickly agreed. "I am going to tell you about Carlos the Cutie," Aurora began. "People called him The Cutie because he was a handsome man. He was thirty-five and I was twelve then, though I looked older. I've had big breasts, hair everywhere, and a round ass since I was eleven."

A continuous, flashing sheet of lightning had been spreading over the sky. Its silver threads entered our barracks through the cracks in the windows. The sound of the rain acted as a background curtain for Aurora's confidences. We listened attentively.

"The Cutie always saw me as a complete woman, never as a naive little girl. I didn't even bleed when we made love for the first time, and it didn't hurt. Well, it hurt a little, but his fine *pinga* was worth the pain. Carlos was very dark skinned. His other women called him *El Mulato de la Pinga de Oro,* the Mulatto with the Golden Dick. Imagine that!

"Carlos began going out with Carolina when I was in the sixth grade. He visited us every day and picked me up at school. Some Saturdays he took the family out: Armando the moron, Carolina, and myself. Armando the moron is my brother, and he *is* mentally retarded, it's not just a nickname."

"Who is Carolina?" asked Marisol.

"My mother," Aurora answered.

"*Ay,* girl!" I exclaimed. "Don't you call her *Mami* or *Mamá?*"

"No."

"And your father, where was he?" asked Marisol.

"I don't know. Carolina kicked him out of the house when I was nine years old. He may be dead by now."

I gasped. Aurora went on, "In the beginning Carlos liked Carolina but soon he became more attracted to me. He told me about his feelings as if I were another adult. I accepted him. He smelled so good . . . His hair, cheeks, neck, and crotch were perfumed with cologne and baby powder. What a guy! He wasn't like many boys I've known since who are sweaty, stinky, and greasy. Yuck!

"The Cutie and I played the daddy-and-his-girl game in front of my family. *Coño*, I was a sneaky little fox! I wouldn't go to bed without Carlos telling me *cuentecitos*, fairy tales, for a while. Then I would ask him to kiss me good night and he would cuddle me right in front of Carolina. I don't know why, but I enjoyed playing with fire."

It stopped thundering. The storm moved away slowly, the air was humid and fragrant. I felt repelled by Aurora's story. *Cochina!* Sleeping with her stepfather! Betraying her own mother!

A mist seemed to surround Aurora. Her voice echoed in the silence of the barracks. "For the first time I felt powerful, important, *una mujer grande*. Carolina had spanked me regularly since I was a little girl. She also hit me with a high-heeled shoe. I still have the marks in my back—*cabrona*! I used to cry and beg her to stop, but after Carlos and I were together, I thought of him and never cried again when she hit me. Never!

"*I am stronger than you*, I wanted to tell her. *You are fat and ugly. He prefers me. My pussy is better than yours!* She accused me of having an insolent expression. And she would beat the shit out of me just for that, *hijas*."

"Did she ever hit you in front of Carlos?" I asked, shivering. Neither *Mami* nor *Papi* had ever beaten me. Grandma Gloria would occasionally whack me with one of her slippers but that wasn't too painful.

"Once. But I bet the bitch wished she hadn't. Carlos called her a perverted mother and slapped her hard. And then *she* cried. Ha!"

Aurora fell silent. Sparse drops of rain hit the zinc roof. A mosquito buzzed in the moist air.

"What? Is that all?" Fat Olga, who had been listening from her bunk bed, asked irritably.

"I didn't want to bore you," Aurora answered.

"Oh, it's not boring at all," Marisol conceded. "You are really ballsy!"

"The Cutie and I were careful when Carolina was around," Aurora continued. "But we took no precautions with Armando. One morning Carlos and I were playing doctor in Carolina's bedroom while she was at the grocery store. The monthly coffee rations had arrived and we knew that the line would keep her there for more than an hour. The surgeon took me to the operating room and the scalpel was already sharpened when Armando's moon face appeared at the door. Don't laugh, *coño!* It wasn't funny at all.

"The Cutie got very nervous and asked the moron to go back to his room. But Armando didn't move an inch. When Carlos advanced toward him, Armando formed a circle with his left hand and put his right forefinger in it. 'Hey,' he said, 'look!'

"'Get out of here, you idiot!' I screamed. Armando turned around and mooned me. I was so pissed off! I could have killed the little *cabrón!*

"'Nice butt, Armando,' Carlos patiently observed. 'Now go to the living room, please.'

"'No.'

"'I'll give you a glass of water with sugar, if you behave,' he promised. 'Lots of sugar!'

"At last we got him out of the bedroom. The Cutie and I got dressed and Carolina returned from the grocery store. That evening, when we were at the table, Armando stopped eating and began to grunt.

"'What do you want, sweetie?' Carolina asked. She always calls him sweetie. I am *la cabrona chiquita*, the damned child.

"He repeated the gesture he had displayed for us in the morning. 'Aurora,' he said, moving his finger in and out the left-hand circle, 'and Carlos, in big bed.'

"'What?!' The bitch screamed. 'What did you say? Aurora—?'

"'Yes, I see them,' he burped. 'See them. Morning.' He chuckled and showed me his long and filthy tongue, stained with egg yolk.

"The Cutie sneaked out of the house. Carolina threw a kitchen knife at me but she missed. 'You are a little whore!' she yelled. 'I should kill you! I should simply kill you, *puta mala,* evil girl!'

"I kicked her and broke a saucepan over her head. We haven't quit fighting since.

"My Golden Dick Mulatto—I don't blame him for leaving after Armando told on us. The stupid chatterbox! I had just turned thirteen and had a lot of boyfriends afterward, but the bitch never again found another man."

No one said a word for a few minutes. Fat Olga broke the silence.

"What happened to The Cutie?" she asked.

"I don't know," Aurora shrugged. "That was the last time I saw him."

"*Coño!*"

"Who is talking in here?" Comrade Katia barked from her bed. "Someone who wants to spend the night outside, I guess!"

Aurora and I curled up together, as usual. Marisol and Fat Olga, unexpectedly reconciled, went to sleep in their own bunk bed.

"Don't you ever feel remorseful for doing that to your *Mamá?*" I whispered into Aurora's ear.

"Not at all! And don't call her my *Mamá!* She didn't feel remorseful when she beat me. Once she tried to toss me off the balcony. Why the hell should I adore her?"

"I didn't say you should *adore* her. I asked you if you ever felt bad about betraying her."

"Betraying my ass! Carlos just preferred me. She was too fat, too cranky, and too old for him."

I loved Aurora. I also pitied her. Not all girls had two caring grandmothers like Grandma Gloria and Grandma Inés, and a loving *Mami*, it seemed. But her affair with Carlos was disgusting. She had no excuse for her indecent behavior. She had really acted like the worst kind of *puta!* I got up and opened the window. The moon was reddish.

Aurora followed me to the window and asked in a raspy voice, "Has your mother ever wished you had never been born?"

"N-no," I stuttered.

She began to cry. I felt too sad to speak and I, too, started crying. Then we hugged each other and went back to bed.

I WAS cleaning the latrines, carrying the shit outside in a tin bucket. Suddenly, a familiar voice said behind me, "Beautiful evening, huh?"

"Papirito!" I exclaimed. "Boy, what are you doing here? I thought you were dead!"

He looked taller, more manly, and seemed to have gained weight. "I was only wounded," he smiled. "But I pretended I was dead so people would stop picking on me. Now I am in Bolivia, fighting with Che Guevara and the *guerrilleros*. Let's go!"

We walked to the creek and began swimming.

"I am very happy to know that you survived, *chico*," I said. "But, how can you be with Che Guevara?" I asked after a moment's pause. "He *is* dead."

Papirito grinned.

Psss. A quiet hissing came from under the water. *Psss.* A swift, treacherous current carried me away. Something viscous rubbed my legs and pulled me down. I recognized the long head and huge horns of the Mother-of-Water moving under the water. I cried for help.

The snake curled herself around my neck and I felt an ineffable pleasure and a terrible fear of death. Then I saw Papirito on top of a palm tree, watching me with the piercing gaze of satisfied hate.

"LOURDES! WAKE up!" I clung to Aurora's voice and opened my eyes. "*Coño*, this damned rain again! And it's leaking onto our bunk bed now!"

❧ CHAPTER XIV ❧

THE DAY AFTER the storm we awoke to a newly clean, sweet-smelling world. The rain had washed away the filth of the barracks. Trees, bushes, flowers, and the little wooden benches shone as if they had been varnished. The grass glittered, dusted with crystal sequins. Our camp, like a canvas painted by a skillful artist, displayed a serene beauty I hadn't observed before.

The fields were flooded. Reluctantly, the principal allowed all the brigades to stay in camp until the soaked earth dried. Even lunch was a step above the usual mess. Hilda and the other *guajira* could not get to the camp but Comrade Katia and Chabela prepared a splendid meal of Russian canned meat, fluffy white rice—cooked in a big pot, for the cooker was never found—and red bean soup. Pancho the Widower sent over several jars of mango jam with Elena.

After lunch, Aurora, Fat Olga, and I sat under the *framboyán*. The tree cast a delicately woven shade over us. Its flowers gleamed scarlet as if the memory of unfortunate Papirito had also been cleansed by the storm. Green, silky, inviting grass carpeted the soil.

"If we didn't have to work so hard, I'd love to live here forever," I said. "With my parents and grandma, of course."

"I'd like to see *you* milking a cow," Aurora snickered. Then she covered her mouth with a handkerchief. Her face had become ashen.

"What's wrong?" I asked.

"I feel like throwing up," she moaned.

"Ask Comrade Katia for permission to stay in camp this afternoon," Marisol suggested. "She won't say no."

Aurora didn't have time to reply. She heaved up her lunch at the base of the *framboyán*.

"Girl, are you pregnant?" asked Fat Olga, smirking. Aurora stood up and walked toward the outhouses without saying a word.

Fat Olga whistled softly. "Hmmm," she said. "Trouble is brewing."

An *aura tiñosa*, a big, black, carrion-eating bird, soared above. A dark feather fell slowly to the ground.

UNFORTUNATELY, THE earth dried too soon. That afternoon our brigade was sent to work in the tobacco field adjacent to the campground. My friends marched grumpily, but I felt ready to *make an outstanding contribution to the glorious conquests of the Revolution*, just as the principal had exhorted us to do.

Old Pancho, cantankerous as a tired ox, claimed he didn't need our help and tried to shoo us away. But we insisted on staying, afraid that if we returned to the camp we'd be told to clean the outhouses. Aurora was among the most vociferous. Little did she know what awaited us!

We were ordered to weed a field of recently transplanted tobacco sprouts of the highest quality—Pancho's pride and joy. The *guajiro* urged our unskilled crew to handle the sprouts with extreme care, but our leader, a lanky, arrogant mulatta, hardly listened to his instructions. As soon as Pancho disappeared, she took control.

"Put your back into it, *chicas*. Pick all the weeds," she yelled. "Everything. We aren't here as ornaments. We have to prove to him that we are the best!"

I started to weed while she strolled among the furrows, shaking a half *cuje* like a whip. "Chabela, be careful. Look at all the stuff you're leaving behind. The furrow has to be clean!"

The damned weeds were glued to the earth. Treacherous thistles hid maliciously among the blades of grass. After the first hour all the workers, accustomed to the coolness of the tobacco house, were tired and sweaty. Marisol and Aurora grumbled and dragged their feet, carelessly planting their boots on the tender green sprouts. The sun radiated daggers of heat that stabbed our necks and backs. I felt as if I had stepped inside a blast furnace.

To boost my morale I reminded myself once more of Che Guevara and his courageous *guerrilleros*. I imagined that I was with them in a jungle, fighting against the imperialist agents, but it didn't help much. Bright yellow particles danced in front of my eyes. My head hurt and burning needles moved up and down my spine. "I wish I *were* cleaning the outhouses now," I whispered to Aurora.

She nodded, panting, her cheeks frightfully red.

However, when Pancho returned less than two hours later, the brigade was ready to proudly report that we had finished weeding thirty minutes ahead of schedule.

"We are the best, Pancho!" the leader remarked. "Look!"

The *guajiro* glanced at the furrows. "*Coño!* I knew it! I knew you would ruin everything! Get out of here!"

"What's the matter, Pancho?" she protested. "Aren't these furrows clean enough?"

Yes, they were clean! Clean of weeds and of unwanted plants and also clean of his precious tobacco sprouts. Clean of the fruits of days of transplanting efforts, by virtue of haste and stupidity.

AN AMPHIBIOUS life began. It rained at least once a day. Storms dissolved into languid, early morning downpours that soon lost their charm since we still had to work. The daily marches became torture. My rubber boots stuck to the damp earth and collected heavy mud with every step. When I arrived at the tobacco house, my feet were already wet and stank like rotten leaves. The boys who picked up *cujes* sank up to their knees in the mud.

The unbearable coldness of dawn became enervating, humid heat by noontime. Every night Aurora and I were soaked by the continual leaking of the roof. When the latrines' stench reached the barracks, even the toughest boys puked. In the kitchen, the wet wood didn't burn and meals were hours late.

Sewing became difficult. The *cujes* were slippery and the needles pricked our fingers. The sticky tobacco leaves oozed a green moisture that transformed the work gloves' fabric into a hard material that slashed the skin.

While I sewed, I tried not to think of Papirito. But how could I stop thinking of him? The *framboyán* and a red drop of blood on my thumb reminded me of his last, fatal leap. Rainy evenings like the one when I had shooed him off, a small *cuje* like those he used to get for Aurora, paragraphs from a book that we had read together— everything seemed to conspire to bring him back.

I couldn't understand it. When Papirito was alive, I didn't care for him much—or so I thought. But now that he was gone, his invisible presence accompanied me day and night. I wondered how the other kids avoided mentioning him. Had they forgotten already? Was I the only one who remembered him? And so I felt relieved to hear Fat Olga sigh one morning, "I wish Papirito were here. He knew how to select good *cujes*, didn't he?"

"Do you miss him?" I asked anxiously.

Fat Olga nodded. "I do. I know he . . . left because of all of us.

Particularly the boys, they are so cruel. I hate them! The poor Mouse, no one loved him."

"I was his friend," I mumbled, feeling again the sting of guilt.

"It's not the same. One always needs a special person. Someone that only loves you."

I surprised myself by asking, "Do you have such a special person, *hija?*"

Fat Olga poked a *cuje* with her needle and finally admitted, "Yes. I have—Marisol."

"But you are just friends!" I played dumb so that Olga would tell me more.

"More than friends, *chica*. Haven't you noticed? We love each other and we are—engaged." She showed me a little tortoiseshell ring she wore on her right hand. "That's our love. Slow but secure, like a tortoise. We fight sometimes, but we always make up. After the reconciliation everything is terrific. Marisol is my *amor*." Olga blushed. She wasn't laughing or grinning. "This is a secret, OK?"

I looked at her and discovered a pensive, sober Olga I hadn't seen before. Under the mask of that chubby, gossipy girl there was a mature woman with solemn eyes, devoted to the woman she loved. Fat Olga's confession warmed my soul just as Grandma Inés's *ajiaco* had once warmed my body. If Olga and Marisol loved each other, maybe Aurora and I, someday . . . Yes, like Dulce and Big Boobs! But Aurora was always bragging about her well-hung boyfriends. Could she be happy with a *pinga*-less partner? It also seemed to me that Juanito didn't want her anymore. She hadn't gone out with him at night for a long time. Could she really be pregnant? *Ay!*

I FELT as if my back had started growing scales. Sometimes it rained after 5 P.M. Our brigade arrived in the camp shaking, cursing, and coughing, a sodden and weary procession of muddy shadows. It was impossible to wander around after six, when the camp shrouded itself in a veil of moisture. Nostalgia for Havana spread quickly like water in the furrows, drowning our hearts and minds.

New robberies marked the rainy season. One morning Comrade Katia discovered that an electric fan that used to be in the principal's office was gone. Just the day before Marisol had complained that a pair of jeans and some underwear that she had washed and left outside to dry were missing. This time no one blamed the kitchen helpers. Both of them were over fifty and looked undernourished and weak. "Can you imagine old Hilda dragging the heavy electric fan through the drenched fields in the middle of the night?" Chabela asked. "Nonsense! Only a man could have carried it!" Then a couple of towels and a flashlight disappeared. We became frantic. The most cautious among us carried to the fields all their valuables, wrapped in kerchiefs or tied to their bodies. Our principal announced that the culprit, once caught, would be taken to the town police station.

An obscure sense of defenselessness and fear oppressed me when I retired to my bunk bed. Chabela said she saw the shadows of sad ghosts. Aurora trembled and asked me to scratch her head. Some girls cried in their sleep and a shy tenth grader wet her bed one night.

WHEN I was a little girl, Grandma Gloria taught me to fear the Nameless Negra, the wicked color thief. The Nameless Negra was so big that she occupied all the space around her. The Nameless Negra saw everything with the one thousand eyes that hung from her black cloak. She sneaked inside the house, into my bedroom, and stole the soft pink of the walls, the white of the sheets, the yellow nose of the Pinocchio embroidered on my pillowcase, the red dresses of my *matrioskas*. The only defense against her was a tiny table lamp that Grandma turned on every night after tucking me in bed. *If you are good and sleep soon, the Nameless Negra will give you back all the colors in the morning,* Grandma Gloria would say. I hurried to close my eyes tightly, hoping sleep would come. Morning brought relief. The Nameless Negra never kept her captives after dawn. But the camp thief wasn't as considerate as my childhood nemesis had been.

"SEE, I can't forget my black T-shirt," Aurora said one evening as the wind blew strongly outside. A little group had gathered around Fat Olga's bunk bed, looking for warmth and gossip. "Don't you remember it? Made of cotton, very good-looking. I bet the thief made off with it."

"And with the rice cooker," sighed Chabela.

"And with a new flashlight," added its unfortunate owner. "What is my mother going to say when I tell her?"

(At that point, I was silently grateful that Jorge had taken my *linterna*. At least I didn't need to worry about a stranger rummaging through my belongings to steal it.)

"Maybe the thief is a sex maniac and that is why he took Marisol's underwear, the towels, and Aurora's T-shirt," suggested Fat Olga.

"*Bueno*, but why would he take the rice cooker and the electric fan?" asked Chabela. "What's the relationship between girls' clothes and those old appliances?"

"Because sex maniacs also eat rice, don't they?" Fat Olga answered. "And they like to cool off in the summer too."

"But the flashlight—" I said.

"That's for the blackouts, *chica*!"

"What will be next?" asked Chabela. "The old Frigidaire?"

"No! The TV set!" Fat Olga yelled.

"Comrade Katia's alarm clock!" Aurora chuckled. "I hate it!"

Other girls joined in.

"Marisol's suede jacket!"

"Lourdes's books!"

"Yeah, what will be next?"

"What? Or *who*?" whispered Marisol who had remained suspiciously silent for a few minutes. "This might be just the beginning. Don't you remember that film when the murderer enters a girls' dormitory with an ax—"

"Oh, my God!"

"And then he starts cutting people up—"

"Shut up, Marisol!"

"He slices off arms and legs while the girls squeal like pigs—"

Chabela ran to the safety of her bunk bed. So did Aurora and I. Soon Aurora began to snore but I stayed awake until midnight. Then I saw Papirito walking around the barracks, his head open like a broken coconut. Later, two huge *santería* dolls armed with axes, their faces covered by black T-shirts, chased me relentlessly until the five o'clock siren sounded.

DAYS PASSED. Bright but still chilly mornings replaced the rainy dawns. Life returned to normal. I stopped worrying about growing scales. But the rains had apparently washed away the last vestige of Juanito's interest in Aurora. They didn't meet at night anymore and he seemed to avoid her in the dining hall. Offended, she began to flirt shamelessly with all the boys in the camp whether they already had girlfriends or not. One of these boys was Natasha's lover, Vladimir the *cojonudo*. As a result, Natasha accused Aurora of being a whore and a sow, while Aurora ridiculed Natasha by calling her Skinny Snake.

It was customary in the School-in-the-Fields for a girl to do her boyfriend's laundry. I didn't have a sweetheart, and since Grandma Gloria loved to spoil me, I sent my clothes home to be washed in Havana every week. But Aurora and my other friends considered themselves fortunate if they got food and a visit some Sundays. They would not even dream of sending their dirty clothes home.

One evening, though, I decided to wash my smelly cashmere sweater. The only empty space in the wooden sinks happened to be beside Natasha, who was soaking a pair of Vladimir's pants.

"My boyfriend is a real pig," she commented in a surprisingly friendly manner, turning to me. "I've been scrubbing these pants for fifteen minutes and they are still as dirty as they were before. And look at this!" Natasha displayed a mud-stained denim shirt. "I never get so filthy. *Cochino!*"

Vladimir showed up at the sinks unexpectedly. Boys were seldom seen there. He carried a big load of bedclothes. Sheets, pillowcases, bedspread, blanket, everything. He laid them by Natasha's side and addressed her in a condescending manner. "Here is something else for you, *mima*. Hurry up! I want you to finish before dinnertime."

"More?" Natasha cried out. "Are you crazy, Vladimir? I only have time for work clothes today. Didn't I wash all your sheets last Sunday?"

"It isn't my fault, *mima*. Tomás sleeps in the upper part of our bunk bed and he never bothers to take off his boots before climbing up there."

"Pigs, simply pigs," she repeated, upset. "I am so tired of scrubbing your shit! *Caramba!*"

"Well, if you are going to complain so much, forget it!" Vladimir replied. "I'll get someone else to do it instead. You are not the only girl in camp, you know."

Natasha stopped washing and grabbed the soapy pants as if she were going to slap Vladimir's face with them. "Oh, really? *De verdad?*

Then why am I wasting my time with you? Here, take your dirty clothes and stick them up your ass!"

People began to crowd around, enjoying the fight, but the *cojonudo* knew better and tried to cool things off. "Hey, don't get so steamed up, *mima*! Please!"

Natasha finally relented. Vladimir smiled his conceited macho grin and walked away, leaving his girlfriend with sheets that looked oddly familiar to me. I discovered a red spot on the pillowcase, leftovers from a jar of guava jam sent by Grandma Gloria the previous Sunday.

"Well, this is what happens when you have a boyfriend," Natasha sighed. "Work and more work. Duties and obligations. But such is life."

I returned to the barracks. Only the thin mattress on top of the wood frame remained on Aurora's side of our bed. She proudly explained that Vladimir was washing all her bedclothes. "I just mentioned to him that my sheets were getting dirty and he volunteered to wash them."

"Do you like him?" I asked.

"Not really," Aurora smiled. "Though he is a good gofer. He is the first guy that has ever washed something for me!"

"So, are you going with him now?" I felt more dispirited than when I learned about her affair with Juanito. What an itching *papaya* Aurora had!

"More or less. I mean, not steadily. But you know how much I dislike this little fool Natasha. I'd do anything to give her a hard time."

"Juanito Lopesanto—" I began. Aurora interrupted me.

"Juanito Lopesanto is an asshole!"

"Did he dump you?"

"Uh—I wouldn't say that," Aurora replied. "I have my pride, *hija*.

A great deal of pride. I am going to prove to Juanito that I do not need him. In a week he will be begging me to return. You will see!"

I did not tell Aurora who was really taking care of her dirty laundry. An hour later, her sheets, pillowcases, and blanket, scrupulously clean, billowed in the cool wind.

The perfume you bought for him,
he wears it when we go out.
The shirt you ironed for him,
he crushed it necking with me.
Alo, alo cua-cua-cuá María Cocuyé, cua-cua-cua—

I DREAMED my School-in-the-Fields service was over. I had arrived home. Grandma Gloria had set up the marble-topped dining-room table and prepared *arroz con pollo*. A dish of tomato and lettuce salad gleamed with oil and vinegar. The hundred eyes of a pineapple winked at me from a glass bowl. The air was redolent of fried onions and chicken soup.

Papi read the newspaper *Juventud Rebelde* in the living room. *Mami* came in from the kitchen and handed me a glass full of mango juice. How yellow, how cold, how sweet it was! I drank it avidly . . .

Aurora moved in her sleep. I woke up and the clutches of fierce hunger grabbed me. Three old crackers dipped in condensed milk comforted my stomach, but then I felt like peeing. That meant going outside. Into the darkness where the thief hid. Although the barracks were only fifteen feet from the outhouse, I spent the following hour torn between my swollen bladder and my fear of the bandit.

Imagine you are in the Bolivian forest with a group of brave guerrilleros. *Imagine your comrades send you to explore the territory. Would you be afraid of the enemy? Don't be a* pendeja. *Go!*

At last I put on a sweater, took a piece of toilet paper, and went out. The path that led to the outhouse seemed deserted. I began tip-toeing when the noise of heavy steps sent me back to the barracks with my heart in my throat. I could not open the door. My only refuge was the *framboyán*. Closing my eyes, I squeezed myself against its trunk and waited, hidden by the leafy shadow of the tree.

Plaf. Plaf. Coño! Who was it? I *had* to see! Slowly, almost unwill-ingly, I opened my eyes and looked. I saw a human figure, but a human figure with four big horns on his head. I bit my hand and didn't move until the apparition, after crossing the fence with one powerful stride, vanished in the distance. Then I discovered I didn't need to go to the outhouse. I had wet myself.

I returned to the barracks, shaking. Had I seen Papirito's ghost, the thief, or the Mother-of-Water?

The next day my cashmere sweater, Aurora's bedclothes, and Vladimir's pants were still on the fence. I didn't mention my encounter with the four-horned beast to any of my friends. No one would believe me. My only witnesses were the *framboyán* and the night, and they wouldn't speak.

⚔ CHAPTER XV ⚕

EVERY FRIDAY MORNING, during the civic act, we saluted the flag and sang the national anthem. I didn't mind the singing, though our squeaky voices seldom blended into a harmonious choir. But the view of the flag never failed to make me feel uncomfortable.

That Friday, after the civic act, Aurora and I marched together to work. She remained silent most of the way, but when the thatched roof of the tobacco house appeared behind the trees like a large, conical straw hat, Aurora turned to me and asked, "Has your period been late before?"

"Well, yes," I answered. "Once or twice."

"Without any reason?"

"Without any reason, of course! I have never *done it!*" I replied, offended. "I am a *señorita!*" I added proudly.

"Big deal," Aurora snorted. "You'll be much happier when you can't say that anymore."

I turned up my nose, refusing to argue.

"Anyway," she said, "how long was your period delayed?"

"When I was sick with ulcers, it was three or four weeks late. And once, in 1980, it didn't come for two whole months. I felt very anxious then. My nerves might have caused it—"

A GIRL LIKE CHE GUEVARA

"Why were you so nervous?" asked incorrigible Aurora. "Love matters? I bet you were having problems with a guy, weren't you, kitten?"

I shook my head. Two years had passed, but I still couldn't talk about it.

1980. THE year of the Mariel boatlift. The year of The Scum. The year I attended a repudiation act with my secondary school classmates and *Papi* became chair of the Political Science department, an unexpected promotion that would later allow him to travel to Moscow, Prague, Berlin—

On the first of April 1980, a van driver broke into the Peruvian embassy in Havana, followed by more than ten thousand people who rushed to the place after security was withdrawn from the zone. The first news about the incident consisted of vague and often contradictory rumors.

"I heard the Peruvians are giving visas to everyone," Grandma Gloria commented. "Free visas to Peru."

"Not exactly," gossiped Marietta. "The butcher told me that a group of dissidents took over a garrison and created a temporary government with Peruvian help. They want Fidel out."

"Nonsense!" *Papi* replied. "It's just a minor mutiny, a few criminals assaulted an embassy, that's all." Then he added, "The CIA is probably behind them."

"My brothers passed by the Peruvian embassy this morning," *Mami* confided to me. "They said it's a human sea. So many people who want to leave the country—They are ready to go to Peru, to *La Yuma*, even to Haiti or to the house of *el carajo. This* may not last long, you know."

117

This meant the government, the system, sometimes Fidel. Only the counterrevolutionaries used such a term. For the rest of us, it was The Revolution. The veiled happiness betrayed by *Mami's* voice puzzled me. Why was she talking like a *gusana*?

Fearing that the mass concentration at the embassy could lead to a serious political revolt, the government opened the Mariel port. Fidel announced that anyone willing to leave the country was welcome to do that. Priority was given to those who were able to prove that they were "antisocial elements," ranging from homosexuals to convicted criminals. Any person leaving Cuba through the Mariel port was automatically labeled as fag, scum, or the ever-present and most feared term, *gusano*, a counterrevolutionary, a worm. Mocking farewell parties were organized for the *gusanos*. They were called repudiation acts.

I took part in one of them. The memories still shame me. The principal had said that all the students should attend a repudiation act after our classes finished. We had to demonstrate in front of a certain house. The people who lived in it were scum, *la escoria*, because they were leaving our country and betraying the revolution. We had been given paper bags that contained rocks, smelly tomatoes, and rotten eggs. But how were we supposed to *demonstrate*? While a huge Cuban flag billowed above our heads, my ninth-grade classmates and I watched a placid, middle-aged pharmacist who lived near our school. As he left the neighborhood drugstore and walked toward his house, our biology teacher, proudly carrying the flag, ordered us to "get him." We hesitated, not sure of what was expected from us.

I stood quietly, staring at Dr. Ruiz, the pharmacist, when our biology teacher turned to me and shouted, "Come on, Lourdes! *Anda!* Throw a rock at him!" She flashed me a wicked smile. "Hit him between the eyes!"

I grabbed the rock but could not raise my hand. Furtively, I dropped the rock back inside the paper sack, picked instead a small egg, and threw it five feet away from Dr. Ruiz. It was as if it were a signal.

"Get out of here, scum!" someone screamed.

"Don't let the door hit you in the ass, worms!"

"Get-out! Get-out! Get-out! Get-out! Get-out! Get-out! Get-out! Get-out! Get-out! Get-out! Get-out! Get-out!"

"*¡Que se vayan! ¡Que se vayan! ¡Que se vayan!*"

Two more eggs exploded like yellow, fetid bombs around the pharmacist. Then came the tomatoes, thrown by bolder hands, which left a reddish trace on his white smock. Finally a rock hit him over his left eye. His blood began to drip.

Dr. Ruiz emitted a shrill, animal sound. "Bastards!" he growled. "Cowards! *Cabrones!*"

Another, bigger rock hit him right on his chest and almost knocked him down. A girl broke into tears and ran away. She was a timid creature with whom I used to talk during recess. The teacher began to sing,

"Jimmy Carter wears panties.
We Cubans wear pants.
And we have a commander
that is a ballsy man."
(*Jimmy Carter usa blúmers,
y los cubanos pantalones.
Y tenemos un comandante
que le roncan los cojones.*)

The pharmacist did not dare to look back. Keeping an arm in front of his face, he ran awkwardly to his house, opened the door with shaky hands, and scurried inside.

Soon the porch was covered with mud, the content of several garbage cans, and smashed rotten eggs. Dr. Ruiz's wife hurriedly shut the windows while we screamed outside.

I returned home confused and tense, but no one seemed to notice. My father was walking around the living room, waiting for a phone call, unable to sit quietly for more than five minutes. He endlessly criticized "the hordes of *gusanos* who were staining the prestige of our revolution" and maintained that they *all* must be thrown in prison until their departure.

"That ungrateful scum!" he'd snarl, pausing beneath the photo of Che Guevara that presided over our living room. "And some of them are youngsters. What a shame! They don't deserve to be called New Men!"

Grandma Gloria shrugged and didn't say a word. *Mami* too kept a stubborn silence, because she—and *Papi*, and the entire family— already knew that her two brothers were leaving through the Mariel port, having presented to the police fake documents attesting to their homosexual condition. That sounded like a bad joke, for my two uncles were both very macho mulattos and incorrigible womanizers. But pretending to be a homosexual was the easiest way of obtaining permission to leave. In our barrio, the *tortillera* Dulce and her friend Big Boobs were among the first neighbors to go. They cleverly escaped at night, fooling those who had dreamed of organizing a harsh repudiation act for them.

The phone finally rang and *Papi* rushed to answer it. A brief conversation followed. When he hung up, his normally pale face appeared illuminated.

"Hey, *compañeras*, now you are allowed to congratulate me!" he announced. "You are talking to the new chair of the Political Science department of Havana University."

"What?" *Mami* gasped. "What did you say?"

Grandma Gloria ran to hug him and exclaimed, "I always knew you'd be something! God bless you, *niño!*"

Papi kissed her, laughing, "That is not a politically correct response, *Mamá,* but it's fine with me. Just don't repeat it in front of anybody." Then he turned to *Mami,* "I said the *new chair.* Do you know what it means? Fewer teaching hours, much better pay, and the possibility of getting a car when the Ladas are distributed among the department heads in November."

He imitated the sound of a car's engine, playfully circling around us. *Papi* didn't look like himself at that moment. He was always so severe, so serious and dignified!

"But how could you be the chair?" *Mami* asked, still incredulous. "What happened to González?"

González was *Papi's* boss and friend, the chair of their department since 1978, the president of the CDR in his block, and a lifelong member of the Communist Party. We treated him as a guest of honor the few times he condescended to visit our house after carefully parking his cerulean Lada in a spot that he could watch from our living room. Grandma Gloria made rice puddings for him, *Mami* ran errands for his stuck-up wife, and I pretended to enjoy talking to his conceited and always overdressed twelve-year-old daughter.

Papi insisted that we befriend the Gonzálezes. He often took his boss out to eat in expensive restaurants like Moscow and La Torre. González, who always wore spotless starched *guayaberas* and a Rolex watch, had very important contacts in the Central Committee. He was "connected."

"González's brother-in-law came from Miami to take him and his family out," my father answered curtly. He regained his composure and added, "I discovered it by pure chance, when I went to his house this morning to pick up the minutes of our last Party meeting. He and his wife were talking about how they would sneak out, pretending they were going to visit a relative in Oriente. I overheard it. The little worm was planning to leave without saying anything until the last moment! But I called the comrade in charge of our Party cell and let him know."

"Did you turn him in?" *Mami* asked in shock. "Oh, Rafael, how could you? I thought that you were good friends, *compañeros*!"

"I am not the friend of scum!" *Papi* answered irritably. "And he is not a *compañero* anymore! Didn't you hear what I said? He is leaving. L-e-a-v-i-n-g. I used to be his friend because I didn't know he was a worm."

"Anyway, this is betraying a friendship," *Mami* whispered.

Papi rolled his eyes, the only gesture that revealed his exasperation. Then he replied with artificial sweetness, "Don't be so silly, Barbarita. *He* is betraying the revolution, and his CDR comrades, and the Party, and all of us. Can't you see it? He's been deceiving everybody all these years. I know that your brothers are leaving too," he continued, caressing *Mami's* back, "but it doesn't bother me. They never pretended they were revolutionaries. I personally believe this is the best thing they can do. Leave and let us build socialism with those who sincerely want to do it, as Comrade Fidel said. But a guy like González, who even went to study in Moscow, who has been given so many opportunities here! He should be arrested and not allowed to go anywhere! I directed his repudiation act. If his house were not a collective property, as it is now, I'd have burned it!"

"And you were appointed to take his place so quickly, my king?" Grandma Gloria asked softly.

"I was the one who warned the Party members and his CDR people before he could take any information out of the house—important university and political secrets. They valued my attitude and I got my reward. Of course, I only did what anybody with a revolutionary consciousness would have done. Besides, the department couldn't be without a head, particularly in the present historical moment, when we all have to be organized to repel imperialist aggression, in case *they* dare to come."

They were the Yankees. The Evil ones.

"Do you think there is going to be a war, *Papi*? Will we be attacked?" The thought of other people throwing rocks and rotten eggs at *us*, burning *our* house, horrified me.

Papi seemed to notice my presence for the first time.

"No, there won't be a war, Lulu," he said soothingly. "It's just a figure of speech. And if there is one, under Fidel's leadership we'll win it. Now, do you know what time it is? It's almost ten o'clock, and you haven't even eaten yet! *Mamá*, give Lourdes her supper and put her to bed. Good night, *niña*. Sleep well."

"Do you think González is really a worm?" I asked Grandma Gloria, as she tucked me in bed.

"I don't know," she sighed. "But if your *Papi* says so, it must be true."

"And are we going to have a blue Lada, now that *Papi* is an important person too?"

"Maybe, princess. Maybe."

OUR BRIGADE had arrived at the tobacco house.

"Wake up, girl!" Aurora shook my arm. "Cat got your tongue or what? You haven't said a word for twenty minutes."

"I was confused, remembering," I admitted. "And a little angry. I am not mad at you," I hurried to say, "but at my father, at myself, at—the world. I don't know."

"I am confused and mad, too," she replied. "That *cabrón* of Juanito—Well, forget it. Let's hope we get small *cujes* today."

⊰ CHAPTER XVI ⊱

ONE OF THE School-in-the-Fields routines I hated was taking a bath on freezing afternoons. We had to fill our buckets with water from the camp's cistern and carry them to the bathhouse. The chilly wind that blew through the cracks in the bathhouse walls didn't help. Fat Olga's idea that the uncaught thief might also be a voyeur watching us from the roof didn't help either. Had I slept by myself, I'd have skipped bathing. But Aurora took a long bath every evening, changed her underwear twice a day, and used deodorant right before bedtime. I didn't want her to call me a pig.

The camp's bathhouse was divided into cubicles the size of telephone booths. The floor was slimy. However, it smelled good, like soap, cologne, and powder perfumed with the little white flowers of jasmine.

I was getting dressed after a quick sponge bath when Aurora called to me from her stall. I tiptoed over. When I entered, I lowered my eyes and noticed her wet, shapely legs. Blood rushed to my face. "What's going on, *chica?*" I asked.

Aurora pointed to her belly, her fingers trembling. "Does it look very swollen? Swollen and big?" she groaned.

"Frankly, no," I said, trying not to stare at a hairy mole under Aurora's navel, a discordant note in the otherwise faultless symmetry of her body. "It is as flat as usual. Why?"

"My period hasn't come this month," she said. "I am fifteen days late."

"It could be a normal delay," I replied. "Maybe you are just feeling tense." Aurora shook her head. "Well, did you tell Juanito?"

"He doesn't believe it's his." Aurora kept silent for a moment. "I hate him! I hate him so much! How am I going to take care of a baby? God, if I come out of this all right, I'll never look at a man again!"

NIGHT WAS falling. Jumbled thoughts whirled inside my mind while Aurora looked dispiritedly through the barracks' windows, staring at the darkness. Getting pregnant in high school was a *jodienda*, a frightful predicament. If Juanito dumped her, what would she do? Would she have his baby anyway?

"Hey, I have an idea!" Aurora exclaimed. "Ask your mother if she knows of any remedy when she comes this Sunday. Would you do that?"

"Sure."

But when Sunday came, I couldn't ask *Mami* a thing. She wasn't there. Only *Papi* showed up, nervous and somber.

I LOOKED forward to Sunday mornings like a child to her birthday party. The parents' bus—rattling, dusty, painted gray—came at about 10 A.M. It had seats for fifty people but more than a hundred passengers would squeeze inside. As soon as the driver parked in front of the camp, the vehicle began to spit out tired-looking visitors carrying enormous bags of food. A swarm of expectant kids ran to meet them and before long the camp bubbled with happy shouts and appetizing smells.

When I saw my father leaving the parents' bus by himself, the first thing that came to my mind was that *Mami* had had an accident. So *Papi's* explanation was almost a relief. "From now on, I'll be visiting one Sunday and *Mami* the next," he said with a false calmness.

"Why?" I asked.

"She is living with her mother now, in Mantilla. But do not be concerned about it, dear. You will not go without a visit, no matter what."

The news didn't come as a big surprise, but I was still shocked. My parents never fought openly, yet for the last three years a strange calm, as tense as a taut silk cord, had marked their marriage. When they talked, it was only about the *niña*, about me. I knew *Papi* had gone to you-know-where behind *Mami's* back. I suspected she kept that black doll soaked in honey to retain him—

"Does it mean that you are going to get a divorce?" I asked *Papi*. I wanted to hear the truth, no matter how painful.

"I am not sure," he answered evasively. "Ask *Mami* when she comes."

"Why can't you tell me now?" I insisted.

"Because I don't know yet."

"You don't know or you don't want to tell me?"

"Don't be silly, Lourdes!" He was getting impatient. "I *can't* tell you because we haven't decided anything. Daughter, you are intelligent enough, almost an adult now, so you've probably noticed that things are not going well between *Mami* and me. We *might* get a divorce—" My face must have reflected more grief than I intended to show, because *Papi* added quickly, "*Bueno*, these problems can still be solved. We are just taking some time away from each other to think about things."

"Are you leaving us?" I asked shyly.

"Leaving *my* house, you mean?" *Papi* looked rather amused. "What a question, *niña*! Certainly not!"

He unpacked the steaks and fried plantains Grandma Gloria had sent, but my usual Sunday hunger had disappeared. For the first time a disturbing idea occurred to me. Someday I might have to choose between *Papi* and *Mami*, between my spacious bedroom at home and Grandma Inés's cramped cabin.

Before he left, *Papi* gave me a wrinkled envelope and told me to deliver it to Chabela. My jaw dropped when I read the sender's name. Why had Crazy Jorge, the monster, written to Chabela? And why had *Papi* brought a message from him?

THE SUN'S feeble rays filtered through heavy gauze clouds. Weekdays advanced as slowly as if Time had decided to take a long siesta.

On Saturday afternoon I was sewing a button on my work shirt, sitting on the edge of our bunk bed. Aurora gazed at the cracks and holes in the zinc roof, both hands resting on her belly. Chabela read *The Countess and the Burglar,* a Corín Tellado romance. Fat Olga and Marisol listened to Pablo Milanés on a battery radio. Unexpectedly, Crazy Jorge appeared at the door and shouted, "Chabela, my bug, here I am!"

Chabela jumped out of her bed, abandoning the countess to her fate. She ran to hug the monster. Then they wandered throughout the camp, holding hands, apparently in seventh heaven.

"Beauty and the beast," Fat Olga chuckled.

"Strange bedfellows," Marisol remarked.

Crazy Jorge used to scare me. Many times I crossed the street when I saw him walking in my direction, even though he ignored me. I thought he must hate me. And he had taken my flashlight! So I was astonished when the monster handed me a package with two steaks, three cans of condensed milk, and a flan that had Marietta's distinctive signature all over its syrupy surface. "Your grandma and my mom sent you this," he said.

"Thanks," I replied. Not able to think of anything else to say, I asked, "How did you get here?"

"I hitchhiked."

"My *pobrecito*," purred Chabela, stroking his hair. "What a trip!"

Camp rules didn't allow visitors to stay overnight, but Crazy Jorge didn't go back to Havana. He convinced Pancho to let him sleep in his cabin. "Frankly, I do not like the arrangement at all," Chabela confided to me, "because he'll be too close to Elena. That girl is dangerous!"

"Oh, she is an innocent *guajirita*," I replied. "What can she do?"

"Many things," Chabela asserted. "None of them good!"

After that Jorge came to the camp not only on Sundays but during weekdays as well. Such visits were not normally allowed, but Comrade Katia and the principal pretended not to notice them. Pancho took a liking to the wild *Habanero* and Elena often invited Jorge to have coffee with them. That made Chabela even more jealous, but Jorge would tell her she shouldn't be concerned. "The *guajirita* isn't interested in a penniless guy like me," he assured her. "She aims much higher." And he laughed out loud.

CHABELA'S NEW boyfriend aroused plenty of gossip. A few girls disapproved but they were just envious. Crazy Jorge's lovers had always been much older women: audacious mulattas in their twenties or young divorcées with their own apartments. This was the first time he'd gone out with an eleventh grader. The others, who had flirted with Jorge for months last year, couldn't accept their defeat.

A couple of nights after his first visit we were already in the barracks by 9:30. My feet felt like two bars of ice. Comrade Katia suggested that we place towels and old papers inside the wall cracks so the cold west wind could not enter. Fat Olga, head and body covered by two blankets, curled up with Marisol. Aurora and I snuggled together, trying to keep warm.

"Our Chabela is a little fox!" Marisol said. "Look at the boyfriend she has now! A decent girl, going out with that *cabrón!*"

"We are all little foxes," Aurora reminded her. "Listen, Marisol, have you ever had problems with your period?"

Marisol answered with a short laugh, "No, *hija*. I do not even notice when it comes. Only when I see the tomato sauce spread all over my clothes."

Chabela entered the barracks, wrapped in Crazy Jorge's blue denim jacket.

"So, you don't know of any remedy to use when it is—a little late?" Aurora persisted.

"I am afraid I don't."

"You haven't wasted time, girl!" Fat Olga chimed in, her round face popping up from under her blanket. "Now you are in trouble. I knew it!"

"I am not in trouble," Aurora mumbled. "But—"

"If you are, ask Elena," suggested Marisol. "She may give you a hint."

"Are you crazy, Marisol? She is a virgin, how am I going to ask her—?"

"How do you know Elena is a virgin?" Marisol retorted. "Have you inspected her pussy? Anyway, *guajiros* know of useful herbal remedies. Folk medicine and the like."

Chabela approached us, "There is more than one little fox in our camp, I'd say. And your friend Elena, the '*sinsonte*,' is one of them!"

"Yes, Elena wiggles her hips too much when she walks," observed

Marisol. "I don't think she is a *señorita* anymore, though she swears she is."

"Girls, do not say bad things about the *guajirita*," Fat Olga warned us. "I believe Elena's mom is dead because people call her father The Widower. It must have been difficult for her to grow up without a mother. She's turned out quite well, for a poor girl living practically alone in this damned Pinar del Río."

We stayed awake for a long time. The cold weather loosened our tongues and made us hungry. I opened one of my cans of milk and passed it around.

"I can't believe you are the girlfriend of that wretch," Marisol said to Chabela as we sipped the condensed milk. "Crazy Jorge is the stupidest, nastiest guy I've ever seen in all my life! I can't imagine him asking you for a date!"

"What do you know?" Chabela snapped back. "You have never spoken to him!"

"Oh! Does he know how to speak? That's good news."

"Well, he is a real stud, *hijas,*" asserted Aurora, who liked to be fair in men's business. "We can't deny that."

"He should be well hung," adventured Fat Olga. "Is he, Chabela? People say that if a guy's middle finger is big, his *pinga* corresponds. Crazy Jorge has the hands of a stevedore."

"Well, he is big. All his person, not only his fingers or his—"

"Yes, but you are *too* different!" Marisol insisted. "Chabela, *chica,* tell me, what do you guys talk about? You are so sweet and nice, and he is so mean and crude."

I suddenly realized that Chabela and Jorge, Aurora and Juanito, and *Mami* and *Papi* were all unlikely couples because they looked so different. The good girl and the bad boy. The teenager and the mature man. The white professor and the mulatta saleswoman. Strange bedfellows, as Marisol had said.

"I don't think they do a lot of talking," Aurora grinned. "And maybe Chabela likes it rough."

"My Jorge is a gentleman!" Chabela said, blushing. "The *pobrecito* has had many problems. You just can't imagine—his father left Cuba when Jorge was a baby. His mother doesn't care for him too much either. But he is very sensitive, though he covers it up."

Marisol added some discourteous observations about where, exactly, Jorge hid his sensitivity. Soon we finished the condensed milk and silence replaced chitchat. But in an evil hour I turned to Aurora and whispered, "I never dreamed Jorge would bring me food or be so civilized. Guess I should thank Chabela for it. Love changes people."

"How naive you are, Lourdes!" She chuckled. "Love, shit! He brought you the package because your *Papi* sleeps with his mother!"

"What—what are you saying?" I stuttered.

"Everybody in the barrio knows they are screwing around," Aurora answered casually. "Didn't you know it, girl? "

Well, I had *suspected* something before, though I had never been able to put it into words. Not even in the privacy of my own mind. It was too horrible.

"I once saw them kissing," Aurora went on. "They were in Marietta's garden, practically in your mom's face. That blonde has cheek!"

Papi was cheating on *Mami* with the slothful floozy, *ay*, and our neighbors knew! They had seen them! How embarrassing! But no. Impossible. How could my proper, decent *Papi* do something so improper, so indecent?

Papi wouldn't cheat! Aurora had to be wrong. Because her parents were nasty and vulgar, she thought all parents were the same. What a dirty mind she had. Disgusted, I turned my back to her.

But at that moment, like a child who puts the last piece of a puzzle in its place and stares, bewildered, at the structure he has seen grow step-by-step, I looked at my home life with new, knowing eyes. I remembered Marietta's frequent visits to our house, and *Mami's* complaints about them. I saw Marietta and *Papi* chat on our patio. I heard them lower their voices when I approached—

Unconnected scenes kept coming back to me. Events that had once seemed too perplexing to even think about added detail to the picture. The flashlight that *Papi* had bought for me, and then given to Crazy Jorge. That day he'd said to Grandma Gloria, "I'll be you-know-where," and asked her to tell *Mami* he was still at the university. You-know-where, I finally understood, was the house next door—How wilfully blind I had been!

Papi didn't love *Mami* anymore. They were not "thinking about things." They were going to split up. I repressed a sob. What else would happen? *Mami* might commit suicide out of desperation. My aunt Mariana had set herself aflame after her husband left her for a Russian girl. But Aunt Mariana had no children. *Mami* had me! I was her *niña*. She still had to take care of me.

Hours passed. The milky clarity of dawn replaced darkness. Aurora snored, unconscious of the turmoil her news had created. I finally fell asleep haunted by a distressing image, my parents' silver-framed wedding picture cut in half by Marietta's lovely, lazy, manicured hands.

⊰ CHAPTER XVII ⊱

THE FOLLOWING MORNING I woke up wrapped in grief and my worn-out cashmere sweater. But I had decided to suppress, or at least hide, my feelings. I wouldn't ask Aurora what else she'd seen. I would try to forget about our conversation. Time would solve everything . . . While having breakfast seated between Chabela and Aurora, I forced myself to smile.

"You girls should follow Lourdes's example," Marisol said to them. "She doesn't miss anybody. She is happy and free."

Happy and free! Ha! My sorrow was no less painful even though the object of my dreams was right next to me. On the contrary, Aurora's presence added a bitter tinge to my confusion.

If only I could have a "special person," as Fat Olga had said. A "special person" who considered me "special" too. A "special person" would protect me from horned monsters, Mothers-of-Water, the fears of life, and the cold weather. But who? I had never had a boyfriend. No one liked me. Neither Aurora nor any boy. I was an ugly duckling.

Perplexing questions plagued me with mosquitolike buzzing. What was love? What *Papi* had stopped feeling for *Mami*? What he felt for Marietta now? What I felt for Aurora? What attracted Chabela to a tough guy like Jorge, and Aurora to Juanito?

★ ★ ★

"*HIJA, YOU* can't continue acting as if you were a seven year old," Aurora admonished me during the morning break, when we escaped from the thick atmosphere of the tobacco house and sat under a palm tree to breathe in fresh air. "At your age, you have to get a boyfriend. And I know who the right person is."

We were chewing small fruits that grew in the nearby trees. Their white, pulpy skin had a sweetish flavor so they were called "almonds." Aurora's assertion surprised me so much that I swallowed my "almond," seed and all. Before leaving for the School-in-the-Fields I had read a Soviet book about telepathy. Were Aurora and I "connected"? After a coughing fit, I managed to ask, "Who are you talking about? No one is interested in me."

"Yes, there is one," Aurora replied. "He doesn't have a girlfriend and you are still waiting for your Prince Charming to come. Why don't you two get together?"

"But who is it?!" I demanded.

"Ssh! Don't shout! It's Ernesto. He is tall, dark skinned, strong, quite good-looking—"

"Ernesto?" I laughed. "You are crazy, girl! He is—he is—" Then I stopped, ashamed, and bit my tongue. The scene I had witnessed in the boys' barracks should remain secret. The principal would kick both boys out of camp if he ever knew.

"He is *what*? Not good enough for you?" asked Aurora. Her expression said too clearly *you pretentious snob.* And it hurt me. I felt like a secondhand pair of shoes because I knew for sure what she thought. I was not a pretty girl. She wanted me to accept a mulatto because I was so ugly, thin, and dark. My mood changed in a second but Aurora didn't notice and kept on talking, "Ernesto gets along with people, he looks clean, and he will treat you well. You have to give him some confidence because—"

"Oh, shut up," I snarled. "You are driving me nuts with your stupid advice."

I was so furious that Aurora dropped all her "almonds," sincerely alarmed. "Are you OK?" she asked.

I nodded, trying to hold back my tears.

"I care for you, Lulu, and I am sorry if I offended you," Aurora said softly. "I didn't intend to say anything mean. But you are, in a way, left behind by most of us. You should give this boyfriend business a fair try and then decide if you want to have one or not. Why did you get so mad?"

My anger and my pain subsided and I finally answered, "I don't want you pitying me because I am not as beautiful as you are. I know I am not, but it doesn't mean I am going to accept the first pig that shows up."

"Oh, you are beautiful enough!" she replied quickly. "Who said you aren't? You have pretty eyes and a fine body, girl. And Ernesto isn't a pig. Where did you get that idea? He is a nice guy and rather handsome too. He is exactly what you need to get your feet wet."

Ay, Beauty, I thought, if you just knew the one that I'd like to get my feet wet with—

Then Aurora sighed. "Lulu, how I envy you now," she confessed. "I wish I was still as innocent as you are. Then I wouldn't suffer so much."

"Do *you* suffer? I thought you were the one who made the boys suffer," I reminded her.

"The boys, perhaps. Juanito—he is different. He can be a real *cabrón* and I sometimes doubt that he'll ever recognize our child. But I still like him. I miss his kisses every night. It's like a pain inside, a void . . ."

A pain inside, a void . . . Didn't I feel that, too? "Are you still in love with Juanito?" I asked shyly.

"Oh yes! If Juanito came to me tomorrow and said, 'Let's get married,' I'd be the happiest woman on earth." Aurora looked at me with a humble smile, completely different from her conceited grin. "I know it sounds ridiculous. Imagine what Marisol would say if she heard me. But I love him. My dream is to live in a big house in El Vedado, with my handsome Juanito and our baby."

"Break is over, girls! Back to work!" shouted the leader.

The fifteen minutes had slipped through our fingers like sand. We returned to the tobacco house but I couldn't sew. My hands were sweating. My heart throbbed. I was confused and exhilarated, depressed and happy, wanting to laugh and cry at the same time.

When I finished my last *cuje* of the day, I had made up my mind. I'd accept Ernesto, even if I didn't like him. Aurora admitted once that she had not been in love with many of her previous boyfriends, that their relationships had simply been "entertainment." "I've learned how to use men," she had said proudly. Well, I would use them too. Ernesto would help me learn about love. He'd help me forget Aurora or—wouldn't that be great?—make me experienced enough so I could win her heart.

It rained for a while during the morning but by lunchtime the sky had cleared. As we walked back to camp a rainbow appeared behind the distant green hills. A hummingbird flew toward it and vanished in the bright mass of color. The somber feelings of the morning had left my heart.

ERNESTO, A tall, strong mulatto who I had once caught in bed with Berto, seemed more serious than other boys. He was reserved but not shy. He dressed passably well. However, the idea of having a dark boyfriend didn't quite fit my plans at first. Deep in my heart

I longed for a very different partner. Someone white. Like *Papi.* Like Aurora.

I knew that a revolutionary shouldn't discriminate against people because of their skin color. Particularly when I was a mulatta myself! But I couldn't avoid it. Some girls liked tall boys, others favored short guys. It was a matter of preference. I simply preferred whites.

The following day, Aurora drew Ernesto and me aside and introduced us. At lunchtime, my prospective boyfriend greeted me bashfully and offered me a seat. Later on he changed places with another boy to be in my supply brigade, and from then on he was usually the one who brought *cujes* to my place. When a leg of the bunk bed I shared with Aurora broke, Ernesto skillfully fixed it.

It was like a game. When Ernesto—encouraged by busybody Aurora—asked me to sit with him on the bench near the boys' barracks one night, I accepted without thinking twice.

"A boyfriend is what you need to pull your socks up," Fat Olga remarked.

"And if you don't like the guy, you can always dump him after four or five days," Aurora said soothingly. "It's no big deal."

"Nothing can be compared to having a sweetheart and loving him," Chabela sighed. "Waiting for him, reading his letters when he isn't around, and even crying over them—"

"Prrrr! Meow! Fu-fua!" interjected Marisol, who wasn't fond of romantic talk. "Get off that cloud, *niña,* before somebody makes you land on earth with a kick in the butt."

Who cared if Ernesto was a mulatto? I wanted "to give the boyfriend business a try."

"TO DO it or not to do it"? I needed to talk about it. But with whom? Aurora was too loose. Marisol and Fat Olga were *tortilleras*. What would they know about boyfriends? Only Chabela could advise me. We found an appropriate place to discuss the matter, under the *framboyán*. Chabela smiled at my first, timid question, "Have you already done it?"

"Yes," she answered proudly, as all "experienced" girls did. "With Jorge."

"Does it hurt?"

"You bet it does! The first time—the first two or three times—it hurts like hell. But later it gets easier and you begin to enjoy it."

"Do you think that I should—" I started, red in the face. She didn't let me finish.

"Now, *hija*," Chabela took the stance of a well-informed little teacher. "I know what you are going to ask, so listen to me very carefully."

"I'm all ears," I whispered.

"You should *not* do it with Ernesto, even if he asks you every day—unless you plan to go steady with him. I had six boyfriends before Jorge but never did it with any of those guys. I wasn't in love with them. There are other things, like necking and kissing, which are also very good. But don't let him push you, because hurrying only spoils things."

"Is it true that boys always want to do it fast but lose respect for you after you please them?" I asked, remembering *Mami's* warnings. "That they dump you and—"

"Some men want it immediately and get mad if they can't get it. That's their problem, though. But even if you feel your *papaya* melting, don't give in too soon. The truth is that if you are too easy, guys don't appreciate it. They may leave you right after doing it and then tell all their friends! It's better to wait a couple of months. Or even more. Until you get to know him well."

That sounded proper and didn't contradict *Mami's* and Grandma Gloria's teachings. I thanked Chabela and promised to follow her advice. Though I felt a nice, slight tingling in my *papaya* when I thought of getting a boyfriend, I wasn't ready to let the "boyfriend" put anything inside it yet.

When I told Aurora about Chabela's recommendations, she laughed out loud. "Chabela doesn't know what she is talking about. Pay attention to her and you'll find a tail growing out of your ears. Listen to *me*. If a guy is going to leave you, he'll leave you anyway. It doesn't matter what you do or don't do. On the contrary, if you do it, he may stay longer with you because of that. Haven't you heard the saying *Dos tetas halan más que una carreta?* Two titties pull more than a wagon! But if you are too inhibited, he'll consider you a child and look for a more obliging girl."

I didn't want to be a child anymore. I longed to be a woman, like the rest of my friends. But, as Chabela herself had pointed out in another conversation, one should not put the cart before the horse. The first step in "getting my feet wet" was to accept Ernesto as a boyfriend.

THE NIGHT of my first date came—

I stood quietly by my bunk bed, while my friends fussed around me taking care of the last minute details.

"Go for it!" Aurora said when she finished combing my hair. "Have a great time and enjoy a good *pinga!*"

"Go for it!" repeated Chabela, applying some of her sticky Maybelline on my eyelashes. "But be extremely careful! Open your eyes and close your legs!"

"Go for it!" urged Fat Olga, sprinkling my clothes with her *Gato Negro* perfume. "So you can tell us later how it was."

"Go for it!" echoed Marisol, as she hung a pretty necklace around my neck.

Aurora accompanied me toward the door of the barracks where Ernesto had been waiting for the last twenty minutes. After a shy greeting, he took my hand and we began to walk nervously around the campground.

During the first hour, Ernesto's sweaty fingers barely touched mine and I recognized in him the familiar symptoms of fear. At the same time, the boy exuded a neediness that attracted me more than typical manly arrogance. After I told him that, yes, I agreed to be his girlfriend, he kissed me quickly on my lips. My first kiss! It wasn't particularly enjoyable, though it wasn't totally unpleasant either. It was like drinking a lukewarm, sugarless glass of milk.

Then Ernesto hugged me. I responded without enthusiasm until I noticed his scent, as I had noticed Aurora's. Ernesto smelled of lilacs and grass and I liked to sniff him. After a few unskilled caresses, he tried to unbutton my blouse. We were near the boys' barracks, in a dark spot. "Look but don't touch" I said, half seriously and half playfully. He obeyed and we continued talking and walking until midnight. My *papaya*, I must admit, remained as dry as a *cuje*.

I had accepted Ernesto not only because of the combined pressure of my snoopy friends, but because we both had a dirty little secret to keep. His was the shameful relationship with Berto the Duck, mine was my crush on Aurora. We were in the same boat.

When I returned to my bunk bed, Marisol whistled softly. "At last! You must have had a very good time, girl!"

"*Coño!* I thought you were not coming back until tomorrow!" complained Fat Olga. "I'm half asleep already!"

"Well, did you like it?" Aurora asked. "How was it?"

"Not too bad," I replied after weighing my answer. "In my opinion, all this boyfriend business is much ado about nothing. Don't you think?"

Aurora looked at me sympathetically. "*Ay, chica,*" she smiled, "it doesn't seem to me that you have learned a lot in your introductory session. You still have a long way to go!"

⊰ CHAPTER XVIII ⊱

THOUGH THE FROG had not turned into a prince after the first kiss, I didn't throw it back into the pond. That was a wise decision. What had started as a bearable duty turned into an enjoyable routine that filled my evenings. I didn't fall madly in love with Ernesto, as some of my friends expected, nor did I dump him after the first week, as others prophesied. We became pals. I found it easy to talk to him. We were a lot alike, a pair of quiet *mulaticos*, though my skin—I never failed to note—was much lighter than his, and my hair less curly.

Our relationship progressed fast. I never enjoyed kissing Ernesto and still thought often of Aurora, but it was pleasant to snuggle with him in the grass behind the boys' barracks after I got accustomed to the gymnastics of necking. Without knowing how it happened, we ended up there like other couples I had seen. Yet naive as I was, Aurora's luckless example and Chabela's lecture prevented me from going further. Ernesto didn't insist on "doing it" either. My *papaya* didn't get hot, not even warm.

I felt a little detached when he touched me "down there," but I tried not to reject him in a rude way. When he asked me if I liked "it," my answers were oblique: "It's OK, I don't dislike it." Ernesto always complied when I told him to stop. Many times he stopped

⊰ 143 ⊱

without being asked, which I appreciated. Because of this, and because Ernesto was very gentle, I came to feel genuine sympathy for him and accepted even his wiry, thicker-than-mine hair.

Despite Ernesto's outward shell there was a softness in him, a surprising tenderness in his manners. When his initial shyness disappeared, he kissed me passionately and repeated, *I love you, mima. I love you so much.* But I knew something was, if not wrong, at least rather phony. What kind of love did he feel for me? The same kind I felt for him, warm but fraternal? Why didn't my *papaya* melt? Chabela and Aurora had told me it would happen sooner than later. Had they lied to me? Was Ernesto a bad lover? Or was it my own fault?

His caresses were enjoyable, sensitive, almost courteous, but they didn't satisfy my deepest desires. Our contact lacked the spicy flavor that Aurora, Fat Olga, and Chabela experienced with their respective partners. On the other hand, I relished our conversations. I only noticed how long they lasted because my dry mouth cried for water and my voice became harsh.

I trusted Ernesto so much that I once told him about the horned beast I had spotted by the outhouse. He assured me that I must have dreamed it. The thief had to be a person. A *guajiro* had probably stolen the rice cooker and the electric fan. As for the clothes and towels, they had been taken or destroyed by one of the girls, either because she liked them or just to annoy their owners. "The Mother-of-Water is an old farmers' tale," he concluded. "You read too many mystery stories. But don't worry because I am here. I will protect you against all the beasts, thieves, and freaks in the world."

I kissed him on the cheek, laughing. "You are right," I said. "I'm such a *pendeja*!"

★ ★ ★

I HAD lived without a true friend. A male friend, that is. Now I recognized how much I had needed him. Our conversations were so different from Aurora's monologues! He never let me down. I couldn't call him "my knight in shining armor," as "knight" was considered a bourgeois term. But he unquestionably was my *guerrillero*.

On one occasion I commented how beautiful Chabela's hair used to be when it was long and straight and how she had ruined it with an awful permanent that left her with a bunch of tarnished locks. "You are envious of white girls' looks," Ernesto said angrily. "Don't you see, my *amor*, that they would do anything to have yours? Why do you think they get permanents?"

I knew I was not the typical, tropical, and tempting mulatta à la Cecilia Valdez. I considered myself plain, too white to be a genuine black, too dark to be a true white. I noticed how proudly black girls carried their velvet-skinned, tiny-waisted, long-legged bodies. Then there were the white girls with their pretty pink cheeks after a day of open-air work in the fields. Blondes or brunettes had long, smooth, easy-to-brush manes. His words raised me in my own estimation.

During the '80s most teenagers had their *quinceaños* pictures taken while wrapped in frilly dresses with their radiant tresses falling to their waists. In my best fifteen-year-old picture—enlarged, framed, and hung on Grandma Gloria's living-room wall—I wore a phony smile, a pink satin dress, and a crown of rigid curls. Fifteen-year-old parties were romantically called "sweet celebrations of the spring of life," but I had hated mine.

A *quinceañera* would put on four or five new dresses on her *fiesta de quince*. Pretentious girls put on fifteen—one dress for each year. The reception took place in the *quinceañera's* house—

recently painted, if possible—or in a banquet room. The tables, ornamented with flowers and balloons, displayed bowls of salads, croquettes, homemade sweets, and a big cake with an elaborate centerpiece. Soft drinks were served for the younger set, and rum, beer, and *mojitos* for the more daring or experienced. Color photos had become extremely popular. They were a novelty in the 1980's. Occasionally a blue dress looked greenish, or blonde tresses turned orange but that didn't matter. The most fantastic photo shoots showed the *quinceañera's* head inside a TV set, the *quinceañera* taking a bubble bath, the *quinceañera* flying on a magic carpet, the *quinceañera* on top of a rainbow, and the *quinceañera* floating on a cloud.

During my *fiesta de quince* I had sixty color photos taken. I put on four new, stiff dresses that I would never wear again because they were too formal and uncomfortable for daily activities. The guests danced and romped in the living room, the dining room, the garden, and even the kitchen. They destroyed five potted plants, an old porcelain vase, two ashtrays, and eleven glasses. They plugged the toilet, killed the fish in Grandma Gloria's aquarium, and vomited in the sink. The party ended at 3 A.M. and left me with a massive headache.

Grandma Gloria woke up the following day complaining that the neighborhood *mulaticas* were responsible for the damage. She had a tremendous fight with *Mami*, accusing her of inviting too many noisy and uneducated kids to the fiesta. When *Mami* pointed out that those noisy and uneducated kids were my friends and classmates, Grandma Gloria yelled, "Well, it's your fault Lourdes associates with the riffraff! It's entirely your fault!" Though *Mami* rebelled sometimes, she was easily intimidated by Grandma Gloria and so she said nothing. I spent long hours trying to figure out what was wrong with my friends until I discovered it. Most of them were mulattas with kinky hair.

★ ★ ★

MAMI AND Grandma Gloria agreed on one thing, though they expressed it differently. Niña, *you've advanced the race, Mami* cooed. *Thank God you didn't jump backward,* Grandma Gloria sighed with relief. Advancing the race and jumping backward, I soon understood, were euphemisms politely used to avoid mentioning the word "black."

Through the years Grandma Gloria had collected a variety of techniques to fight my frizzy hair. *If you want it to grow fast and straight, you must cut the ends off on the Day of Candelaria.* So on February 2, rain or shine, she would take me to her hairdresser. She knew of extraordinary potions, of funky-smelling blends that allegedly smoothed the most rebellious hair. *Mix cold cream with butter and oil. Apply the mixture to your hair before you go to bed and it will be silky and shiny in the morning. Rub an egg yolk all over your head—*

I brushed my hair one hundred times every night. I closed my eyes and dreamed. *Fancy french braids. Blonde ponytails. Waist-long manes. Cute pigtails. Copper curls. Long, flowing tresses. Goldilocks.*

Though I was the lightest complexioned of Grandma Inés's grandchildren, she never paid my "whiteness" any special attention. If being dark was OK for the *orishas,* it should be OK for people too, she'd say. This often annoyed *Mami,* the only one of Grandma Inés's five children who had a white spouse.

Until I was seven years old, *Mami* used to iron my hair once a month as if it were a piece of clothing. I hated the tormenting heat treatment so much and so persistently resisted it that it was very difficult for her to keep my head motionless on the ironing board. "For God's sake, hold still, Lourdes!" she would yell. "If you were quiet, we could have finished an hour ago."

Steam struck my face. I tried to keep a safe distance from the tiny hot clouds that made my eyes teary and itchy. "But I don't like it!" I whimpered. "It hurts!"

"Don't be a liar!" *Mami* barked. "It's just a little uncomfortable, but you make it much worse with your stubbornness. Would you like to have short and thick hair like your cousins?"

I couldn't care less at that time about having curled or straight hair. Some days I even said I'd prefer not to have hair at all. But *Mami's* ultimate admonition was always, "*Niña*, I am not going to comb any kinky hair! Either you let me finish or I'll have your head shaved! What a *jodienda* it is dealing with this girl!"

When she would pretend to look for a razor I'd yield. Despite my bravado, the vision of a bare and gleaming head was more intolerable than the painful heat of the iron.

In the meantime, Grandma Gloria stayed close by. Though she never attempted to interrupt the torture, she always had some tidbit ready for me when the treatment was over. I loved her *arroz con leche*, a mulatto dish of white rice and sweet brown cinnamon.

"I know it's unpleasant," she would say. "But it's for your own good, my princess. It is positively for your own good."

Papi didn't approve of the procedure and repeatedly asked *Mami* to stop it, but hairstyling was a woman's issue. *Mami* ignored his complaints as she did mine.

Until *la mierda* hit the fan.

During one afternoon of kicking and squirming, my skull was scorched by the edge of the iron. *Mami* left the house clothed only in her dressing gown and rushed with me to the Lawton Pediatric Hospital. "Second-degree burns," the doctor said to my weeping mother. "How in the world did it happen?"

I don't know what she told him.

When *Papi* returned home and learned of the accident, he was enraged. For the first and only time in their married life he slapped

Mami in the face, then smashed the iron against the wall, and forbade her to iron my hair again.

Despite the disastrous finale, *Mami* always credited the way my hair turned out to her determined ironing: it was frizzy at the ends but more or less straight around the roots. I didn't share her enthusiasm. Big deal! What had I gotten after all? A *mulatica*'s hair!

CHAPTER XIX

M Y ROMANCE WITH Ernesto colored my boring life. I
had someone who really cared for me, and for whom to
wear my nicest camp clothes, put on makeup, and do my best to
look pretty. As our relationship became known, my prestige
increased. More girls nodded at me in a friendly way and a few boys
noticed my presence for the first time. "You are now one of us,
hija!" Aurora said, enchanted, patting my back. "You are already a
woman, *una mujer!*"

At that point I feared that the news of my *noviazgo* would reach
my parents' ears and get me in trouble. Grandma Gloria had
admonished me a long time ago, "I don't want any secrets. Once
you have a sweetheart, let us know immediately. That's the right
thing for a well-behaved *señorita* to do." However, the idea of discussing a sex-related topic with *Papi* made me blush. After carefully
preparing a "speech," I awaited *Mami's* visit.

"You'd better keep quiet," Aurora warned me, "or your mom
will start watching you and giving you all sorts of shitty advice. She
may even ground you when we get back to Havana."

"My *Mami* will never ground me!" I replied. "She trusts me and
I trust her!"

"I trust nobody," Aurora said curtly.

"Well, I've always told *Mami* everything—or almost everything."

"Fine," Aurora shrugged. "Go show your ass and you'll get it kicked."

THE FOLLOWING Sunday, while she heated the juicy chicken breasts sent by Grandma Inés, *Mami* started preaching a long and bitter sermon. A mulatta, she stated, should never fall in love with a white guy, because dark women suffer too much in such romances. They seldom ended like the nationally produced soap operas did, with the *mulatica* nurse and the handsome white doctor getting married in a communist wedding at *La Plaza de la Revolución* and living happily ever after.

"You may be too young to know about this stuff," *Mami* said, "but I have to tell you now, *niña*, so you don't end up like me. Cuckolded and kicked out! Better find a mulatto like yourself, even a Negro. It doesn't matter if you don't advance the race, or if you have a jump-backward, kinky-haired child. Anything is better than to be replaced with a lazy, good-for-nothing *puta* just because her hair is better than yours!"

I had never seen *Mami* so angry. "So, you are not returning to Grandma Gloria's?" I asked.

"Never!" she replied with an icy determination. Her lips quivered. I had a sudden glimpse of her fights, sorrows, and defeats. I could only imagine the humiliation of having to leave our house, of going back to the Mantilla cabin packed with her mother, sisters, nieces, old memories, and the invisible presence of their *orishas*. For a moment *Mami* disappeared and I saw in her place a dumped, vulnerable teenager. I hugged her and said, "I love you, *Mami*. I don't care what *they* (I didn't dare say *Papi* and Grandma Gloria) think or do. I really love you."

Mami wiped away a tear, cleared her throat, and smiled weakly, "Come on, eat your chicken. We are not at a wake!"

I waited a few minutes, then hesitantly confessed, "I have a boyfriend, *Mami*. I wanted you to know about it because—I like him a lot."

"A boyfriend? So soon? You are still a *niñita*!" She pretended to be worried, but her eyes brightened. "And who is that lucky boy?"

"Ernesto."

"Ernesto," *Mami* repeated. "Not the mulatto who lives in a San Mariano Street tenement, I hope."

"Well, yes."

Mami pouted with the same disappointed grin that twisted her face when I got a low grade at school. "*Ay*, Lourdes!"

"What's wrong with him?" I demanded. "That he is a *mulatico*? But you just said—"

Mami lowered her head. "I know, I know what I said," she murmured. "But I didn't expect you to take it so literally. You should leave him at once," she added sharply.

I felt angry and betrayed. Aurora was right.

"*Bueno*, I won't prohibit you from seeing Ernesto, because you are going to be together here, anyway," *Mami* went on, in a softer tone. "We parents don't have much authority over our children anymore. But let me tell you that Ernesto's father is almost black, with kinky hair. If you bring a dark baby to Gloria's—"

"I have kissed Ernesto only a couple of times!" I protested. "And you are already talking about babies!"

Mami soon recognized that her concerns were premature. "I am sorry, Lourdes. I am so confused myself," she admitted. "Do you love him?"

I shrugged, still hurt. Then she invited my boyfriend to share our lunch.

Ernesto had a brother in another camp and rarely received a visit. He quickly accepted the invitation, thanked *Mami,* and sat next to me. While the three of us ate and talked, Aurora left the barracks, walked toward the bathhouse, and glanced at our group with a pensive, crestfallen air. She passed by a painted mural that read *Homeland or Death* and the red, big letters of the word Death loomed over her as if written in blood.

SLOGANS WERE everywhere. We chanted them in school, before and after classes, and during political marches. *Men die but the Party is immortal. Down with Yankee imperialism!* Slogans could be found on billboards, walls, magazine covers, restaurant menus, textbooks, in hotel lobbies, and on school message boards.

Man is more than white, more than mulatto, more than black read a mural above the colossal bust of Che Guevara where the Pioneers— elementary and secondary school students—left garlands of white roses every Friday. Mural and bust adorned the barrio communal park, the *parque.*

I heard the first public criticism of my parents' marriage in the *parque* when I was eight years old. It happened on a Friday afternoon after the flower offering. Two of our neighbors, María Juana and Luisa the Gossiper, were seated on a park bench. When I realized they were talking about *Papi,* I hid behind the big Che bust and listened to them, curiously at first, indignantly later.

"People say that Rafael is," Luisa made the sign of cheating—the pinkie and the index fingers erect, the three other fingers bent, "on Barbarita. Do you think it is true?"

"It has to be," María Juana answered. She was the president of our CDR—the Committee for the Defense of the Revolution.

"Isn't he the professor? A handsome, green-eyed guy that looks like a foreigner? And Barbarita is the mulatta who lives with him, huh? I am not even sure they are married."

Old *cabrona*, I thought. Of course they were married!

"Neither am I. She has such *bad hair*," Luisa stated, wrinkling her long nose.

"And she is so—" Here María Juana rubbed her right index finger on the back of her left hand, meaning "colored." "I can't stand these couples of white men and black women nor of white women and black men, which is more serious. *Cada oveja con su pareja*. Marry your own kind. I am not a racist, you know. I am a real, sincere revolutionary, but, between you and me, if my son married a mulatta or a black woman, I would kick him out. I don't want a tribe of *negritos* running like cockroaches all over my house!"

That incident haunted me for years. But I never told anybody about it. I felt too embarrassed. Now, I trusted Ernesto enough to confide it to him.

"Do you think *Papi* was cheating on *Mami* even then?" I asked. We were under the *framboyán*, surrounded by the amorous noises of other couples. I noticed how his body blended with the soft darkness of the night. "Is she too ugly for him?"

"Neighbors always gossip," he replied. "You shouldn't pay any attention to them. Barbarita looks good."

"But I wish she were white!" I exclaimed. "Or that *Papi* were black. Well, not that, because then I'd also be black. I wouldn't like that either. Though it's so difficult being in the middle. Neither fish nor fowl."

He nodded gravely. "Blacks have less problems. A black guy gets a black girl and it's OK. If he snags a blonde all his friends look up to him. Of course white guys can choose whomever they want."

He shrugged. "But if a mulatto gets a black girl, his family protests, and if he gets a white one, then *her* family raises hell and calls him an opportunistic *mulatico*."

"My *Mami* and I are *mulaticas* ourselves. That's why I sometimes fantasize about being whiter," I confessed. "I dream that we both have long, blonde hair like the Bolshevik girls who appear in the magazine *Soviet Woman*."

"*Mierda*, you don't need long hair!" Ernesto protested. "Bolshevik girls are way too chubby! You are much prettier!"

A warm current of pride ran through my body. "Thanks! But—do you ever wish that your parents were lighter?"

"My parents are both mulattos. In fact, my dad is *very* dark," he answered. "But I wouldn't change them!"

It was easier for him. Ernesto had no close white relatives to compare himself to, but I had Grandma Gloria and my father in front of my eyes every day. "I wouldn't change mine either," I sighed. "I mean, I wouldn't change my *Mami*. I would only change the way she looks."

"Then she wouldn't be your *Mami*," Ernesto asserted.

I was going to reply when Berto arrived. "Hey, Nesto," the Duck said without even greeting me. "You need to go to the barracks right now. We are having a meeting with our leader." He took Ernesto by the arm. My boyfriend hurried to explain that their leader was a weirdo who always scheduled production meetings at bedtime. "See you tomorrow, love," he muttered. He barely had time to kiss my forehead before Berto dragged him off to the boys' barracks.

The aromas of the night became fetid, the romantic buzzing of the other kids a senseless cacophony. A meeting at eleven o'clock! *Hmm*.

I sniffled and returned to the girls' barracks. Then I realized that Berto was never far from Ernesto. They were in the same brigade, they went together to the dining hall and to the bathhouse. The Duck called him "Nesto" and he didn't like me.

I had not forgotten the bunk bed episode. I had not forgotten the two bodies squirming, Ernesto's voice calling the Duck *maricón*. Were they still partners? Would my boyfriend tell Berto the secrets I had shared with him? Would they make fun of me? I should have been distrustful and hard like Aurora. "From now on I'll trust nobody," I vowed.

⤝ CHAPTER XX ⤞

A LIGHTNING FLASH CROSSED the sky, followed by the deep growling of thunder in the distance. There was an odd silence—the silence of the birds. The air felt dry and brittle, as if it had turned into glass.

"I can hardly breathe," Aurora complained. "What's going on?"

Less than a minute later, furious strokes of lightning traced a luminous net in the sky and thunder rumbled over and over above our heads.

"Everyone run to the barracks!" Comrade Katia shouted. "Hurry up!"

While we all ran in panic from the dining hall queue to the barracks, in my mind I went back home, to the "Traveling Christ" room. The Traveling Christ was an image that had originally presided over the living room in our house. This I learned from Grandma Gloria, because by the time I was born, the blood-dripping, open-heart Jesus painting had been replaced by Che Guevara in the famous Korda photo, enlarged and elegantly surrounded by an oak frame. The Sacred Heart image had been transferred to Grandma Gloria's bedroom, but later, following *Papi's* suggestions, it was moved from there to the storage room. *Papi* explained to us that because some of his friends' daughters came to play with me and might enter Grandma's bedroom, comments could be made about the religious portrait. Since *Papi* taught Political Science, such remarks might damage his reputation at the university. No one objected, and he himself baptized the nomadic painting as the Traveling Christ.

Once the Traveling Christ had been accommodated in the storage room, I noticed that, occasionally, Grandma Gloria went in there, closed the door and spent a few minutes inside, all by herself. Afterward, I realized that *Mami* did the same. The storage room became the "mystery room." I'd wonder what on earth *Mami* and Grandma did behind the closed door, though always at different hours. They never seemed to coincide.

Grandma Gloria kept the door locked, but on one of the days that she devoted to housecleaning, I got to peek inside. The Traveling Christ was there, as I already knew, half hidden in a corner. In front of it, I saw a round table with a glass of dusty water on top. In the corner opposite stood the statue of a young woman dressed in red and white, with a sword in her slender hand, a golden crown on her head, and a countenance that was fiery and at the same time dignified. She was at least a foot tall. Flanked by candles and with another glass of water beside her, the statue stared defiantly at the Traveling Christ, who wouldn't take his probing eyes off her.

A few days later, a thunderstorm struck our neighborhood. It was more terrifying than a regular storm. Blazing streaks of light crossed the indigo sky, followed by earsplitting sounds that reverberated in the distance with a drumlike resonance. Since I was already twelve, it didn't look proper for me to get under the bed, as I used to do. Feigning indifference, I sat on the sofa, turned my back to the living-room window, and tried to read a book. Then, realizing that *Papi* was out of sight and that *Mami* and Grandma Gloria were probably busy in the kitchen, I decided to tiptoe to my bedroom and get—well, maybe not under the bed, but at least on it.

I walked through the hall, where all the doors that opened to the inner court-yard had been closed. It was humid and uncomfortably hot, but I wouldn't even think of going outside. Yet I knew there were people in the streets at that moment, people who went on with their businesses and didn't pay much attention to the thunderstorm. Was I an incorrigible *pendeja*?

Then I heard the voices. Grandma Gloria's, high pitched and angry, and *Mami's* more muffled but equally irate. They came from the storage room. And with them came a poignant smell. Something was burning there, I realized, and ran to the room.

"How in the world can you say that crossing two knives in front of a Santa Bárbara image is going to protect us from thunder?" Grandma Gloria asked, chortling. "That is so silly! Just the opposite, *my dear*. Knives are made of steel and they are more likely to attract a stroke of lightning than to repel it. The right thing to do is burn palm leaves blessed on Palm Sunday. Learn, *daughter,* learn from me."

She pronounced the words "my dear" and "daughter" with a sarcastic intonation.

"Burning palm leaves is sillier than placing knives in front of Changó," *Mami* replied. "Probably worse, as the Catholic Church doesn't distribute palm leaves for such practices. You are misusing them—*Mother.*"

"What do you know about the Catholic Church? Do you believe in Jesus Christ?"

"I believe in the *orishas*."

"My God! Listen to her! What are the *orishas*, would you please tell me? Invented, false gods that no one knows about, except for a small group of uneducated folks here in Cuba, the *culo* of the planet, if you will. While Jesus is adored all over the world, by all sorts of people."

"If you adore Jesus so much, why don't you keep his painting in the living room?"

"You know perfectly well why I moved it here. Because I care for *my son*. I'd do anything for him. But maybe you can't say that you'd do the same for *your husband*."

They stopped arguing as soon as they saw me. Only ashes remained in a porcelain dish placed next to the candles. Two knives that formed a cross lay at the feet of the young saint dressed in white and red whose name—I felt confused—was it Santa Bárbara or Changó?

"IT IS OK to burn blessed palm leaves to keep the thunderstorm away from our house," Grandma Gloria told me that night. "I learned that when I came to Cuba, many years ago, and my house has never been hit by a stroke of lighting, so it must be true. But your mother is crazy, princess. She changes the name of the saints, calls Santa Bárbara—a Catholic saint and a virgin—a male name, Changó. The ignorance! The stupidity of these mulattos, *uff!*"

"Who is Changó, grandma? An African saint?"

"Don't ask me! I don't know!"

"Changó is the *orisha* of thunder and war, of love and passion," Grandma Inés explained to me later. "He isn't a woman, but a very macho man, a lady killer. He used the disguise of Santa Barbara and passed as a woman to protect himself from the whites. When the Yoruba people were brought to America as slaves, they were forced to become Christians. Their masters wouldn't allow them to worship our *orishas*. Then the slaves looked at the Catholic saints that their owners kept in the churches' altars and guess what? They discovered that the *orishas* were hidden within the white saints' clothes and ornaments. Yemayá, Oshún, Changó, all of them, had crossed the ocean with their people. They had come from Africa and now used the Spaniards' saints to disguise themselves. They are so smart! That is why we honor Obatalá as Our Lady of Mercy, Changó as Santa Barbara, and Yemayá as the Virgin of Regla."

Changó used the disguise of Santa Bárbara and passed as a woman to protect himself from the whites. Just like my uncles had pretended to be homosexuals to leave Cuba during the Mariel boatlift—

The *santeros* would say, "Ungrateful people only remember Santa Bárbara when it thunders." They also have their sayings, their "religious mottoes," just like the government had *Homeland or Death*. Grandma Inés told me that the *orishas* demanded to be worshipped always, not just in times of trouble. She propitiated them with offerings of fruits, candles, and tiny toys. She placed a two-inch silver boat in front of an image of the Virgin of Regla, patroness of the sea, the day my uncles left Cuba through the Mariel port. She was a devotee of Babalú Ayé and once walked on her knees from the door of El Rincón—*San* Lázaro's Catholic church—to the main altar to keep a promise she had made to her saint.

Grandma Inés prayed to the *orishas* to keep them contented. Their relationship was pragmatic. "The *orishas* can't live without our offerings," she explained. "They need us as much as we need them." In *santera* Sabina's house, honey, candles, and flowers were offered to Yemayá in exchange for protection. There was no need for me to behave in any particular way so as not to lose the goddess's favors. I had just paid for them.

Oshún: Our Lady of Charity rules over streams and rivers. Goddess of the Most Powerful Papaya, *she teaches women how to keep the love of their men. She is the patroness of desire and love. Her symbol is a mirror. Offer her sunflowers, honey, and cinnamon.*

San Lázaro: Babalú Ayé is the doctor-saint of the blessed crutches. He heals the sick with fresh waters and leaves. He carries all the fruits of spring inside his burlap sack. Offer him a white hen and two coconuts on a silvery tray.

Changó: Santa Bárbara is the god and goddess of thunder, war, and big pingas. Santa and Santo of the fighters, lord and lady of the sword. Offer him melons, pineapples, and a big glass of rum.

I WAS taught at school that *religion is the opium of the masses.* However, *Mami* openly resorted to the *orishas* in more than one emergency. "Giving a couple of bananas to a saint has never harmed anybody," she'd said. "It can't offend the memory of Che Guevara." She kept those black dolls hidden inside a drawer. I had not forgotten them. Maybe she was also a clandestine *santera*, an undercover witch!

Papi boasted of being an atheist but he always crossed himself—very discreetly—when he passed a Catholic church. "It's a child-hood trauma," he would say to justify himself, a little embarrassed, "because I attended a Jesuit school from the age of five."

Grandma Gloria offered glasses of water to the Traveling Christ, and said that I should respect Jesus and *Papa Dios.* She'd advised me to pin a brooch with the image of Santa Lucía on my brassiere. "The saint will protect your eyesight and you'll never need to wear glasses." She didn't believe in the *orisha* Changó but respected his counterpart, the Catholic Santa Bárbara.

Grandma Gloria did have certain rules. They were simple. Good girls obey their parents and grandparents, don't smoke or fight, and don't touch themselves "down there" because all this offends *Papa Dios*.

Papa Dios sees everything and is everywhere. He knows all you do, all you think, and where you put your hands and your eyes. There are no secrets from him. If you entered a dark cave, your parents and I wouldn't be able to see you, but Papa Dios would.

Papa Dios might have been everywhere but I failed to notice his presence. The Traveling Christ, who was very quiet, didn't seem to intervene in our human affairs. On the other hand, the *orishas* had saved my life, or so Grandma Inés said. And they were definitely present in the School-in-the-Fields.

Ernesto and his family believed in all of them, particularly in *San Lázaro*, who was a miraculous saint, though very demanding.

"If you promise him something, he'll give you whatever you want," my boyfriend told me gravely. "But you cannot break your promise, or the Old Man will punish you and hit you in the head with his crutches. He is a short-tempered *orisha*!

"*Mamá* wanted to call me Lázaro, but when *Papá* went to record my birth in the Identity Registry offices, the clerk explained to him that I'd be better off with a revolutionary name. Only the bourgeois named their children after old saints. So I was named Ernesto, after Che Guevara. Lázaro is my middle name. Anyway, in my house they call me Lazarito."

When I showed him my *azabache*, he kissed it and said, "*Mamá* also gave me a charm before I came to the camp. It got lost. Good thing, because I didn't dare throw it away myself. I didn't want to snub the saints, but I didn't want anybody to discover that I was wearing an amulet either."

Later I found out that Chabela had an *azabache* identical to mine hidden under her work shirt. She admitted that her grandmother had made her bring it to the camp "just in case."

Aurora didn't believe in anything. "Carolina says that she has God in heaven and no one on earth," she remarked. "But if God is there for her, he certainly won't help me. And I know nothing about the *orishas*, nor care for them. They have never done a thing for me."

It was obvious, though, that Aurora could use the *orishas*' protection, or at least that she should ask for it. Her period hadn't come yet. Juanito kept ignoring her. I felt sorry for her when she lay in our bunk bed at night and sighed from time to time. What would she do if she was pregnant and her lover refused to help her? She didn't have grandmothers. No one knew where her father lived. And her mother—

Yet Aurora wouldn't openly cry or complain about her bad luck. Grandma Inés would say that my friend was a daughter of Changó, a child of Santa Bárbara. Proud and strong, belligerent and sassy, hard to break.

⊰ CHAPTER XXI ⊱

MARCH CRAWLED TOWARD April. Time had certainly passed, even if it often seemed immobile. The *framboyán,* which had lost most of its flowers during the rainy season, was now covered with blushing pink buds, frail and delicate as a promise of love.

There had been some changes in our lives too. Aurora passed through alternative states of flirting, fever, and vomiting and desperation. Crazy Jorge became a habitual guest in camp. I became accustomed to working. The *cuje* needle in my hands turned into an efficient, though rather painful tool to use. I felt comfortable in my new "girl with boyfriend" status. Like other couples, Ernesto and I had our own little bench of boredom, our special spot under the *framboyán*, our favorite song. Only one thing bothered me during those quiet days, and that was his unwavering loyalty to Berto the Duck.

Patriotic slogans taught us how to think politically, religious sayings transmitted the old commands of saints and *orishas*, and there were also many maxims intended to control our sexual conduct. *A decent woman should be a* señorita *until her wedding day.* Aurora and my other friends weren't decent women, of course. From Grandma Gloria I had learned that *The one who has a hen, watches over her. The one who has a cock, sends him into the street.* So we hen-girls had to be extremely cautious! She also maintained that if I touched my tits in an improper way or worse, played with my *papaya*, I would end up crazy, confined to an asylum where doctors would have to tie my hands to the bed.

Che Guevara, Jesus Christ, and *Papa Dios* scorned *maricones*. Proof of it were the labor camps, where gays were sent to make men out of them, and the blazing hell Grandma Gloria had told me about, where all people who did dirty things burned forever. I didn't know what the *orishas* thought about *maricones*, but I imagined it was nothing good, either.

A popular belief stated that if an unguarded boy allowed another male to touch his buttocks or—horror!—to insert a finger in his anus, he would be lost forever and become a *maricón*, hopelessly and absolutely. And everyone knew that *A homosexual man is the shame of his family*. Confronted with the possibility of having a gay son, many parents would scream *Better dead than* maricón!

Because of these widespread opinions, I couldn't bring myself to ask Ernesto about his relationship with Berto. It could ruin everything. I knew that the easiest way of insulting a guy was to question his masculinity. Yet I had shared with him many embarrassing episodes of my own life. Shouldn't he trust me?

One Friday after lunch we were celebrating the selection of our camp as the most productive among all the Havana high schools. The brigades were spared a half day of work. The principal allowed us to have a *bailable* until bedtime.

Elated with the prospect of a long, cool afternoon for ourselves, Ernesto and I felt closer and happier than ever. We walked around the camp arm in arm. The loudspeakers blasted "Loving you is where I belong." Comrade Katia had become a fan of Harry Belafonte, even though he was from the *bad* country, after the musician had visited Cuba and declared his support for the Revolution. Ernesto whistled and tried to repeat the English words.

Suddenly, a wave of courage came over me. I will ask him, I silently swore. After a net of gentle intimacy had wrapped around us, I began. Why did Berto always have something "very important" to say to him in private when he found us together? Why did he behave so impertinently in my presence? Ernesto tried to excuse The Duck but did not sound convincing. Then, lowering my voice, I mentioned what I had once seen from the window. "I didn't mean to snoop, but I saw and heard . . . " I said.

I expected an indignant denial or a violent outburst, but Ernesto didn't look upset or even surprised. Perhaps he was grateful for the opportunity to discard his macho disguise. After a tense silence, he muttered that he and Berto had *done it* twice.

"Did you like it?" I asked, almost jealous. "Better than necking with me?"

"Can't you tell, *amor?*" Ernesto answered, blushing. "You are the first girl I've gone that far with, and we haven't done the whole thing yet. I know that I love you." I looked at the serious face of my honest mulatto and knew he wasn't lying. "I like girls," he continued, squeezing my hand. "I like both, boys and girls. I don't understand why, but that's how it is." He squeezed my hand again with a stronger pressure.

"So, are you a—?" I stopped before pronouncing the offensive term.

"No!" he exclaimed. "*Cojones*, no! I am always the one that penetrates Berto. It's like doing it with a woman. But I never permit The Duck to probe my ass or to pat me on the buttocks. I am not a *maricón!*"

There was a lengthy silence. The deafening music of the loudspeakers sounded like a distant babbling. When Ernesto spoke again, he hugged me and said, "I am happy you asked me, instead of talking about it behind my back."

"Thanks for telling me," I replied.

We continued walking silently. I was still concerned about the moral implications of my boyfriend's conduct. Even if Ernesto didn't consider himself a *maricón*, he had made love with another guy. He had touched his buttocks. He wasn't a New Man. He would never be like Che!

SOON THE DUCK'S insolence vanished. He often joined Ernesto and me for our afternoon walks, though he prudently stayed away after dark. The three of us talked and joked together. Because Berto was witty, his clever remarks added a spark of humor to our chats. We strolled around the camp telling stories and laughing at Berto's refined gestures and effeminate diction.

"Do you know, *chicos*, what my life dream is?" he asked us once. "I want to perform in a Tropicana show wearing a white, tiny, fluffy feather bikini and singing 'Fumando espero' like Sarita Montiel."

Ernesto listened thoughtfully. Sometimes Berto consulted me about delicate matters, like what to do with the hair growing on his chest. Should he use wax to get rid of it or simply a razor?

"Leave it alone," I teased him. "Then you'll be a hairy man, *un hombre de pelo en pecho*. How would you like that?"

"Don't make me vomit, please! How would you like to grow a beard yourself?"

Happy, funny, and peaceful days. Unfortunately, they were not destined to last.

⊰ CHAPTER XXII ⊱

OMRADE KATIA'S LIPS moved steadily. They were reddish and fleshy. Her tongue, pink and long, came out every
two seconds and expelled tiny saliva bubbles. The teacher brandished
her Marxism manual and wagged her right index finger in the air.

While Comrade Katia spoke, words danced a crazy rumba in
my head. The sound of the *orishas'* drums mixed with the trumpets
of a military march. For anti-imperialist solidarity, peace, and
friendship we will all light a candle tonight. Blessed *San* Lázaro,
always toward victory. An *azabache* is our best weapon against
Yankee aggressions. Mister Imperialist, we have absolutely no fear
of you. We'll be like Che. Offer a good, fat chicken to Yemayá.
Homeland or Death. Siacará.

It was 10 P.M. and we were still attending a political workshop led
by Comrade Katia, that pretty brunette whose rump attracted more
interest from male students than all her political discourses. Her
polyester pants wrapped her hips and buttocks so tightly that
Vladimir asked her once, "Teacher, are you by any chance in favor
of capitalism?"

"Me?!" Comrade Katia huffed. "Of course not! How do you
dare to ask this idiotic question?"

He pointed to her imposing butt. "Well, because you always keep the masses so oppressed."

We met in a small brick construction adjacent to the principal's office. The students sat on wooden benches and the teacher stood in front of our group. A world map, the Cuban and Soviet flags entwined, and the ubiquitous Che Guevara poster decorated the dusty walls. A fluorescent lamp lit the room.

The workshop had begun with an excerpt from Engels's *The Origin of the Family, Private Property and the State*, in which, talking about the regularization of sexual relationships after the imminent suppression of capitalism, the German philosopher prophesied a new generation of men and women who would never use sex as a commodity in exchange for money.

After she finished reading the passage, Comrade Katia respectfully closed the Marxism manual, laid it on her desk, and addressed us. "You should know, kids, that before 1959 many girls your own age," she pointed to Aurora and Chabela, "had to work in brothels as the only means of buying medicines for their impoverished families, as the only way to be clothed and fed. The benefits that you now take for granted, like a portion of food for everybody and equal, free education, were a dream for those poor girls. Now, thanks to the conquests of socialism, prostitution, once a national stigma, has forever disappeared from our country and will never return."

"Some girls slept with Juanito in exchange for good marks," Aurora whispered to me. "It wasn't his fault but the girls'. They pestered him. But weren't they prostitutes too?"

"How do you know?" I asked.

"Juanito himself told me."

"Pay attention, Aurora and Lourdes!" Comrade Katia yelled. "Nothing is more important than the ideological education of our socialist youth!"

Prostitution was a salacious topic. It raised a million questions. How much did those girls charge? Did they work every day? How many hours? Where? With whom? Then Vladimir asked if there were still prostitutes in other countries.

Comrade Katia nodded. "In capitalist nations, yes," she said. But the balance of power was changing for good, the teacher declared, pointing to the map where socialist countries were colored red. A bright red reigned in Europe, led by the colossal Soviet Union and backed up by its Eastern allies in such a compact block that France, evil Germany, and even Spain appeared as tiny, modest blue specks.

"Look at the former Dark Continent," she indicated. "It is surely going to become red with our internationalist help. Look at Angola, at Ethiopia. Now, look at Asia. Socialist China, communist Vietnam. And in the Caribbean, we, victorious Cuba, the first to defeat imperialism in America. There will come a time when the whole map will be red. The world is closer to communism than some of you are aware."

"Will there still be School-in-the-Fields when we have communism?" Ernesto asked.

"Yes. At least in Cuba. The School-in-the-Fields is our practical application of the Marxist principle of combining work and study," Comrade Katia explained.

"And the United States, will it become communist?" Fat Olga inquired with a slightly mocking tone.

"I do believe it will. Perhaps through armed struggle, or inspired by the success of the Soviet Union. But it will surely happen by the end of this century."

"That's not so soon," somebody groaned.

"Yes, it is, my child," Comrade Katia said patiently. "We are talking in historical terms. What are twenty, or even fifty years, when measuring world changes?"

"That's true," Aurora sighed. "Time flies."

"Not in the School-in-the-Fields," Chabela replied. "A day here has forty hours instead of twenty-four. Time doesn't fly, it crawls."

"Do you believe what Comrade Katia said?" Aurora asked Marisol in a whisper.

"That *La Yuma* is going to be communist someday?" Marisol shrugged. "Nonsense!"

"But if it were true," I said, "then we could visit it."

Fat Olga laughed. "*La Yuma* will always be *La Yuma*, girl. The country of Coca Cola, Hershey bars, and McDonalds, where nothing is in short supply and you can eat as much as you want without a ration card."

"Wait a moment, kids, wait a moment!" Comrade Katia clapped. "You should speak in order. Raise your hands. Do you have a question, Lourdes?"

"Yes," I said. "When the States become communist, will we be able to travel to Miami?"

"Definitely," she replied. "The Yankees won't be our enemies anymore and we'll be able to go—"

"To the *bad* country where the *good* things are made," Fat Olga muttered. Comrade Katia heard her.

"It won't be a *bad* country anymore," she said sharply. "It is bad now because of a corrupt socioeconomic regime. Once it has become communist we won't have to be afraid of the ideological distortion that consumerism causes. About the *good* things, I am not sure that they are so good, either. Do they have color television? Well, the Soviets have color television too. And great cars, washing machines, satellites, rockets—What about Yuri Gagarin? Remember the sputniks? The Soviets have absolutely no reason to envy the Yankees."

"Except films," said Aurora under her breath. "Have you ever heard of anybody able to endure a Russian film?"

"I bet Comrade Katia likes them," I replied and raised my hand again. "Teacher, do you like Russian films?"

Suffocated giggles crossed the room.

"*Soviet* films," Comrade Katia corrected me. "It was Russia in the time of the czars. And yes, I do. They are remarkable. How many of you have seen *Battleship Potemkin*?"

Her question generated an embarrassing silence. Vladimir broke it, "I saw it, teacher. Great movie. Better than all the American crap some people like to watch."

"But Vladimir listens to American music all the time," Chabela said.

"Oh, he's trying to impress Comrade Katia," Fat Olga chuckled.

"*Hija,* boys are all absolutely dumb," Aurora concluded.

By the end of the session my eyes itched and my eyelids weighed a ton. I was so tired that I fell asleep, and woke up only when Comrade Katia called my name. What a shame. I wanted to be a soldier like Tania La Guerrillera, to fight for the freedom of countries that were still oppressed by the imperialists. And I couldn't even keep alert during a political meeting.

"You need to learn how to analyze Yankee films," Comrade Katia was saying. "Avoid their poisonous Hollywood appeal and you'll be worthy Young Communists in the future." She paused, and then added with a resolute expression, "We'll watch the Saturday night movie, and then discuss it in our next workshop."

There was a black-and-white TV—a Soviet Electron—in the dining hall, but the principal personally controlled its use. He didn't allow us to get close to it except on Sunday mornings, when only cartoons were on. I had not seen even one Saturday night film— which were always American—since our arrival at the camp.

With a resounding "Viva Comrade Katia!" we all marched to our barracks at 11:30. I was so drowsy that I forgot to give Ernesto his good-night kiss.

AMERICAN FILMS lie. They portray a false life, a life that can't be true. It can't be true that there are supermarkets full of steaks, chicken breasts, bananas, chorizo, apples, Spanish olives, condensed milk, chocolate bars, oil. It can't be true that people don't have to wait in line to get all this. It can't be true that they don't even need a ration card. It can't be true that they can buy hamburgers and sodas on every corner. It just cannot be true.

Hollywood is a Yankee trap. Disneyland is a myth. There are no dishwashers, no cordless telephones, no instant color photos, no car dealerships. It is all science fiction. It doesn't happen here. Not on this planet. In another world, maybe.

"DO YOU have somebody in *La Yuma*, girl?" Marisol asked me the next morning during our break in the tobacco house.

Pedro and Juan, *Mami's* brothers, were *marielitos*. Though *Papi* and I had criticized them and called them traitors, *Mami* and Grandma Inés still wrote to them. But acknowledging the existence of relatives in the United States could spoil a student's chance of a university career. *The university is for the revolutionary*, a slogan said. And the revolutionary didn't keep up ties with the *gusanos*, the defectors who had fled to *La Yuma*. "No," I answered. "I don't have anyone there. What about you?"

"Neither do I," Marisol said, her response about as sincere as mine. I knew that her grandparents lived in *La Yuma*. They sent her

Lee and Levi's blue jeans, Mickey Mouse T-shirts, brightly colored backpacks and authentic Adidas tennis shoes.

"Do you have somebody in the *bad* country, love?" I asked Ernesto that evening.

"I have a cousin," he admitted after a brief hesitation. "He left on a raft in 1978. Now he lives in New Jersey and has an awesome car, a silver Mazda. Last year he went to Spain and sent us photos from Madrid, Seville, San Sebastián—Lucky guy!"

"Why lucky?" I protested, upset. "Don't you know that black people are discriminated against in *La Yuma?*" I remembered a two-line verse shouted at the blacks leaving Cuba, during the repudiation acts:

"Those niggers that defect,
may the Ku Klux Klan beat them."

"Supposing this is the case—where aren't blacks discriminated against, can you tell me?" Ernesto replied. "Even in Africa, where they are the majority, they have apartheid. And here! Aren't we discriminated against here too?"

"No. This is a communist society. We are all equal," I quoted *Papi*. "We all have the same rights."

"If we are all equal, why do you want your *Mami* to become 'lighter'?" he retorted. "Why do you want to have blonde hair?"

I stayed silent for a while. "But we don't have to pay when we go to the hospital, Ernesto," I answered at last. *Papi* always praised the achievements of our socialist medicine. He had explained to me that we had the best health-care system in the Americas, even better than the Yankees. "And there are no prostitutes here."

He smirked.

In spite of the teachers' admonitions—or because of them—the *bad* country was present in many of our thoughts and conversations.

We liked its films and music. We listened to Barry Manilow, Cindy Lauper, Kenny Rogers, The Rolling Stones, Michael Jackson, and Kool & the Gang, because dissimilar as they looked at first sight, they all had something in common. They were all from the *bad* place, *they* were *La Yuma. La Yuma* of Saturday night movies, a faraway country where people drove and crashed shiny sport cars just for fun, lived in impressive mansions, drank Coca Cola, and ate ham and cheese sandwiches as a natural thing. *La Yuma*, an evil paradise despised by Che Guevara. A paradise with subways, swimming pools, and all kinds of food. But an imaginary, fake paradise, as Comrade Katia said.

The morning after the political workshop, Comrade Katia went to the classroom to pick up her books and discovered that the fluorescent lamp had disappeared. Adding insult to injury, the thoughtless thief had stepped over the Marxism manual and left it, dirty and damaged, in a corner. The world map and the Che Guevara poster had suffered a few smudges too.

Comrade Katia's frantic cries resonated throughout the camp. A special meeting was held. The principal established a permanent guard of teachers and students to avoid the repetition of these outrageous incidents. An old chain was installed to reinforce the kitchen door.

"Guards won't help a bit," said Marisol. "'When shitting is the problem, green guavas are useless.'"

On Friday morning the TV set was gone. It vanished from the dining hall just like the rice cooker and the other items. We never watched the promised Yankee film. Comrade Katia, her eyes flaming, swore by Fidel's life that she would have revenge.

⊰ CHAPTER XXIII ⊱

TINY WARM BUGS of light frolicked over my face. They stroked my nose, brushed my eyelashes, caressed my forehead. I raised my hand to grab them. The bugs escaped and I woke up. Rays of sun entered through the window. It was already 9:30, and, I remembered, in shock, that it was a Monday morning. The five o'clock siren had not sounded that day.

Aurora, Fat Olga, and Marisol were still in bed, disconcerted by the unexpected change in our schedule and the nervous comings and goings of the teachers. We saw *La Flaca*, with the look of a frightened hen, leaving the barracks with a paper bag hidden under her blouse. When she returned, the package was gone. Fat Olga found it later, inside a latrine hole. She opened the bag with the help of a stick and discovered that it contained a bunch of expensive aromatic cigars.

"Perhaps she's decided to quit smoking," Fat Olga said, doubtful.

"But *La Flaca* doesn't smoke," Marisol replied. "What was she doing with those cigars?"

That morning Juanito sent for Aurora and appeased her, humbly agreeing to all her demands. Yes, he would recognize their baby, he would marry her as soon as we returned to Havana, he would never again leave her. In the meantime, would she mind hiding a box full of cigars under her bunk bed?

Aurora camouflaged the box between our suitcases. She didn't know what the problem was. She didn't care. "I'll help him, of course!" she announced. "I can't let Juanito down now! Poor thing!"

"*Poor* thing? Juanito? I thought he was an asshole," I reminded her.

"*Ay*, Lourdes!" she huffed. "You don't understand anything!"

But I did understand. I knew that there was something wrong with the cigars. Maybe they had been stolen from an unfortunate *guajiro*. I tried to convince Aurora to get rid of the box but she called me a first-class *pendeja* and stubbornly kept it.

There was no civic act that morning. When Marisol, Fat Olga, and I showed up in the dining hall for a belated breakfast we were pleasantly surprised. Marmalade and a piece of cheese had been added to our regular slice of bread. Later, we sat in the sun like rich bourgeois women vacationing in *La Yuma*, free for one day from *cujes* and the tobacco house, lazily stretching our legs and counting the petals of the daisies.

Comrade Katia appeared at 10:30 riding pillion on a young police officer's motorcycle. He parked in front of the camp, raising a cloud of dust. Comrade Katia's butt overflowed the backseat, but she jumped off with great dignity and marched straight to the principal's office. He followed her outside.

"What a cute cop!" remarked Aurora. The newcomer was twenty or twenty-two years old, serious and handsome in his dark blue uniform. He stared at us and obviously did not know how to begin his task. He appeared bewildered in the presence of the principal, and confused by the avalanche of words that Comrade Katia, Juanito, and the *guajira* Hilda were directing at him.

Aurora and I witnessed a clever tactic. Patting the officer's back, Juanito invited him to have a cup of coffee. They sat under the *framboyán* to talk, away from Comrade Katia's disquieting presence. Juanito acknowledged that a few, not very valuable, pieces of clothing and old gadgets had disappeared. But none of the missing articles amounted to anything, he said. Though the TV set was worth at least five hundred pesos, Juanito didn't even mention it. He described the rice cooker as "an old pot."

"I found a lightbulb hidden on the kitchen shelf," the teacher commented casually. "Comrade Katia thought it had been stolen but she was wrong. There is no need to waste our revolutionary police's precious time with such insignificant episodes. They are just teenagers' pranks."

The principal joined them and explained that Comrade Katia—earnest, conscientious Comrade Katia—had hurried to bring "The Law" to the camp because, being a very devoted teacher, she got nervous whenever a trivial incident seemed to threaten the kids. "You know how women are, don't you? But I am in control here. I can guarantee you that everything is just fine." The cop nodded and sipped his coffee.

Two hours went by peaceably. The other teachers were all smiles. The principal turned into an amiable pig and grunted affectionately when he met our brigade in the dining hall. Lunch included an unusual dessert; a delicious caramel pudding that Elena had made. We were also given the afternoon off.

At 4:30 the cop left on his motorcycle after shaking hands with Juanito. The principal and teachers refused to discuss the thefts anymore. A serene, starry sky brought the day to a close.

IT SEEMED Comrade Katia had taken the loss of the TV set personally. She'd gone to town at dawn, promising to put an end to the counterrevolutionary robberies we had suffered for weeks. She didn't know that the other teachers had established a secret trade with the *guajiros*, exchanging clothes and household articles from Havana for pork, vegetables, and high-quality Pinar del Río cigars. But

Pinar del Río cigars were considered export items. Their sale was prohibited, so they could be sold in the capital for three times their value in the countryside. It became clear that except for Comrade Katia and the principal, all the adults in camp were in on the conspiracy. Though Juanito swore that he and his partners had nothing to do with the thefts, they feared that a search of the camp could create difficulties for all the parties involved in the "cigar trade."

That night the boys lit a fire in the middle of the campgrounds. Small groups sat around it, talking and sharing the buttered crackers that Juanito distributed after dinner as an "extra."

"I feel as if I were in *La Yuma*, girl," Fat Olga purred. "This is luxury."

The logs burned with a sound of muffled snaps. Scarlet flames warmed feet and spirits, inspiring nostalgic *cadencia* singers and snuggling couples. Nervous fireflies darted through the darkness. The most daring landed on heads and clothes, creating a moving aura that danced from one shadow to another. The camp looked like a glittering, giant float ready to join a parade.

Ernesto and I exchanged short remarks about the amazing events of the day.

"They almost got their asses in jail. Just for a bunch of smelly cigars—"

"Holy smoke!"

The principal sat with us for a while, his legs stretched by the fire and a false smile pinned on his plump face. Elena was curled up next to him, her fine profile lit up by the flames. I watched them. Were the principal's fleshy hands searching under the *guajirita*'s skirt? No, I *had* to be wrong. When I looked again, the old man had left. Aurora and Juanito were out of sight too. Whispered comments and the tangy smell of burning logs filled the air.

"Comrade Katia is crying her eyes out in the barracks," Chabela murmured. "The principal scolded her, said that her duty was to protect us from the *bad* country's influence instead of encouraging us to watch Yankee films. *Pobrecita!*"

"Why *pobrecita?*" Natasha cackled. "If that silly cop had found out what is really going on here, she'd have been 'the star of the film.' She wanted to show off, but she fell on her ass."

"At least it's big enough to offer her a good cushion," Fat Olga observed. "I wonder what she's going to say in the next political session, provided there is one."

Marisol chuckled, "I've got an idea, girls!" She ran to the workshop room and returned with a book. "I'm going to burn this shit," she announced. "We won't have to stay awake until midnight anymore listening to science fiction stories!"

"*Ay*, don't do that," I pleaded. "It's a valuable textbook, written by Konstantinov. And if Comrade Katia finds out—"

I tried to stop her but she pushed me away. The book landed in the fire, producing a cascade of orange sparks and a flurry of applause. The ghost of the Marxism manual floated sadly in the air, then dissolved into the sky.

⊰ CHAPTER XXIV ⊱

O NE MORNING I came out of the barracks earlier than usual—the siren hadn't sounded yet—and discovered that the green foliage surrounding the camp had disappeared. Most of the trees were gone, too, only the powerful silhouette of the *framboyán* rose out of the deserted chalky earth. Where were the boys' barracks? And the bathhouse? The world had melted away. A dense, cool mist surrounded me. Everything was silent and dead. Shivering, I approached the place where our dining hall should have been.

In the midst of the oppressive white mist, a ghost walked toward the fence. Mesmerized, I followed at a respectful distance. The ghost stopped and so did I. A weak ray of sun broke the clouds and turned the ghost into Elena. Before I could call to her, the *guajirita* crossed the fence and left. Then the siren sounded. The fog vanished, the trees returned, and our camp came back to life.

The temperature fell to ten degrees Celsius. On our way to the tobacco house we tramped around in the mud with mouths, noses, and ears covered by wool kerchiefs, scarves, and hats. It was no longer necessary to wait in line to take a bath, for no one spent more than five minutes inside the bathhouse. In the dining hall, food got cold as soon as the *guajiras* served it. A chorus of lamentations sounded every night.

"This dreadful winter!"

"Why didn't we come here in June?"

"My balls have become a pair of green peas. I can't even feel them anymore," Ernesto complained. But that "dreadful winter" gave us a glimpse of other worlds, the frosted wonder of an unexpected hailstorm. I had never seen one, as it seldom hailed in Havana. The opaque pieces of ice created a milky wave that undulated magically throughout the camp, making it look like the Christmas landscape in a *La Yuma* postcard.

Aurora and I rubbed against each other to keep warm. Despite the inconveniences caused by the cold weather, I cherished those wintry nights. When The Beauty fell asleep, I tried to stay awake as long as possible to enjoy the contact with my friend's soft skin and the rubbing of her thighs against my *papaya*. Sometimes I thought Aurora enjoyed it too, but I immediately rejected the idea. If she ever suspected my feelings, she'd move to another bunk bed at once.

BECAUSE CHE Guevara had warned revolutionary youth against consumerism, I didn't care too much for dresses or perfumes. (Certainly, thanks to *Papi's* trips, I had more clothes and shoes than most of my friends. And he had just bought that fancy *pitusa* that waited for me at home.) But the cold weather prompted me to ask *Mami* for a jacket. The old cashmere sweater that had belonged to Grandma Gloria was the warmest item I possessed. The following Sunday, *Papi* delivered a note from *Mami* promising me a new coat. During the days that followed I kept thinking about it. It would be black, elegant, velvety, and smooth. It would disguise the weakest features of my body and enhance the best ones.

Usually we wore clothes that could be discarded after the

School-in-the-Fields term or stored until next year. Shabby pants, discolored shirts, darned socks. Only a poor *guajirita* like Elena would admire them! But a few girls wore nice clothes even in Pinar del Río. Marisol, for example, owned an impressive wardrobe. Aurora envied the beautiful suede jacket and the Levi's sent from *La Yuma* by Marisol's grandparents. She often borrowed a tight Betty Boop T-shirt which displayed a generous amount of cleavage. Marisol wasn't selfish and she loaned her belongings to anyone who asked for them. I couldn't understand Aurora's passion for borrowed finery. How ridiculous, I thought, to show off in a nice piece of clothing when everybody knew it wasn't hers. "I like to be in style, you little fool," she'd reply when I criticized her. "Who cares about *whose* T-shirt this is? The important thing is *how* I look in it. And I look pretty good!"

As my relationship with Ernesto strengthened, certain flaws in Aurora's character became obvious and even bothersome. Silly, vain girl! Clothes, makeup, and boys—that was all she cared for. She might have the body of a woman but she had the brains of a mouse.

My boyfriend and I talked about *serious* issues. Issues I couldn't even mention to Aurora because she'd laugh and call me a book-worm. Ernesto was smart and thoughtful. I still didn't enjoy kiss-ing him, but I *liked* him. If things continued the way they were, I asked myself, will I end up forgetting about Aurora and falling in love with Ernesto? Will I ever want to feel his *pinga* inside me? His *pinga*, which I had seen just a couple of times, resembled a big brown sausage, a *perro caliente* like those that came from Czechoslovakia in yellow cans.

In the evenings after taking a shower I huddled under two blan-kets waiting for dinnertime. I curled up in a warm spot that pre-served Aurora's scent. Ernesto stood by the window above my bunk bed wearing an oversized black pullover and a red Pioneer beret. I once told him that he looked a lot like Che Guevara but he didn't take it as a compliment.

"I wear this silly beret because I do not have anything else," he replied.

Sometimes I feared he didn't want to be like Che at all.

I felt particularly baffled when he told me about his growing resentment of the School-in-the-Fields. He also needed a coat but his parents couldn't afford it. He went to bed hungry every night because his family didn't have enough money to get the food sold *por la libre*—in addition to the ration-card quota but at very high prices—or on the black market. Even buying bus tickets to Pinar del Río was a financial strain for his parents, who had come to camp only once. I needed long explanations to understand my boyfriend's complaints. *Papi* made five hundred pesos a month at the university, *Mami* earned a good salary at the clothing store where she worked, and Grandma Gloria had a widow's pension. They seldom talked about money.

"When people don't talk about money, it means they have plenty of it," Ernesto asserted. "In my house we are always talking about it, particularly at the end of the month when the ration-card food is gone and *Mamá* says, 'What am I going to give you for breakfast tomorrow, *niños?* There is no sugar, no coffee, no milk, no *nada!*' It's not easy."

"What does your father do?" I asked.

"He's a construction worker."

"Has he ever traveled to the Soviet Union or to other socialist countries?"

"Once he went to cut cane in Las Villas for five months. He worked harder than anybody else and was chosen as a *machetero vanguardia*. But only his brigade's overseer got the prize, which was a trip to Bulgaria. My *Papá* got nothing."

"That's unfair!" I exclaimed. "How did it happen? Why?"

"Because the other guy was the boss, and white," Ernesto answered bitterly. "I work very hard here too," he went on. "They just gave me another certificate saying I am an outstanding worker, a *vanguardia*. So what? I can't buy a pound of rice with it. I can't get another glass of milk in the morning. The certificate is not even good to wipe my ass with, because it's way too hard."

After discussing the matter extensively, Ernesto and I came up with several questions and answered them together. My responses were based on Comrade Katia's lectures, on Che Guevara's teachings, and on *Papi's* comments. Ernesto's contribution was very different. I wrote them down in my green notebook, with my feeble replies. Since I didn't know how to argue with him, I'd ask *Papi* as soon as we got to Havana. He'd clarify everything.

- Why do we have to come to the School-in-the-Fields, wake up at five o'clock in the morning, eat badly, and get cold? (Ernesto asked.)

  Working in the fields is the least we can do for the revolution, a revolution that is educating us and giving us free housing and free health care, (was what I said.)

- But Pancho says we are useless here. How are we supporting the revolution with our work? (Ernesto asked.)

  The principal told us that our work is a symbolic gesture to pay homage to Che Guevara, I answered.

- The principal doesn't work himself. Most teachers don't work either. Why?

  They are not good communists. Was my answer correct?

- Were the people involved in the "cigar trade" paying homage to Che Guevara?

  They were trying to eat better because we aren't given enough food here.

- If our society is egalitarian, why do some families have more money and eat better than others?

  Because white people make more money and have more opportunities than mulattos and blacks.

- What's the difference between racism here and in *La Yuma*?

  Blacks there have cars.

SHADOWS. WHIMPERS of nervous ghosts. The pungent, bitter-sweet smell of the night. The aroma of the forget-me-nots mixed with bat guano. The moon grinning behind a cloud. The trees whispering menacingly above us. A bat that flew dangerously close to my shoulders. An owl that hooted in threatening tones.

A kitchen worker had sent Fat Olga and me to ask Pancho for firewood because she didn't have enough fuel to cook dinner. What an errand to run after dark! The *guajiro*'s cabin wasn't far from the camp but the walk seemed interminable. A somber atmosphere surrounded us as we made our way through the tobacco fields. I thought that invisible beings lurked in the palm trees. "I don't know how Elena can stand living here," I said with a shudder.

Fat Olga nodded. "At least we have company in the camp. But she is alone most of the time while her father works in the fields."

When we passed by the creek the waters rose, bubbling with an internal, evil life. A loud hissing came from the bushes. "¡A correr!" Fat Olga cried. "Let's run!"

So we did, only stopping when we bumped into the principal on the muddy path leading to Pancho's home.

"What are you doing here, *cabronas*?" the old man barked. "Don't you know it's against the rules? Wait until I talk to your parents on Sunday!"

Fat Olga explained why we were there, but he ordered us to return to the camp at once. "I just talked to Pancho and he's bringing the wood," he said. "Go back! And don't come here again without my permission! I don't want to see you again near the *guajiro*'s house!"

The principal escorted us back to the kitchen. He lumbered by our side, a furious ball on feet.

"I wonder why he is so interested in keeping us away from Pancho's," Fat Olga murmured when we returned to our barracks. "I smell a rat here, Lourdes. A big, fat, ugly rat."

When Pancho came to deliver the wood, Elena accompanied him and stayed to eat with us. Later the *guajirita* sat with our group and bragged about her plans. She would definitely go to Havana by July. She'd buy new dresses, skirts, perfumes, and maybe a Hungarian leather purse, she announced, smoothing her good hair.

"Go to Yumurí," Aurora advised her. "There you can get good stuff without the clothing-ration card. But Yumurí is very expensive. Fifty pesos for a blouse! One hundred for a pair of shoes! You have to sell the eyes out of your face and even the little eye of your ass to buy anything there."

"There is a store called Centro where food is sold *por la libre*," Fat Olga added, smacking her lips. "Cream cheese, chocolate cakes, ham, soft drinks . . . The only problem is that you have to wait in line for three or four hours to get in. You need to get there by five A.M. at the latest."

"I'd sure like to taste a soft drink," the *guajirita* sighed.

"But you told us that you had no relatives in Havana," Chabela said, looking at Elena suspiciously. "Where are you going to stay?"

"I can't tell you yet," she replied. "But I won't sleep in the streets, believe me."

That sounded odd—as odd as the feline smile that appeared for an instant on the *guajirita*'s cherry lips. Fat Olga winked at me and smiled knowingly.

⊰ CHAPTER XXV ⊱

MONOTONY DESCENDED OVER the camp like a thick curtain of dust. The bored flies buzzed a litany to dullness. The birds repeated the same song over and over. What a tedious evening! Aurora had gone out with Juanito. Chabela was busy writing a long letter to Jorge. Ernesto didn't feel well. I left the barracks wishing I could do something exciting, different, new . . .

Fat Olga had found an old issue of *Sputnik*. A small crowd soon gathered around her to look at the popular Soviet magazine. We sat and began turning pages, waiting for dinnertime. Unfortunately, the magazine was written in Russian. Although we had all taken three courses in Russian in secondary school and two in high school, our knowledge of the language left a lot to be desired. No one could understand more than a few isolated words on each page. All we could do was look at the pictures. One showed two spotted animals with rounded ears, black noses, and sharp white teeth. "Weird tigers," Natasha commented, giggling.

"Where are the tigers, shit eater?" Vladimir roared. "Can't you see they are big dogs?"

"Neither dogs nor tigers," I said. "They are hyenas. I saw them at the zoo."

"Hyenas, *mierda!*" Vladimir shouted. "They are dogs! Dogs!"

"They are hyenas!" I yelled back. "Read a natural science book! They are hyenas! Hyenas!"

The bystanders laughed.

"*You* are the hyena," Vladimir snapped. "Bony Ass!"

He snatched the magazine from Fat Olga's hand and tried to hit me with it. I ran away. He chased me around the camp. Ernesto came out of the boys' barracks, watched us for a while, and finally confronted him. "What's the matter with my girl, man?"

"I was just joking, dude," Vladimir replied. "Come on!"

Ernesto walked away. That was the beginning of my misfortunes. Or perhaps they had begun much earlier, the day Vladimir spilled Papirito's *arroz con leche* and I did nothing to help him.

Curled up in my bunk bed I burst into tears, convinced that everybody was talking about me and calling me Bony Ass. Worst of all, I felt betrayed. Ernesto had completely disappointed me. I'd expected him to be my defender, my champion, my loyal *guerrillero*. Why hadn't he punched Vladimir in the face?

Aurora went to the barracks and cajoled me to have dinner with our brigade. I reluctantly followed her to the dining hall.

"I'm sorry, *hija*," Chabela consoled me. "Vladimir is a jerk. Don't pay any attention to him."

I ate with my eyes glued to the table. Since Aurora remained silent, apparently concerned, I commented with a false air of detachment, "Vladimir is so immature! I don't understand how Natasha puts up with him."

"Natasha will put up with a bald scarecrow just to say she has a boyfriend," Aurora answered. "But next time don't run away, Lourdes. Don't let Vladimir know he's hurt you. If I were you, I'd get even with him. I'd embarrass him in front of everybody too."

"How would that help?" I cried.

She replied, "Vladimir is testing you. If you let him kick your ass once, you'll have to let him kick your ass a hundred times afterward. Listen to me, and get even with that *cabrón* before it is too late."

I shook my head.

"*Bueno,* Lourdes," Aurora said solemnly. "But you'll regret it."

How right she was!

Nothing else happened that night, but Vladimir took to screaming "Hey, Bony Ass!" whenever he saw me, and making faces behind my back. I pretended to ignore him. But it turned out to be the wrong strategy. The bully became bolder. He'd pull my hair and run away. He'd pinch my arms. Some people began to say he had a crush on me. Only occasionally would Ernesto confront him. Vladimir always told him he was "just kidding" and promised "not to do it again." The fact that my boyfriend accepted such lame excuses made me mad. I realized that he was afraid of the bully. *Pendejo!*

That bothered me, although not as much as the reconciliation of Aurora and Juanito did. After the stir created by the "cigar trade," his indifference of the previous weeks dissolved and the couple made up. They went out every night as if nothing had happened. He would whistle, she'd run outside, and he'd take her to the grass behind the boys' barracks. Fat Olga swore she had seen them making out under the *framboyán.* "Those two are crazy," she told us. "If the principal or Comrade Katia caught them, they'd now be in deep shit."

"Maybe that's what Aurora wants," replied Marisol. "If they are caught, Juanito will have to acknowledge their relationship publicly. Didn't you say she is pregnant? Then he'll recognize their baby too. She's no dummy."

No, she was smart and beautiful. She had confidence, long hair, and a big rump. I loved and envied her at the same time.

★ ★ ★

"JUANITO IS in my clutches, girls," Aurora announced as she got dressed. "I've grabbed him by the balls and I am not letting him go!"

"If he wants to leave you again, he will," I answered back.

"Look, *niña*," she purred, "first, I could denounce him for his participation in the 'cigar trade' at any time. Secondly, according to the law, I am still a minor. If I accused Juanito of taking advantage of me, he may end up in jail. Elena explained it to me."

I gulped. Aurora had trusted Elena enough to tell the *guajirita* about her affair! *Caramba!*

"Men need to be punished," Aurora added, glancing at her mirror with a satisfied air. "If you want a man to respect you, cheat on him. Shit on him. Abuse him. Betray him. Escape with his best friend. Spend all his money. Break his heart. Drink his coffee. Eat his meat. Call him *cabrón* and *maricón*. Kill him. Burn him. And then he'll love you more than ever."

Fat Olga and Marisol clapped.

Aurora went out. I couldn't help but notice the way she used her power. Like *Papi*. When *Papi* said "Barbarita, do this or that," *Mami* always obeyed him (or at least she used to.) Vladimir possessed the same ability. Aurora, *Papi,* Vladimir, all so different, had something in common. *Mami* and poor Papirito didn't have it. Neither did I.

It saddened me to think that I'd never be a total revolutionary, an heir of Che, because of my weakness. I lacked the skills to confront others. If I couldn't defend myself from a kid like Vladimir, would I ever be chosen to fight in other countries? Would I be able to free the oppressed masses of the world?

I needed to talk to someone about it, but Ernesto always managed to change the subject whenever I brought it up. He didn't want to get involved, period. Though Aurora listened to me, she didn't understand. "Just slap Vladimir in the face," she'd suggest, "or kick him in the balls." As if it were so easy!

Should I complain to Comrade Katia or to the principal? Should I tell them about Vladimir's harassment? I knew that Comrade Katia would defend me. But if the other kids found out, they'd call me a *chivata*, a tattletale. They'd despise me.

When no one was around, I sat in front of the greasy Che poster that adorned the wall of our barracks. I silently talked to him. I asked him for advice, but he never responded. He just stared at me with his eerie, bright eyes.

⊰ CHAPTER XXVI ⊱

L IFE IS ONE spoonful of sugar, another one of salt, Grandma
Inés would say. The Sunday that *Mami* brought me the promised coat she looked depressed and tired. Her shoulders were bent,
and her head drooped. She told me that *Papi* was already living with
Marietta. Grandma Gloria seemed enchanted with the arrangement. She cooked for the slothful floozy, spoiled Jorge, and addressed
him as "my new grandson."

"Can you imagine it, Lourdes?" *Mami* fumed. "After she's called
him 'a monster' for years! Seeing is believing!"

Radio *Bemba*—Big-Mouth Radio, as the officious barrio gossipers were called—had hurried to inform *Mami* that Marietta
spent most of the day with Grandma Gloria, seated in our inner
courtyard, eating flans and chatting. "Probably criticizing me," *Mami*
sighed. "*Ay!* I'll never set foot in that house again!"

When I asked her where I'd live after returning from Pinar del
Río, *Mami* answered quietly, "It will be up to you to decide, *niña*.
You know there isn't a lot of room in *Mamá* Inés's place, nor as
many nice things as Gloria has. But would you like to see Marietta's
face every day, obey her, put up with her son's insolence?"

For the first time in my life I felt the weight of responsibility, and it was not a pleasant feeling. I tried to dilute it with a bashful question, "*Bueno, Mami*, what do you want me to do?"

"Of course I'd like for you to stay with me, but I know it's going to be tough. You are not accustomed to living with other children. Mantilla is very far from your high school. It is not a quiet neighborhood like Lawton. So *you* have to decide, dear, not me."

I had always been afraid of my cousins, the ones that I had seen only three or four times a year. The ones that Grandma Gloria called dirty *mulaticos* when they visited the Vista Alegre Street house. "They may have lice, do not get close to them," she would warn me. The dark, noisy, poor relatives. Those who had kinky hair. Those who could only afford ration-card food. Those who could never buy clothes and toys in Yumurí, nor food in Centro.

We hadn't even invited them to my fifteen-year-old party. If I went to live in their house, how would they treat me? Would they pick on me? Would they beat me up? Should I stay with Grandma Gloria? But things had changed—a lot. Would I become a second-rate granddaughter, now that she had "adopted" Crazy Jorge? What kind of stepmother would Marietta be?

Mami stroked my hair and said, "Well, you don't need to decide right now. Let's wait until you go back to school. Now look at your new coat. Try it on!"

I put it on obediently, while all my hopes dissolved like hail under the sun. The coat was heavy and smelled of glue. Its phosphorescent blue color hurt my eyes. The synthetic material, rigid and abrasive, scratched my neck. But *Mami* didn't notice. "You look like a Little Blue Riding Hood," she cooed.

Little Blue Riding Hood, my ass. I looked like the wolf! But I couldn't offend *Mami* by telling her I did not like her present. It would keep me warm, no doubt, though it was too hot to wear on a sunny morning. I assured her that I would put on the coat at night, as it always cooled off after dark.

"I knew you would like it," *Mami* said proudly. "It's an expensive coat. It cost eighty-five pesos in Yumurí!"

I took the coat to the barracks and locked it inside my suitcase.

The disappointments I suffered that ill-fated Sunday didn't end there. At 1:30, a big truck showed up and almost hit the parents' bus, which was parked in front of the camp. The truck contained fifty students from a nearby encampment. The earlier hailstorm and persistent rains had rendered the other camp's barracks uninhabitable. The latrines had flooded. They'd run out of drinking water. Overwhelmed, their principal had decided to evacuate the camp and distribute its inmates among neighboring facilities.

When the new arrivals entered the campground, Ernesto was sharing an avocado salad with us. *Mami* had placed a tablecloth on the grass, picnic-style. Three chicken legs grilled happily on the portable brazier. Ernesto and I took turns taking long, warm drinks of *café con leche* from the thermos. The truck didn't attract my boyfriend's attention at first. He slowly chewed the yellow avocado slices soaked in vinegar and salt. He cleaned his mouth neatly with a handkerchief before drinking the milk. *Mami* smiled at him, obviously pleased with his manners. Despite the fact that he was a dark *mulatico*, she had come to like him.

"My brigade collected five hundred *cujes* last week," Ernesto commented. "Did you girls sew that much?"

But before I could answer, my boyfriend stopped eating and stood up. He stared at the line of student refugees stumbling toward the barracks, dragging their suitcases and bags. When I asked him if he knew someone there, he said no. But he forgot all about the salad. About our conversation. About me. I couldn't figure out what was going on.

As if awakening from a dream, Ernesto placed his dish on the ground and muttered, "I have to go. Excuse me, Lourdes. With your permission, Señora Barbarita." And he ran toward the new-comers' line.

"We have bad luck with men," *Mami* declared sadly, shaking her head. "That's what you inherited from me, *pobrecita*, along with your wiry hair and brown sugar skin."

"Why do you say that?" I asked her. "He'll come back soon. He probably went to greet an amigo."

"Amigo or *amiga*?" she sneered. "Don't be silly, Lourdes." *Mami* pouted, an embittered wife. "How long have you been together? Just a few weeks. You don't get to know a man, not even after you've lived with him for twenty years. If you give this kid a chance, he'll raise a leg and take a leak on you. All men are exactly the same. Like dogs."

"*Mami*, stop it." I felt like crying. "Please."

"Yes, men are all the same," *Mami* went on, her eyes wet and lost in the distance. "They can't be happy with one woman. They need two or three. *Cabrones!* The best one deserves to be hung by the balls. I can tell you right now, this guy is leaving you for good."

I began to chew my chicken leg without much appetite. Although I also found Ernesto's behavior odd, I tried to appear calm. *Mami* had created a tempest in a teapot. She probably thought Ernesto was like *Papi*. But he was not!

I looked at the sky. The sun. The hills. The wind. The clouds that passed so fast over the camp.

Mami left in midafternoon. I waited for Ernesto. But my boyfriend, who used to chat with me until dinnertime after the parents' bus departed, didn't show up. I sat under the *framboyán* while *Mami's* warnings hummed inside my head with the dogged persistence of a summer cricket.

He couldn't be talking with a refugee, not for three hours. Was he making love to The Duck? Were they both under Berto's blanket, kissing and calling each other *maricones*? Ernesto would have to decide: either Berto or me, I resolved. I wouldn't put up with their affair anymore. I had been too tolerant, too naive.

At 5:30 it cooled off. I put on my new coat and went out to look for Ernesto. I peeped inside the boys' barracks. I walked around the outhouses. I entered the dining hall, now silent and empty. I passed by the kitchen, with its permanent smell of burning wood. Finally, downhearted, I returned to the girls' barracks and lay down on my bunk bed. Marisol and Fat Olga chatted with a new girl—a short-haired, bright-eyed brunette. Aurora laughed outside, flirting with two handsome newcomers. Chabela wandered around with Crazy Jorge. All my friends were having fun. I was lonely and forgotten. I hated everybody, especially The Duck.

At 6:30 Ernesto still hadn't appeared. My heart full of fear, I kept walking around the camp, rushing from the *framboyán* to the barracks. *Pobrecito* Ernesto! Something must have happened to him! That Mother-of-Water that Elena had told us about . . . I was sitting dejectedly on the edge of my bed when Aurora came in to apply more lipstick.

"Juanito is jealous!" she giggled. "He saw me talking to the new boys and hasn't stopped circling around us. Now he will see! I'll make him pay for all his *mierditas*!"

"I thought you loved him," I said weakly.

The Beauty observed her face in Chabela's mirror. "I don't need more rouge, eh? Yes, I do love him, but I want him to love *me* more, that's why I am going to punish him for a while. Doesn't he deserve it?" She took Fat Olga's bottle of *Gato Negro* and generously sprayed perfume on her neck. Then she ran toward the door leaving behind a sweetish fragrance.

What if Ernesto also wanted to "punish" me? Had I done something to upset him? Could he be angry at me or at *Mami*? Tired of me? Was I too silly for him? Too plain? Should I go out once more or wait for him to come? Maybe I couldn't find him because he didn't want to be found. No, I wouldn't chase him. He owed me an explanation, didn't he?

With the commotion and noise created by the refugees, the evening turned out to be particularly turbulent. Girls ran wildly about the barracks, charging up and down the aisles. Intermittently, loud disputes occurred when a newcomer tried to take over a bunk bed that was already occupied.

"Get out of my bed, refugee! Didn't you see my stuff on it?"

"Sorry, Comrade Big Ass. I thought this was just junk."

"Your *papaya* is junk!"

"*Cochina!*"

Several portable radios, tuned to different stations, played at the same time. Outside, the clouds still flew over the camp. Faster. Darker. Taking with them the promises that men made to women to win their silly hearts.

The blue coat was too big and limited my movements. After Aurora left, I replaced it with the cashmere sweater and, swallowing my pride, went to look for Ernesto one more time. I entered the principal's office, a small room located next to the dining hall. The old man had decided to sleep there after the third week of the term. He complained that the barracks were too noisy. Needless to say, the boys applauded his decision.

Elena was cleaning the office. "Do not worry, *Habanera*," she patted my arm soothingly. "Your sweetheart hasn't run away. Keep looking and you'll find him."

I asked other kids but no one had seen Ernesto. To make things worse, Vladimir noticed my distress and yelled, "Bony Ass lost her boyfriend! Anybody have a spare one for her?"

"Forget it, babe," an impertinent refugee chuckled. "Boyfriends are now rationed like sugar, coffee, and rice."

"You'll have to wait in line to get another guy, Bony Ass!" Vladimir laughed. "Or ask your daddy to bring you one from Moscow!"

I went back to the barracks with tears of hate and impotence running down my cheeks. Then I went out again. In and out. Pointlessly. Hopelessly.

I had lost track of time when Berto appeared near the boys' bath-house. The antipathy I felt for him dissolved as soon as we bumped into each other. We screamed at the same time, "So he wasn't with *you!*" The Duck seemed as concerned and nervous as I did. He had not seen Ernesto after lunchtime and had walked around the camp looking for him during the last two hours too.

"You think he ran away?" Berto asked. "He hates the School-in-the-Fields."

"If he leaves, he would be a defector," I replied. "What a shame! And he will never be able to go to the university. No, Ernesto knows better. Let's look for him again."

At 7:30 Berto and I considered reporting Ernesto's disappearance to Comrade Katia. He might be lost, wounded, or sick. The Mother-of-Water might have attacked him. However, he could have gone to town or to a *guajiro*'s house. Escaping from camp, even for a few hours, was a serious offense and the fugitive would be severely punished, maybe expelled. "I don't know what to do," I confessed.

It was dinnertime, but neither of us felt like eating. We decided to wait until eleven. If Ernesto had not showed up by then, we'd ask Comrade Katia for help.

When Berto went back to the boys' barracks, I noticed the small queue that had formed in front of the dining hall. Waiting lines were shorter on Sunday nights because only those who had not had visitors that morning showed up for the collective dinner. Could Ernesto be there? My heart raced as I approached the waiting line.

Yes, there he was. My mulatto. He wasn't sick, he wasn't lost or wounded. And he wasn't alone either. The Mother-of-Water had not kidnapped him, but one of the refugees, a tall girl whose skin was much darker than his, had.

My throat filled with fluid, choking me. Ernesto—with a *negra*. They were talking. He held her hand. She smiled at him. *Men are all the same. They can't be happy with one woman, no. They need two or three.* Cabrones! *The best one deserves to be hung by the balls!*

I didn't want them to see me. I tried to return to the barracks but my stubborn feet carried me directly toward the couple.

"Lourdes!" Ernesto's voice echoed in a strange, ghostly way. *Lourdes! Lourdes!* "I was trying to find you." *To find you—to find you*—"This is Isobel," he went on. "Isobel, Lourdes is my best friend." *My best friend—my best friend*—

"Hi, Lourdes," Isobel said affectionately. Ernesto's expression was a mute plea for silence. "Nice to meet you."

The waiting line advanced.

"Hey, move!" Someone yelled behind me. "I'm hungry, *coño*! If you are not, get lost!"

Finally, as if coming out from under a spell, I turned my back to the queue and walked to the girls' barracks. Ernesto caught up with me on the way. "Thanks, Lourdes," he mumbled. "We'll talk it over later, *bueno*?"

Making a superhuman effort I agreed, "*Bueno*."

I never knew how I got to my bunk bed that night. I hid under the blankets and wept inconsolably. Wept as I used to weep in my childhood after being scolded by Grandma Gloria. Wept as if I had lost one of my *matrioskas*. My sparkling, newly found adult world was coming to an end.

What had I done to Ernesto? I liked him, I was falling in love with him when without warning, wham! He dumped me. He left me, not for a pretty blonde like Marietta but for a much darker girl. Why? Because *we have bad luck with men. That's what you inherited from me,* pobrecita, *along with your wiry hair and brown sugar skin.*

"What's the matter, Lourdes?" Aurora bent over me. "Are you sick? Why are you crying, dear?"

Nothing could console me, not even Aurora's gentle inquiries and caresses. *Mami* was right. Men were all the same. *Cabrones!* I again compared Ernesto with Aurora, who was concerned about me, kind and sweet. Aurora, whom I had almost forgotten. Oh, if she had been my girlfriend, she wouldn't have acted so inconsiderately. She would have never dumped me in such an awful way.

I didn't notice the disappearance of my blue coat until the morning. But the loss didn't affect me very much. I had come to regard the coat as an omen of bad luck and didn't even report the theft to Comrade Katia.

⌐ CHAPTER XXVII ⌐

Having fallen from the high perch of "girls with boyfriends" to the black pit of dumped *pobrecitas*, I passed through the following days in a blur of tears. Gone was the comforting certainty of being loved and cared for. I avoided leaving the barracks so as not to suffer the sight of Ernesto and Isobel, who seemed to show up everywhere I went. I would sit crying by the window and watching the distant hills dissolving in the soft darkness of the evenings.

I shed tears of fury. Tears of sorrow. Tears of hate. "Don't cry," Aurora said, "men don't deserve our tears." How could I avoid crying? My throat was plugged, my lips burned. "Despise him," she advised me. "And swallow your tears. If you keep them inside you, they'll heal your heart. Swallow them!"

I did. I swallowed them every evening when Ernesto trotted around the camp with Isobel and hid with her behind the boys' barracks.

Ay, Isobel! What did she have that I lacked? When we met, I angrily scrutinized her face and body. She was darker than I was, but prettier. She had a narrow waist, inviting red lips, and the long legs of a runner. "She looks like Aurora's black twin," Fat Olga remarked once.

Ernesto would greet me briefly, but he didn't seem to remember I had once been his girlfriend. He behaved as if our relationship had never existed. Berto said with a bitter tone of jealously in his squeaky voice, "Memories are short." The Duck had been discarded too.

Aurora still went out with Juanito. After flirting with several newcomers, she decided Juanito had been "punished" enough and they resumed their encounters. She stayed out with him until three in the morning. She came back to our bed with love bites on her neck and dead leaves tangled in her hair, happy and tired.

In the meantime I withered. The cold, boring, and dreary afternoons crawled into cold, boring, and dreary evenings. Vladimir kept teasing me. As if all this were not enough, the most difficult decision of my life waited for me at the end of the School-in-the-Fields term. The tribe of my dark cousins stood menacingly on one side, Marietta and Crazy Jorge on the other one. Had I been able to discuss it with Ernesto, it would have helped. But I wouldn't approach him now to complain about my miseries.

One night my need for an escape valve was so strong that I made a few comments about what my friends already knew, that *Papi* was having an affair with Crazy Jorge's mother and that *Mami* had left our house because of it. While I spoke, Aurora gently patted my hand under the covers.

"So I don't know what I'm going to do now," I concluded. "Because I love *Papi* and Grandma Gloria. I like living so close to the high school. Can you imagine me moving to Mantilla? I'll have to take a bus every day to go to school. *Uff!* But I feel sorry for *Mami*. I don't want to hurt her."

Fat Olga came up with a solution I hadn't thought of. "You don't have to live all the time with one family," she pointed out. "You can spend the weekdays with your *Papi* and the weekends with your *Mami*. Or the other way around. That's what most kids of divorced parents do."

"Then both sides will spoil you and try to make you happy so you'll prefer them," Marisol added. "I know from experience. You see, I live with *Mamá* but visit *Papá* and my stepmother every two weeks. And *niña*, they stuff me with good food every time I go there. *Papá* was a pain in the neck when he lived with us, but now he buys me all I want and doesn't nag me as he used to. My step-mother cooks for me and practically kisses my ass to make *Papá* happy. And *Mamá* doesn't complain for a couple of days, no matter what I do, when I've just come from the other house."

"Lucky you!" Fat Olga sighed. "When my parents scold me, I don't get any help and have to put up with their crap. Wish I had an 'other house' to go to too!"

Aurora shook her head and replied with unusual seriousness, "*Ay*, hija, don't say that! It's no fun when your folks break up, believe me. It's very hard to spend the rest of your life missing your father and—crying for him."

"Why crying? Doesn't your mom allow you to go to the other house?"

"Which other house? I don't even know where my *Pipo* is now."

"What do you mean?" I asked.

"It's such a sad and long story," Aurora said quietly, "that I am not sure you want to hear it."

"Oh, yes!" Fat Olga exclaimed. "Tell us, girl!"

"Well, if you insist. My *Pipo* was a drunkard, the drunkest of all the drunkards in our neighborhood. When he arrived home at night, I heard the sound of the key in the lock and I knew imme-diately if he had been drinking or not. If he had, the lock made a *Crack-pa-rra-lan* and Carolina jumped from her bed. 'Out!' she yelled. 'Get out of here, you son of a bitch! Out!'

"Out he would stay for an hour or more, scratching and struggling and cursing. After he had awakened half of our neighbors, Carolina got up and let him in screaming, 'Agustín, *carajo*! I am going to kick you in the balls to teach you to waste money on booze! Now, come in.'

"You tell me, girls," Aurora asked, "if she was going to let him in anyway, why didn't she do it at first? Why didn't she avoid the uproar?"

"Some people like to talk big, but they do nothing," Fat Olga said.

"She probably took pity on him," I suggested.

"Pity, uh? But she never took pity on us, *chica*! It never occurred to her that my brother and I couldn't sleep with that racket. Then, if she had been quiet once *Pipo* came in, it wouldn't have been so bad. But the real show began *after* he was inside. The nightly concert! Carolina howled and kicked *Pipo* and the furniture. The neighbors laughed, whistled or cursed us."

"*Uff*, that is pretty bad," commented Marisol. "But why did your folks stay together?"

Aurora looked at her sadly. "I think they liked to live that way. Carolina always threatened *Pipo* with divorce, but never meant it. I feared that one day she would hurt him if I was not around, but nothing ever happened. And it went on and on for years. Three nights a week at least, they offered the barrio a free concert. What a life.

"It was a fucking comedy, I realized much later. The day after a fight *Pipo* would clean the bathroom or fix anything that needed to be fixed and she would cook a nice supper for him. They didn't argue again until the next binge."

While Aurora talked Chabela left her bed and walked toward the door.

"Things wouldn't have changed if that coffeemaker had not exploded," Aurora continued. "*Pipo* began to make coffee one night when he was drunk, then went to bed and forgot all about it. The coffeemaker blew up and started a fire that spread to the bedrooms, scorched doors and walls, and filled the entire building with ashes and smoke.

"I woke up coughing and saw flames coming from the kitchen. *Coño!* I ran to the stairs in my pajamas. *Pipo,* half naked, limped behind me, while Carolina dragged my brother, the moron, and cried for help. Then came the screams, the siren of the fire engine, the neighbors watching and protesting, the *jodienda*—

"A few days later Comrade Ana, the president of the Committee for the Defense of the Revolution, stormed into our apartment. She said that there had been too many complaints about our fights. The fire was the last straw. Either *Pipo* went or the whole family would be thrown out of the building. The secretary of Popular Power had made the decision in the last Neighbors' Meeting, which we hadn't attended, of course."

The barracks were silent, except for Aurora's muffled voice. Suddenly, Chabela rushed in and collapsed on our bunk bed. "I saw a—a shadow outside! A big, long shadow! *Ay!*"

The horned monster! I trembled, too terrified to say a word, but the other girls weren't impressed with Chabela's report. Fat Olga replied disdainfully that there were hundreds of shadows at night, all over the place. Chabela insisted it was a *walking* shadow, perhaps the Mother-of-Water herself.

"You just had a nightmare!" Marisol laughed.

"Do you want to go out and see it?" Chabela suggested. "It may still be around."

"Thanks a lot!"

"Go back to bed, Chabela," Fat Olga advised her. "There is nothing outside. And, if there is a Mother-of-*Mierda*, leave it alone."

I couldn't be so skeptical. What had Chabela seen? The same

creature I had spotted once? A ghost? The snake from the creek? A thief?

"What a shit eater this girl is!" Marisol grumbled, after poor Chabela returned to her bunk bed in tears. "Go on, Aurora."

"What comes now is so ugly . . ." she sighed. "I don't feel like talking about it."

"That's not fair!" protested Fat Olga. "What happened later? What did your mother do?"

"Yes, finish, please," Marisol urged her.

"Plea-se," Fat Olga whined. "Plea-se!"

"*Bueno*," Aurora agreed, clearing her throat. "The president of our CDR hated *Pipo*. She hated other women's husbands because no man ever wanted to marry her. People called her Ana the Ogress and said she was still a virgin at sixty-five. The old, mean, fat cow!

"I can still see her in her olive green pants, with her red-and-black *miliciana* armband. She stood in our charred living room yelling at Carolina and ordering her to kick *Pipo* out. She threatened us with eviction, the police, and even jail if we didn't obey her.

"My brother and I hid under the sofa, which smelled of *Pipo*'s urine. Carolina cried and pulled her own hair out saying, "I'm going to kill myself! It's all my fault! I'm such a failure as a wife, as a mother, as everything!"

"That was the last time I felt sorry for her.

"After Comrade Ana left, Carolina asked *Pipo* to move out. Then I thought that she had no choice. But now I know she could have protested. She could have convinced the secretary of Popular Power to give *Pipo* another chance.

"*Pipo* got on his knees, begged, promised he would never again get drunk, but the bitch had made up her mind. She would not kill herself. She'd rather get rid of him to please the Ogress.

"I wanted the fights to end. The problem is, I also loved *Pipo*.

When he wasn't drunk he played with me and treated me better than Carolina did. And he never hit me. I pleaded with Carolina to forgive him. But the bitch kicked him out. It was the seventh of June, two days before my birthday. *Pipo* had just bought me a pink dress and a little stuffed dog. I still have them both.

"A week later he came back. Completely drunk, *borracho perdido*. That night Carolina did not let him in. He fell asleep at our threshold after pounding on the door for two hours. In the morning she collected the last of the clothes *Pipo* had in their closet and threw them at him. I tried to wake him but couldn't. A purple ring circled his right eye and his shirt was torn.

"Comrade Ana came down to snoop. Carolina asked her to inform 'that drunkard,' when he woke up, that he no longer belonged in our apartment. Delighted, the Ogress promised she'd call the cops if he came back."

Aurora breathed deeply.

"At least the nightly concerts stopped, didn't they?" Marisol said.

"Girl, he is her *dad*!" replied Fat Olga. "My old man also likes to drink but if *Mamá* kicked him out of the house, she'd have to kick *me* out too!"

"So, what happened to your father?" I asked. "Did he come back again?"

"He did, once or twice," Aurora answered. "Comrade Ana called the police every time, saying he was drunk and trying to abuse Carolina. What a liar! The cops already knew him and said, 'Agustín, *carajo*, you are disturbing these comrades again. We have a bed ready for you. Move.' I felt so guilty, girls, when I saw him being shoved and pushed inside the police car.

"One night Carolina noticed I had been crying and slapped me in the face. 'If you miss the *cabrón* drunkard you can go and live with him in the streets,' she hissed. I hated her from that day on. It was then that I began calling her Carolina instead of *Mamita*.

"In the end *Pipo* gave up and stopped knocking at our door. But he remained in the neighborhood for about a year. I would see him resting on a park bench or seated on the sidewalk, sleeping or drunk. *Pipo* wearing a muddy, buttonless shirt and shoes without socks. *Pipo* smelling of alcohol, old sweat, and vomit. Poor *Pipo*!

"Sometimes he walked toward me and mumbled, 'Aurora, tell your mother that I am coming home. Tell her to make coffee and to fry two eggs for me.' I never answered. I was so sad and embarrassed that I just went on walking. But generally he didn't even recognize me. He remained drunk for weeks. Each time I saw him he seemed more and more wasted, looking fifty years old when he was thirty-five. *Ay*, if things could be done over I would take him with me and *mierda* on Carolina and Comrade Ana! I would fight for him!

"One day he disappeared. Then Carlos the Cutie began visiting us. But I still missed *Pipo* and couldn't understand why he didn't return.

"Last year I found the phone number of *Pipo*'s mother and I called her. Though the old woman dislikes Carolina and acts as if my brother and I don't exist, she was decent enough to talk to me. She said that *Pipo* had left Cuba during the Mariel boatlift. You know that all the criminals who wanted to leave the country in 1980 were allowed to go. *Pipo* had been picked up by the police after a street fight and thrown in jail. Once the Mariel port was opened he headed for Miami.

"A neighbor who went to *La Yuma* six months ago came back saying that a man who looked a lot like *Pipo* was working in a grocery store in Miami and driving a blue Ford. This was the last we heard of him. But if *Pipo* is still the guy he used to be, there is no way I can imagine him riding a bicycle, let alone driving a car.

"My *viejo*! If he had not drunk so much—if the coffeemaker had not blown up—if the Ogress had not stepped in—how would things be now? He and my mother might still be fighting like cats and dogs, but together, *coño*, together! I shit three times on Carolina, on Comrade Ana, and on the whole world!"

Marisol sighed loudly. Fat Olga blew her nose.

"I know men don't deserve our tears," Aurora sobbed. "Not even my *Pipo*. But—I just can't help it."

I stroked her hair until she fell asleep. Her story changed the way I thought about my parents' separation. Actually, it had shed a different light on my whole life. *Papi* never drank. People respected him. *Mami* didn't curse me. Most neighbors looked up to us. I had two good grandmothers. Oh, I could have been so happy—if Ernesto had not dumped me.

◄ CHAPTER XXVIII ►

WHILE WE WERE having breakfast Chabela told every-body about the "walking shadow" she had seen. She later asked the teachers to explore the creek and its surroundings. She warned them that the snake had come out, but no one took her seriously. The principal scolded her and called her account "a fairy tale." Juanito and *La Flaca* paid no attention to her. Comrade Katia had gone to Havana again and wouldn't return until the following week.

Kids laughed at Chabela and said that she was nuts. A refugee hid a dead lizard under her breakfast tray. When our brigades went together to the tobacco house, Vladimir tried to shove her into the creek and shouted, "The Mother is going to get you, chicken!"

During the break I sat with Chabela and asked her for details. Did the shadow have horns? Chabela couldn't tell. The monster had escaped very fast, but it looked big.

"How big?" I lowered my voice because Fat Olga was watching us with the inquisitive glance of an incorrigible snoop.

"Taller than any of the boys," Chabela answered. "Do you think it was the Mother-of-Water?"

"I would not doubt it," I whispered. "She was probably walking on her hind legs."

Elena confirmed our suspicions later, explaining that Mothers-of-Water were extremely curious creatures who once in a while abandoned their liquid homes and wandered around to pry and rob. "If a Mother-of-Water likes something—let's say, a mirror, a watch, or any object that glitters—she takes it with her," the *guajirita* said. "Though she looks like a snake, she is a woman in her feelings. She is conceited and nosy. And very smart."

"You mean she was the one who stole the clothes, the rice cooker, and our TV set?" asked Fat Olga. "Does the Mother have electricity under the water to watch TV? Maybe she has a radio and a Frigidaire, too."

We all chuckled.

"Laugh now, you'll cry tomorrow," Elena warned us.

"Have the neighbors ever tried to hunt her?" I asked.

"Are you out of your mind?" replied Elena severely. "If a man harms, or God forbid, kills a Mother-of-Water, he will die that very day before sunset. And everybody knows that without a Mother-of-Water in the creek, it will dry up."

Hilda, the cook, told us that when they were out of the water, Mothers didn't attack people unless they were attacked first. However, she wouldn't advise anyone to approach them. "Their eyes glow in the darkness," she said. "They are like living lightbulbs, like bright summer stars. *Cuidado!* Don't ever look at them!"

They have hypnotic powers, the other *guajira* added. No one knew what might happen to the unfortunate human who fell under the influence of a Mother-of-Water's deadening stare.

No, it wasn't wise to go outside after dark anymore. All the couples got the message and the grassy land behind the boys' barracks was deserted at night. Nevertheless, at 11:30 I stood bravely under the *framboyán*, quivering every time I heard a leaf move, but determined to stay. Though a confirmed *pendeja*, I had decided to behave for once like a ballsy girl. Besides, the *orishas* were watching over me, or so I thought.

Hidden among the bushes, a cricket sang its monotonous song. The breeze carried a subtle fragrance, bits of grass and the remote sound of a barking dog. As I gazed at the clear sky, the vague concept of "infinity" made sense to me for the first time. Space was indeed infinite and so were the number of stars. The stars. Where had they come from? I had never seen so many in the city, but in the fields they covered the firmament with a hieroglyph of light. Lacy clouds veiled them for a few minutes, but soon moved on and the stars gleamed again. The serene atmosphere enfolded me; nothing bad could happen on a night like this.

I was waiting for Ernesto. At dinnertime he had dropped a note on my tray. "Please, let's meet tonight after the lights are off. I need to talk to you. Ernesto." All my resentment faded instantly and I nodded. That note could only mean that he wanted me back.

I had carefully braided my hair and asked Fat Olga for some of her perfume. I'd borrowed Aurora's bandana and a copper bracelet from an obliging refugee. My hopes were as high as the most faraway stars. Despite Che Guevara's teachings, I definitely believed in Oshún, goddess of love and sweet *papayas*, and in all the protective *orishas* that Grandma Inés worshipped.

Eleven-forty. Ernesto would come soon, asking for forgiveness. First, I'd let him know he had made a mistake. I'd be stern and cold. After "punishing" him with my indifference for a while, I'd allow him to kiss me. Then he'd dump Isobel. (Maybe he had already done it.) We'd be together again. Forever.

That evening I had taken a shower, rubbed my body with cinnamon sticks, and applied honey to my skin as if it were a cream. I had silently asked Oshún to give me Ernesto back. Just in case, I'd repeated *Siacará* several times. When Marisol and Fat Olga entered the bathhouse and got inside a booth together, I dried myself and left, wondering if my plea would be answered.

Did the *orishas* really exist? Did they listen to our prayers? Was Che Guevara among them? The fact that *Mami* hadn't been able to keep *Papi's* love briefly cooled my enthusiasm. But, two hours later, Ernesto's note was in my hands. Hurray!

Twelve o'clock. *Coño!* I decided to wait ten more minutes. If Ernesto didn't come, I'd go to bed. But he had to come. He couldn't do this to me!

Then I noticed the lights. Two of them. They were about the size of five-cent coins and jumped in the grass at my feet. I had almost forgotten about the Mother-of-Water. With a shudder I recalled Hilda's words, *Their eyes glow in the darkness. They are like living light-bulbs, like bright summer stars.* Cuidado! *Don't ever look at them*!

The lights got closer. One moved to the left, the other to the right. They were dancing. And there were three, five, eight more lights. A luminous ballet was being performed for me, its enchanted and only spectator. Oh, the stars had descended on the camp! The moist grass brimmed with them. One daring green spark reached my shoe. I bent to touch it, and then I heard Ernesto's voice, "Sorry I am late, Lourdes. I tried to get here sooner but couldn't. Are you tired?"

The fireflies ran away, leaving behind a trail of twinkles. I felt an immense sadness. And then it dawned on me. A sudden flash of truth lightened my mind like the fireflies had lightened the dark night. I didn't want to be Ernesto's girlfriend anymore. I felt humiliated because he had left me for Isobel, but I did not love him nor did I want to "punish" him.

Ernesto waited for my answer. I shook my head. He was such a great friend to talk to in the evenings. A gentle, patient buddy. But I had never "missed his kisses." I hadn't enjoyed them at all. Neither the kisses nor the other caresses. Now he wanted me back. What was I going to do? Accept him? Tell him that I couldn't forgive him?

"I have been thinking of you all these days," he began shyly.

"I have thought of you, too," I murmured.

"I'm really sorry about the way I treated you," he said, leaning back against the *framboyán*. "There was no need to act in such a— childish way."

"Oh, it was not childish." It was cruel, I wanted to add. But I didn't.

"I apologize for running away from you. Any other girl would have raised hell and insulted Isobel and me. You behaved like a real woman though."

"Thanks," I answered, blushing with pleasure. That was what I had missed, Ernesto's kind, flattering remarks.

"You must know something, Lourdes," he went on. "Isobel was the first girl I liked, the only one I ever thought of making love to. I liked her for many years but never dared to ask her out. I feared my parents wouldn't be happy if I had a black girlfriend. But my folks will have to understand. She is—special."

"What's so special about her?" I demanded, appalled. Didn't he want *me* to be his girlfriend again? Why did he bring the *negra* up?

"She is very black!"

"I know she is black!" Ernesto replied defiantly. "Precisely. She is so beautiful because she is *so* black."

Were we going to end up fighting? Oh, that *cabrona* Oshún had cheated me, making me believe she had answered my prayer and then finally kicked me in the ass. I hated her. I hated Yemayá, Babalú Ayé, and all the saints. I hated Ernesto, too.

Then Ernesto took my hand and kissed it. "You are also special," he said warmly. "Things I have said to you I'd never share with Isobel or anybody else. Lourdes, you and I will always be friends. The best of friends. I know—I know you never liked me very much, as a boyfriend, I mean. You wouldn't even let me touch your *papaya*."

"That's true," I admitted. "Yet I felt bad when you left me."

"I felt bad too. But now we are going to continue being friends, aren't we? Like two guys."

A tear rolled down my right cheek. I quickly wiped it off. "Yes," I agreed. "Like two guys."

We walked together to the door of the girls' barracks. The fireflies followed us. I remembered the words spoken by Sabina the *santera* and when he said softly, "Good night, Lourdes," I replied, "Good night, Ernesto. Light be with you!"

⊰ CHAPTER XXIX ⊱

A FIELD OF SUNFLOWERS blossomed unexpectedly beside the creek, splashing the landscape with brown and yellow strokes. We discovered it one afternoon when our brigade returned from the tobacco house. The flowers were splendid and tall, about the height of a five-year-old child. Chabela took three stalks to the camp and placed them inside a tin can by her bunk bed. The following morning they opened like little suns.

With every day that passed the weather was warmer and I needed to wear fewer clothes. Spring hadn't arrived yet but I could already feel its fragrant breath. The end of the term was close and I sometimes thought with anticipated nostalgia of the serene beauty of the fields, so different from the crowded, smoke-filled city streets and houses.

One Sunday evening, Aurora and I sat on the grass with Chabela, Marisol, and Fat Olga to share the food brought by our families that morning. Olga had gotten a bag filled with chocolate kisses after promising her mother that she would not devour them all by herself. "Please, girls, leave some for tomorrow," she begged from time to time, possibly regretting her generosity as the sweet kisses melted in our mouths at a dangerous speed.

"They will spoil," replied Marisol, licking her fingers. "Better keep them safe in my belly instead."

Aurora was in a rapturous state. After we emptied the bag, she announced that Juanito Lopesanto planned to marry her as soon as we returned to Havana. "You all are going to attend our wedding, aren't you?"

Their wedding!

"Teachers are not allowed to marry their students," Chabela pointed out. "It's against the law."

"Oh, I can change to another school," Aurora replied nonchalantly. "It's no big deal. *No hay problema!*" I crumpled a chocolate wrapping. Aurora would be leaving our high school, leaving *me*. "I'll move in with Juanito. His parents live in Oriente, on a farm, but he has an apartment in Havana."

Fat Olga opened her big, expressive eyes. "An apartment?" she repeated. "Where?"

Aurora hesitated. She thought for a moment and finally said, "Uh, somewhere in El Vedado. Near the Coppelia ice-cream parlor—"

"With whom does he live?" Marisol asked. "If he's renting a room in his third-cousin's house, like most *guajiros* do when they go to Havana, I doubt you will be welcome."

"I don't know who he lives with. He hasn't told me yet." Aurora seemed a little put out. "Besides, what does that have to do with anything?"

"A lot!" Marisol snapped back. "How can you talk about marrying a guy when he hasn't even taken you to his house, girl? Come on!"

Aurora ignored her and went on with the description of the ceremony that would take place in the El Prado Palace of Marriages. "We'll have a *La Yuma*–style wedding with lots of flowers, a white convertible, one hundred color photos and a three-layer meringue cake!"

Marisol suppressed a laugh and winked at Fat Olga.

"Is Juanito Lopesanto going to support you while you go to the university?" I asked. I knew my eyes looked red though I wasn't crying—yet. If Aurora got married that would be the end of my dreams of her, perhaps the end of our friendship, too.

"Who cares about the university?" Aurora wrinkled her pretty little nose. "I don't know if I'll even finish high school. Anyway, I'll be too busy after November. I won't have time to open a book."

"What's the problem with November?" Chabela asked, intrigued.

"The baby. That's the problem. I'll have to stay home to take care of him." Aurora's eyes brightened when she said "home."

"I knew it!" Fat Olga exclaimed.

"Don't tell me that you already—"started Chabela.

"Yes, *hija,* yes," Aurora chirped. "I am going to be a *mamá.* Just don't make a fuss about it yet."

A refugee joined our group and we changed the topic. I went to the barracks and fell into bed, the chocolate kisses and Aurora's upcoming wedding torturing my aching belly and my broken heart.

BEFORE LONG, Aurora began to retire early. "Juanito isn't feeling well," she would explain. "He's sick with the flu and needs to rest. It's better for him to avoid the cool night air, *pobrecito.*" She prepared chamomile tea for him in Chabela's portable brazier. She asked Elena for a needle and embroidered Juanito's initials on a cotton handkerchief.

He must have caught a very bad cold because days passed and they did not resume their nocturnal meetings. Then Aurora acquired a very tedious habit. Every night she would regale us with lengthy, boring descriptions of her wedding plans and future family life. I pretended to be asleep but she didn't notice, babbling freely, curled by my side. Once she talked nonstop for three and a half hours, until the other girls hissed in exasperation and *La Flaca* ordered her to shut up.

The next morning, the atmosphere in the tobacco house was stifling and gloomy. The greenish leaves looked like solid puke. The *cujes* resembled long turds. The whole world stank. I felt hurt and resentful. Both Aurora and Ernesto had deserted me. I'd grow old without a partner. I'd die alone and forgotten. Nobody loved me.

But soon I was pulled out of my somber mood. Aurora had gone outside to get a *cuje* when Marisol remarked, "People say love is blind, but it must be deaf and mute, too. Your friend talks about Juanito, believes he is going to marry her, tells everybody about their wedding—and the man was making out with Comrade Katia last night!"

"With Comrade Katia?" I repeated, incredulous. "Are you sure, Marisol?"

Marisol replied, "She likes Juanito. And he likes her, of course. The guy is an assflower!"

"A what?"

"An assflower! Don't you see he's always turning his head toward the biggest piece of ass? I just hope Aurora finds out before it's too late. I'm sorry for her, but I'm also fed up with her stories about Juanito's house and the El Prado Palace of Marriage. Psst!"

Aurora returned with a long slippery *cuje*, cursing the boys in our supply brigade. I went back to work inhaling with pleasure the pungent aroma of the tobacco leaves. How beautiful and green they looked now.

That night, when Aurora launched into a detailed description of her embroidered wedding dress, I knew there would be trouble. At lunchtime we had all seen Juanito in the dining hall, with no symptoms of flu, chatting with Comrade Katia. Aurora shamelessly lingered around their table. Once she even tried to break into the teachers' conversation but they ignored her.

"The dress will have a long trail and lots of lace around the skirt," The Beauty mused. "I don't want the guests to notice my belly. We'll get married by July and spend a couple of weeks in Varadero. A summer wedding! How romantic, *verdad?*"

"Hush!" grunted Marisol. "I'm sleeping!"

"Later, Juanito wants to travel to Oriente," Aurora went on, imperturbably. "His father manages a farm there and I'll eat eggs, steaks, chickens. Then I'll have a baby boy and name him after his *Papi.* Juanito II!"

Marisol uttered a loud groan.

"We'll have more kids later, at least three. And I will be a good mother, not a nagging bitch like Carolina."

While Aurora talked, a quiet, discreet, and low voice—that of common sense—whispered into my ear. It reassured me. Yet not all voices were quiet or discreet in our barracks. The third time Aurora detailed her intended honeymoon on the beach, a drowsy and angry Marisol cut her off. "For Lenin's *cojones, hija,* shut up! I do like your stories when they are real-life stuff, but this Juanito thing is getting old. The guy isn't marrying you."

"What are you saying, Marisol?" Aurora nervously bit the knuckles of her right hand. "Are you serious?"

"I *am* serious! By the time we get to Havana he won't even remember your name. Wake up, woman!"

Aurora remained speechless for a long time. We all waited for her reaction. Would she shrug? Would she cry? Would she laugh?

"What do you know about love?" she asked at last in a strange, hoarse voice. "You are an envious, frustrated dyke. An ugly *tortillera!*"

"Yes, I am a *tortillera,* but you are a whore!" Marisol roared. "You have sucked every *pinga* in this camp!"

Aurora stood up and grabbed Chabela's tin vase.

"Hey! My flowers!" Chabela shouted. "Stop!"

The sunflowers landed on the floor and the can on Marisol's head.

"Aurora! Girls! Please, calm down!" pleaded Chabela. "There is no need to fight over this!"

Marisol got up and threw the can back at Aurora, but missed.

"What's going on, *cabronas chiquitas?*" yelled *La Flaca* from her bunk bed. "Be quiet!"

The can flew through the window, crashing noisily against the *framboyán*. Chabela ran outside to retrieve it.

"Aurora and Marisol, go back to your beds!" shouted Comrade Katia, rushing into the barracks. "Now!"

A warm breeze came from the tobacco fields. Chabela wept over her sunflowers while putting them back in the makeshift vase. An angry rooster crowed in the distance. Two cats meowed loudly on the zinc roof, their piercing cries proclaiming the arrival of early Cuban spring.

⊰ CHAPTER XXX ⊱

T HE DAY HAD begun badly. When we arrived in the tobacco house Katita, our pet owl, didn't greet us from her corner as she usually did. We whistled and called her but she didn't show up. At noon I heard the boys of our supply brigade yell and laugh. I hurried outside, followed by Chabela. Dark feathers were scattered all over the place and a small bundle lay under the mango tree.

"Chicken yesterday, feathers today," Vladimir said with an ugly smirk. He kicked the bundle and added, "We used it as a ball until the insides came out."

Someone had tied a rope around Katita's body, which was cut in the middle and smeared with blood and mud. Chabela burst into tears. The owl's large eyes, clouded but still open, seemed to stare at the world with an imploring look.

Chabela and I went back to the tobacco house and told the other girls about the sad end of Katita. They listened to us in terrified silence. Fat Olga was the first one to react. She ran outside, grabbed a rock, and threw it at the boys. "I hate you, *cabrones!*" She shouted. "I hate you all!"

We soon followed her example, furiously attacking the boys with more rocks, rotten mangoes, and even *cujes*. The supply brigade fled, having suffered an ignominious defeat.

Misfortunes never come singly. That evening when we left the tobacco house, I forgot to take my work gloves with me. I only remembered after we were in camp.

"Now I have to go back," I said to Aurora. "If a *guajiro* finds my gloves, I'll never see them again."

She tried to dissuade me, "They will be there tomorrow, girl. Take it easy." But I insisted on going, even though Aurora didn't offer to accompany me. What a friend, I sighed, walking fast by the creek. *I'd* have accompanied her!

I bumped into our supply team. Vladimir immediately yelled, "Bony Ass is going to work until midnight! She wants to be a *vanguardia*!" No one laughed. The other boys looked ashamed. When I passed by the mango tree, I noticed that a few withered jasmine flowers had been scattered over the owl's body.

A dense dimness reigned in the tobacco house; all the windows had been closed before we left. I cursed myself and the work gloves, and bent to look under the *cuje* pegs. A slamming of the door made me jump. "Is it you, Aurora?" I asked, happy to have her company. "Come in!"

No one answered. A nauseating smell filled the room. It got darker. Frightened, I drew back to a wall and didn't dare to move. The stink became more offensive. Could it be the Mother-of-Water's fetid breath?

I shrank against the wall. Someone (or something) had sneaked into the house. It kept moving around. Panting. Trying to get me.

Minutes passed. It could have been an hour. Finally I mustered enough courage to leave. I tiptoed toward the door when something hit me right in my face. It was soft and warm. It was large and smelly. It was a big *plasta de vaca*, a pile of cow manure. I screamed. A familiar, hated laugh answered. Vladimir ran away.

The shit was in my eyes. Blinded, I crawled out of the house.

Feeling my way I walked a few feet, stumbled over a bush, and fell to the ground. There I stayed, weeping, until help came from the most unexpected source. Crazy Jorge, who had just arrived from Havana, found me on his way to our camp.

"Hey, Lourdes!" I heard him exclaim. "Are you OK?"

I leaned on him and got to my feet, sobbing. Jorge guided me to the creek. With surprising gentleness he cleaned my face with his handkerchief.

"What happened to you?" he asked. His voice was deep and soothing. He didn't sound like a monster at all. "*Pobrecita.*"

How could I tell him about Vladimir? I hung my head and mumbled, "Nothing. I just fell right in the middle of the cow shit."

We returned to camp together. Later, Chabela and Aurora assisted me in the unpleasant task of washing my stinky clothes.

Grandma Gloria had sent me a package of food with Jorge. "Here, honey," he told me affectionately, "stuff yourself." We sat together and chatted. He gave me news about *Papi* and Grandma Gloria, but did not talk about his mother or *Mami*. Quite sensitive after all!

That night I thought a lot of Crazy Jorge. He had not made fun of me. He had come to my rescue like a knight in ragged jeans. I remembered his hands kindly wiping the *plasta de vaca* off my cheeks. Despite his previous obnoxious behavior, despite the fact that his mother was a slothful floozy, despite my loyalty to *Mami*, I felt a tentative, grateful sympathy for him.

Though I had asked my friends not to talk about the incident in the tobacco house, the news spread quickly. Vladimir made sure everybody else knew why my work clothes were still damp the following morning. Most kids pretended to commiserate with me, but I perceived mockery in their comments. Because of his easy victory over me, Vladimir's fame grew. And I ended up with a new nickname, Lourdes Turdface.

"Defend yourself," Fat Olga advised me. "Tell the teachers, throw a rock at Vladimir, do something. You'll be known as a geek, like Papirito, if you don't!"

I swore to myself that it wouldn't happen.

Like a lonely *guerrillero* hidden in the Bolivian forest who knows he won't be seeing his city comrades for a long time, and prepares himself for a cold winter by collecting all available fruits, I started stockpiling mental reserves of courage. I'd talk back to Vladimir the next time he harassed me. I'd call him *cabrón*. I'd convince Ernesto to fight with him. *I'd* kick his ass. But my brave resolutions evaporated when I was in the bully's presence. All my reserves of courage would melt away.

Despite the fear Vladimir caused in me, the day he threw a live cockroach in my face I decided that I had had enough. I called Comrade Katia and told on him. Incensed, she ordered my tormentor to help Hilda in the kitchen for a week—a disgrace to his macho reputation, no doubt. But it didn't deter him from harassing me. "Don't get the wrong idea. I'll get even with you, Turdface," he promised.

He was true to his word. The punishment only made things worse. That very night he waited for me behind the barracks and pulled my hair savagely. The next morning I discovered my dress shoes had been stolen and my two bags of food emptied.

Fat Olga was right. I had become Papirito's heir. Despite my sincere desire to join the *guerrilleros*, I hadn't learned how to fight. I could not slap Vladimir. I could not break a *cuje* over his head. Comrade Katia wasn't always around, the other teachers didn't care. And I'd rather die than tell *Mami* and *Papi* about my predicament.

Aurora attempted to defend me on one occasion. Vladimir was pinching my buttocks when she got between us and yelled at him, "Leave Lourdes alone, *cabrón*! You pick on her because she is just a child. Try to abuse me and I'll cut off your balls and hang them from the *framboyán*."

To be called "a child" was humiliating enough, and to be called that by my *amor* was even worse. But the ultimate insult came when Vladimir pretended to attack Aurora—though with more libidinous intentions—and she laughed and enjoyed it.

The situation became so intolerable that I decided not to go outside in the evenings anymore. Sometimes Ernesto talked briefly about confronting Vladimir, but absorbed by his romance with Isobel, or afraid of the bully, he soon forgot his promise. And there were no other male friends willing to take my side. Ah, why didn't I have a brother—or a boyfriend—like Crazy Jorge?

In vain I looked at the Che Guevara poster and asked him to grant me the courage that a true *guerrillera* should possess. In vain I shut myself up inside a shower stall and asked Changó, the *orisha* of thunder and power, to become my warrior and protect me. In vain I kissed the polished surface of the *azabache* and my Outstanding Communist medal. In vain I leafed through *Che's Journal*. In vain I made terrible promises, like not eating ice cream for a year or not looking at Aurora while she changed clothes, if Vladimir would stop taunting me. In vain I whispered *Siacará* and *Homeland or Death*.

April warmed up slowly. But the beauty of the season only depressed me more as I compared the splendor of Nature with my miserable life. Aurora didn't love me, Ernesto had dumped me, my parents were getting a divorce, everybody made fun of me. I was harassed during the day, I had nightmares at night. Neither Che Guevara nor the *orishas* had listened to me.

One day the slogans painted on the camp's mural sent me a secret message. *Homeland or Death. Socialism or Death. Death to the Enemy. Victory or Death. Death, Death. Death.*

Death! *La Muerte!* Yes! I knew Chabela had a bottle of alcohol that she used in her portable brazier. I'd steal it, pour it over myself, and light a match. I'd set myself aflame like Aunt Mariana did after her husband left her. Then, adios School-in-the-Fields. Adiós laughter, adiós abuse. Adiós *Mami* and *Papi*, Grandma Inés, Grandma Gloria, Aurora, Ernesto, adiós!

The evening that I found a dead black butterfly on my pillow, which had been placed there by one of the girls—perhaps by Aurora herself!—since boys weren't allowed inside our barracks, my resolve was confirmed. I'd do it the next day. I'd ask Comrade Katia for permission to stay in camp, pretending I was sick. Then I'd write a letter blaming Vladimir for my death and I would kill myself in the sunflower field. When I saw Papirito again, I'd tell him how well I understood his anguish. The anguish that made him fall from the *framboyán's* tallest branch . . .

I went to sleep with total peace of mind and had no nightmares that night.

CHAPTER XXXI

M AN PROPOSES AND God disposes, as the saying goes. The next morning we weren't awakened by the five o'clock siren but by Comrade Katia's screams, "Open your ears, *cabronas!* There is a thief among us. But I am going to find her. I am going to take her to the police station myself. Enough is enough." It was uncomfortably cold and the air smelled like rain. I got up shivering, sleepy, and disconcerted.

Comrade Katia's alarm clock had disappeared during the night. Convinced that it was still in the barracks, she began a meticulous inspection of all bags and bunk beds. The search took place amid continual yawning and timid protests. Aurora looked at her watch. "It's only four o'clock," she hissed. "I shit on Katia's mother!"

Comrade Katia quickly examined my suitcase. Satisfied, she was going to proceed to Aurora's belongings when my grammar notebook attracted her attention. She opened it and started to read. Head pounding, I remembered the "questions" written there, my work and Ernesto's, those subversive comments. . . .

"Shame on you!" The teacher slammed the notebook down on my bunk bed. "So the School-in-the-Fields is a waste of time. Our socialist society is *not* egalitarian. We are racist—What does this mean?"

I remained silent, not sure if I was awake or in the middle of another nightmare.

"Come with me!" Comrade Katia ordered.

Aurora stared at us, amazed. I followed Comrade Katia's butt as it wagged threateningly inside her denim pants. We made our way through the deserted campgrounds, sprinkled with the first drops of a light, chilly rain. *This isn't happening*, I thought. *I can't have such bad luck.*

As soon as we entered the workshop room the teacher closed the door. I sank into a chair, under the Che Guevara poster. She stood in front of me, her eyes burning with fury behind her gold-rimmed glasses. "What's wrong with you?" Comrade Katia asked sharply. "I thought you were a revolutionary. I'd have recommended you for the Young Communist League. You have really disappointed me!"

"I—I am a revolutionary," I stuttered.

Comrade Katia went on, ignoring my remark, "I'd have answered any question you had about the inequalities that, unfortunately, still exist in socialist societies. But you didn't ask me. Instead, you chose to draw your own stupid conclusions, 'What's the difference between racism here and in *La Yuma*? Blacks there have cars.' What evil rubbish!"

My mind worked at full speed. Comrade Katia trusted me. I had always been a good student. I had participated in all our high school political marches. If I told her that Ernesto had come up with most of the "answers" she'd believe me. Besides, that was the truth. Though it might ruin Ernesto, it'd certainly save me.

"Now, Lourdes, be honest." She looked me right in the eye. "Why did you do it? Who put these ideas into your head?"

As a flash of lightning lit up the room, a wicked but wonderful idea popped into my mind. I remembered the *plasta de vaca* all over my face, the cockroach, the black butterfly. I remembered Papirito and the night of Valentine's Day. I remembered Aurora calling me a child. And I answered, "Vladimir."

"Vladimir!" Comrade Katia repeated, astonished. "It can't be!"

"His spelling is terrible so he forced me to write the 'questions' down," I explained. "He was going to beat me up if I didn't—" I started to cry. I cried from pain, real pain that caused real tears, recalling the bully's abuse.

"You mean he asked himself all the questions first?"

Comrade Katia didn't seem convinced. A slightly different approach had to be used. I looked at the world map that adorned the wall and said, "He and his long-haired buddies are always listening to American music. Some of the questions are taken directly from Yankee songs, translated by a hippie. Vladimir wants to share them with more people, with his *gusano* friends."

Comrade Katia muttered, "This is making sense, now."

I felt more confident as the teacher's tone became kinder. "He dictated everything to me," I whimpered. "He told me I should keep the notebook until the end of the term and give it to him in Havana. But I planned to ask *Papi* to look at the note-book first. My *Papi* is a scientific communism professor at the University of Havana," I added quickly. "He would tell me for sure if the 'questions' were counterrevolutionary. If he said they were, I was going to take the notebook to our high school and hand it to you."

"But why wait until our return?" Comrade Katia asked. "Why not here?"

"Because I was afraid of Vladimir," I replied. "He's threatened me many times. He's always picking on me. You can ask anybody in the camp if you think I am lying."

Comrade Katia's eyes had become soft as green tobacco leaves. "Poor Lourdes!" she sighed. "How is it possible that a good *compañera* like you has been subjected to that kind of treatment? Why didn't I notice it before?"

"Oh, it's my fault," I murmured. "I should have told you. I should have called the principal or another teacher."

"Yes, you should have trusted us, *niña*. But better late than never. Now, tell me everything you know about Vladimir. Don't be afraid, because I will not allow anything bad to happen to you."

That morning I didn't go to work. All the brigades left but I stayed in the office talking to Comrade Katia. Later we met with the principal and with the other teachers. My story sounded better and more credible each time I repeated it.

What followed these conversations was like a dream. Vladimir was called in and I repeated my accusations. For Papirito, I thought. Revenge for all the times you made him cry and humiliated me. For Papirito and for *me!*

Vladimir protested and called me a liar. Despite his macho façade, he sobbed like a child when Comrade Katia questioned him. But his denials didn't do him any good. The teachers knew he was a bully. He did have hippie-looking friends. Besides, he was baffled and perplexed. How could he avoid being perplexed, the devil, who never in his life had put together two ideas about politics? How could he avoid being baffled when words like "egalitarian" and "pay homage" weren't even in his limited vocabulary?

The principal tried to diminish the importance of the matter but Comrade Katia wouldn't back down this time. "We are dealing with a case of ideological deviation," she stated. "Either we are communists or we are pro-Yankee!"

The old man relented. A special, closed-door meeting was held with Vladimir, Natasha, and myself as the star witnesses. To my surprise, Natasha didn't even attempt to defend Vladimir. She admitted that her boyfriend had long-haired, maybe *gusano* friends. "They all listen to rock music, collect empty Salem and Marlboro packs, and read foreign magazines," she confessed.

"*Foreign* magazines!" Comrade Katia exclaimed. "Capitalist propaganda! This is worse than I thought!"

The following day Vladimir's parents were contacted and he was sent, in custody, to a reeducation center in Las Villas.

After Vladimir had left, all my macabre suicide fantasies vanished as well. A new life began for me. I wasn't a geek anymore, but Comrade Katia's ally, an exemplary *compañera*, a trustworthy comrade. Students and even teachers treated me with more respect than they had before. Some labeled me as a *chivata*, a malicious informer, and feared me. But I had found out that it was better to be feared than to be despised.

However, I couldn't avoid a tinge of remorse when I thought of Che Guevara and his high concept of what a revolutionary should be. I had lied to Comrade Katia. I had falsely accused Vladimir. My only consolation was that he deserved it. I had acted in self defense.

Only to Aurora did I confess the truth. She complimented me by shaking my hand and calling me a real *cojonuda*. In return, I learned that she had thrown Comrade Katia's alarm clock down a latrine because its rackety ticktock had prevented her from sleeping.

I recalled the first prophecy of the *santera*. *There will be a lot of malice, my daughter, but you'll conquer it by the power of your mouth.* Sabina had been precise in the first prediction—would she be as accurate in the second one? Would I ever be loved by Aurora? And why then would I be dissatisfied?

⚔ CHAPTER XXXII ⚔

OUR *FRAMBOYÁN* SANG a purple hymn to the spring. Sunflowers blossomed, girls sighed, and boys panted. The trees were green explosions over the cocoa brown earth. After work Chabela would gather daisies and lilies and weave them into necklaces. Tiny wildflowers traced pink, blue, and yellow streaks in the grass.

It was a bright, pleasant spring and my life was brighter and more pleasant than ever. After Vladimir's expulsion I became Comrade Katia's pet. She often asked me to run errands, thus freeing me from sewing *cujes* in the tobacco house. She suggested to Hilda that the kitchen *guajiras* serve me bigger portions because I looked too thin. She watched over me like a protective *orisha*. The next time *Papi* came, they had a long chat about communist values. My friendship with the teacher raised my status in camp. Aurora jokingly called me an ass kisser and a shameless brownnose, but I didn't care. Better ass kisser than butt of jokes!

One Sunday afternoon, after the parents' visit, Comrade Katia summoned me to the workshop room and said, "*Compañera* Lourdes, a true revolutionary not only should be able to obtain the best grades at school, but also make the right decision at the right moment. Do you plan to become a Young Communist someday?"

"Of course." I answered. "I've always dreamed of being a *guerrillera*, too," I added shyly. "Like Che Guevara."

"Then you must remember that Che wanted his *guerrilleros* to be cold killing machines," Comrade Katia asserted seriously. "If you choose to follow his example, you shouldn't fear to kill, burn, or shoot the enemy. You shouldn't fear to resort to revolutionary violence. You have to destroy the oppressors by any means possible."

I nodded. Yes, I had heard that before in our Marxism classes.

"You are a good student and a loyal revolutionary, but you still need to boost your self-confidence and leadership abilities," Comrade Katia went on. "You will need them if you are sent on an internationalist mission as a *guerrillera*. I've decided to place you in charge of a tenth-grade-girls' brigade."

I made a bashful comment about being too shy for leadership work, but she replied, "Nonsense! Be strong and demanding from the first moment and all your underlings will show you the proper respect. This way you'll prepare yourself to fight in the continental revolution."

The following day I entered the tobacco house as a leader. My subordinates immediately liked me. They called me little boss, *jefecita,* because of the way Comrade Katia introduced me to them, "Here is your new leader. And I must tell you that Lourdes will not tolerate any disorder. She is a tough little boss."

Soon I forgot her advice to be "strong and demanding." For the most part, I allowed the girls to do as they pleased and to take frequent breaks. They were fourteen-year-olds, docile, and respectful, and never challenged my authority.

From another leader I learned a few tricks that turned our brigade into a *Vanguardia Socialista,* an exemplary company. Regardless of how many *cujes* were sewn, I would write down a very impressive number at the end of every shift. Since no one came to count the finished *cujes*, which were stored together with the *cujes* sewn by the rest of the teams, mine was twice chosen as the most productive brigade of the camp. The *Vanguardia* certificates, printed on gray cardboard and signed by the principal, made *Papi* feel as proud of me as if I had already been accepted in the Young Communist Cuban League.

But even exemplary leaders were not above buying Yankee products. One evening Fat Olga showed me a can of condensed milk full of a saffron-colored paste. "It is the Michael Jackson lotion," she boasted. "I'm selling it for *only* fifty pesos."

Around the time we had left Havana, a concoction known as the Michael Jackson lotion became the latest fashion among dark-skinned people. The lotion, allegedly used by the American singer to whiten his skin, was a thick yellowish ointment with a funky smell. A small bottle cost eight hundred pesos. A fortune!

As soon as I heard of the *maravilla Americana* I wanted to try it. But *Mami* didn't trust foreign potions as much as her own heroic measures, namely the "ironing treatment" for the hair. "Remember your *fiesta de quince*, how much we have already spent this year," she would say when I begged her to buy the lotion. "Don't even think about it!"

Grandma Gloria wasn't too well-disposed toward the purchase either. "How do you know it will work?" she asked. "There is a sucker born every minute, my child!"

Oh, but the Michael Jackson lotion *did* work miracles! Who hadn't heard the story of a mulatta *Guantanamera* who became so white that she had to change her ID picture? And the other one about a baby whitened by his mother two days after his birth? He was later rejected by his father, a black man who did not want to believe that such a fair-skinned boy could be his offspring. Fat Olga, a clever salesgirl, assured me that Marisol had received a big bottle of ointment directly from her *La Yuma* relatives. "It's authentic," she emphasized. "Made in the USA!"

Marisol had decided to make some money by selling the froth in small portions because she was happy with her own color, Fat Olga said. Marisol's skin was also brown, though lighter than mine. She could have passed as a dark-haired white, but proudly acknowledged a black grandmother from whom she had inherited her strong will and broad ass—her only beauty, according to the boys.

I hesitated. My parents had given me one hundred pesos as emergency money. Half of this sum didn't seem an outrageous price to pay for whitening my skin. But if *Mami* found out I'd be in trouble. And I might need the money later. . . .

"Hurry up!" Fat Olga prodded me. "I know lots of girls who are ready to buy the froth. They would pay twice as much for it!"

Finally, I offered Olga forty pesos and two guava bars. She accepted and I even thanked her for thinking of me first.

"Now, don't talk to Marisol about the lotion because she doesn't want people to know it belongs to her," Fat Olga warned me after the deal was closed.

Soon my face and neck were coated with the stinking yellow paste. But I did not mind its smell. The Michael Jackson lotion would change my life. Neighbors would see me in the barrio and ask each other, "Who is that pale girl? Have you ever seen her? She looks like a Russian." The same thing would happen at school. Boys—maybe girls too—would be impressed by my new appearance. I'd be more popular and well liked. Oh, if I could just buy the entire bottle!

"Phew, what kind of cream is that?" Aurora held her nose when she approached our bunk bed. "It smells like shit!"

"No, it doesn't. That's the smell it should have."

I said no more, despite Aurora's loud complaints. I planned to surprise her the next morning with a newly whitened complexion. Would she like me more? And Ernesto, what would *he* say? He might ask me to go back to him but I would reply, "Forget it! You threw me away, now you can't pick me up. And I don't go out with *mulaticos* anymore!"

While I lay dreaming Aurora climbed up to her own bunk bed and slept there with a perfumed handkerchief over her nose.

When the five o'clock siren jolted me awake I immediately looked at the little mirror that hung from a bedpost. The same brown sugar *mulatica* I saw every morning smiled at me, but my forehead and cheeks itched and felt warmer than usual. "It means the froth is working," Fat Olga reassured me. "First it itches and then it whitens. You'll see results soon."

After washing my face I covered it again with another, thinner layer of cream.

"You should wipe that crap off before walking in the sun," Aurora advised me as we marched to the tobacco house. "It may cause a bad reaction. And it still stinks!"

Offended, I turned my back to her and joined my new brigade.

By lunchtime my cheeks were intolerably hot. Not only did they itch, they burned. When the brigades returned to camp at noon my whole face was red and swollen. I hurried to the sink and washed the ointment off.

"*Ay*, Lourdes, ask Comrade Katia to take you to the doctor," Fat Olga urged me, staring guiltily at my poor face.

Comrade Katia touched my forehead and recommended that I apply cold-water compresses to the swelling. It didn't help. Night came and I couldn't sleep, tormented by incessant itching. The next morning I almost fainted when I looked at the mirror. A crop of green pimples had sprouted on my face like moss on the barracks' walls after a heavy rain.

"You are having an allergic reaction," Comrade Katia said, worried. "Let's go to Los Palacios and see a doctor there."

Los Palacios, the closest town, was about twenty miles from the camp. Pancho offered to take us. At 10 A.M., after an hour drive, his asthmatic Ford stopped in front of the dispensary. It was a small concrete, tin-roofed house. Comrade Katia knocked at the unpainted door several times and finally a disheveled nurse opened it. "The doctor is in a Popular Power assembly," she grunted. "Could you return another day?"

"No," Comrade Katia replied angrily. "We'll wait for her."

The nurse allowed us to enter the dispensary. The waiting room smelled like coffee, old dirt, and mice. Two metal chairs and a three-legged pine desk furnished a dusty corner. A poster of Fidel in the Sierra Maestra Mountains covered a broken window. *Health, a right of the people* read a big banner nailed to the flaking wall.

The doctor—a young, fleshy *guajira*—arrived at three o'clock. She sat behind the desk and looked at me with the unsympathetic expression of one who is viewing an ugly, maybe dangerous, bug. "What's the problem with this girl?" she asked, grabbing a piece of paper and a pencil. "What in the world does she have on her face?"

"That's for you to find out," Comrade Katia snapped back. "Do you think we'd have come all the way from the camp if we knew?"

Ten minutes later the doctor dismissed me with a hurriedly scribbled prescription for a zinc oxide lotion and a loud *awh*.

"Lazy bum! *Zángana!*" Comrade Katia thundered as we left the dispensary. "In a capitalist country, a country girl like her would have never been able to study medicine. These young doctors don't have the slightest idea of the sacrifices our government makes to train them. They act as if they are doing the patients a favor."

I remembered how much *Papi* had praised our socialist medicine. For the first time in my life I disagreed with him. I wished he had been in the dispensary with Comrade Katia and me. I wished Che Guevara had been there too.

"We've already missed our chance to eat lunch at the camp. Let's look for a restaurant," Comrade Katia suggested, sighing.

There were no restaurants in Los Palacios. We ended up in a grimy, chairless cafeteria where we waited fifteen minutes at the food-stained counter before the waitress grouchily asked us what we wanted. Comrade Katia bought two hard pieces of bread spread with a mysterious substance that tasted like decayed fish.

The zinc oxide lotion wasn't as helpful as the remedy Pancho gave me when we returned from Los Palacios. Looking like *San Lázaro, Babalú Ayé* of the magical herbs, the *guajiro* brought some sweet-smelling sage and told me to apply it to the pimples. The cool leaves soothed my painful face. They cleansed my skin and my soul. They sang to me: *You silly* mulatica, *aren't you happy to go back to your smooth brown sugar skin? Brown sugar isn't worse than white sugar.* I went to sleep lulled by that soothing voice, comforted by the leaves' healing touch.

The next day my friends gathered around the bunk bed where I lay down, my face coated with zinc oxide and wrapped in sage.

"I'm *so* sorry, Lourdes. I thought the stuff was harmless. I didn't want to make you sick," Fat Olga apologized, remorseful.

"Why the hell did you say *I* had given you that crap?" Marisol yelled at her. "Let me tell you, *hija,* that I didn't have anything to do with Olga's Michael Jackson lotion! I didn't even get to see it!"

"I am sorry," whined Fat Olga again. "I will give you the money back, Lourdes. I can't return the guava bars because—because I already ate them—but here are your forty pesos." She handed me two crumpled bills.

"So, what was the Michael Jackson lotion made of?" Aurora asked.

"Oh, just butter, condensed milk, sunflower petals, water, and cereal," confessed Fat Olga, looking at me with a repentant air. "Lourdes, you aren't going to tell on me, are you?"

"It'll serve you right!" Marisol barked.

"No," I said weakly. "Don't worry, girl."

Why should I accuse Olga? It had been my own fault. I was a mulatta, the daughter of another mulatta, and the granddaughter of a *negra*. Better accept that fact and learn to live with it.

"I still can't understand why you bought the froth, Lourdes," Aurora said. "You have such nice skin. It's permanently tanned, so pretty and dark."

A wall fell silently in the darkness of our barracks and strange landscapes appeared on it. I saw the Ivory Coast and the Port of Vigo, where my ancestors had lived and from where they had departed, voluntarily or not, to start a new life on the other side of the Atlantic. I saw Grandma Gloria clean floors and my black great-great grandmother cut cane. I saw *Mami* break her bonds and leave the Vista Alegre Street house with a suitcase in hand, her cinnamon skin gleaming proudly under the sun . . .

Outside the barracks Chabela sang a *cadencia* that seemed to have been written especially for me.

Dicen que lo negro es feo,
yo digo que no es verdad.
El cielo de noche es negro
y mira qué bello está.
Alo, alo cua-cua-cuá María Cocuyé, cua-cua-cua.
(They say that black is ugly
I say it isn't true.
The night sky is black
and look how pretty it is.)
Alo, alo cua-cua-cuá María Cocuyé, cua-cua-cua.

⊰ CHAPTER XXXIII ⊱

M ANY YEARS AGO, *Babalú Ayé, disgusted with the other orishas' ways, decided to retire to the woods and live there by himself. He didn't approve of all the love affairs going on around him because he was, and still is, a very austere saint. He found out that Changó was a womanizer—he even went after his own mother, Yemayá! He heard that Oshún had two or three lovers at the same time. He angrily realized that men and women were led astray by the orishas' bad example. And he held all of them in contempt.*

So he took his burlap sack and left Ilé-Ifé, the orishas' kingdom. He went to a distant cave and remained there, ignored and alone. At first his presence wasn't missed, but after a while the other orishas noticed that the trees were losing their leaves. Herbs and flowers withered and died too, because they lacked the blessing of Babalú Ayé, the lord of plants and seeds.

Frightened, the orishas sent messenger after messenger to Babalú, asking him to return to Ilé-Ifé. Yemayá pleaded and offered him a chest full of ocean pearls and pink seashells. Changó brandished his powerful sword and threatened to set Babalú's cave on fire with a thunderbolt. Oyá meekly promised they would mend their wicked ways. Everything was in vain, as wise Babalú Ayé knew they would not bridle their improper passions. He remained in the woods and sent all the emissaries away with irate words.

Three long months passed. The trees lost all their leaves and only naked, brown branches swayed sadly in the cool air. The tasty yellow mangoes, the red papayas, and the mouth-watering bananas had all disappeared from the earth. The orishas shivered, and they went hungry for the first time since the beginning of the world.

Then Oshún, tired of the general scarcity, swore she'd make Babalú come back. The orishas doubted it, as she had provoked Babalú's anger more often than anybody else with her tempestuous romances. How could fatuous, flirtatious Oshún succeed where brave Changó, prudent Yemayá, and smart Oyá had failed? Bah!

Oshún paid no attention to the orishas' gloomy predictions. She took a hollow pumpkin, filled it with honey, and went to the woods in search of Babalú. Once she found him, she didn't say a word. She started to dance, looking him in the eye, and offered him from time to time her fingers dipped in honey. Entranced, Babalú Ayé followed her out of the woods and returned to Ilé-Ifé. The mangoes, papayas, and bananas came back with him. The trees grew green again and their branches were soon covered by new leaves.

After fickle Oshún left him, Babalú stayed lonely forever. Once a year he goes back to his cave to cry for Oshún's lost love, and all the fruits and greenness of the trees go with him. But he always returns to Ilé-Ifé, bringing the young sap of the spring in his burlap sack. Though he remains a chaste saint, he has never asked the other orishas to mend their ways again.

WHY DID I recall Grandma Inés's story when I saw Elena walk toward our camp? Maybe because the *guajirita* carried a basket on her head, as I imagined Oshún had carried her honey-filled pumpkin. Or because she reminded me of the slender, beautiful mulatta image of our Lady of Charity that Grandma Inés worshipped.

As Elena came closer, it dawned on me how little I knew about her. Since our arrival at the camp, I'd gotten to know most of my friends, classmates, and even teachers quite well. But the *guajirita*, with her enigmatic blue eyes and her too innocent smile, remained veiled in mystery.

I was in the girls' barracks by myself, looking out of the window. Comrade Katia had insisted that I take three days off. She wanted to make sure that my skin sores were completely healed, after the disastrous experiment with the Michael Jackson froth.

I watched Elena enter the principal's room. The old man wasn't there. He had gone to town earlier, accompanied by Juanito Lopesanto, to report on the brigades' production. When the *guajirita* emerged from the office, I waved to her and shouted, "Hey Elena! Come here for a minute. Do you have some time?"

She walked over to the barracks and soon was by my side.

"Were you looking for the *viejo*?" I asked her. "He won't be back until lunchtime."

"I brought him a few tamales," she said. "*Papá* Pancho told me to prepare them for him. You know, they are good friends." She opened her basket and took a bottle out. "He also sent him coffee but there is no point in leaving it in the office. It will be cool in ten minutes. Let's have some."

"Oh, I've never had coffee without milk," I answered. "My grandma says that it doesn't look proper in a young woman."

"But your grandma isn't here to watch you," Elena replied. "Drink it. It's good coffee, ground at home. It's not mixed with peas like the shitty packages they sell at the grocery store." She poured coffee into my tin cup and then took a long sip from the bottle.

"I thought you had classes in the mornings," I commented, after savoring the strong, sugary drink.

She shrugged. "There are classes, but I don't want to go to school anymore. I just show up a day or two every week, so the teachers don't have to take me off the list. They will pass all of us, anyway. Thank God I am in my last secondary school year. Once I am through with it, I will never enter a classroom again."

It surprised me to hear that Elena was only in the ninth grade. She looked older than fourteen. "*Coño!*" I exclaimed. "So you are not a *quinceañera* yet?"

"I'll be seventeen in July." The *guajirita* smiled. "I'm still in secondary school because I missed several years. When I was fifteen *Papá* Pancho was given two cows, and I had to milk them every morning and make butter later. Who feels like going to school after an hour of squeezing old cows' tits?"

"Did you really milk cows?" I gasped.

"Milked cows, fed pigs, sewed tobacco leaves, you name it," she sighed. "You think it's hard to sew a few *cujes* every day, but let me tell you, *niña*, that you *Habaneras* have an easy life. I used to wake up at five o'clock, when it was still dark, and spend a long hour with Lola and Cuca, our cows. Girl, did my hands hurt when I was done. Then the pig—"

"You had a piglet?!"

"What piglet? A big, fat, rotten oinker. He'd root around under my feet and make me fall, he was always so eager to get close to his food, the dirty beast. God, I hated that animal! I was so happy when *Papá* Pancho slaughtered him. At least we got some bacon out of him."

"What? Did you eat a pig you had taken care of?" I asked, baffled. "*Pobrecito!*"

"*Pobrecito*, my ass!" Elena laughed out loud. "That is why we have pigs, to eat their meat and get cracklings, bacon, and lard."

"Didn't you feel sorry for him?"

She shook her head. "*Ay*, Lourdes! I felt sorry for *myself*. What do you think we get in Pinar del Río with our ration card? I've heard that you are given a pound of meat every month in Havana. Here, half a pound, and that is in the good months. January, February, March, and April are bad ones this year. Popular Power makes us share our food with you guys, so we get even less. I haven't seen a steak since last November."

"Well, we also have problems in Havana," I said defensively, and began telling her about the toilet paper my family had stored for me and the use of our ass rags. But she didn't commiserate with me.

"You sure are spoiled, *Habanera*!" she remarked, grinning. "Toilet paper! I don't even remember when I last saw a roll. Here, my friend, we clean our behinds with tobacco leaves."

"Does it hurt?" I cringed.

"Not if they are soft enough," she said casually. "One shouldn't use very green leaves, though. They are too crisp. But that is the least of our problems," she added. The *guajirita* must have noticed my sympathetic expression because she patted my hand. Hers was strangely cold. "I am hoping we'll have water piped in this year. *Papá* Pancho has been asking Popular Power for it since I was five. Now we have to get water from the creek, where the Mother lives, you know. Some women take baths there but I have never done it." She lowered her eyes. "That's wrong."

Poor Elena. I sincerely pitied her. How lucky I was, having been born in *La Habana* where we had bathtubs, a few steaks, and a roll of toilet paper every month. The contrast between the city and the countryside was too obvious, almost offensive. I knew we had not attained communism yet, but shouldn't these differences be less marked in a socialist society? Why hadn't Fidel solved at least some of the problems that the *guajiros* had?

"As for the gas supply—forget it," Elena went on. "We cook with wood, like you do here in camp." The *guajirita* tilted her head, uncovering the scar that crossed her left cheek, which she usually kept hidden under her long curls. "I got this chopping wood. The ax got stuck in a log. One of those hard pieces of oak. When I tried to free the ax, it bounced back. Guess I should be thankful it didn't hurt my eyes." She hid the scar again. "Do you want more coffee? If I drink all this I won't be able to sleep tonight."

"But what were you doing with an ax?" I asked stupidly as she refilled my tin cup.

"Someone had to chop the wood, Lourdes. At home, it's just *Papá* Pancho and me. And he can't do everything. He works hard in the fields, and must help when the School-in-the-Fields brigades are here. Sometimes I don't see him for days."

"And your mother?"

No sooner had I pronounced these words than I realized what I'd done. The Michael Jackson lotion had not only affected my skin, but my brain as well. I'd heard that old Pancho was a widower, so Elena's mom must be dead. What a lack of sensitivity on my part. I was going to excuse myself for my indiscretion when the *guajirita* replied calmly, "She's somewhere in *La Habana*. I don't know where. She left one day, when I was a little girl, and she never returned. I don't blame her, though. *This* is not life, Lourdes. And she was very pretty, everybody says so."

I couldn't tell if she was being sincere. Had *Mami* left *me* in such an awful place and gone to the city, I would have never forgiven her.

"Fat Olga told us she'd died," I said. "Then why do people call your father The Widower?"

"It was my stepmother who died. She went to the creek to swim and the Mother-of-Water got her. We found her drowned and headless."

"Headless?" I repeated. "*Ay!*"

"Yes, we found her body one day, and her head a week later, half eaten by the fish." Elena's eyes gleamed, but there were no tears in them. Her voice was flat. "Our neighbors started gossiping and said she had been killed. The police came and looked around, but they couldn't find the murderer. Of course, there was none. The Mother-of-Water must have been really angry," she added with an odd smile. "But that *cabrona* deserved it."

"Why?"

"During the three years we lived together, I went hungry all the time. When *Papá* Pancho wasn't looking, she ate my food, hit me with a leather belt, and ordered me around as if I were a slave. She drank all the cows' milk and only gave me water with a spoonful of sugar for breakfast." Elena took the empty coffee bottle and threw it in her basket. "I got as thin as a lizard. She'd make fun of me and call me skinny cat, *gata flaca*. What a bitch!"

"Like Cinderella's stepmother, huh?" I tried to make a joke but my voice cracked. Elena's expression when she described her stepmother's death had frankly frightened me.

"Who's Cinderella?"

She'd never heard of Snow White, Cinderella, or Little Red Riding Hood. I soon found out that Elena hadn't even read a children's book. Any book, in fact. She didn't like to read.

"I can't really do it very well," she confessed. "It takes me a long time to understand the words, and when I get to the end of the page, I've already forgotten what was written at the beginning. That *puta* of my stepmother used to hit me when I got low grades at school, but she never thought of helping me with my homework. I am so happy she's dead and buried! Ha!"

I offered to tell her all about Snow White. I wanted to change the subject because our conversation made me feel extremely nervous. She didn't seem interested in fairy tales, though. She cut me off with a loud yawn even before the Seven Dwarfs appeared. "Better tell me something about *La Habana*. Tell me about the nice places where *Habaneros* go to eat. Is it true that the guys who serve you wear uniforms and ties? Are they handsome?" she asked eagerly.

"You mean in the restaurants?" I asked. It was my turn to impart information. "Yes, the waiters wear uniforms, black pants and tie, and a white shirt. Some of them are handsome, others are ugly and fat."

"What kind of food can you get in restaurants?"

"It depends. *El Mandarín* and *El Polinesio* have Chinese food, while *La Romanita* and *Montecatini* serve Italian dishes: pizza, spaghetti, cannelloni . . . But everything is rationed, so you can only get one dish of pizza and one of spaghetti. And they don't let anyone have seconds. But their food is so good. Their lobster pizzas! Their ham-filled cannelloni! Mmm!"

"Wish I could eat a pizza." Elena's blue eyes had become dreamy. She smacked her lips. "And the clothing stores, are they beautiful?"

I didn't consider the Havana clothing stores to be particularly beautiful. Not compared to those that appeared in Yankee movies, replete with mirrors, carpets, and ornamented windows full of glittering merchandise. "Well, some of them are *more or less* OK," I replied. "The new ones, where you can buy things without the clothing-ration card, are not that bad. There are some nice Vietnamese dresses and blouses. There are good Bulgarian perfumes. And those Soviet radios of the *Selena* brand. And Chinese electric fans."

"Are the stores opened all day?"

"No. They close at five-thirty."

She paused briefly and then asked, "Don't people go there at night and steal things?"

"Uh—no. Not very often, that I know of," I answered, surprised. "Why?"

"Well, you *Habaneros* must be real fools," Elena grinned, "or

first-class *pendejos*. A clothing store with dresses, radios, and perfumes wouldn't last one night here. It'd be emptied in less time
than a cow needs to switch her tail."

She looked as if she quite liked such an idea. I privately thought
that Elena herself wouldn't mind sneaking inside a store after it
closed and making off with a few things.

"And the beach? Have you gone to the beach? I've seen post-
cards of Varadero," she bragged. "I know that it is blue and much
bigger than our creek. But is it very deep? Is the water warm? How
does it taste?"

Her stark ignorance shocked and at the same time amused me. I
couldn't believe how little the *guajirita* knew about things that I'd
always considered a normal part of life.

"I go to the Guanabo beaches very often, they are closer to the
city. And I've *been* to Varadero," I told her, trying not to sound stuck
up. "My parents and I stayed at the *Hotel Internacional* last summer.
Yes, Varadero is blue, green, and white, and there are pink shells in
the sand. The water is warm, clean, salty and ... " I didn't know how
to continue. How can you describe Varadero?

"What else?" she asked. She looked anguished and curious, hanging on my every word.

"It smells like pickles," I said. "But not everybody is allowed to
go there and stay at the hotel," I went on. Maybe Elena wouldn't
feel so badly if she knew that not all *Habaneros* had gone to
Varadero. "We did because it was a reward that the Party gave to
my father."

"The Party is like the government, isn't it?" Elena frowned, as if
she were not very sure. "And Fidel is the owner of it?"

"Well, Fidel is—the leader. The commander in chief."

I wished Elena wouldn't ask me questions about politics. I had a few doubts myself. Fortunately, a motorcycle that had stopped in front of the camp attracted the *guajirita's* attention.

"It's Albertico!" she exclaimed. "He came early today. Look, someone brought him. See you later, Lourdes."

"Thanks for the coffee," I said.

She ran outside. I wondered who Albertico was. A boy? A *guajiro*? I had never heard that name in camp. I returned to the window. Elena and the principal walked together to his office, went inside and closed the door.

Now he'd eat the tamales, I thought, feeling envious and hungry. How silly I had been! I should have asked Elena to save a tamale for me.

Since nothing else was available, I turned to my provisions and began nibbling an old chocolate cookie. Two hours later, at lunchtime, I suddenly recalled that Alberto was our principal's first name. Strange that Elena had called him "Albertico," a familiar diminutive. Yet I didn't think she meant to be disrespectful. She simply had no manners, but it wasn't her fault.

In the evening, when the brigades had returned, I entertained my friends with a detailed account of my chat with Elena. I repeated some of her funniest questions about our city, the restaurants, the beach.

"So she hasn't even finished secondary school." Fat Olga shook her head. "*Coño!* And Comrade Katia called Elena a future developer of communist agriculture. Well, I'd say that with 'developers' like her, our communist agriculture is going to be in deep shit. Twenty years from now, we'll be getting half a pound of potatoes every month, instead of five."

"I still can't believe it!" cackled Marisol. "That girl has never eaten out. Pinar del Río is definitely the ass-end of the world."

"*Bueno*, I've been in a restaurant only three or four times in my life," Aurora replied. "And always with a guy. In my house there is never enough money to throw away on such luxuries."

"But you should have heard all the questions she asked me about the stores, and the food." I said. "As if she were from another planet. She thinks that *La Habana* is the most wonderful place on earth!"

"Everything is relative in this world," gravely asserted Fat Olga, who was in a philosophical mood that day. "When you think you are in trouble, you can always find someone who is in a much worse situation than you are. For these poor *guajiros*, *La Habana* is what *La Yuma* is for people like us."

CHAPTER XXXIV

ISPS OF GRAY clouds flew over the camp. *Framboyán* flowers and leaves fell like a steady rain to the earth. Swept by an invisible broom, the leaves danced. Sunflower petals, paper bags, old newspaper pages, cigarette butts, straw hats, and purple flowers danced with them.

The strong wind that blows in mid-April is called by the old people the Lent wind, *el viento de Cuaresma*. Grandma Gloria hated the Lent wind and closed all the windows and doors as soon as it started blowing. "When I was young, I didn't leave my house during Lent except to go to church," she would say. "The Lent wind makes people do wild things. It runs between the legs of women and inside the pants of men. It carries the germs of madness and lust."

I seldom noticed the wind at home. In humid, hot Havana any kind of breeze is welcome. In Pinar del Río I discovered the rhythm of the seasons which passed practically unnoticed in the city. And life was agitated in the city, no question. The following Sunday, when *Mami* visited me, I noticed the effort she had to make to carry the bags of food and clothes from the bus. Her arms and wrists were almost as thin as mine. For a moment I feared that the wind would blow her away, she looked so fragile. Her expression had changed, too. She seemed more determined and at peace.

We didn't talk much. *Mami* avoided any mention of Grandma Inés's house. I knew she didn't want to press me about moving to Mantilla. But I had to decide. Only three weeks were left and once in Havana, where would I go? My kingdom of dolls in Grandma Gloria's was certainly more inviting than the *orishas'* nest at Grandma Inés's.

THE LENT wind blew with particular force every evening when we waited outside to enter the dining hall. A film of dust covered our lips while our stomachs growled with repressed hunger. The ever-present smell of burned rice came from the kitchen and we cursed the queue and the lazy *guajiras*.

One evening the dining hall line was advancing at the leisurely pace of a well-fed snail as the wind slapped my face and particles of dirt blew into my eyes. I looked for Aurora. She hadn't showed up yet, though she was generally on time when it came to food. I asked Fat Olga to keep my place and went to the girls' barracks. Aurora wasn't there either. I had flopped onto our bunk bed to rest for a few minutes when the door opened and two people came in.

In the light of the dying lamp I recognized Juanito and Aurora. Male teachers and boys were forbidden to enter our barracks, but the couple walked in holding hands, as if they were strolling around Malecón Drive. Shutting my eyes, I pretended to be asleep. Juanito and Aurora got into Chabela's bed, giggling and kissing each other.

"Juan, are you really going to marry me?"

"Sure."

"And we'll live in your house, won't we?"

"Yes, *mima*, yes. Whatever you want. Hmmm!"

At that moment Juanito became aware of my presence. But

Aurora said, "Oh, Lourdes sleeps very soundly. Don't worry. She can't hear us."

One minute later they were making out again. I couldn't avoid listening to Juanito's moans and to Aurora's scared warning, "Be careful of the baby!" And I couldn't avoid silently cursing them both while anticipating the finale, the ultimate rapture, the great ecstasy I had heard about for so long but never experienced myself. A reluctant witness filled with envy, disgust, and curiosity in equal parts, I waited without daring to move or make a sound.

The explosion came, though not the way I had expected it, in a torrent of lewd sighs. "What on earth is going on, Juan?" Comrade Katia screamed.

Chabela's bunk bed squeaked loudly as Juanito and Aurora became unglued. I heard Aurora's agitated breathing. Then Juanito's boots and Comrade Katia's sandals moved away quickly, but not so fast that I couldn't also hear his feeble attempts at justification, "Katy, let me explain to you what we were—"

And Comrade Katia's irate reply, "Go to *el carajo* with your explanations, man!"

I opened my eyes. Aurora was quickly buttoning her blouse. "Why did you bring him here?" I asked her. "You shouldn't have done that!"

She shrugged.

From our window I saw Comrade Katia and Juanito. They had stopped under the *framboyán*. Comrade Katia spoke with a frenzied rage that I never suspected she could feel, except against Yankee imperialism. The wind brought her words to the barracks as clearly as if she were still standing inside. "You are a *cochino*, Juan! A depraved, dirty womanizer! *Cabrón!*"

Aurora and I looked at each other.

"See? Comrade Katia is mad now," I said. "She is probably going to scold you too."

"Scold me? Why?" Aurora replied, angry. "Did I borrow her pussy? And why is she screaming at my man? The fat, myopic, envious broad!"

Obviously that was not the right moment to inform Aurora about the relationship between Juanito and Comrade Katia. We joined our brigade in the waiting line. The *guajiras* had prepared a magnificent supper of canned Russian meat, sweet potatoes, and flan but Aurora hardly nibbled the dessert.

"You should eat everything on your tray," Chabela advised her, "even if you don't feel like it. Now you have to eat for two."

"I wish I could," Aurora whispered.

I remembered a certain night when I had also been unable to eat. How things had changed. How I had changed. I feasted on Aurora's untouched meal.

By 9:30 all the brigades had finished eating. Fat Olga and Marisol played cards. Chabela heated a can of evaporated milk on her portable brazier. Aurora rested on her bed, silent and frowning. I tried to read *Che's Journal* but couldn't concentrate.

Comrade Katia approached us. Aurora turned pale, but the teacher didn't even look at her. "Can you come with me, Lourdes?" she asked.

"Yes, Comrade," I said obediently.

Then she noticed that one of the refugees was smoking and ran to scold her. *"Hija,* be careful what you say," Aurora begged. "Don't tell on us."

"Don't worry," I reassured her. "I'll defend you."

I followed Comrade Katia's butt. It didn't wag menacingly anymore but swayed humbly behind her. Once we were in the workshop room, the teacher took her eyeglasses off and I realized she had been crying. Her eyes were red and she blew her nose into a checkered handkerchief.

"What happened today is inexcusable and shameful," she began. "Of course, Aurora is not an innocent little girl but Juan Lopesanto is an adult. He should have been more responsible. Now, what do you know about them? Did she seduce him? Or did he lead her astray?"

Two voices resounded at the same time inside my head. *Tell Comrade Katia that it was Juanito's fault! Save Aurora!*

Save Aurora? What did she do when Vladimir was picking on me? She laughed!

"Lourdes, tell me the truth," Comrade Katia pleaded. "I need to know who is to blame in this scandalous affair."

The truth is that she is a puta, *teacher.*

Say that and you'll lose Aurora. Not only will she hate you, but Comrade Katia will kick her out of school and you won't see her again.

I took a deep breath. How many lies had I told already? One more didn't matter. I finally answered that Juanito had been after Aurora for a long time and that she had always rebuffed him. "He followed her to the barracks and chased her," I said. "She tried to stop him but—"

"OK, I believe you," Comrade Katia cut me off. "I'll cover up the whole thing, for our high school's reputation and for Aurora's sake," she added with a sigh. "Do the same, please."

Back in the barracks I told Aurora about the result of my interview with Comrade Katia, embellishing the story slightly. "Thanks, Lourdes," she hugged me. "Thanks, little sister, thanks!"

I avoided looking at Che's poster. I could not stand the silent reproach of his burning, magnetic eyes.

❧ CHAPTER XXXV ❧

DESPITE MY SILENCE and Comrade Katia's, the following day everybody in camp knew about the affair. Not a soul was ignorant of even the most embarrassing details, though an inaccurate version stated that the principal, not Comrade Katia, had caught the couple in the act. Aurora's alleged pregnancy was also discussed at length.

"Who is the father of her baby?" Natasha grinned. "Juanito? Tomás? A *guajiro*? Probably that whore doesn't know herself!"

Fresh gossip, like mud, filled the barracks. Carried by the Lent wind, the mud flew throughout the fields and spread a layer of slime during the breaks. Juanito didn't come close to Aurora but she excused him. "He's probably waiting until things cool off. *Pobrecito!* They can even kick him out of the school system!" she complained, weeping. "It's not fair. We love each other. Do you think he will lose his job?"

"No, he'll be fine," I comforted her. "Comrade Katia is not that kind of person. Our teachers are good at covering up for each other. Remember what happened when the cop came?"

Aurora didn't think about herself. She wasn't the same girl who had once threatened to accuse Juanito of taking advantage of her so as to send him to prison. Still under her lover's spell, she acted like a devoted, loving wife. But in the end, it made no difference.

Envy, which at one time had been disguised as admiration, revealed its true, ugly face. Poisonous comments came out of the gossipers' mouths, destroying what was left of Aurora's reputation. Things had happened so fast that it seemed as if a wicked fairy had turned the former Beauty into the Dumped Slut with a quick wave of her wand. The most ill-natured girls would talk about "mad *papayas* that cannot stay still." Others prohibited their boyfriends from exchanging a word with "that *puta*." Only Elena, Fat Olga, and I defended Aurora. "She hasn't done anything that you wouldn't have done, if you had had the opportunity!" I yelled. Being a leader, even if just for a couple of weeks, had made me bolder.

"Everybody screws around here!" Fat Olga proclaimed. "She had bad luck, but it could have happened to anyone."

Elena added, "You *Habaneras* are so mean."

Plain, quiet girls savored their vindication. In the last political workshop Comrade Katia brought up the topic of prostitution again. While the audience laughed and winked, Natasha stood up and emphatically asserted that not all prostitutes lived in capitalist countries or worked for money. They were found everywhere, she remarked, and the worst among them would just do it *gratis*, for free.

Poor Aurora! I still loved her, but my love had been tainted with pity and contempt. I caught myself secretly rejoicing in the difference between our positions, all the advantage being on my side. Thanks to Comrade Katia's protection I was now a popular leader. Because of my relationship with Ernesto, even though it had ended, people didn't see me as a child anymore. But I had something precious to guard. I was a *señorita*, a virgin, and it made me more desirable for a serious relationship than Aurora, pregnant and ridiculed.

Aurora foresaw gloomy consequences for the nights spent in the grass behind the boys' barracks. Her self-assurance and haughtiness melted day by day as our return to Havana approached. Gone were her wedding plans and the honeymoon in Varadero. Gone was the house in El Vedado. Gone with the Lent wind, vanished like Juanito Lopesanto, who one evening sneaked out of the camp without saying good-bye to anybody, not even to his lover.

CERTAINLY PEOPLE would never treat Aurora the same. She represented an easy target for the boys, a warning for us girls. And after Juanito's flight, she had lost even more of her prestige. She wasn't the beauty of the camp anymore, but the abandoned pregnant mistress of a spineless guy.

I spent so much time consoling Aurora that I practically forgot about Ernesto's desertion, my parents' divorce, and most of my own difficulties. Aurora often said, holding my hands, "Lulu, you are a real friend, the only one who's always been there for me."

Certainly people would never treat *me* the same. The principal himself had praised my work when I received the *Vanguardia* certificates. Those who considered me a *chivata*, a telltale, were careful not to cross my path. My subordinates showered me with candy, offered to clean my rubber boots, and openly brownnosed me.

I felt proud of all the attention I received, not only from my friends and the other kids, but also from Crazy Jorge. Despite the odd position in which we were placed by *Papi's* and Marietta's relationship, I had come to like Jorge. After Vladimir's expulsion he had congratulated me for getting revenge for the *plasta de vaca* incident. "Well done, Lourdes!" he said. "Let people know that if they don't fuck with you, you won't fuck with them, but if they do—" And Jorge finished his statement with a very expressive gesture. Though his vocabulary wasn't precisely "refined" I appreciated his support.

Then he handed me a package sent, I assumed, by Grandma Gloria. But when I opened it in the girls' barracks, I was delighted to discover that it contained the Russian flashlight *Papi* had bought for me.

"I don't view Jorge as a monster anymore," I confessed to Aurora, "I guess that we are going to be like brother and sister, don't you think?"

"Brother, my ass, Lourdes!" she replied with her most slutty smile. "Such a handsome guy. If I were you, I'd already be flirting with him."

"But he is Chabela's boyfriend," I reminded her.

"So?"

When I saw Jorge the following week, I unconsciously looked him up and down. Aurora was quite right. For the first time I realized how good-looking he was, six feet tall, with short, brown, wavy hair. I admired his broad shoulders and tight muscles. Hmmm.

"Don't tell me you don't like him," purred Aurora, pinching my arm. I blushed. "Silly Chabela is so lucky. And you, little fox, are you trying to snatch him, as I advised you to do?"

I immediately denied the accusation but she replied, laughing, "There is nothing wrong with it, *hija*. You are a woman. The problem is, you haven't found the way to your *papaya* yet. You need some help from a more experienced hand. Who knows, you may be getting it quite soon."

Aurora went to the barracks, leaving me intrigued. Some help. . . . What had she meant by that?

☙ CHAPTER XXXVI ☚

AN EARSPLITTING VIBRATION spread through the barracks like a drop of black ink in water. The shrill sound of the
camp siren woke me up. My face and crotch felt wet. I had been
dreaming but couldn't remember what my dream was about. Yet I
knew I had seen a familiar face in it. Aurora's? Jorge's? Lazily, I got
out of bed and put on my work clothes.

It was Monday. On Mondays our breakfast tasted worse than on
other days, the *cujes* looked heavier and bigger, the tobacco needles
turned into daggers. Amiable conversations degenerated into loud
arguments. Most of the fights at the School-in-the-Fields happened
during anger-filled Monday mornings.

In the cramped dining hall Aurora bumped into Natasha's
chair. "*Estúpida!*" Natasha shouted, furious. She pointed at the
white stream of spilled milk running toward the edge of the table.
"Now give me yours. I am not going to go without breakfast
because of you."

She grabbed Aurora's tray. Aurora pushed her away and yelled, "I
didn't do it intentionally, you idiot!"

"*Tu madre!*" Natasha replied.

Aurora slapped her in the face. A circle of spectators surrounded
them at once. *Tu madre* was the ultimate insult. Those who failed to

answer it with a good blow to the head were labeled as *pendejos*. Even if Aurora didn't feel much sympathy for her mother she couldn't let it go. It was a matter of honor.

"*La galleta,*" someone shouted, delighted, meaning "the slap" and by association, a fight. Natasha tried to kick Aurora in the stomach but missed her target. Aurora seized Natasha's ponytail. Our dining hall became a battlefield. The onlookers cheered their favorite fighter, insulted the other one, or offered advice.

"Hit her with your tray, Natasha!"

"Go, Aurora! Kick her flabby little ass!"

"Hey, girls, don't play dirty!"

Fights at the School-in-the-Fields were great entertainment. They combined the immediate emotion of a fierce scuffle with the prospect of long, succulent gossip in the aftermath. A good quarrel's shock wave would help dissolve boredom for a week.

"I'm going to drag you by your kinky hair!" Aurora roared. "Now *I* shit on your mother three times, bitch!"

Natasha retreated. The two girls glared balefully at each other like angry cats in a staring match.

Every time I saw a fight, I'd think of the one I had witnessed at home, between *Mami* and Grandma Gloria. I remembered *Mami*, noisily sporting her *chancletas*. Her *chancletas* were unpolished sandals consisting of a piece of wood and two plastic straps. The *cha-ca-ta* sound of the sandals clapping on the tiled floor never failed to annoy Grandma Gloria. Inside the house Grandma Gloria wore only flannel slippers she had knit by herself that produced a gentle *fla-fla-fla*.

Cha-ca-ta. *Mami* went around our living room watering the plants and dusting the wicker chairs. Grandma Gloria sat at the dining table in front of a copper pot full of rice. Carefully she put aside the bad grains and crushed the offensive rice weevils, the *gorgojos*. *Cha-ca-ta*.

"Barbarita, you should change out of those *chancletas*. *Dear*, they make a horrid noise. And I have a headache," complained Grandma Gloria while *Mami* busied herself with the dusting cloth.

Grandma Gloria's voice sounded sharp and shrill like a fingernail scratching a slate. Whenever the *chancleta* issue was brought up, *Mami* would reply that she liked to be comfortable while doing the house chores. Chores that no one else would do, she emphasized. Grandma Gloria pronounced "dear" with a particularly sarcastic intonation. *Papi's* philandering had already electrified the atmosphere, making it ready to explode.

"DON'T RUN, *cabrona*!" Aurora barked. "Come here and I'll kick your ass!"

Natasha stopped, facing Aurora with an unexpected exhibition of courage, "You and who else?"

"I don't need help to crush a roach like you."

"A roach, huh?" Natasha spat at her. "A roach like the one Juanito Lopesanto said you have under your belly button?"

This was Aurora's secret. Not a real secret, as she couldn't conceal her hairy mole when we had to bathe and change clothes in each other's sight. But we all knew she was ashamed of this minor flaw on her otherwise perfect body. Natasha had gone too far, and mentioning Juanito's name had added insult to injury.

"LOOK, *VIEJA, no me joda más!*" *Mami* cried. "If you want to clean the house in high heels, do it yourself! But do not bother me when

I am working like a mule and you are seated with your *papaya* undisturbed!"

"Indecent!" Grandma Gloria rose slowly from her chair. "Curse all you wish in the tenement where you were born, but hold your tongue here!"

"It doesn't come out of my ass to hold my tongue!" *Mami* tore the dusting cloth into two pieces. "And I am not working anymore today. I am not the housemaid."

"No, you are the queen," retorted Grandma Gloria. "Queen Shit! Of course, I never expected much of a dirty mulatta like you, but you are definitely out of control."

"Now, I am dirty," *Mami* screeched. "Sure. What about you, old woman? Your farts don't stink, huh? Oh, they smell like roses!"

"As a matter of honor, I won't lower myself to argue with you," Grandma Gloria drawled. "I just want you to leave my house immediately," she added. "Right now!"

AURORA POUNCED on Natasha. Before anyone could move or do a thing to avoid it, they were squirming on the floor. She twisted Natasha's arms and slapped her again. Natasha gave out a long wail. A few girls laughed while Chabela and I attempted to separate the contenders. Suddenly, Natasha freed her right hand and searched inside her pocket.

"Watch out!" I yelled. "She has a *cuje* needle!"

The tiny, sharpened metal rod went straight to Aurora's face. A chorus of frightened screams sounded but no one dared come close to the fighters. Natasha chortled. A drop of blood stained Aurora's work shirt. Chabela ran out crying for the teachers.

"Now, tell me about my mother!" Natasha gasped, momentarily victorious. "Call me *cabrona* now, come on!"

"SHUT UP!" *Mami* gritted her teeth. "Clean your mouth before talking to me, old *pendeja!*"

"Get out of here! Get out!" Grandma Gloria squealed hysterically. "Dirty mulatta! Out!"

Mami grabbed a broom and brandished it shouting, "Who is going to kick me out?"

Grandma Gloria seized the copper pot and menacingly approached *Mami*. "*I* am going to do it! Have you forgotten who the owner of this house is?"

AURORA RECOVERED. She punched Natasha in the chin and threw her backward.

"What is this?" Comrade Katia rushed into the dining hall. "Unbelievable! Aurora, *you* are fighting again?!"

"She started it, teacher," Natasha sobbed from the floor. "She hit me first!"

"*Chivata!*" Aurora snarled. "Cry baby! Chickenshit!"

PAPI, WHO had been working in the garage, hurried to the living room. "Barbarita! *Mamá!* What are you arguing about?" he asked, getting between the two enraged women. "What's going on?"

"This old bitch!" *Mami* screamed.

"This mulatta *de mierda*!" Grandma Gloria yelled.

He tried to pacify them with hushes and nervous gestures toward my bedroom, where I had witnessed the scene through a crack in the door. My heart was torn into two pieces like *Mami's* dusting cloth.

⚜

"IF YOU get into another fight, Aurora, you will be expelled," Comrade Katia warned her. "You are impossible! Now, both of you are going to stay in camp and clean the outhouses. And I want to see them spotless when I return."

Natasha accepted her punishment humbly, but Aurora gave Comrade Katia the finger behind her back.

"Calm down, *hija,*" said Chabela soothingly, taking Aurora by the arm. "You are worse than Jorge. He used to get into fights all the time because he was mad at the world. But he is a guy. Why do you—?"

"Don't you think that I have good reasons to be mad at the world too?" replied Aurora somberly. Her brown eyes were dark puddles of hate.

⊰ CHAPTER XXXVII ⊱

THE WALLS DANCED with the ceiling. Long *cujes* swirled around like giant ballerinas' legs. Green garlands of tobacco leaves moved rhythmically in the air. Even the wind whistled a *quinceañera* ballad. Chayanne sang *"Tiempo de vals"* on the radio and the world stopped as my favorite song played.

I saw myself waltzing with *Papi* in our living room, the hem of my long pink satin dress coyly held in one hand. I saw *Mami* in a corner, trying not to sway her hips like a *rumbera* while Grandma Gloria served *ponche de huevo* in her Bohemian crystal punch bowl.

Someone had sneaked a portable radio into the tobacco house and *"Tiempo de vals"* took me back to Havana on its magic carpet of harmony. But the song ended and I returned to Pinar del Río. The *cujes* came back to their pegs, the leaves fell down, I donned my earth-stained denim pants and wrinkled shirt again—

My only duty as a leader was to make sure that the *cuje* girls kept busy sewing. Our brigade worked in the rear of the tobacco house, far from the other girls' sight. Every morning I took a book with me and sat in a corner to read, but I would walk around every half hour to inspect my subordinates' work. "Is everything OK?" I'd ask first.

"Yes, *jefecita*."

"I'll check it out soon," I'd alert them. "In five minutes." They all looked really busy when I passed by them.

At 10:30 a girl reported that our company had run out of *cujes*. Three more brigades were in the same situation. The supply teams had been transferred to a distant field and no one knew when they would return. I had not forgotten the principal's prohibition about visiting the *guajiros*, yet my underlings had to—at least—give the impression that they were doing something useful. I could have given them the day off, but it wouldn't look good on our monthly report. And if the other companies followed my example and work stopped completely, then we'd all be in trouble.

After thinking about it for a while, I volunteered to go to Pancho's cabin and ask him for a new batch of *cujes*. Maybe Elena would offer me *arroz con leche*, a piece of homemade cheese, or, if nothing else, a cup of strong coffee.

A tenuous fog softened the landscape. It smelled like fresh rain and forget-me-nots. The silky grass under my feet reminded me of the plush carpets that covered the *Hotel Internacional's* floors. I breathed in deeply, enjoying the morning fragrance, glad to be out of the stuffy tobacco house. But it was also a cool, windy day. Crossing the dew-sprinkled fields, I missed my lost coat for the first time.

I hurried by the creek, the Mother-of-Water's aquatic home. I thought of Elena's headless stepmother, killed by the beast. It couldn't be a lie. Hadn't Chabela seen it too? The waters seemed innocent, though. As innocent and placid as Elena's blue eyes. . . .

The closer I got to Pancho's cabin, the poorer and more dilapidated it looked. It stood amid tall bushes and small trees like a big, deformed frog. A dirty jute curtain covered the only window. Next to the half-open door breathed a barrel filled with garbage, blanketed with flies. I followed the star-shaped prints that a turkey had left in the muddy pathway and stopped on the threshold. Music came from inside, the familiar signature tune of a Yankee cartoon.

"*Hola!*" I said. No one answered. I tiptoed in. Once in the house, the first thing I saw was a TV set. Our camp's TV set, placed on a plywood shelf facing the front door. On the screen, in a beautiful *La Yuma* parlor, Sylvester ran after Tweety Bird. I looked around and spotted the fluorescent lamp that used to be in our workshop. And the three chairs that had once furnished the principal's office were also there. And the old electric fan. But the biggest surprise came when Elena returned from the backyard wearing—my blue coat.

For a moment both of us were silent. The *guajirita* spoke first, asking in a defiant tone, "Why did you come here? You are not allowed to leave the fields."

"It doesn't matter why I came," I said curtly. "Now I want to know what you are doing with my coat."

"This coat is mine, shit eater!" Elena replied insolently. "My father got it for me."

"That is not true!" I yelled, shocked by her brazenness. "My mother bought it. And you stole it."

The sympathy that I had once felt for Elena vanished, eclipsed by my anger and by the drastic change in her. Her face was now crimson, her lips tight, and her blue eyes gleamed like a wildcat's. Instinctively, I backed off. The *sinsonte* had turned into a spider.

"Are you calling me a thief?" Elena took a bellicose stance. "Get lost or I will take my machete and cut your fucking head off. It won't be the first time that I've done it," she murmured, as if talking to herself.

With a shiver I recalled the story about her beheaded stepmother. Chabela was right, the *guajirita* had a woman's eyes. Actually, she had an *old* woman's eyes, stern, embittered, and cold.

But she isn't bullying me, I told myself. Neither Elena nor Vladimir nor the Mother-of-Water. Never again!

The memories of other affronts helped me recover from my initial shock. I calmly told Elena, "Look here, *guajira*. Comrade Katia is a friend of mine. When I tell her where she can find the TV set and the electric fan, she will call the police again. You know what happened to Vladimir. How would you like to keep him company in the reeducation camp?"

Elena knew it would be impossible for her to hide everything before the teacher came. After a moment's pause, she took off the coat and quietly handed it to me. I felt bolder and asked for Aurora's black T-shirt. Without a word, the *guajirita* disappeared behind a faded flowered curtain. When I looked at the TV again, Granny had entered the room and was chasing Sylvester with her broom.

An appetizing red bean soup boiled in the kitchen. I peeked in. The camp's rice cooker stood on top of the wood oven. *Coño*, the only reason Elena hadn't ransacked the outhouses was because there was nothing but shit in them.

The *guajirita* came back and gave me the T-shirt. "You are not going to take the cooker, too, are you?" She added in a plaintive voice, "You guys are leaving soon. Why would you care for these old things? They weren't yours in the first place."

The fact that they weren't hers either didn't seem to bother Elena. She also offered me her Slava watch and a bottle of perfume. "I want nothing," I said. "Just tell me how you carried the TV set and the electric fan out of the camp."

"I took the clothes and *Papá* Pancho brought home the big items," she answered, glancing at the Slava, probably stolen, too. We returned to the living room and she opened the door. "Well, now you have your coat and the T-shirt. Adiós!"

"Wait a moment! I will not go back to the camp until I know

the whole truth," I replied with my best imitation of the tough guys who appeared in American films. "I saw a monster once, after dark. It was big, ugly, with four horns. What did you have to do with it?"

"A monster?" she shrugged. "*Papá* Pancho went to the camp at night, but he never took anybody with him. With four horns— Could it be my *viejo* holding a table or a chair over his head? You thought it was the Mother-of-Water, huh?"

Elena erupted in laughter. The comical side of the situation struck me and I started laughing too. My past terrors dissolved. The monster! The Mother-of-Water! The ghost! Ah, Elena, *guajirita cabrona*! Ah, sly *mulatica*, little Oshún! You are the worthy daughter of the Mother-of-Water, smart and cunning, a snake in woman's clothes.

"These foolish *Habaneras*—" Elena sneered. But she kept looking at her watch, evidently concerned. "Lourdes, you have to go now. Please!"

Tweety Bird was back in his cage, safely singing "I tawt I taw a puddy tat" when I left.

I wondered why Elena was so anxious to shoo me away. Feeling both shrewd and wicked, I hid in the nearby bushes and waited. Ten minutes later, our principal walked straight to the *guajiro*'s house, panting and stumbling over the damp rocks of the pathway. I saw Elena go out to meet him. I saw the old man pat her breasts and kiss her on the lips. That kiss turned my stomach. They went inside the house together and closed the front door.

Like a bonfire in the darkness, the truth shone vividly in my mind. I remembered the night I saw the principal search under the *guajirita*'s skirt. He'd been close to her at the Valentine's Day celebration, too. She'd brought him tamales, cleaned his office, and called him Albertico—Elena was a *puta*! Worse than Aurora. Aurora loved Juanito, but Elena couldn't love our ugly, crotchety, fat principal. She had just used him to get a few ragged clothes and some gadgets. Pancho, that severe and dignified *guajiro*, was his daughter's pimp and a vulgar thief. And the principal, so serious and stiff, always talking about revolutionary values, was a lecherous old bastard.

Comrade Katia had said that *Now, thanks to the conquests of socialism, prostitution, once a national stigma, has forever disappeared from our country and will never return.* Had she lied to us? No, she hadn't. I knew she was sincere. Sincere but wrong. *Papi*, too, was wrong when he considered our health-care system the best in the Americas. How many other lies, or half-truths, had I been told throughout my life?

And then, Elena's sinister words, "Get lost or I will take my machete and cut your fucking head off. It won't be the first time that I've done it," kept ringing in my ears. Was she just bragging or—? Had she killed her stepmother? Was she a thief *and* a murderess?

No, that was too much for me. I could deal with political issues. I could challenge *Papi*. I could reconsider Che Guevara's ideas. I could change my beliefs. But I still wasn't ready to confront death. Not that kind of death, at least. I'd rather not know, for my own peace of mind.

On my way back to the tobacco house I passed by the creek without the slightest fear. The world of fantasy and monsters, of ghosts and snake women, had been drowned in its waters. A part of me also lay there, the trusting, childish girl who had arrived at the camp in January.

Common sense decreed that I should make no comments about my discoveries. It would be foolish, even dangerous, to talk about them. Yet common sense is the least common of all senses. The burden of silence proved too heavy for me to bear. The secret annoyed me like a swollen pimple yet I didn't want to tell Aurora. She

wouldn't give it the importance it deserved. She had her own troubles. And she liked Elena. (Though she'd probably change her mind
if I told her where I had found her black T-shirt.) Fat Olga was a
chatterbox. But Chabela had disliked Elena since the beginning.
She had seen the "shadow" too. She wouldn't gossip. I asked her to
sit with me under the *framboyán* and whispered, "If you promise to
keep mum, I'm going to tell you about something—something
really awful, *niña.*"

Chabela pricked up her ears. "Go ahead! You know you can trust
me. Speak, *hija,* speak."

I told her everything, except for Elena's threat of cutting my
head off. When I finished my story Chabela stood up and spat on
the ground hissing, "*Cochino!* Dirty pig!" Her reaction took me by
surprise because her anger was not directed against the *guajirita*, but
against our principal. "He perverted her, Lourdes," she said angrily.
"Not that Elena was a saint before, but it is his fault, not hers. The
guajiros are poor and can't buy anything here, that is why he took
advantage of her. The old man calls himself a communist and he is
prostituting that girl. What do you plan to do about it?"

"Nothing," I answered, amazed. What did Chabela think *I* could
do? "Why?"

"Well, our principal is supposed to be an example for us," she
replied. "And what is he?"

"A *cabrón,*" I admitted. "An immoral *cabrón!*"

"Then he ought to be denounced!" Chabela concluded.

I should have agreed with Chabela. Che Guevara had stated that
a loyal revolutionary must struggle against crime and injustice, and
denounce them at once. But I was afraid of the principal. Afraid of
Elena, too. And somehow Che's words didn't impress me as they
used to. After all, he had been defeated in Bolivia. He had led his
comrades to death. He had fought against prostitution, inequality,

and corruption, but they still existed in Cuba. What did it really mean, to "be like him"?

"Do whatever you want," I finally told Chabela. "Just don't get me involved in anything."

"I won't. But my conscience orders me to denounce what is happening. This is an act of prostitution, Lourdes! A shame for our high school!"

ONE MORNING I woke up and Comrade Katia wasn't in camp anymore. We would be returning to Havana in ten days, so I assumed she had gone ahead. But Chabela sat with me at lunchtime and murmured, "Now the old bastard will be exposed. Comrade Katia went to Havana to take care of the matter."

⚜ CHAPTER XXXVIII ⚜

BODIES SWAYED, HIPS rocked back and forth. The air was filled with the smells of cologne, jasmine, crushed leaves, cigarette smoke, rum, and sweat. That Saturday the *bailable* started at five. Couples spun around, dancing away fatigue accumulated during the last months. The beating drums of Los Van Van, the red-and-blue garlands, a barrel of lemonade, and three meringue pies bought by *La Flaca*, created a carnival-like atmosphere in our camp.

The teachers joined in the revelry. *La Flaca* danced with the principal. Berto sang in a funny soprano voice. I smiled sincerely at Isobel and Ernesto when they passed by me holding hands. Everything seemed lovely because it was the last Saturday in camp. Only a dejected Aurora stood aside. "I am not in the mood for partying, *hija*" she said, and went to bed at seven.

IT HAD been a long, lonely, sad Sunday. The Saturday *bailable* had drained all the energy from us. Because we were returning to the city the following Friday, most parents—*Papi* among them—had skipped the last visit.

I consoled myself thinking that Havana was just a few days away.

Havana meant summer clothes, Grandma Gloria's rice puddings, chocolate ice creams in Coppelia, and all my books. I ought to have been happy anticipating my return, but I was not. The painful question kept haunting me. Would I live in the Mantilla cabin or in the Vista Alegre Street *casona*? Oh, why did I have to decide? Why couldn't someone do it for me?

I walked around the camp, vaguely uneasy, until my bunk bed looked more inviting than the deserted outdoors. Aurora joined me and asked, "What are you going to do when we get home?"

"I want to go to *La Moderna Poesía* bookstore," I answered. "And have a facial at Suchel, the new beauty salon in El Vedado. And eat a good fruit salad. Oranges, melon, tangerines, papaya, mango—I'm dying for fresh fruit. What about you?"

"I'll have to see Juanito first," Aurora sighed. "Unfortunately." I felt her despair. She didn't even look pretty anymore, with dark circles around her eyes. She seemed older and weary.

"You'll come out of this," I told her confidently. "We are neighbors, remember? Next-door neighbors. If there is a problem with Juanito or your mother, you don't need to worry. You can come to my house and stay with us. We have so much space that my grandma won't mind."

Aurora smiled sadly. "Thanks, Lulu. I'd love to have my baby and live in my own house, away from Carolina. But, in case that doesn't happen," she said quietly, "would you accompany me to the hospital to—you-know-what?"

"I will."

"I've always been careful with all my previous boyfriends. But Juanito hated using a condom. I tried to use the rhythm method and—it didn't work." Although I had no idea what she was talking about, I nodded. "Do you think Juanito is going to marry me?" Aurora asked eagerly. "Do you think he—loves me?"

TERESA DE LA CARIDAD DOVAL

She looked so depressed that I didn't mind lying a little. I had become quite good at it. And the truth would hurt her too much. "Juanito will be waiting for you in Havana," I answered as cheerfully as I could. "Then we'll go together to rent the wedding gown. You'll have a big party in the Palace of Marriages and invite everybody except that little viper, Natasha."

"The little viper, that's a good name for her! The little viper, the little—" Suddenly her voice faltered. "Oh, Lulu, you have been so nice to me all the time," she sobbed. "And I've been such an asshole! Such a stupid, conceited little viper myself! You defended me and lied to Comrade Katia. You haven't made fun of me and Juanito. You found my T-shirt. You were always helping me when we were in the same brigade. . . ." She sniffled.

"I've done it because—because I like you," I murmured. I was going to say "love" but the word didn't come out.

"I like you too, Lourdes," Aurora said, wiping her eyes. "A lot."

"No, amiga. I mean, I'd like *to be with you*. I do not want to offend you, but—you are my *amor*." I stopped, horrified. Now I had said it. What was she going to do? *Please, Yemayá, help me!*

"I know that, Lourdes." Aurora's pensive face turned mischievous. She recovered her usual, impish grin. "I've known it for a long time. I once read a letter—a love letter you wrote to me."

I gasped. "When?!"

"About two months ago. Papirito had called you. While you were outside with him I found the letter. I wish you'd given it to me then," she added. "Maybe it would have kept me out of trouble—who knows?"

"Well, I've liked you since the first time I saw you," I confessed, hiding my face in the pillow. "When you sat next to me on the train. But it is so wrong. . . ."

Aurora caressed my back. "Why wrong?" she asked sweetly.

"Because we are both girls," I sighed. "And you only like men with big *pingas*. You don't care for me."

"Lulu, there is nothing wrong with liking another person. One can't control that." Aurora put her arm around my shoulders. "And I *do* care for you. I've loved many guys in my life, and many more have been after me, but," she smoothed my ponytail, "none of them was ever as considerate and helpful to me as you were. You deserve to be loved more than any of them."

"I didn't expect you to. . . ."

"That's what I like about you, that you never expect a thing. My patient, dear Lourdes! My pretty *mulatica*!"

For the first time being called a *mulatica* didn't upset me. I looked up and shyly asked her, "Can we go outside, *amor*?"

Arm in arm we walked to the boys' barracks and curled up on the grass behind them. Then Aurora gave me a tangerine kiss while her breasts quivered like sunflowers blossoming in my hands. I smelled the wild breath of the countryside. The fragrance of the forget-me-nots around us mixed with Aurora's scent of violets and her gaze had a newer softer gleam as she looked at me. A curtain of *framboyán* flowers fell down over us like a bride's veil.

"WHERE IS the letter, Lulu?" Aurora asked when we went back to the barracks. "I'd like to keep it, if you don't mind. No one has ever written a love letter to me before. And I always wanted to have one."

When I gave her the letter, she put it carefully inside her suitcase.

We lay down in the bunk bed. Time passed slowly. I relived our encounter, recalling that Aurora's lips were sweeter than ripened mangos and that her hips had more music within them than all the Los Van Van songs.

"You'll go out with boys, Lourdes," she said after a long silence. "They will dunk their bread in your *café con leche*. And you'll enjoy it, as I do, because you are a woman. But I've learned something tonight. We girls understand each other better than the most sensitive guy does. We should get together and create a *Papaya* Federation. It'd be more powerful than the Communist Party!"

She grinned, kissed me on the cheek and went to sleep smiling. We cuddled like little sisters, Aurora's arms innocently wrapped around my neck and my head resting on her shoulder.

❧ CHAPTER XXXIX ☙

ON WEDNESDAY MORNING after breakfast, all the brigades received unexpected and welcome news: we wouldn't go to work that day. The principal stood nervously in front of us, flanked by a couple I had never seen. The visitors were a fat peroxide blonde and a thin bald man. Their neat clothes and a red Lada, parked outside the camp, proclaimed that they had just arrived from Havana. The bald man rubbed his hands every two seconds. The peroxide blonde wouldn't stop eating french fries from an oily paper bag. Marisol said they both worked "*en el Ministerio,*" for the Ministry of Education.

"Comrades!" The principal yelled after the first announcement was made and greeted with hurrahs. "Comrades, students, teachers! These *compañeros* have come from Havana to clear the name of our high school. Someone spread a rumor about the morality of our pupils—"

"*Ay, coño,*" Aurora mumbled. "They already know all about Juanito and me!"

"Accusing me of having an affair with a minor, apparently a female student at this camp." The principal frowned when he said the word "minor." "I urge you to declare if this is true or false, as all of you know it is untrue."

Aurora relaxed. Fat Olga winked at Marisol. Chabela was in the first row, her eyes shining with a firm resolve. A couple of boys whistled. Though the principal struggled to appear unconcerned, he couldn't hide his distress. The blonde swallowed a handful of french fries and had a coughing fit. The bald man glared at us.

"Since no one has anything to say," the principal concluded, "we assume that you all agree this is a noxious lie which doesn't even deserve another minute of our time. Thank you, comrades! Homeland or Death!"

A few timid voices answered with the perfunctory *Venceremos* while a wave of giggles rocked the assembly. The principal hurried to leave the platform, followed by the visitors. The brigades began to disperse.

Then Chabela climbed up on the platform and began to talk. At first no one understood what she was saying because of the excitement that reigned in the campground. But soon we all heard her indictment, as loud as she could produce, "He isn't involved with a student but with Elena the *guajira*! Go to her house and you'll see the TV set and all the stuff she and her father stole from the camp. This is not a slander. It's the truth!"

The peroxide blonde and the bald man pushed Chabela into the workshop room. Our principal disappeared. An hour passed, every minute filled with questions, laughs, gossip, and conjectures.

"The principal and the *guajira*? Can you believe it?

"He's old enough to be her grandfather. It can't be true!"

"I bet it is. The dirty bastard groped me once—"

When Chabela returned to the barracks, the blonde accompanied her. She wouldn't leave her side until the three of them—Chabela, the blonde, and the bald man—got into the Lada and left the camp.

But Chabela had found a moment to go to the latrines. After she returned, she threw a piece of paper onto my bed. *They say I will be expelled from our high school*, I read. *Explain that to Jorge. He will be here today.*

There were no more speeches that day and we loitered until bedtime. Aurora's disgrace was practically erased from all our minds, much to her happiness, by this new and more succulent scandal.

Darkness spilled over the hills quickly. A dazzling full moon floated above the *framboyán* like an incandescent ball. Surrounded by an odd, unnerving silence, I waited for Jorge near the camp's fence.

I felt guilty, scared, and more confused than ever. Those comrades who worked *en el Ministerio*, weren't they revolutionaries? Obviously, they had not come to "clear the name of our high school," but to defend the principal, to cover up for him. They hadn't even gone to Pancho's house.

What would happen to Chabela? The principal was not a witless boy like Vladimir, but a smart adult. He had power and friends, well-connected friends. Chabela had dreamed for years of becoming a psychologist. Now, unless Comrade Katia saved her, she wouldn't be allowed to go to the university. The expulsion would mar her record forever. But she hadn't done anything wrong. She had just denounced a crime—as Che Guevara had exhorted us to do—and she had been rewarded with a kick in the ass! No one had questioned Elena or Pancho. The principal was still the principal. What kind of world was this?

Jorge showed up. He didn't seem surprised by the relationship between the principal and Elena, which made me suspect he already knew about it. But it took him a while to figure out why Chabela had ended up involved in the affair. When he finally got it, his face turned red, then dark. "The damned old man," he grunted. "The *cabrón*—"

Jorge swore he'd take revenge. He didn't say how and I didn't ask him either. He shook my hand and disappeared, blending into the night.

After dinner everybody went to the barracks. We could have stayed outside until much later, as the principal had locked himself in his office and nervous *Flaca* didn't pay any attention to us. But no one felt like playing around that night.

I sank into my bunk bed and tried to read an old issue of the magazine *Bohemia*. But I couldn't avoid my thoughts, the bloody scenario my mind kept painting. Which Yankee horror movie would Jorge imitate to get even with our principal? Would he wait, hidden behind a tree, for the old man, and then butcher him? Would he appear one day in our high school with a machine gun and shoot the *cabrón viejo* in front of all the students? *Ay!*

The sound of the tree branches crashing against each other acted as an ominous accompaniment to my fears. Had Chabela's banishment been my fault? If something happened to the principal, would it be my fault, too? *Coño*, I had only shared a secret with a good friend. I never wanted to harm anybody. But what pandemonium I had unleashed by opening my mouth. "Evil will surround you," Sabina had said. Evil—for the first time I sensed its presence, dangerously close to me.

At dinner, after we commented on Chabela's bravery with admiration, Natasha had the wicked idea of bringing Aurora's misfortune to public attention again. "Chabela is a real woman. She challenged the principal. She stood her ground. Quite different from Aurora! The *puta* is alone now, so she may be planning to steal someone's boyfriend. Mine isn't here anymore but you better be careful, because that broad doesn't know what respect is."

"How can you say that? She is still in love with Juanito," Fat Olga protested. "And he is the father of her baby."

"Bah, she's surely forgotten all about him already." Natasha grinned. "I bet she is looking for a sucker to take care of the cow—and of the little calf."

"But where there is smoke, there is fire," argued another girl. "Aurora and Juanito love each other, don't they?"

"Love each other, shit!" replied Natasha, implacable. "She was in heat and he—well, he is a man. What could he do when she chased him around and grabbed him by his *pinga*? Actually, Juanito is tired of her. He's been going out with Comrade Katia."

"You are kidding!"

"It's true," Marisol said. "I once saw them together."

"Hush!" I looked over my shoulder. "Here comes Aurora! Hush!"

WHERE THERE is smoke, there is fire. Yes, Aurora still loved Juanito. She sobbed, her head buried in our pillow. I patted her hand. It was all I could do, given the circumstances.

After a while Aurora turned to me and said, "You know what I did today, Lourdes? When I heard the story about the principal and Elena, I went to warn her. Had she come here people would have given her a hard time, like they did me. She invited me to have lunch with her. They have such a cute little house."

"Cute little house?" I repeated, astonished. "That is a hovel, girl!"

"*Papá* Pancho came and he was a real sweetheart, too—"

"Did you call him *Papá*?!"

"Why not? It would be so good to have a father like him. Remember the day when your skin was so sore and he brought the sage for you?" Aurora paused briefly and then went on, "Elena told me about their deal with the old man, and how you discovered it. But I don't know how Chabela found out. She isn't *that* smart. You didn't tell her, did you?"

"Oh no!" I lied. "I didn't even know Elena and the principal were screwing around. I just knew about the stuff she stole. And I didn't even mention it to you. I am not a *chivata*, *hija!*" I added with great dignity.

"Only when you need to be," Aurora chuckled. "Well, tomorrow will be another day. Good night!"

I stayed awake for a long time. It was not a restless, tormented vigil, but a quiet recounting of the last events. Up until then, I had idolized Aurora as a distant star. Even after realizing she was vain and conceited, I kept worshipping her until that night when we met under the *framboyán*. At that point, something changed.

I still thought she was pretty but I didn't desire her anymore. Tall, sexy, and big-assed, Aurora represented my ideal. She was the girl I had wanted to be for a long time, the beautiful white woman I'd never be. But the halo my imagination had placed on her had fallen away.

Jorge's face appeared intermittently in the middle of my reflections. My handsome neighbor, the "boy next door" with his broad, square shoulders and big hands. What had Fat Olga said about the connection between a guy's middle finger and his *pinga*? I knew so little about *pingas*. I couldn't even remember Ernesto's. How would Jorge's be? How would it feel inside me? Oh, I shouldn't think that way about him. But it felt so good down there, in my *papaya*—

A SOUND like the rustling of tobacco leaves rubbing against the *cujes* awakened me. The smell of burning wood invaded the barracks. Immediately afterward, the siren emitted a piercing howl. A chorus of screams echoed it. I jumped out of bed. "It's the office!" someone yelled.

The principal's room was on fire. The wind had blown sparks onto the grass and flames quickly approached our barracks. *La Flaca* ran from bed to bed, waking people. Some girls hurried outside in their pajamas.

"Help me get dressed!"

"My eyeglasses—"

"Get out!" The teacher shouted. "Leave the barracks at once, everybody! Get out!"

"Where are my clothes?"

"Forget your clothes, get out!"

I ran toward the door, followed by Aurora and pushed by a crowd of frantic, half-asleep girls. In the confusion I stumbled over a suitcase and fell to the floor. The smoke filled my nostrils. I coughed. My vision blurred and my throat closed. Cotton-wrapped noises reached me from a remote place. Someone tried to drag me. I fought.

The barracks became a crazy kaleidoscope. I saw streaks of blue as clear as the Mother-of-Water creek. A mist as white as an afternoon cloud. Ribbons as red as the Pinar del Río earth. Purple sparks that gleamed like the *framboyán*'s flowers. And floating above all, the cold, indifferent April moon—

Dried leaves under the trees. Couples under the trees. Tiny tobacco plants. Green and brown. Rancid food. Touch me here. All men are pigs and now it rains. It rains. Wet leaves under the trees. Couples under the trees. Oh. More. Burned milk. Stale bread. Sticky hands under the blankets. Couples under the trees. Lurking monsters that crawl around us. Fear. Dried leaves under the trees. Touch me again.

THEN I saw Aurora. Her clothes were covered with soot. She had leaned over me and caressed my cheeks, "Are you OK, Lulu?"

I nodded and sighed. "I thought I'd had a nightmare."

Aurora replied, "There was a fire in the camp. Don't you remember? You fainted and I pulled you out of the barracks."

I reached for her hand and said, "Thanks."

The fresh morning breeze bore a heavy layer of ashes. I stood up painfully and looked around. The principal's office was completely destroyed, as well as the workshop room and the dining hall. But the rest of the camp had suffered less. Three walls of the girls' barracks were intact and the boys' barracks had been barely touched by the flames. Scattered groups of kids loafed about. An ambulance was parked near the gate. "How are the others?" I asked.

"Everybody is fine," Aurora said, "except the principal. The fire began in his office, you know." I nodded again. I knew, yes. I knew too much. "They're taking him to the hospital. I wondered how it happened. Strange, huh?"

When I saw the principal still breathing but half fried, I suddenly realized the magnitude of Jorge's crime. *He* had acted like "a cold killing machine." Not to free another country, not like an internationalist soldier, not for the continental revolution, but with the same outcome. Destruction. Violence. Maybe death. Crazy Jorge the monster, the high school dropout, was the one who actually ended up being like Che.

And what about Elena? Comrade Katia had once called her "a symbol of the peasant children of our revolution." What a symbol! Had she resorted to "revolutionary violence" too, against her hated stepmother? I didn't know and I didn't *want* to know. One thing I did know, though, was that I would never be like Che Guevara. Why had I ever wished to be like him? I hated fighting. I wouldn't be able to become "a cold killing machine." I loved my life and I loved other people, with the exception of a few bastards like Vladimir. I doubted even Comrade Katia could be a *guerrillera*.

My head began to spin. Then I vomited up all the slogans *Health, a right of the people; Homeland or Death; With the Revolution, everything. Against the revolution, nothing* that had filled my mind and mouth during the many years I had actually wanted to be like Che.

We wandered around the camp trying to rescue our charred possessions. After searching through sheets reeking with smoke, broken bedposts, and crushed suitcases, I recovered my cashmere sweater. It was dirty and ripped but wearable. Later I found my boots which were only slightly scorched. Aurora retrieved her lipstick, all that survived from her cherished makeup kit.

We didn't go without food, thanks to the *guajiros*' charity. At lunchtime Elena and Pancho brought us rice and black beans. Hilda came later with more rice, bread, and chicken soup, plus used clothes and shoes to replace our pajamas. I got a denim work shirt and a pleated red skirt. Fat Olga wrapped herself in a checkered cotton gown. Aurora showed off in a frayed, yellow sequined dress and asked, "Do I look like Cindy Lauper, girls?"

"DON'T YOU wish we were already in Havana?" I asked Aurora later.

"Not really," she said gloomily. "I have nothing to do there. I can't go back to our high school. You see how people treat me here. And when Carolina finds out—"

"She won't find out until you and Juanito get married," I replied. "Then it won't matter. Aren't you going to live with him?"

The wind blew a burned *framboyán* flower and it drifted to her feet. Aurora picked it up. "Juanito, shit! He isn't marrying me. I heard what Natasha and Marisol said yesterday about him and Comrade Katia. I suspected it before but I didn't want to admit it." She crushed the flower and then kicked it toward the boys' barracks. "He isn't interested in me anymore. It is true I chased him but I won't do it again. It would be useless. He is—trash."

A big truck arrived for us at 5:30. From the back of the vehicle, leaning on the railing, I took a long look at our camp. The *framboyán* towered above its ruins. It was blistered and leafless but as magnificent in its death as it had been when its branches brimmed with gleaming flowers. Like a petrified giant, it still reigned over the camp.

I took another look at the creek, forever free of the feared presence of the Mother-of-Water. And I took a longer, more intense look at Pancho's wooden house. Aurora stood at the door waving at me while the truck drove away from the camp, toward the Pinar del Río train station, toward family and peace.

CHAPTER XL

LAZILY, AS IF in slow motion, the train drew closer to the capital. Fat Olga rested her head on Marisol's shoulder. Natasha and Berto chattered. Other girls sang. *La Flaca* dozed. My seat was by the window yet I couldn't see the Pinar del Río landscape nor the curved hills that framed it. I still saw Aurora's face, and her impish grin when she had announced, "I am not going to Havana, Lourdes. I am staying here."

"What do you mean?" I asked. "Are you going to live outdoors? In the tobacco house?" I laughed. "Or in the creek with the Mother-of-Water?"

"No. With Elena and *Papá* Pancho."

"Aurora the *guajira*," I chuckled.

"Lourdes, I am not joking."

I almost fell to the floor. "What are you going to do in this place, the ass-end of the world?" I lifted my arms in horror. I felt like adding "with a pimp and a killer, great company for you," but I shut up. "These *guajiros*—why stay with them?" I asked, baffled, after a moment's pause. "Who put this idea in your head?"

"Elena. When I went to her house she was so thankful, the poor thing, and then she said, 'You are welcome here anytime, Aurora. My house is your house.'"

"That is just a saying, *hija.*" I shrugged. "A way of speaking. Very nice, but it really means nothing. They aren't taking you in. Forget it!"

"Yes, they are!" Aurora replied. "I've already talked to *Papá* Pancho. He told me I could stay. If there is food for two mouths, there is food for three, he said. Don't you see, Lourdes, that I cannot go home? Carolina hates me. I do not have a father. Juanito is gone. No one cares about me. Elena and I will help each other now."

"How can you say no one cares about you?" I asked, hurt. "So, I don't count? I, too, told you that you could live in my house."

"You *do* count, Lulu." Aurora squeezed my hand. "You are the best friend I ever had. But you are going to have your parents' divorce to deal with. You may move to another barrio. And I need to get away from Carolina, at least for a while."

"What are you going to do with—the child?"

"I don't know yet," she sighed. "Maybe have him. I don't know."

When I heard Aurora's faltering voice I recalled how she had exuded self-confidence and courage. How much I had wanted to be like her, to order people around, to be a beauty, a ballsy girl, and the camp's queen. Now I realized that no one is all that eternally. The higher you fly, the harder you fall.

"Well, whatever your decision is, whether you choose to stay here or to go back to Havana, I'll always be there for you," I said, and I meant it.

"I know, Lourdes." Aurora squeezed my hand again. "I've always known that."

THE RHYTHMIC *cras-cras-trac-trac cras-cras trac* of the train sounded like a hospitality chant. Welcome Lourdes, the train sang, welcome home. *Cras-cras-trac-trac cras-cras trac.* Welcome home. Welcome home.

I didn't want to think of Aurora again. I forced myself to remember *Mami's* coconut smile and *Papi's* greenish eyes.

They would be worried because of the news of the fire. They would be pacing the waiting room of the train station as they had done the day of my departure. Despite the troubles caused by their separation, they would both beam when I jumped from the train. They would run to hug me. They would ask the inevitable questions, "Are you tired, *niña*? Have you lost much weight? You didn't wash your hair with cold water, did you? What do you want to eat?"

There would be a delicacy hidden in *Mami's* purse, a bar of chocolate or two, chicken croquets made by Grandma Gloria.

Grandma Gloria! I loved her as much as I loved *Mami*. Or more. How could I live without her cuddling, without the sugary *café con leche* she brought to my bed every morning? But she didn't like *Mami*. She had never liked her. Now she had blonde Marietta. And Jorge. Would she still love me?

Cras-cras-trac-trac cras-cras trac. Welcome home. Welcome home.

I longed to see both my parents, but maybe only *Mami* would be waiting for me, wearing her loose polka-dotted dress and carrying a cheap vinyl purse in her hand. My little frumpish *Mami* who didn't straighten her hair anymore and seldom used makeup.

I longed to see both my parents, but maybe only *Papi* would be waiting for me, clean shaven and neatly dressed in his white *guayabera*, carrying a Russian leather briefcase. *Papi* calm and proper, reassuring me. Saying that their problems could still be solved. Solved? And Marietta?

Cras-cras-trac-trac cras-cras trac. Welcome home. Welcome home.

If I went to the Vista Alegre Street house, supper would be warm and ready. A lavish, delicious meal prepared by the expert hands of Grandma Gloria. A breaded pork steak. Or maybe a chicken leg smothered in onions. The wonderful french fries that only Grandma Gloria could make, crispy and salty, which crackled inside the mouth. Chicken soup. And the dessert. The dessert! Flan, guava jam, rice or chocolate pudding. At last, a ceremonial glass of milk and coffee with little grains of sugar dusting the top.

A bath would follow supper. A bath that would clean the reddish dust and reeking memories from me. A bath with lukewarm water in our marble bathtub. A scented powder puff, my pink towel, the pajamas *Papi* had bought for me in Moscow. My silky, flowery pajamas that wouldn't smell like tobacco leaves or dampened earth.

Grandma Gloria would accompany me to my room, tuck me in bed, caress my forehead. I would go to sleep covered with an immaculate blanket and holding my familiar little pillow, the one with Pinocchio embroidered on the pillowcase.

The next day I would wake up to a well-deserved week off. A week to sit on the patio, to catch up on the Brazilian soap opera and neighborhood gossip. A week to read, to watch TV until midnight, to eat ice cream in Coppelia. A week to miss Aurora.

A week to talk to Jorge, too. We'd see each other often if I stayed on at Vista Alegre Street. We shared a secret now. I knew he had burned the camp and *he knew that I knew*. The thought of our complicity tickled me in an odd, pleasant way. He was the slothful floozy's son and Chabela's boyfriend. He was a criminal. But—

Cras-cras-trac-trac cras-cras trac. Welcome home. Welcome home.

HOW WOULD it be to go to Grandma Inés's? People talked about long blackouts that darkened the nights in the poor suburbs. Grandma Inés collected candle stubs and had an old kerosene lamp. She cooked with wood, like the *guajiras* did in camp. However, her *ajiaco* would be just as delicious as any of Grandma Gloria's dishes.

Grandma Inés's little cottage had its own rural charm. I liked the balmy breeze that came in from the patio. I even liked the statuettes of her saints with bananas and oranges arranged around them. Smells of onions, coffee, fruits, and cigars. Candles burning at the *orishas'* feet. Grandma Inés singing an old song—*"Babalú"*—while she peeled the potatoes. The soft sound of the rain falling outside, cheering the bougainvillea. The stone well where the stars could be seen at night when I looked down. Tiny blue butterflies that only flew around the forget-me-nots.

But I did not like the smoky kitchen. I hated to use the small, windowless bathroom. It didn't have a bathtub, only a wooden washtub, a bucket for water, and a slippery untiled floor. And where would I sleep? On a borrowed cot? On the floor? How would my cousins receive me?

Cras-cras-trac-trac cras-cras trac. Welcome home. Welcome home.

The memory of Grandma Inés's cabin took me back to the *santera's* house. Like Grandma Inés's, it had a pretty bougainvillea on the porch and an *orishas'* altar near the door. I remembered the light of the candles casting odd shadows on the wall, the mulatto Jesus hanging from the crucifix, the shells of divination clattering on the table—the cleansing work with honey and flowers. The *azabache.* The prophecies.

Yes, life had put a few obstacles in my way. My parents' divorce, Ernesto's abandonment, Vladimir and the other kids who had made fun of me—Yes, I had used the power of my mouth when I lied to Comrade Katia and sent that damned boy to the reeducation camp. I wondered what the saints thought about it, supposing they existed. *Coño,* what I had done to Vladimir was wrong, even if he deserved it. It would have been easier for Yemayá to spare me his harassment. Why had she allowed him to pester me and smear me with the *plasta de vaca* in the first place?

Yes, Evil had been surrounding me. Sweet Elena turned out to be a whore and a thief. Maybe something worse. The principal was a pig and a liar. Juanito had cheated on Aurora. Chabela, who had tried to act honestly, would be expelled from our high school. Crazy Jorge had burned the camp. We had all killed Papirito.

(But Evil didn't dwell only in camp, I had to admit. I had participated in that shameful repudiation act and thrown a rotten egg at helpless Dr. Ruiz. *Papi* had denounced his friend and colleague, González. *Mami* had stuck a rusty pin into a *santería* doll dressed like Grandma Gloria. Grandma Gloria had kicked *Mami* out of the house. *Papi* and Marietta had cheated on *Mami. Uff!*)

Yes, I had "gotten" Aurora, and yet I hadn't felt completely happy in the end. But I knew that neither honey nor the *azabache* had made it happen. She had come to me simply because she wanted to. Because I had been good to her. Because she was curious, perhaps.

Actually, what had the *orishas* done while we were in camp? Not a thing! They couldn't save Papirito. They didn't protect me from Vladimir. They wouldn't defend poor Chabela. Despite my prayers to Oshún, Ernesto never came back to me. The saints hadn't lifted a finger to help me or anybody else. And Che Guevara—well, he wasn't my hero anymore, but certainly the *orishas* wouldn't occupy his vacated place.

I carefully took the *azabache* and my Outstanding Communist medal off my silver chain and slipped them in my pocket. I'd give the *azabache* back to Grandma Inés. I'd put the medal in a box with my *matrioskas* when I got home—

Home? *Which* home? Aurora had already solved her problem, but I hadn't decided anything yet. Time was running out. I couldn't put off my decision any longer. Even if *Papi* and *Mami* were both waiting for me at the train station, I could leave with only one of them. Which one?

It was nearly dawn in Havana. I saw the first paved streets, a crowded bus, and a few buildings, but within my mind the images of the green leaves of tobacco, the charred barracks, and Aurora's pensive face remained.

A strange woman waited for me at the station. She resembled *Mami* but seemed thinner and taller. She looked like *Mami* in photos taken several years ago. She wore makeup—red lipstick and black mascara—and a new, rather short and tight blue dress. *Papi* wasn't there. His absence disappointed me at first, but later I sighed with relief. I didn't need to decide anything. He had already made the decision for me.

My brand new *Mami* smiled and kissed me. Then she asked a thousand questions. Was I hurt, hungry, afraid? Had the fire been as terrible as people said? Why hadn't Aurora returned? Did I know that Comrade Katia had been kicked out of the education system?

How many things I'd have to tell her! (How much *should* I tell her?)

Mami talked fast and nervously. I felt closer to her than ever before. It hit me for the first time how much I loved her, my young, anxious, and troubled mother. I took her arm and said, "I'll tell you everything, *Mami*. Everything. Believe me, there is enough material to keep me talking until tomorrow. I hope the buses aren't very crowded at this hour. Where do we get the one to Mantilla?"

We walked together to the nearest bus stop.

While we waited for the Number 34 bus, *Mami* looked at me guiltily and whispered, "Lourdes, your father doesn't know about the fire yet. The school clerk contacted me at my work and I didn't tell him. He still thinks you are coming back this Friday." I froze for a moment. *Mami* went on, "I did it because I was so nervous—God, I need you more than he does. But you can still go and live with him if you want to. I'll take you to Vista Alegre Street now, if you like. I can't offer you even half of the things he and your other grandma have."

I saw her tears and hugged her. "Don't worry, *Mami*," I said. "I'll talk to *Papi*. I'll visit him sometime this week. But I am staying with you. I need you too, *vieja*, didn't you know that?"

An hour later, while riding on the bus that would take us to Mantilla, to the house that would become "my other house," to the up-until-then strange people, noises, and smells that would accompany me for years, I couldn't keep my eyes off the Leyland's exhaust pipe. The whitish puffs that followed the bus hung ghostlike in the air. I began to try to fix in my memory old faces and events, scenes as fugitive and ephemeral as smoke, the lost pieces of a childhood that was being inexorably left behind.

⊰ GLOSSARY ⊱

a correr: let's run

adiós: good-bye

ajiaco: vegetable and meat stew

aldeanas: villagers

amor: love

anda: get going

arriba: at the top

arroz con leche: rice pudding

arroz con pollo: chicken with rice

aura tiñosa: carrion-eating bird

ay: ouch

azabache: jet stone

bailable: dance

barbudos: bearded ones. Refers to Fidel Castro and those who fought with him in the Sierra Maestra Mountains

bembé: initiation party in santería

borracho perdido: completely drunk; drunk as a lord

bueno: good

cabrón(a): bastard (vulgar)

cadencia: four-verse song

café con leche: coffee and milk

carajo: damn it. Ir a casa del carajo: go to hell

caramba: rats

carnicería: butcher shop

cartucho: brown paper bag

casona: big house

cascarilla: a powder made with eggshells

CDR (Comité de Defensa de la Revolucion): Committee for the Defense of the Revolution

centavos: cents

chancletas: flip-flop sandals

cheo/a: old-fashioned

chica: girl

chicharrón: pork rind, crackling

chico, chica, chiquita: boy, girl, little girl

chivata: informer, rat

chorrera: mushy, soup-like consistency

cochina: dirty, pig

cojones: balls (vulgar)

cojonudo: ballsy

compañero/a: comrade

congrí: rice and black beans

coño: damn it

cuentecitos: short tales

cuidado: watch out

cuje: dried stick of wood

culo: ass

daño: harm

¿de verdad?: really?

dios mío: my God

el mulato de la pinga de oro: the golden dick mulatto

el profesor: the professor

el responsable: the person in charge

el viento de Cuaresma: the Lent wind

estúpida: stupid

fiesta de quinceaños: fifteen-year-old party, similar to a "sweet sixteen" fiesta

flaca: skinny

framboyán: tropical tree

fuera: out

galleguita puta: little Galician whore

gata flaca: literally, skinny cat; bony person

Gato Negro: black cat (Bulgarian perfume)

gorgojo: rice weevil

guajiro/a: peasant, country folk

guayabera: traditional man's loose embroidered shirt

guerrillero/a: guerrilla

gusano/a: literally, worm; in Cuba, counterrevolutionary.

Habanero/a: one from Havana

hija: daughter; also used as a term of endearment

hijo: son

hola: hello

ileke: beaded necklace

indecentes: perverts

jamón curado: cured ham

jefecita: little boss

jodienda: (a) screw up

Juventud Rebelde: Cuban newspaper; literally, Rebel Youth

ki ki ri kí: cock-a-doodle-doo (also quí-qui-ri-qui)

la cabrona chiquita: the damned child

la comida: food

la escoria: the scum

la galleta: the slap

la muerte: death

La Plaza de la Revolución: Revolution Square

La Yuma: the United States

las casonas: the great houses

linterna: flashlight

llorando miserias: complaining, asking for things

los pobrecitos: the poor things

los trapitos de culo: the rags used for wiping the rear

machetero vanguardia: outstanding cane cutter

Mamá: mom

Mami: mommy

Mamita: mommy

manejadora: babysitter

maravilla Americana: American wonder

maricón: fag (vulgar)

marielitos: Cuban refugees who arrived in the United States in 1980, during the Mariel boatlift

matrioskas: Russian nest dolls

mi rey: my king

mierda: shit

miliciano/a: militia member

mima: mom

mojito: alcoholic drink

muerte: death

nada: nothing

negritas: black girls

niña: little girl

no hay problema: no problem

no me joda más: stop fucking with me (vulgar)

no tengas pena: don't be embarrassed

noviazgo: courtship

orisha: African god or goddess

panadería: bakery

Papá: dad

papaya: pussy (vulgar)

Papi: daddy

parque: park

pastelito: pastry

patria o muerte: Homeland or Death (Cuban revolutionary slogan)

pendejo/a: literally, pubic hair; figuratively, coward (vulgar)

periquitos: little parrots

perro caliente: hot dog

pinga: dick (vulgar)

Pipo: dad

pitusa: blue jeans

plasta de vaca: cow pie

pobrecito/a: poor one

ponche de huevo: eggnog

por la libre: not rationed

puta mala: low-class whore

puta: whore

que se vayan: get out of here

quinceañera: fifteen-year-old girl

quinceaños (fiesta de): fifteen-year-old (party)

radio bemba: literally, big mouth radio; figuratively, the voice of street

ropa vieja: stew (literally, old clothes)

rueda de casino: Cuban dance

rumbera: rumba dancer

san: saint

santería: Afro-Cuban religion

santero/a: santería practitioner

señora: Mrs., lady

señorita: literally, Miss; also, a virgin

Siacará: interjection used in santería practices

sinsonte: mockingbird

tiempo de vals: waltz time

torrejas: fried slices of bread, a kind of French toast

tortillera: lesbian (vulgar); literally, a woman who makes tortillas

tu madre: your mama (vulgar)

uff: ugh

un buena gente: a nice person

un hombre de pelo en pecho: literally, a man with a hairy chest; figuratively, a brave man

una mujer grande: a big or mature woman

vanguardia: outstanding

venceremos: we will win (Cuban revolutionary slogan)

verdad: truth

vieja: old woman, sometimes used affectionately

viejita: little old woman; also term of endearment when referring to one's mother

viejo: old man

viejo cabrón: old bastard

zángano/a: literally, drone; figuratively, lazy.

⊰ MY LIFE IN CUBA ⊱

THE HAVANA OF my childhood, as I remember it, is wrapped up in a curtain of rain. I am sure it did not rain every week or even every month, but in my memories there is always a rainstorm and I can hear my grandmother say, "Cover all the mirrors, quick, before it starts thundering." We lived in a big, rather dilapidated house where the roof leaked so badly that a variety of containers—among them a porcelain chamber pot—were strategically located in different rooms to collect the water.

The 60's and 70's were times of scarcity. The ration card (still in existence today) regulated the amount of food and clothes each family received. The barrio butcher used to trade a few pounds of meat for other equally scarce items. I remember an old GE electric fan that my grandfather exchanged for 15 pounds of steak.

When I was 6 years old we moved to an apartment which was modern and much closer to downtown, in Centro Habana. The president of the CDR (Committee for the Defense of the Revolution) lived in the same building and CDR meetings were held downstairs once a month. Every family had to be "on duty" regularly and patrol the neighborhood to make sure that nothing improper happened. One night my mother and another "cederista" were guarding the entrance of the grocery store. At midnight they ran to our apartment, terrified. They had seen "a strange man with a bottle." The following morning they discovered that the man was the barrio drunkard. But had he been a thief, he could have rummaged throughout the entire grocery store as the "cederistas" were not going to lift a finger to prevent it.

I attended an elementary school located in an old family house. It had only one bathroom that was used by students and teachers alike. We girls used to shout "Hay hembras" (there are girls) when we were using the bathroom but boys were not always careful to announce their presence when they were inside. The dining area where we had lunch occupied what had been the basement of the house. It always smelled of burned peas and slightly of mice.

I grew up hearing "We'll be like Che" at school and "Down with Fidel" at home and among trusted friends. Soon I learned to say the first statement aloud and to whisper the second one.

Up until my last year of elementary school I was a typical nerd, complete with eyeglasses and heavy black orthopedic boots. Around my eleventh birthday I changed to contact lenses but I kept the boots until I was fourteen. "Fiestas de quinceaños" were popular among girls my age but I preferred not to have one and got a stack of books instead. Then I exchanged my birthday present, a Bulgarian make-up kit, for the complete works of Edgar Allan Poe.

I was an only child and lived with my parents and maternal grandparents. My mother is a medical and pharmacy doctor and my father was a mason with a 12th grade education. The apartment belonged to my mother's family and she made most of the important decisions. My dad, a quiet man, was a relatively obscure figure at home.

Participation in the School in the Fields was compulsory but I did not go to all of them because my mother managed to get medical certificates for me. I was exempt in two occasions. When I did go, thanks again to the medical "certificates" I seldom worked in the fields, but was assigned to the self service brigade. I stayed in camp and found out some interesting details about the activities of students and teachers that I would use later when writing *A Girl Like Che Guevara.*

Unlike the main character in my book I never wanted to "be like Che." Since I was fifteen years old, I dreamed about coming to the U.S. I took English classes with a private tutor. Access to language schools was limited and only those who worked in tourism were allowed to learn English. Russian was the only foreign language taught in most high schools.

In 1980, during the Mariel boatlift, a Miami-based relative sent a yacht called Rio India to take the whole family to the U.S. It traveled with a Dominican Republic flag and was not allowed to enter Cuba—only those ships with American flags were permitted to come into port. I did not participate in any repudiation act, as my own family was expecting to leave, but I did witness some of them. Those that happened in our neighborhood were less callous than some staged in other barrios. Ours was considered "a gusano nest," I later learned.

Upon finishing high school, I went for a BA in English Literature and Language and completed it in 1990. By then English was taught in more high schools and the Department of English Language had been created at the University of Havana. Later on I pursued an MA in Spanish Studies.

From 1990 to 1995 I taught English at the ISPJAE (Instituto Superior Politécnico José A. Echeverría) and at the Dentistry School in Havana. I also taught a few beginning courses in Spanish Grammar at the School of Fine Arts. My experience as a professor was essentially different than it had been as a student. We were told to give good grades to every student so as not to affect the "promotion emulation" which was a competition among the departments of the university. If a department had too many students with 3 (the equivalent of C) or 2 (F) its members would not be eligible for the distribution of TV sets, electric fans and alarm clocks. Every year the faculty attended a department meeting where the right to buy such gadgets was discussed. It was called "Meetings of Merits and Demerits." Some professors spent a whole semester writing down what others did wrong (not to attend political marches or fail to show up for "voluntary" work.) Then they unloaded their findings during the meetings. Friendships and trust were destroyed because of the right to buy a Russian radio which might not even be for sale in the local stores after all.

When socialism collapsed in Europe, scarcities increased in Cuba. In 1991 the "Special Period" (euphemism for crisis) began. In 1993 I was still working at the university and my salary was 280 pesos a month—the equivalent of 8 dollars. Many of my colleagues who had also graduated from the Language School moved to the tourism sphere either legally, as hotel employees and tourist guides, or illegally, as female prostitutes (jineteras), their male counterparts (pingueros) or clandestine taxi drivers. They made twenty times more money than I did.

I continued working at the university and joined a meditation group until two if its members committed suicide in the Escambray mountains, looking for the Shamballa. Afterwards I became part of a Quaker group. We got together once a week and meditated for one hour. It was during that time that I met my husband, Hugh Page, who went to Havana as a member of the Pastors for Peace. Hugh has been involved in social causes most of his life. He worked with the American friends Service Committee in California. He is a writer, too, and has a Ph.D. in psychology.

A year after we met, Hugh and I got married in Havana, in 1995. In 1996 I came to the U.S. We lived for six years in San Diego, CA, where I taught Spanish as a part-time instructor in several community colleges and through UCSD Extension. In August 2002 we moved to Albuquerque, NM, and I started taking classes at the University of New Mexico. This spring I was accepted in the doctoral program in Spanish Literature.

My husband has always been very supportive of me. We argue—occasionally—about politics but our relationship is solid and of mutual respect, despite the differences in backgrounds, culture and age. He is 78 years old and I will be 37 this October.

Teresa de la Caridad Doval